STRANGE Academy

First Class

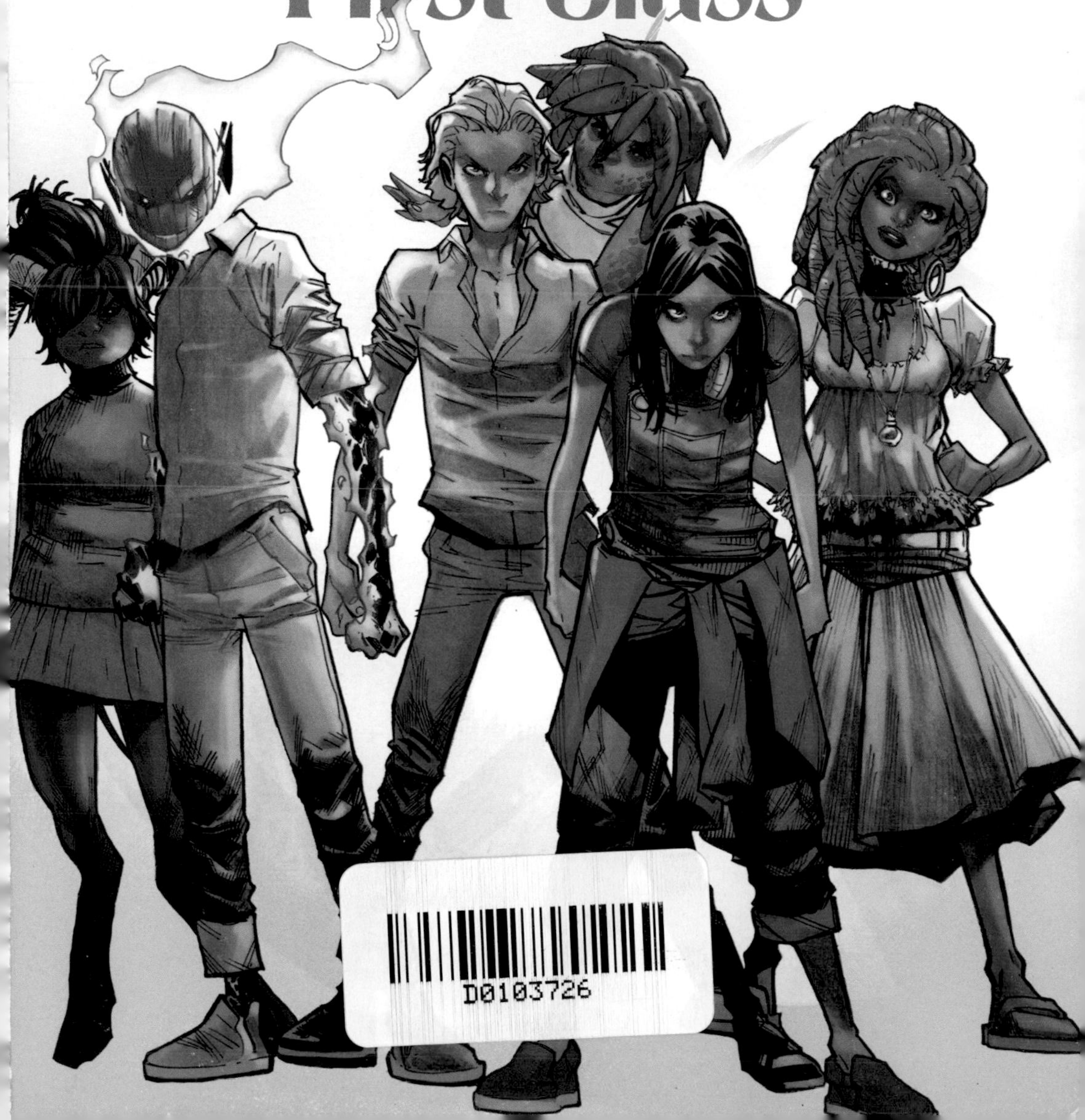

First Class

EMILY BRIGHT
DOYLE DORMAMMU
SHAYLEE MOONPEDDLE

ALVI BRORSON
IRIC BRORSON
DESSY

ZOE LAVEAU
TOTH
GUSLAUG

GERMÁN AGUILAR
CALVIN MORSE

STRANGE Academy

Skottie Young WRITER

Humberto Ramos ARTIST

Edgar Delgado COLOR ARTIST

VC's Clayton Cowles LETTERER

Humberto Ramos &
Edgar Delgado COVER ART

Jared K. Fletcher LOGO DESIGN

Danny Khazem ASSISTANT EDITOR

Kathleen Wisneski ASSOCIATE EDITOR

Nick Lowe EDITOR

Doctor Strange
CREATED BY **STAN LEE** & **STEVE DITKO**

Jennifer Grünwald COLLECTION EDITOR

Daniel Kirchhoffer ASSISTANT EDITOR

Maia Loy ASSISTANT MANAGING EDITOR

Lisa Montalbano ASSISTANT MANAGING EDITOR

Jeff Youngquist VP PRODUCTION & SPECIAL PROJECTS

Jay Bowen BOOK DESIGNER

David Gabriel SVP PRINT, SALES & MARKETING

C.B. Cebulski EDITOR IN CHIEF

STRANGE ACADEMY: FIRST CLASS. Contains material originally published in magazine form as STRANGE ACADEMY (2020) #1-6. Second printing 2021. ISBN 978-1-302-91950-4. Published by MARVEL WORLDWIDE, INC., a subsidiary of MARVEL ENTERTAINMENT, LLC. OFFICE OF PUBLICATION: 1290 Avenue of the Americas, New York, NY 10104. © 2020 MARVEL No similarity between any of the names, characters, persons, and/or institutions in this magazine with those of any living or dead person or institution is intended, and any such similarity which may exist is purely coincidental. **Printed in Canada.** KEVIN FEIGE, Chief Creative Officer; DAN BUCKLEY, President, Marvel Entertainment; JOE QUESADA, EVP & Creative Director; DAVID BOGART, Associate Publisher & SVP of Talent Affairs; TOM BREVOORT, VP, Executive Editor; NICK LOWE, Executive Editor, VP of Content, Digital Publishing; DAVID GABRIEL, VP of Print & Digital Publishing; JEFF YOUNGQUIST, VP of Production & Special Projects; ALEX MORALES, Director of Publishing Operations; DAN EDINGTON, Managing Editor; RICKEY PURDIN, Director of Talent Relations; JENNIFER GRÜNWALD, Senior Editor, Special Projects; SUSAN CRESPI, Production Manager; STAN LEE, Chairman Emeritus. For information regarding advertising in Marvel Comics or on Marvel.com, please contact Vit DeBellis, Custom Solutions & Integrated Advertising Manager, at vdebellis@marvel.com. For Marvel subscription inquiries, please call 888-511-5480. **Manufactured between 5/28/2021 and 6/29/2021 by SOLISCO PRINTERS, SCOTT, QC, CANADA.**

1 0 9 8 7 6 5 4 3 2

1

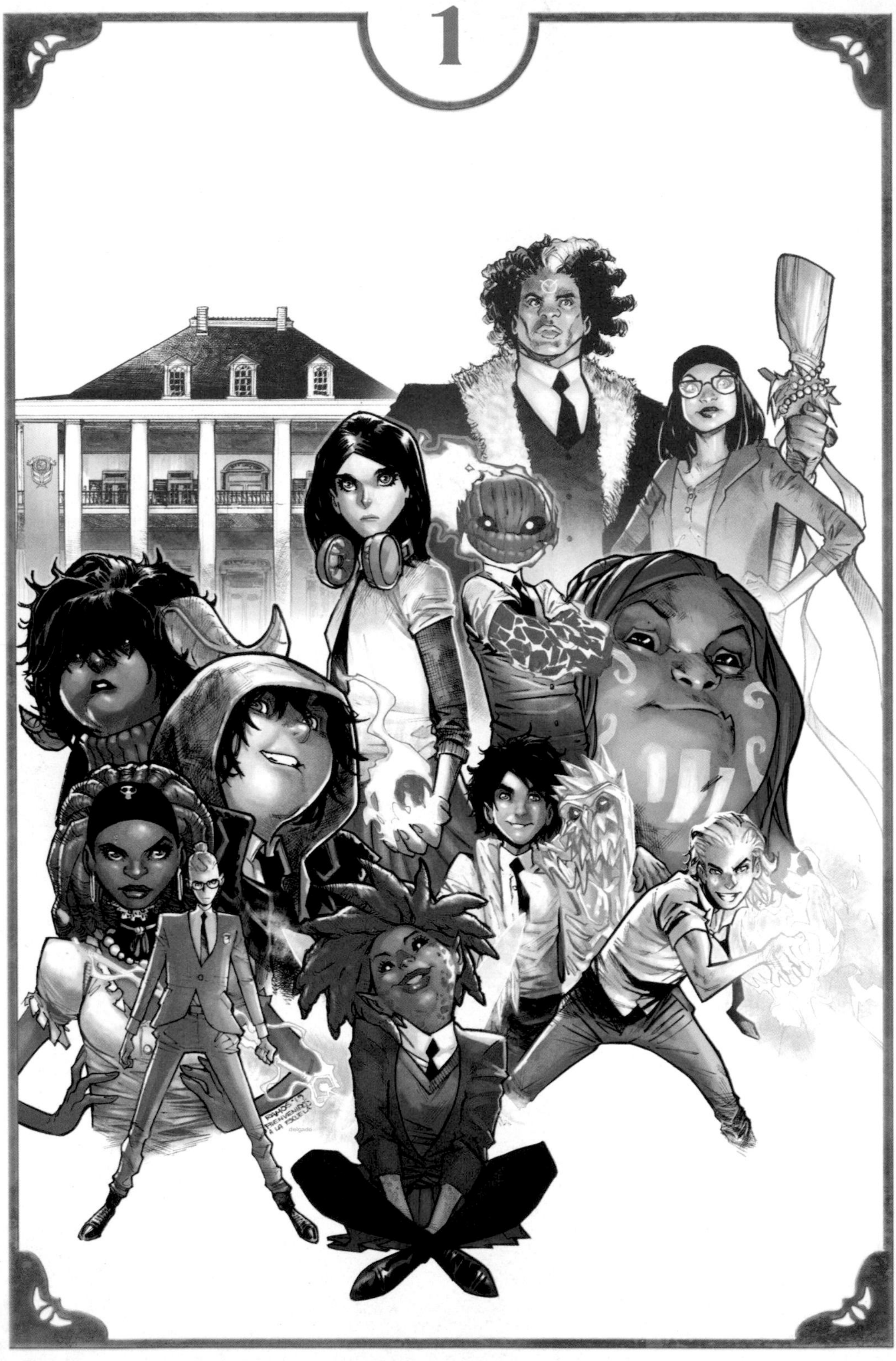

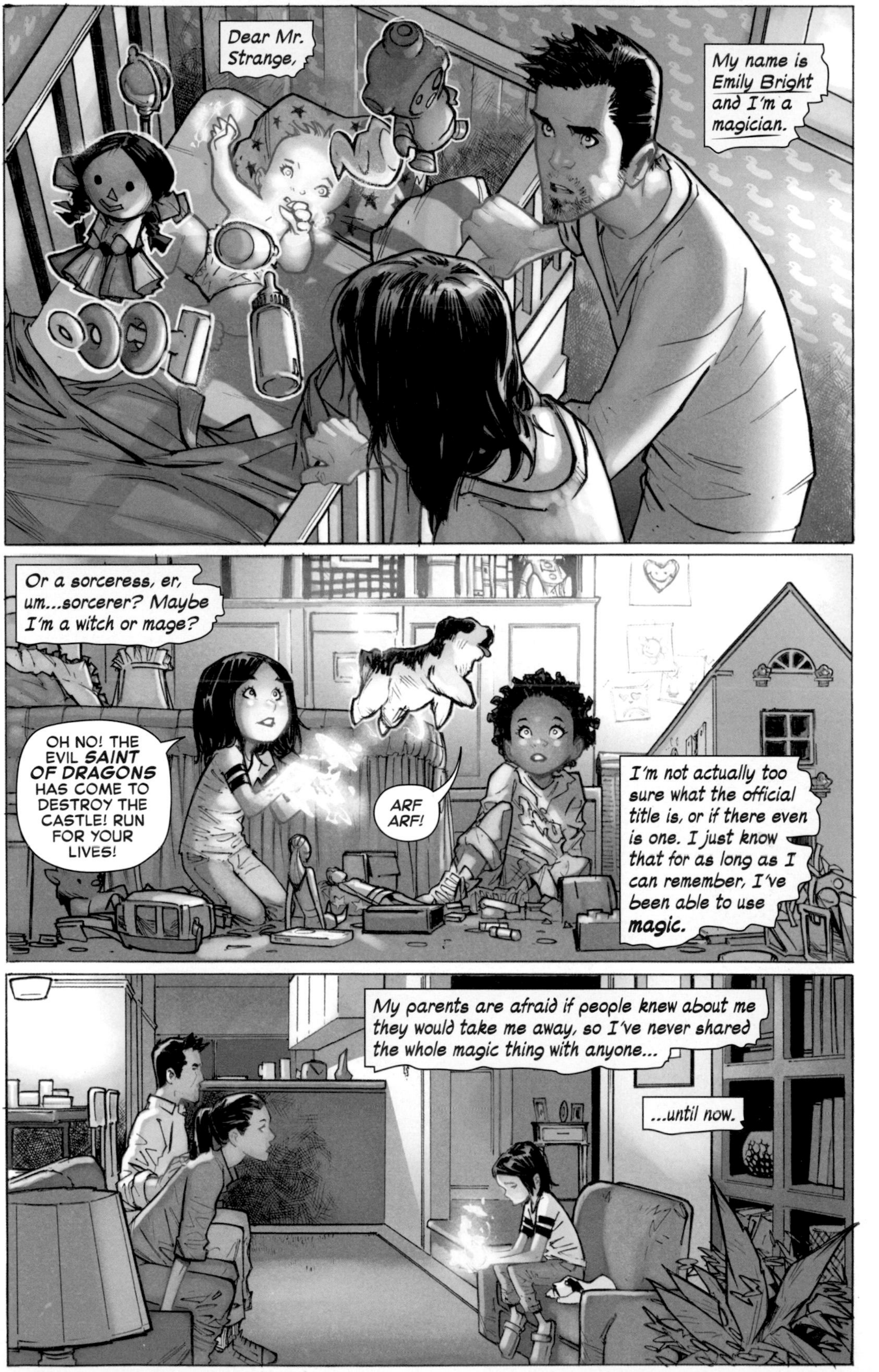

Dear Mr. Strange,
My name is Emily Bright and I'm a magician.
Or a sorceress, er, um...sorcerer? Maybe I'm a witch or mage?
OH NO! THE EVIL SAINT OF DRAGONS HAS COME TO DESTROY THE CASTLE! RUN FOR YOUR LIVES!
ARF ARF!
I'm not actually too sure what the official title is, or if there even is one. I just know that for as long as I can remember, I've been able to use magic.
My parents are afraid if people knew about me they would take me away, so I've never shared the whole magic thing with anyone...
...until now.

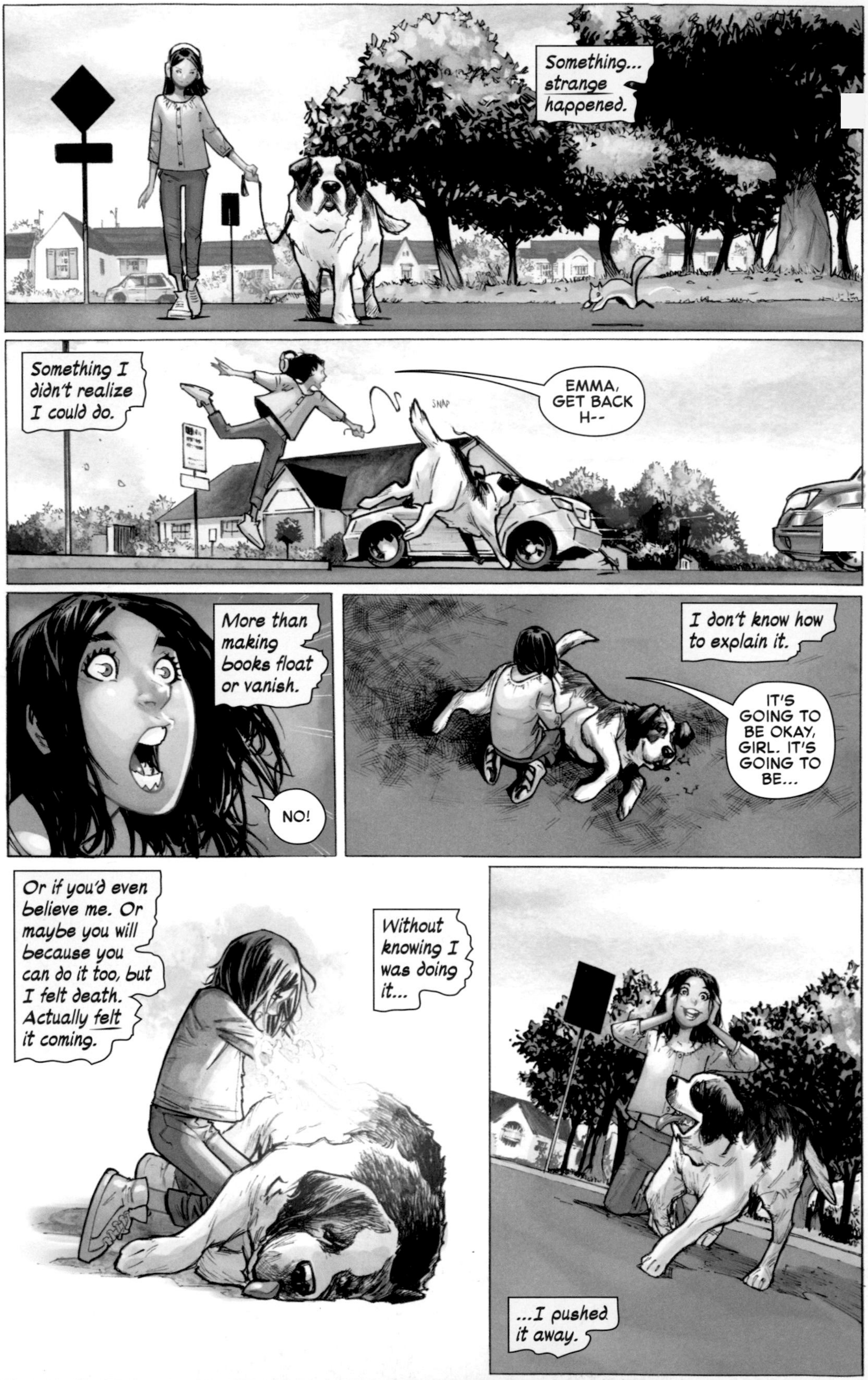
Something... strange happened.
Something I didn't realize I could do.
SNAP
EMMA, GET BACK H--
More than making books float or vanish.
NO!
I don't know how to explain it.
IT'S GOING TO BE OKAY, GIRL. IT'S GOING TO BE...
Or if you'd even believe me. Or maybe you will because you can do it too, but I felt death. Actually felt it coming.
Without knowing I was doing it...
...I pushed it away.

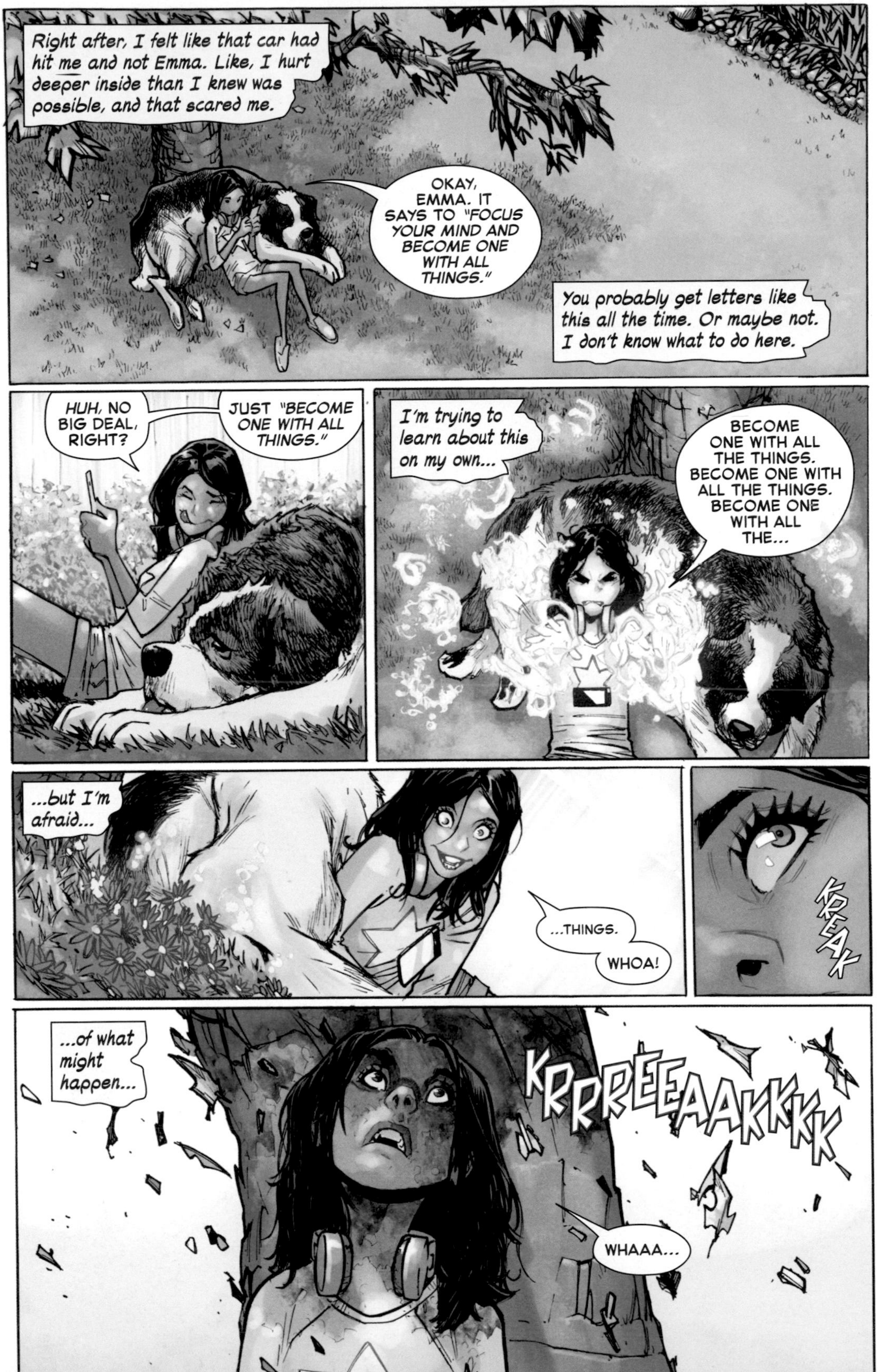

Right after, I felt like that car had hit me and not Emma. Like, I hurt deeper inside than I knew was possible, and that scared me.
OKAY, EMMA. IT SAYS TO "FOCUS YOUR MIND AND BECOME ONE WITH ALL THINGS."
You probably get letters like this all the time. Or maybe not. I don't know what to do here.
HUH, NO BIG DEAL, RIGHT?
JUST "BECOME ONE WITH ALL THINGS."
I'm trying to learn about this on my own...
BECOME ONE WITH ALL THE THINGS. BECOME ONE WITH ALL THE THINGS. BECOME ONE WITH ALL THE...
...but I'm afraid...
...THINGS.
WHOA!
KREAK
...of what might happen...
KRRREEAAKKKK
WHAAA...

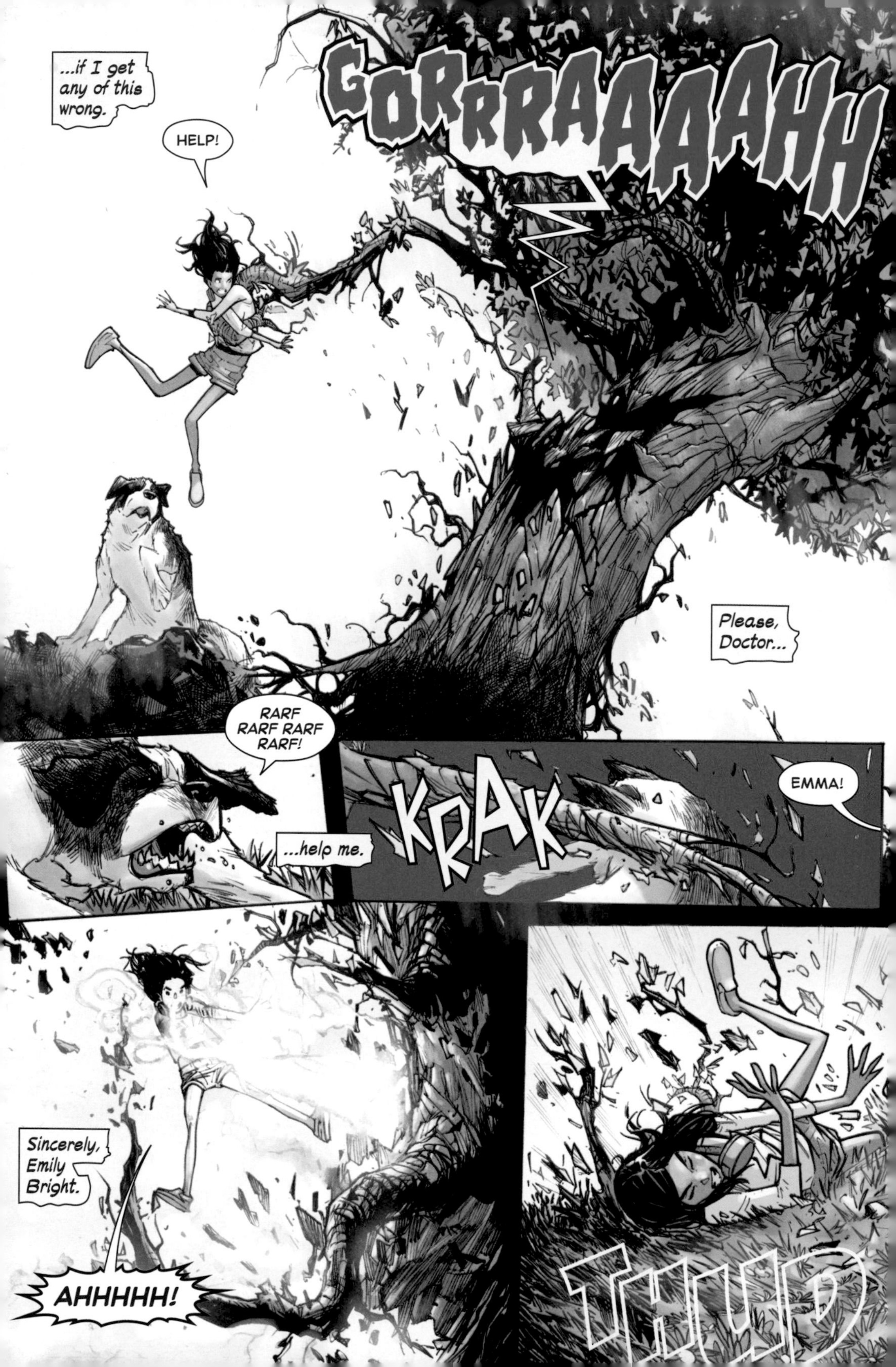
...if I get any of this wrong.
HELP!
GORRRAAAAHH
Please, Doctor...
RARF RARF RARF RARF!
...help me.
KRAK
EMMA!
Sincerely, Emily Bright.
AHHHHH!
THUD

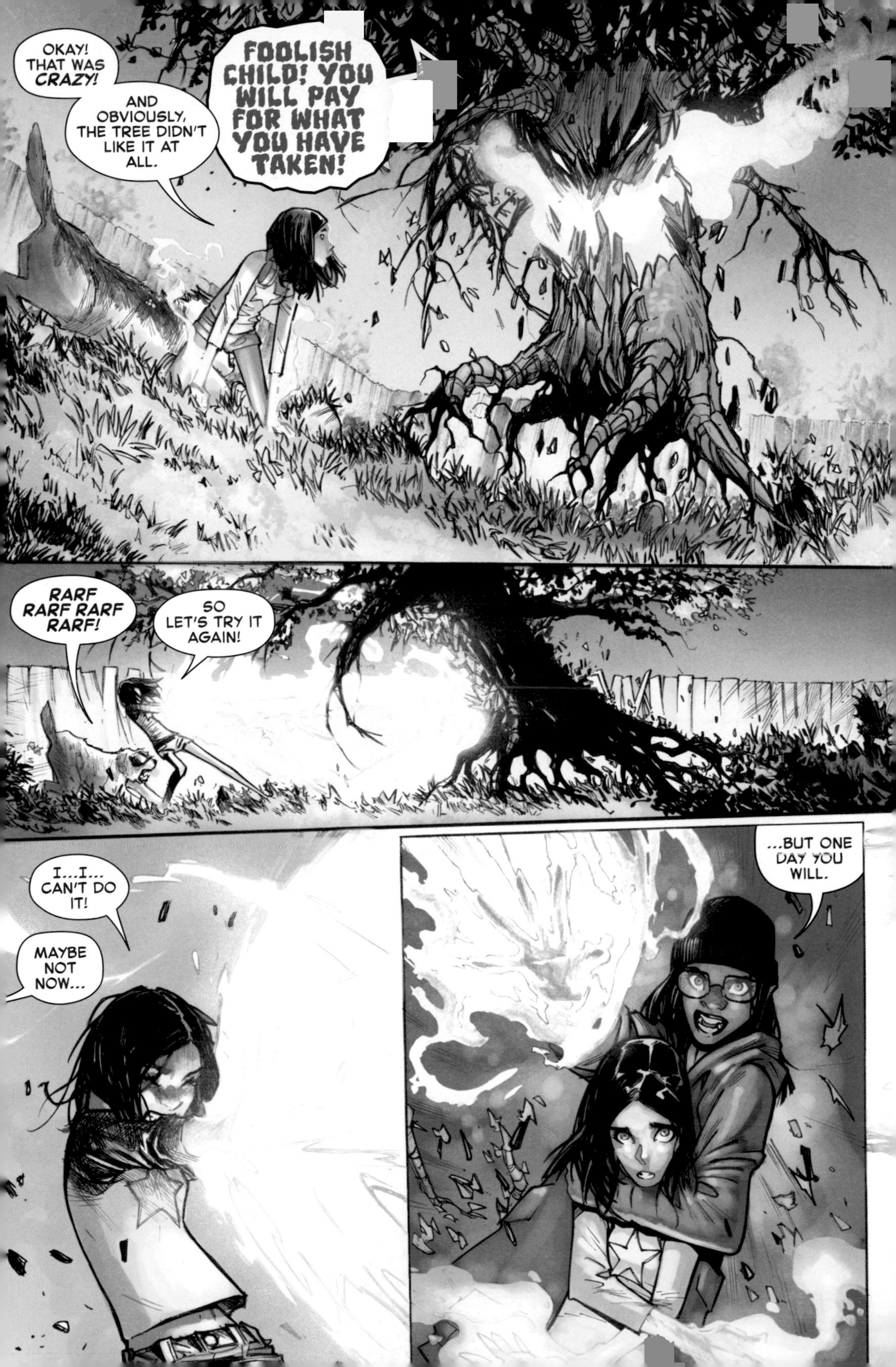
OKAY! THAT WAS *CRAZY!*
AND OBVIOUSLY, THE TREE DIDN'T LIKE IT AT ALL.
FOOLISH CHILD! YOU WILL PAY FOR WHAT YOU HAVE TAKEN!
RARF RARF RARF RARF!
SO LET'S TRY IT AGAIN!
I...I... CAN'T DO IT!
MAYBE NOT NOW...
...BUT ONE DAY YOU WILL.

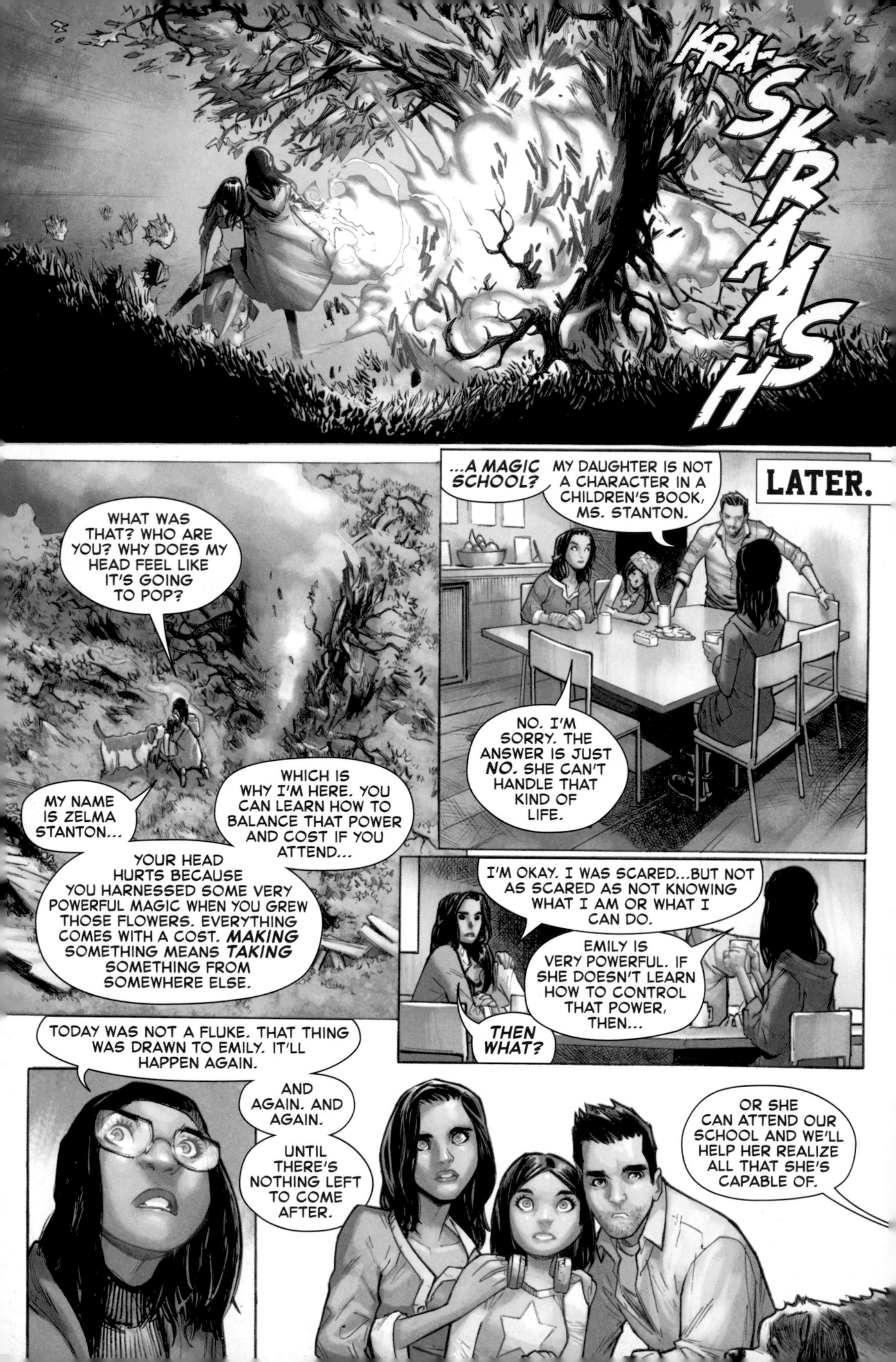
KRA-SKRAASH
WHAT WAS THAT? WHO ARE YOU? WHY DOES MY HEAD FEEL LIKE IT'S GOING TO POP?
MY NAME IS ZELMA STANTON...
YOUR HEAD HURTS BECAUSE YOU HARNESSED SOME VERY POWERFUL MAGIC WHEN YOU GREW THOSE FLOWERS. EVERYTHING COMES WITH A COST. *MAKING* SOMETHING MEANS *TAKING* SOMETHING FROM SOMEWHERE ELSE.
WHICH IS WHY I'M HERE. YOU CAN LEARN HOW TO BALANCE THAT POWER AND COST IF YOU ATTEND...
...A *MAGIC SCHOOL?*
MY DAUGHTER IS NOT A CHARACTER IN A CHILDREN'S BOOK, MS. STANTON.
LATER.
NO. I'M SORRY. THE ANSWER IS JUST *NO.* SHE CAN'T HANDLE THAT KIND OF LIFE.
I'M OKAY. I WAS SCARED...BUT NOT AS SCARED AS NOT KNOWING WHAT I AM OR WHAT I CAN DO.
EMILY IS VERY POWERFUL. IF SHE DOESN'T LEARN HOW TO CONTROL THAT POWER, THEN...
THEN WHAT?
TODAY WAS NOT A FLUKE. THAT THING WAS DRAWN TO EMILY. IT'LL HAPPEN AGAIN.
AND AGAIN. AND AGAIN.
UNTIL THERE'S NOTHING LEFT TO COME AFTER.
OR SHE CAN ATTEND OUR SCHOOL AND WE'LL HELP HER REALIZE ALL THAT SHE'S CAPABLE OF.

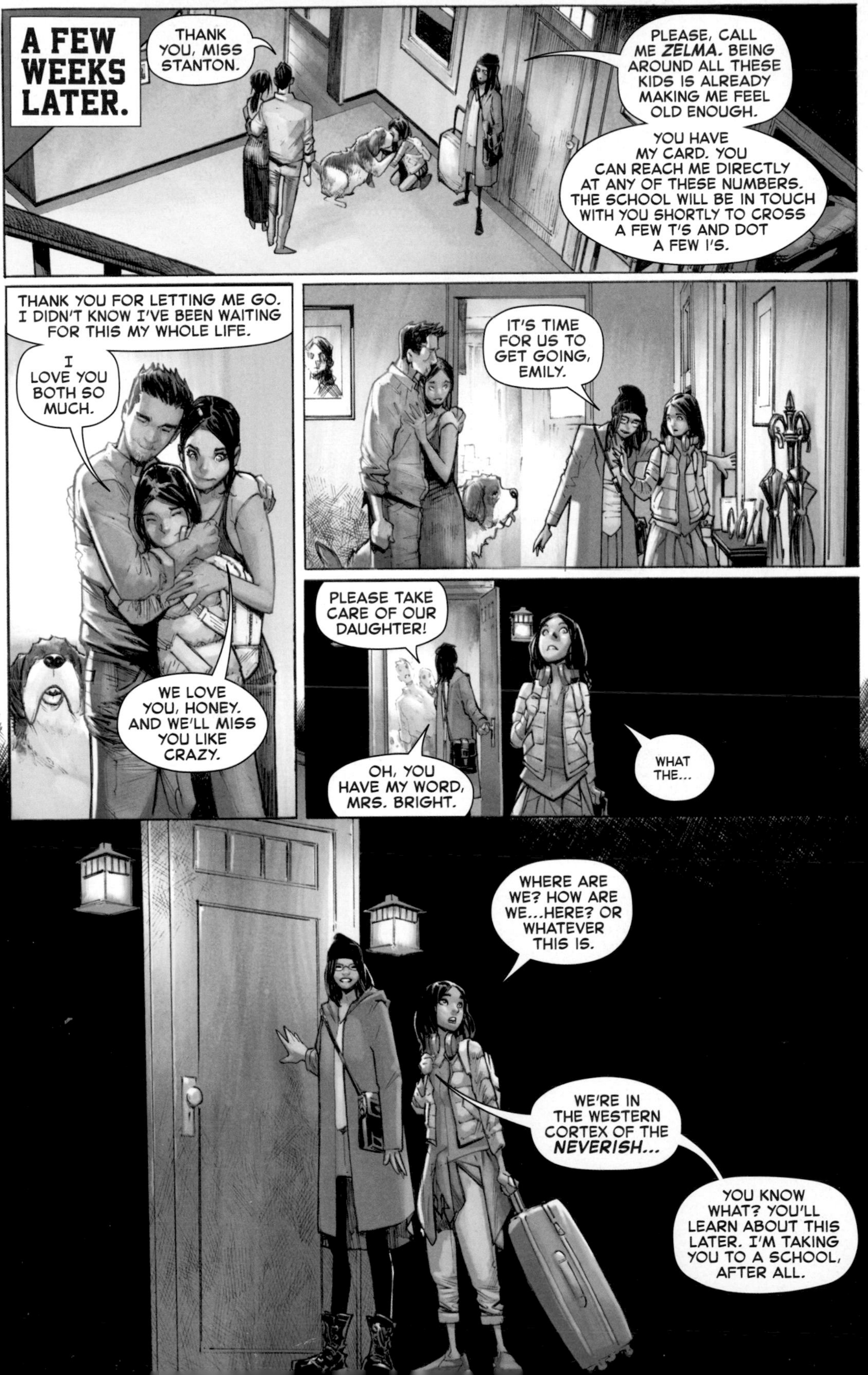
A FEW WEEKS LATER.
THANK YOU, MISS STANTON.
PLEASE, CALL ME ZELMA. BEING AROUND ALL THESE KIDS IS ALREADY MAKING ME FEEL OLD ENOUGH.
YOU HAVE MY CARD. YOU CAN REACH ME DIRECTLY AT ANY OF THESE NUMBERS. THE SCHOOL WILL BE IN TOUCH WITH YOU SHORTLY TO CROSS A FEW T'S AND DOT A FEW I'S.
THANK YOU FOR LETTING ME GO. I DIDN'T KNOW I'VE BEEN WAITING FOR THIS MY WHOLE LIFE.
I LOVE YOU BOTH SO MUCH.
WE LOVE YOU, HONEY. AND WE'LL MISS YOU LIKE CRAZY.
IT'S TIME FOR US TO GET GOING, EMILY.
PLEASE TAKE CARE OF OUR DAUGHTER!
OH, YOU HAVE MY WORD, MRS. BRIGHT.
WHAT THE...
WHERE ARE WE? HOW ARE WE...HERE? OR WHATEVER THIS IS.
WE'RE IN THE WESTERN CORTEX OF THE NEVERISH...
YOU KNOW WHAT? YOU'LL LEARN ABOUT THIS LATER. I'M TAKING YOU TO A SCHOOL, AFTER ALL.

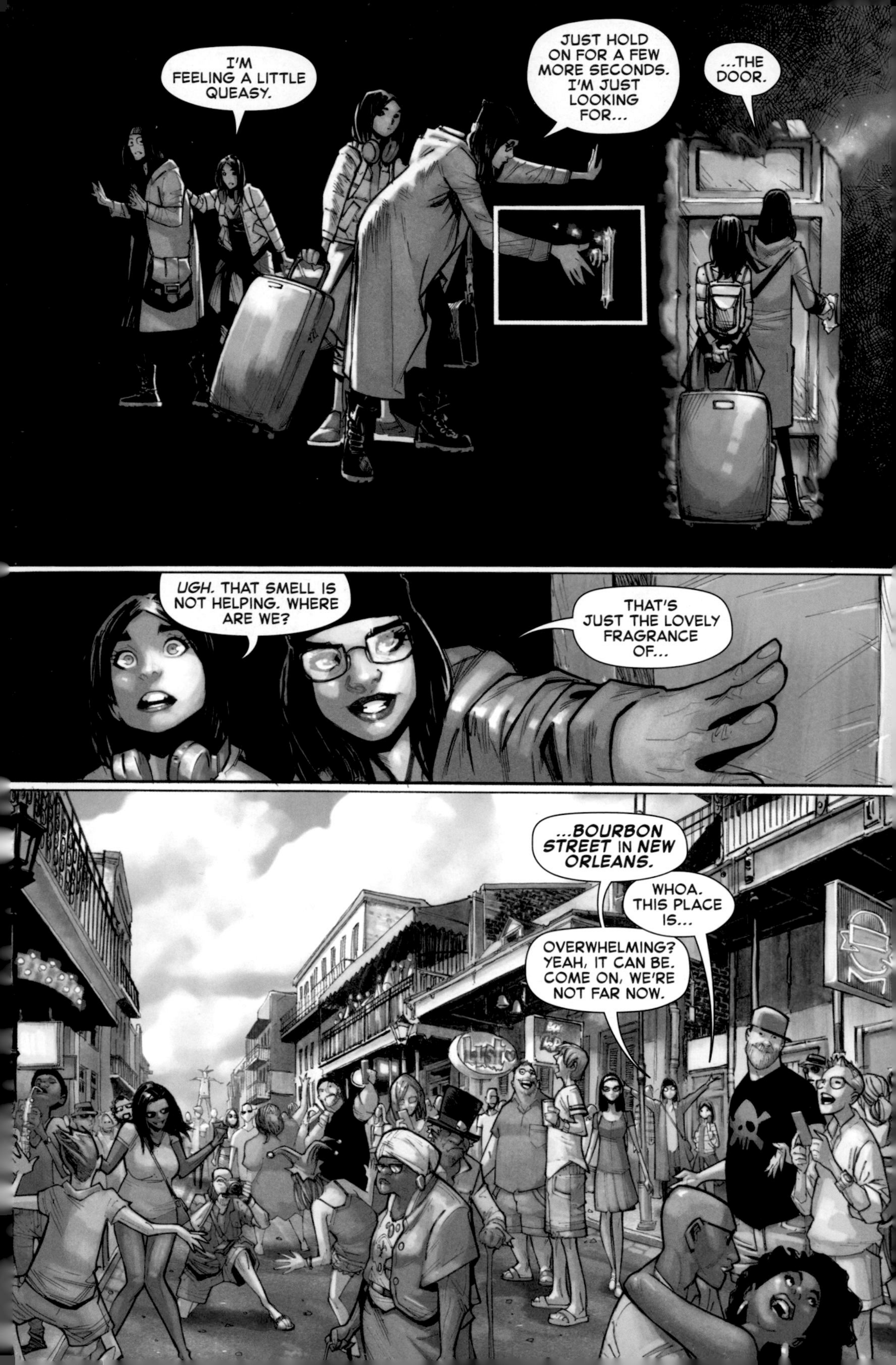
I'M FEELING A LITTLE QUEASY.
JUST HOLD ON FOR A FEW MORE SECONDS. I'M JUST LOOKING FOR...
...THE DOOR.
UGH. THAT SMELL IS NOT HELPING. WHERE ARE WE?
THAT'S JUST THE LOVELY FRAGRANCE OF...
...***BOURBON STREET*** IN ***NEW ORLEANS.***
WHOA. THIS PLACE IS...
OVERWHELMING? YEAH, IT CAN BE. COME ON, WE'RE NOT FAR NOW.

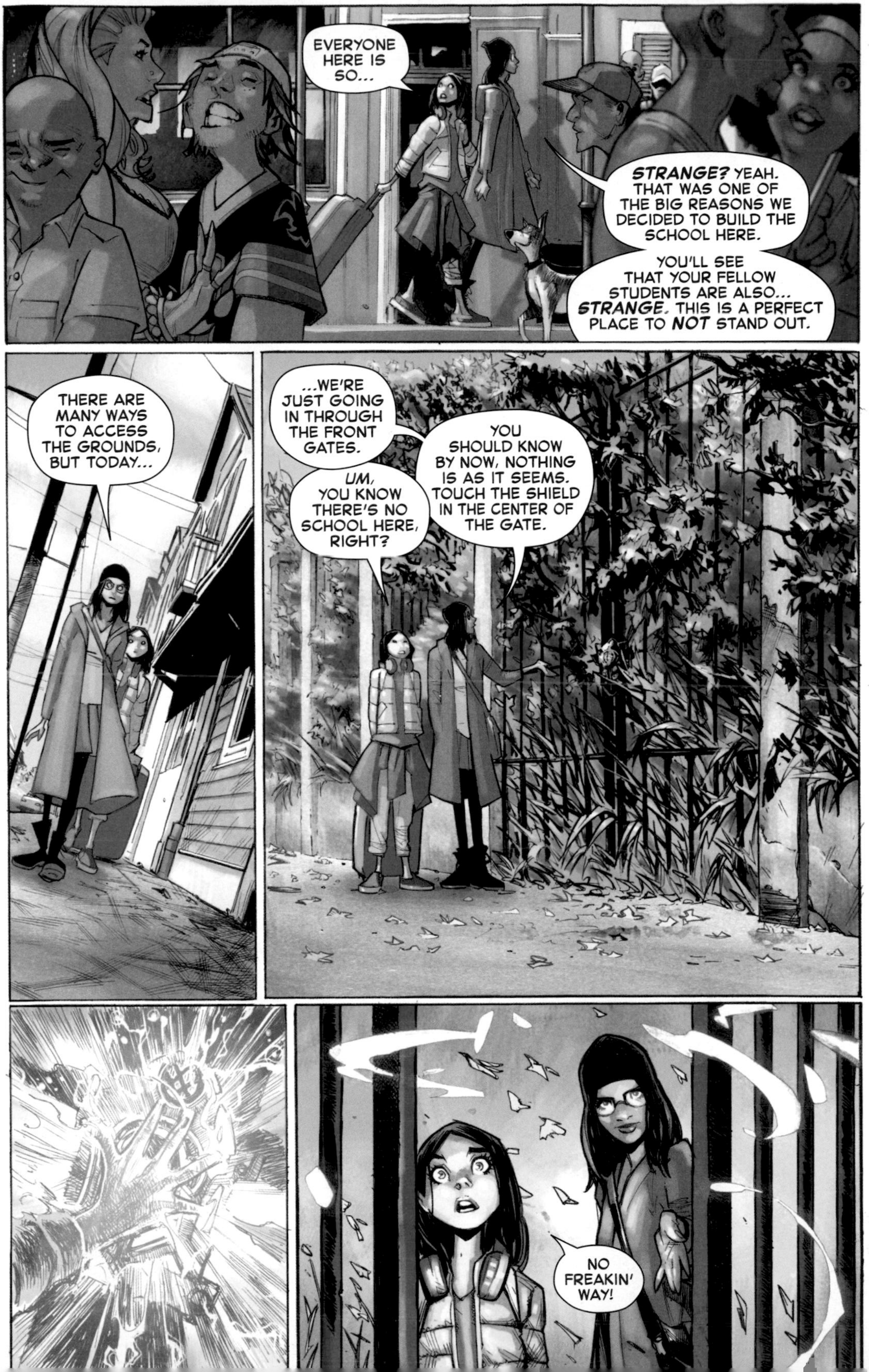
EVERYONE HERE IS SO...
STRANGE? YEAH. THAT WAS ONE OF THE BIG REASONS WE DECIDED TO BUILD THE SCHOOL HERE.
YOU'LL SEE THAT YOUR FELLOW STUDENTS ARE ALSO... STRANGE. THIS IS A PERFECT PLACE TO NOT STAND OUT.
THERE ARE MANY WAYS TO ACCESS THE GROUNDS, BUT TODAY...
...WE'RE JUST GOING IN THROUGH THE FRONT GATES.
UM, YOU KNOW THERE'S NO SCHOOL HERE, RIGHT?
YOU SHOULD KNOW BY NOW, NOTHING IS AS IT SEEMS. TOUCH THE SHIELD IN THE CENTER OF THE GATE.
NO FREAKIN' WAY!

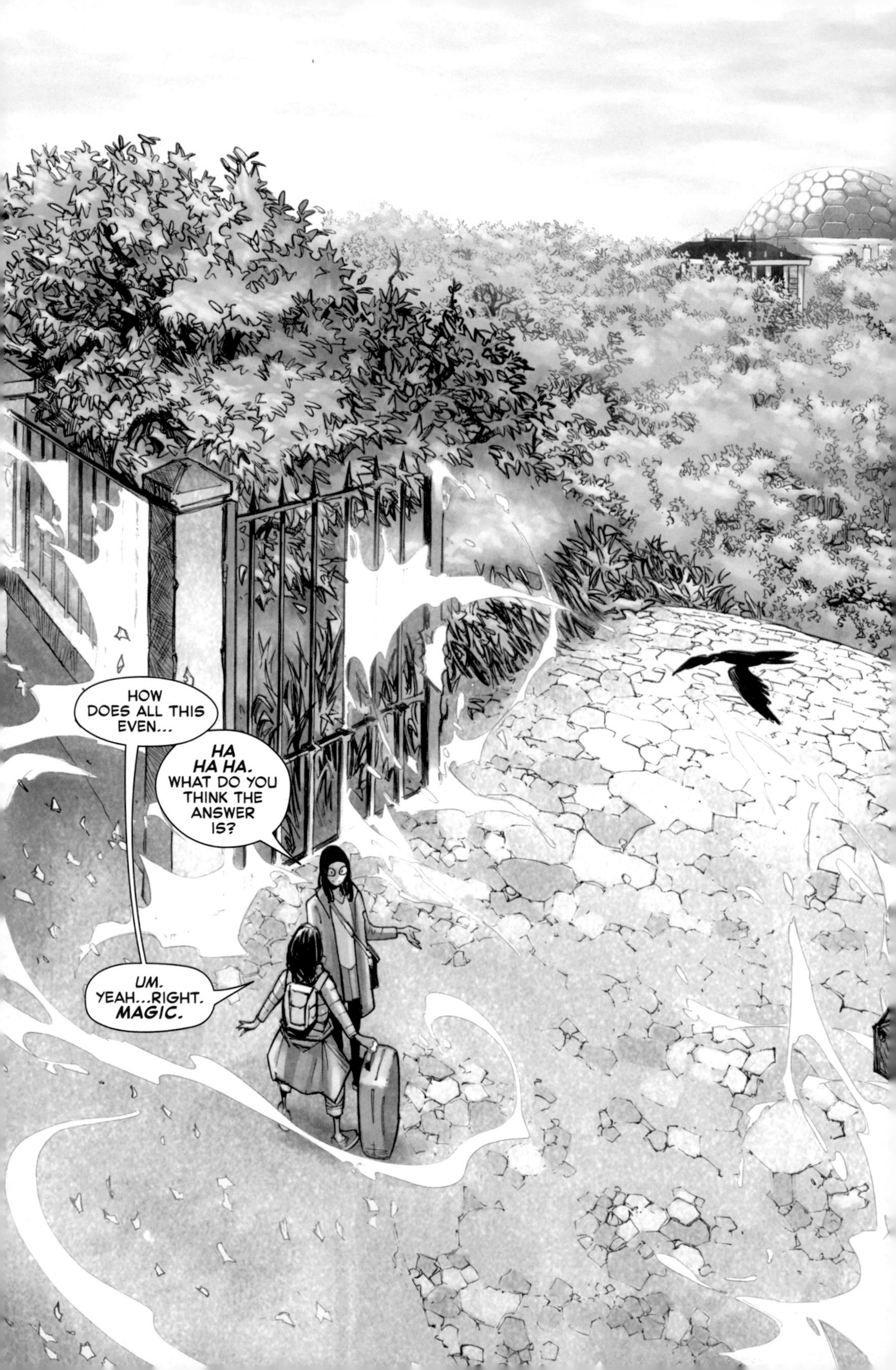
HOW DOES ALL THIS EVEN...
HA HA HA. WHAT DO YOU THINK THE ANSWER IS?
UM. YEAH...RIGHT. MAGIC.

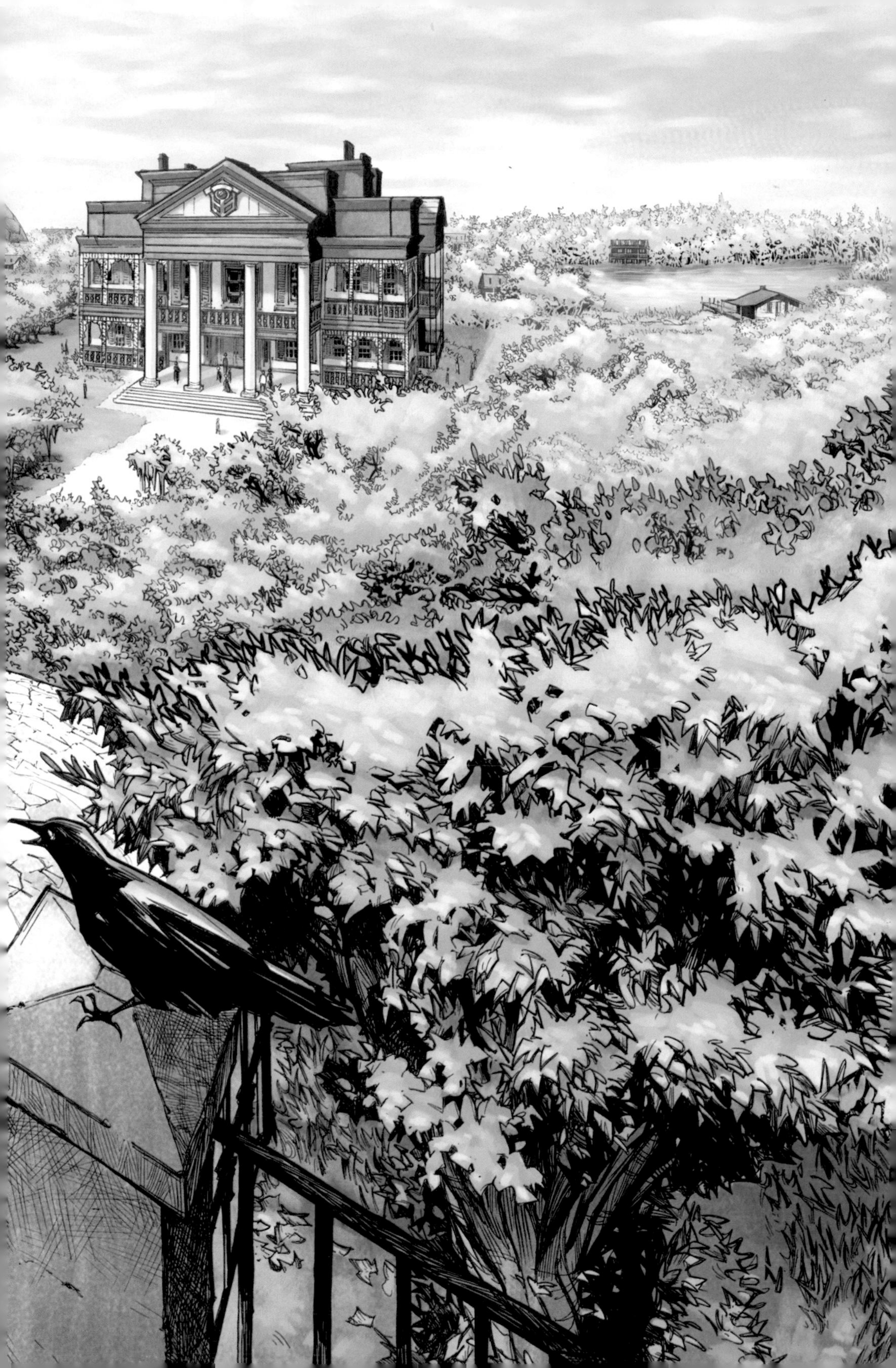

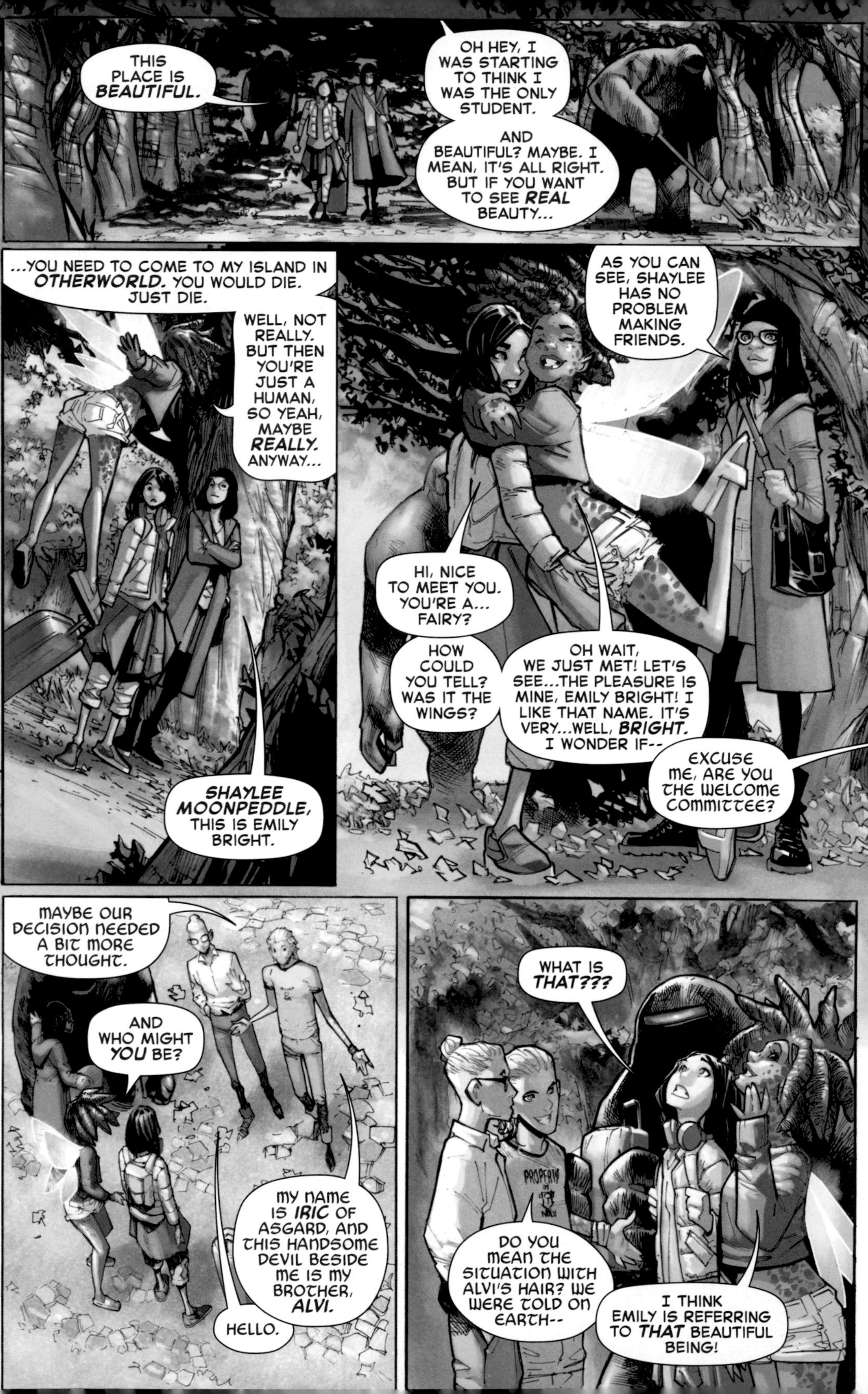
THIS PLACE IS BEAUTIFUL.
OH HEY, I WAS STARTING TO THINK I WAS THE ONLY STUDENT.
AND BEAUTIFUL? MAYBE. I MEAN, IT'S ALL RIGHT. BUT IF YOU WANT TO SEE REAL BEAUTY...
...YOU NEED TO COME TO MY ISLAND IN OTHERWORLD. YOU WOULD DIE. JUST DIE.
WELL, NOT REALLY. BUT THEN YOU'RE JUST A HUMAN, SO YEAH, MAYBE REALLY. ANYWAY...
SHAYLEE MOONPEDDLE, THIS IS EMILY BRIGHT.
AS YOU CAN SEE, SHAYLEE HAS NO PROBLEM MAKING FRIENDS.
HI, NICE TO MEET YOU. YOU'RE A... FAIRY?
HOW COULD YOU TELL? WAS IT THE WINGS?
OH WAIT, WE JUST MET! LET'S SEE...THE PLEASURE IS MINE, EMILY BRIGHT! I LIKE THAT NAME. IT'S VERY...WELL, BRIGHT. I WONDER IF--
EXCUSE ME, ARE YOU THE WELCOME COMMITTEE?
MAYBE OUR DECISION NEEDED A BIT MORE THOUGHT.
AND WHO MIGHT YOU BE?
MY NAME IS IRIC OF ASGARD, AND THIS HANDSOME DEVIL BESIDE ME IS MY BROTHER, ALVI.
HELLO.
WHAT IS THAT???
DO YOU MEAN THE SITUATION WITH ALVI'S HAIR? WE WERE TOLD ON EARTH--
I THINK EMILY IS REFERRING TO THAT BEAUTIFUL BEING!

AHHH! THAT IS A FROST GIANT!

ARE YOU SEEING THIS, BROTHER?

KIND OF HARD *NOT* TO SEE SOMETHING THAT BIG AND DISGUSTING.

BOYS, BOYS, BOYS...

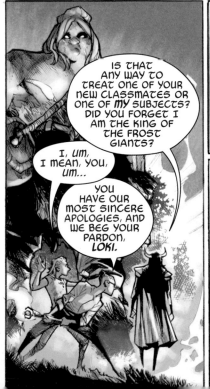

IS THAT ANY WAY TO TREAT ONE OF YOUR NEW CLASSMATES OR ONE OF *MY* SUBJECTS? DID YOU FORGET I AM THE KING OF THE FROST GIANTS?

I, um, I MEAN, YOU, um...

YOU HAVE OUR MOST SINCERE APOLOGIES, AND WE BEG YOUR PARDON, *LOKI.*

KIDS WILL BE KIDS.

IT'S VERY GOOD TO SEE YOU AGAIN, ZELMA. I DIDN'T REALIZE HOW MUCH I--

SHHH. THAT'S ENOUGH. I'M AT *WORK.*

WELCOME, GUSLAUG.

I DON'T MEAN TO INTERRUPT *KING HUMBLEBRAG...*

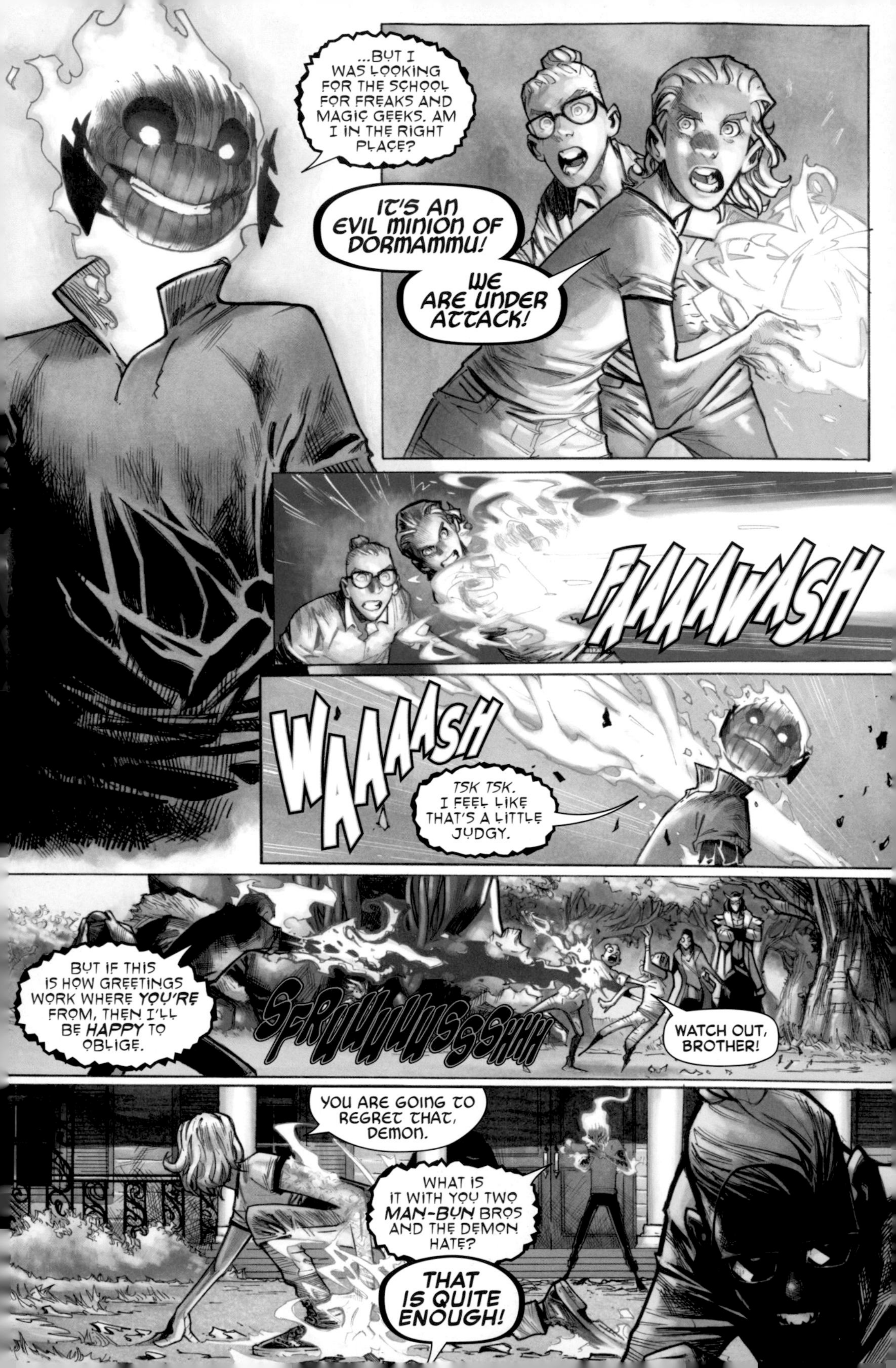
...BUT I WAS LOOKING FOR THE SCHOOL FOR FREAKS AND MAGIC GEEKS. AM I IN THE RIGHT PLACE?
IT'S AN EVIL MINION OF DORMAMMU!
WE ARE UNDER ATTACK!
FAAAAWASH
WAAAAASH
TSK TSK. I FEEL LIKE THAT'S A LITTLE JUDGY.
BUT IF THIS IS HOW GREETINGS WORK WHERE YOU'RE FROM, THEN I'LL BE HAPPY TO OBLIGE.
SFRUUUUUSSSHH
WATCH OUT, BROTHER!
YOU ARE GOING TO REGRET THAT, DEMON.
WHAT IS IT WITH YOU TWO MAN-BUN BROS AND THE DEMON HATE?
THAT IS QUITE ENOUGH!

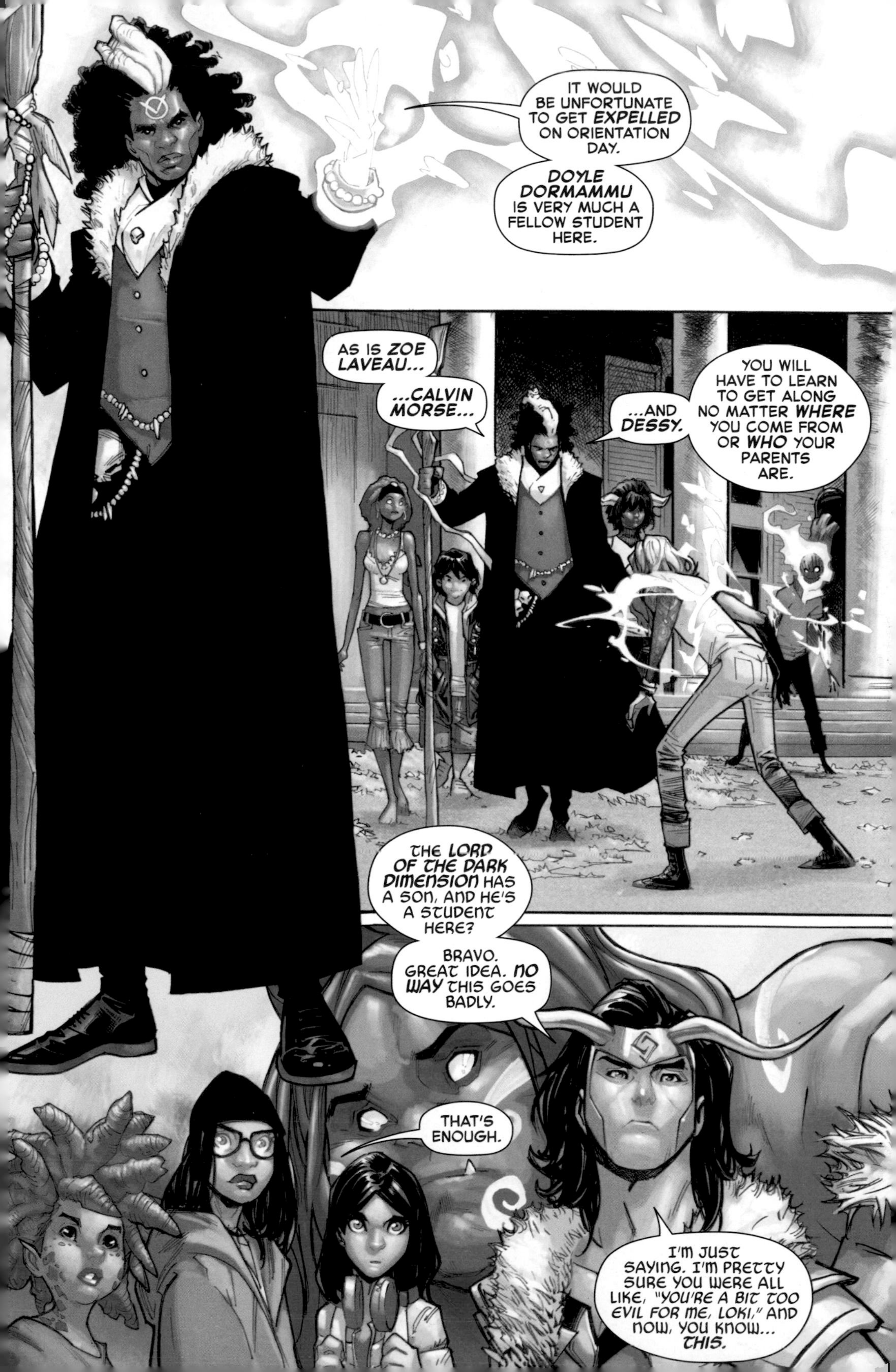
IT WOULD BE UNFORTUNATE TO GET EXPELLED ON ORIENTATION DAY.
DOYLE DORMAMMU IS VERY MUCH A FELLOW STUDENT HERE.
AS IS ZOE LAVEAU...
...CALVIN MORSE...
...AND DESSY.
YOU WILL HAVE TO LEARN TO GET ALONG NO MATTER WHERE YOU COME FROM OR WHO YOUR PARENTS ARE.
THE LORD OF THE DARK DIMENSION HAS A SON, AND HE'S A STUDENT HERE?
BRAVO. GREAT IDEA. NO WAY THIS GOES BADLY.
THAT'S ENOUGH.
I'M JUST SAYING. I'M PRETTY SURE YOU WERE ALL LIKE, "YOU'RE A BIT TOO EVIL FOR ME, LOKI," AND NOW, YOU KNOW... THIS.

"OKAY, IF WE'RE DONE WITH THIS LITTLE SPAT, ZELMA WILL SHOW YOU AROUND CAMPUS."

WOW, HOW OLD IS THIS PLACE?

SOME SAY IT'S BEEN HERE LONGER THAN THE CITY ITSELF.

ZOE'S PARTIALLY RIGHT. *THIS* LOCATION HAS BEEN A SANCTUARY FOR THOSE IN THE MYSTIC ARTS SINCE BEFORE RECORDED HISTORY.

I THINK THE OLDEST THING WHERE I'M FROM IN KANSAS IS THE BURGER SHACK.

THE BUILDING ITSELF WAS BUILT IN THE 1800s, AND, LIKE YOU ALL NOTICED WHEN YOU WERE OUTSIDE THE GATES, NOTHING HERE HAS EVER BEEN WHAT IT SEEMS.

FOR EXAMPLE, YOUR CLASSROOM FOR *THE MAGIC OF THE COSMOS...*

...ISN'T WHAT YOU MIGHT EXPECT.

IS THAT--

SPACE? YES, IT IS.

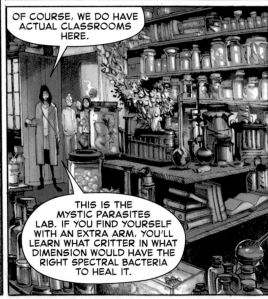

OF COURSE, WE DO HAVE ACTUAL CLASSROOMS HERE.

THIS IS THE MYSTIC PARASITES LAB. IF YOU FIND YOURSELF WITH AN EXTRA ARM, YOU'LL LEARN WHAT CRITTER IN WHAT DIMENSION WOULD HAVE THE RIGHT SPECTRAL BACTERIA TO HEAL IT.

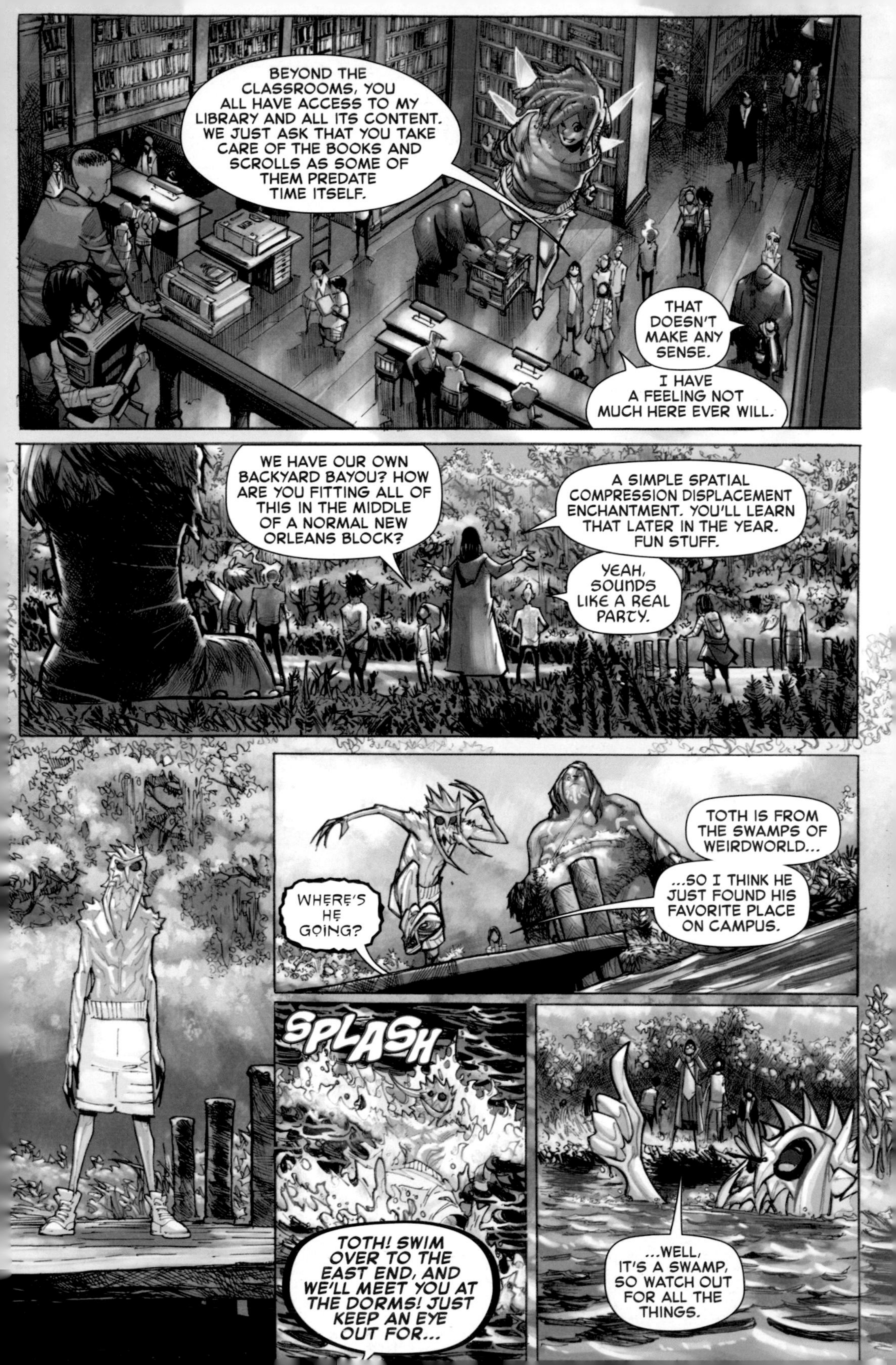
BEYOND THE CLASSROOMS, YOU ALL HAVE ACCESS TO MY LIBRARY AND ALL ITS CONTENT. WE JUST ASK THAT YOU TAKE CARE OF THE BOOKS AND SCROLLS AS SOME OF THEM PREDATE TIME ITSELF.
THAT DOESN'T MAKE ANY SENSE.
I HAVE A FEELING NOT MUCH HERE EVER WILL.
WE HAVE OUR OWN BACKYARD BAYOU? HOW ARE YOU FITTING ALL OF THIS IN THE MIDDLE OF A NORMAL NEW ORLEANS BLOCK?
A SIMPLE SPATIAL COMPRESSION DISPLACEMENT ENCHANTMENT. YOU'LL LEARN THAT LATER IN THE YEAR. FUN STUFF.
YEAH, SOUNDS LIKE A REAL PARTY.
WHERE'S HE GOING?
TOTH IS FROM THE SWAMPS OF WEIRDWORLD...
...SO I THINK HE JUST FOUND HIS FAVORITE PLACE ON CAMPUS.
SPLASH
TOTH! SWIM OVER TO THE EAST END, AND WE'LL MEET YOU AT THE DORMS! JUST KEEP AN EYE OUT FOR...
...WELL, IT'S A SWAMP, SO WATCH OUT FOR ALL THE THINGS.

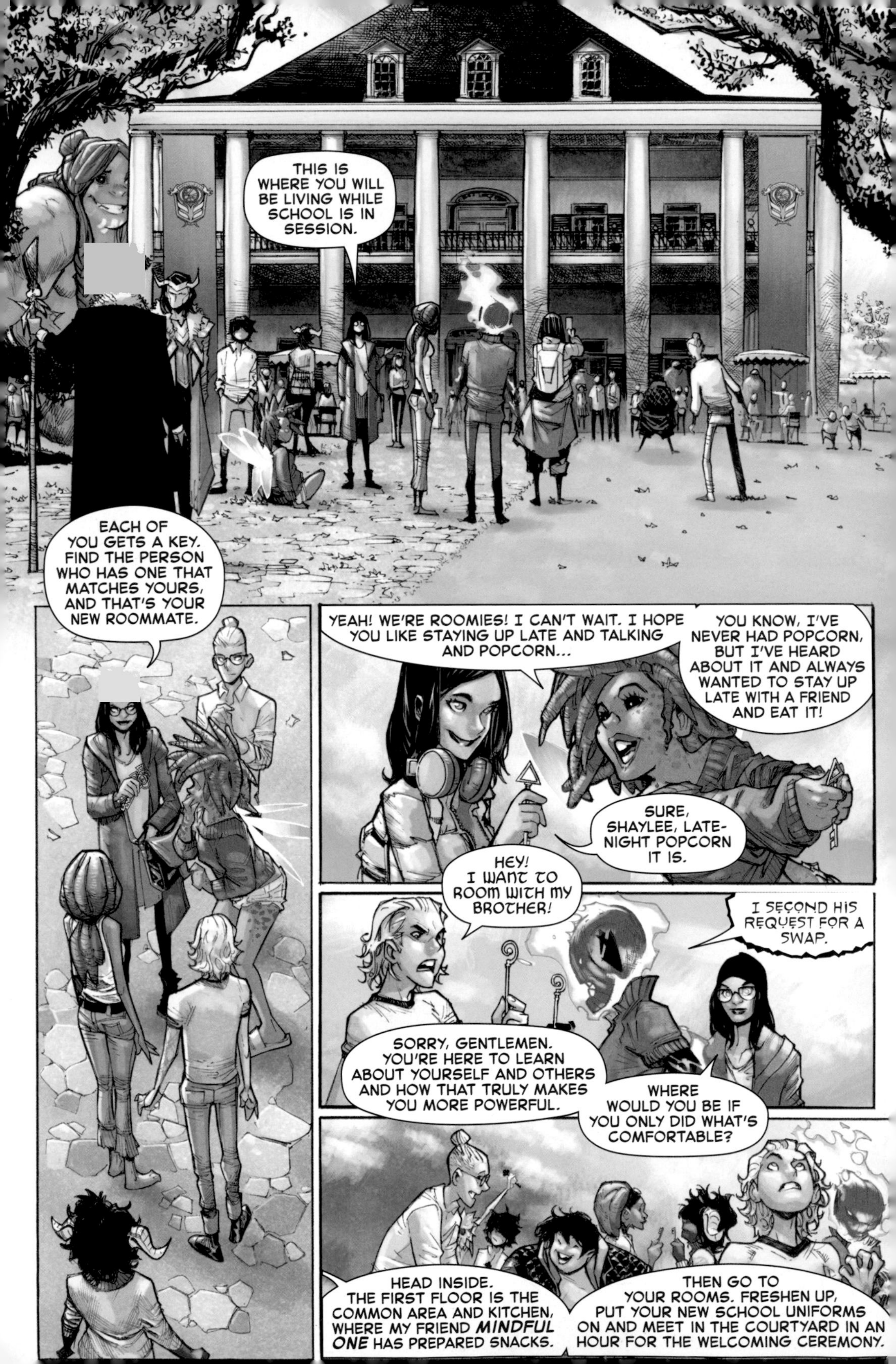
THIS IS WHERE YOU WILL BE LIVING WHILE SCHOOL IS IN SESSION.
EACH OF YOU GETS A KEY. FIND THE PERSON WHO HAS ONE THAT MATCHES YOURS, AND THAT'S YOUR NEW ROOMMATE.
YEAH! WE'RE ROOMIES! I CAN'T WAIT. I HOPE YOU LIKE STAYING UP LATE AND TALKING AND POPCORN...
YOU KNOW, I'VE NEVER HAD POPCORN, BUT I'VE HEARD ABOUT IT AND ALWAYS WANTED TO STAY UP LATE WITH A FRIEND AND EAT IT!
SURE, SHAYLEE, LATE-NIGHT POPCORN IT IS.
HEY! I WANT TO ROOM WITH MY BROTHER!
I SECOND HIS REQUEST FOR A SWAP.
SORRY, GENTLEMEN. YOU'RE HERE TO LEARN ABOUT YOURSELF AND OTHERS AND HOW THAT TRULY MAKES YOU MORE POWERFUL.
WHERE WOULD YOU BE IF YOU ONLY DID WHAT'S COMFORTABLE?
HEAD INSIDE. THE FIRST FLOOR IS THE COMMON AREA AND KITCHEN, WHERE MY FRIEND MINDFUL ONE HAS PREPARED SNACKS.
THEN GO TO YOUR ROOMS. FRESHEN UP, PUT YOUR NEW SCHOOL UNIFORMS ON AND MEET IN THE COURTYARD IN AN HOUR FOR THE WELCOMING CEREMONY.

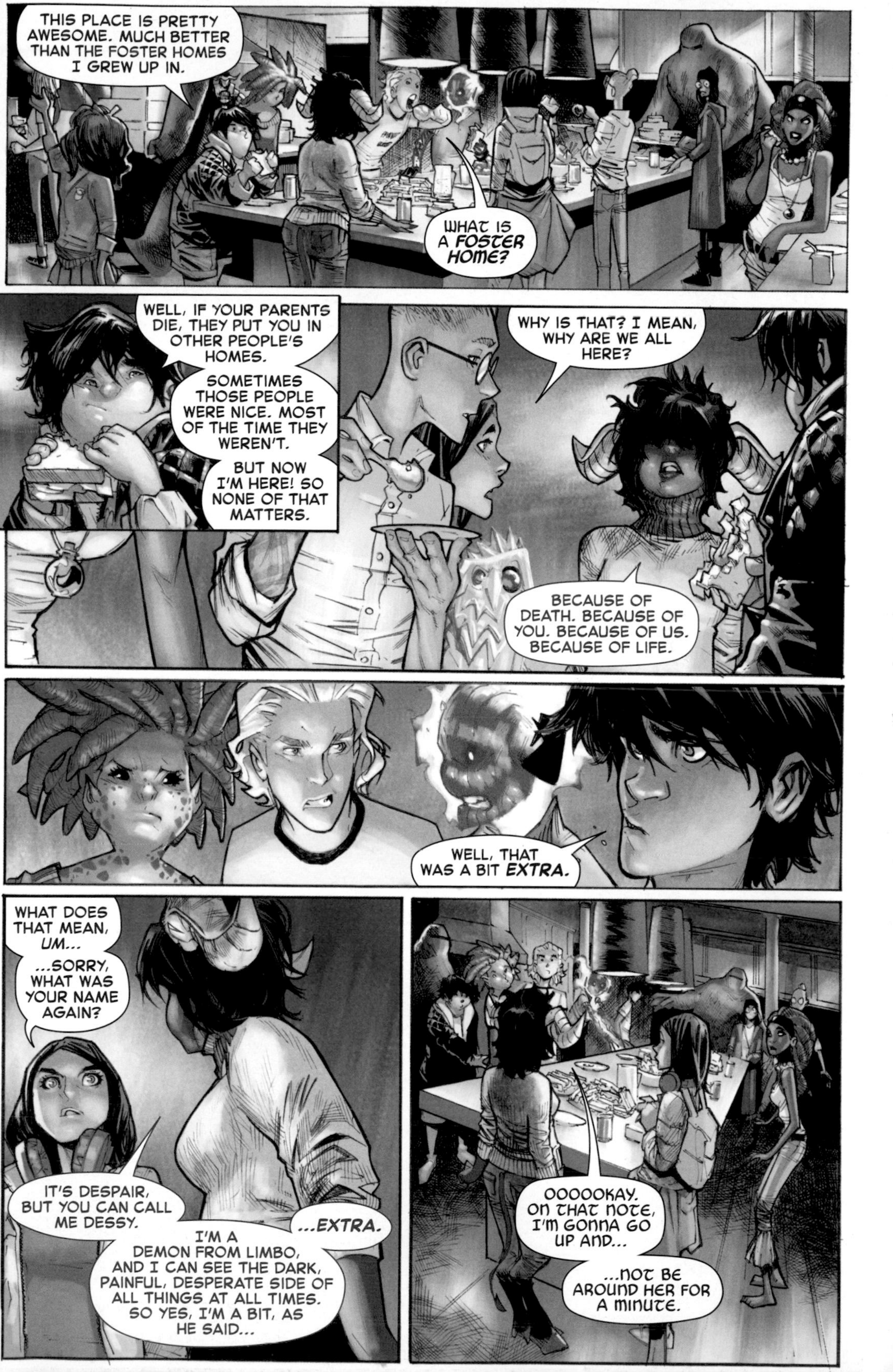
THIS PLACE IS PRETTY AWESOME. MUCH BETTER THAN THE FOSTER HOMES I GREW UP IN.
WHAT IS A *FOSTER HOME?*
WELL, IF YOUR PARENTS DIE, THEY PUT YOU IN OTHER PEOPLE'S HOMES.
SOMETIMES THOSE PEOPLE WERE NICE. MOST OF THE TIME THEY WEREN'T.
BUT NOW I'M HERE! SO NONE OF THAT MATTERS.
WHY IS THAT? I MEAN, WHY ARE WE ALL HERE?
BECAUSE OF DEATH. BECAUSE OF YOU. BECAUSE OF US. BECAUSE OF LIFE.
WELL, THAT WAS A BIT *EXTRA.*
WHAT DOES THAT MEAN, *UM...*
...SORRY, WHAT WAS YOUR NAME AGAIN?
IT'S DESPAIR, BUT YOU CAN CALL ME DESSY.
I'M A DEMON FROM LIMBO, AND I CAN SEE THE DARK, PAINFUL, DESPERATE SIDE OF ALL THINGS AT ALL TIMES. SO YES, I'M A BIT, AS HE SAID...
...EXTRA.
OOOOOKAY. ON THAT NOTE, I'M GONNA GO UP AND...
...NOT BE AROUND HER FOR A MINUTE.

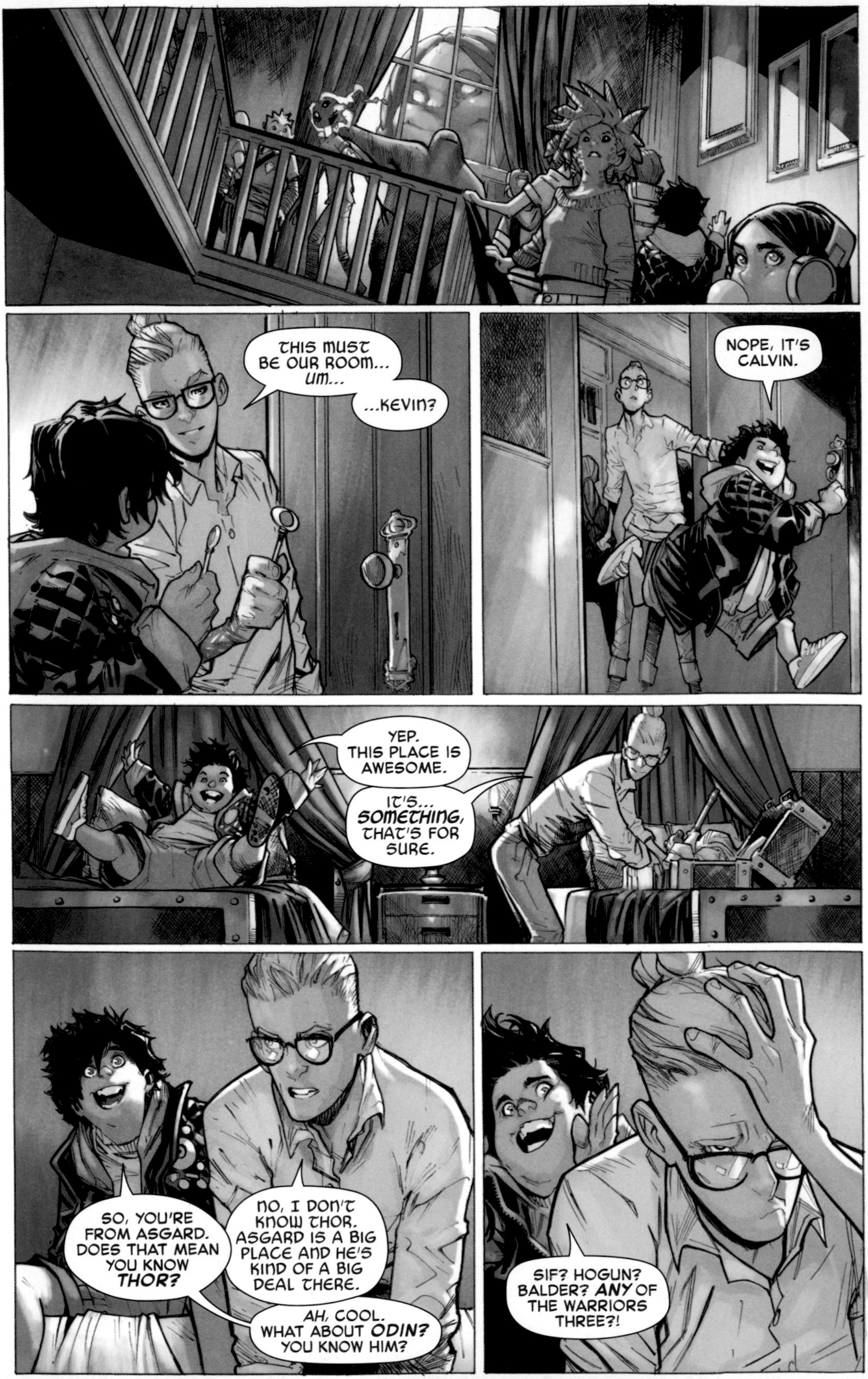
THIS MUST BE OUR ROOM... UM...
...KEVIN?
NOPE, IT'S CALVIN.
YEP. THIS PLACE IS AWESOME.
IT'S... SOMETHING, THAT'S FOR SURE.
SO, YOU'RE FROM ASGARD. DOES THAT MEAN YOU KNOW THOR?
NO, I DON'T KNOW THOR. ASGARD IS A BIG PLACE AND HE'S KIND OF A BIG DEAL THERE.
AH, COOL. WHAT ABOUT ODIN? YOU KNOW HIM?
SIF? HOGUN? BALDER? ANY OF THE WARRIORS THREE?!

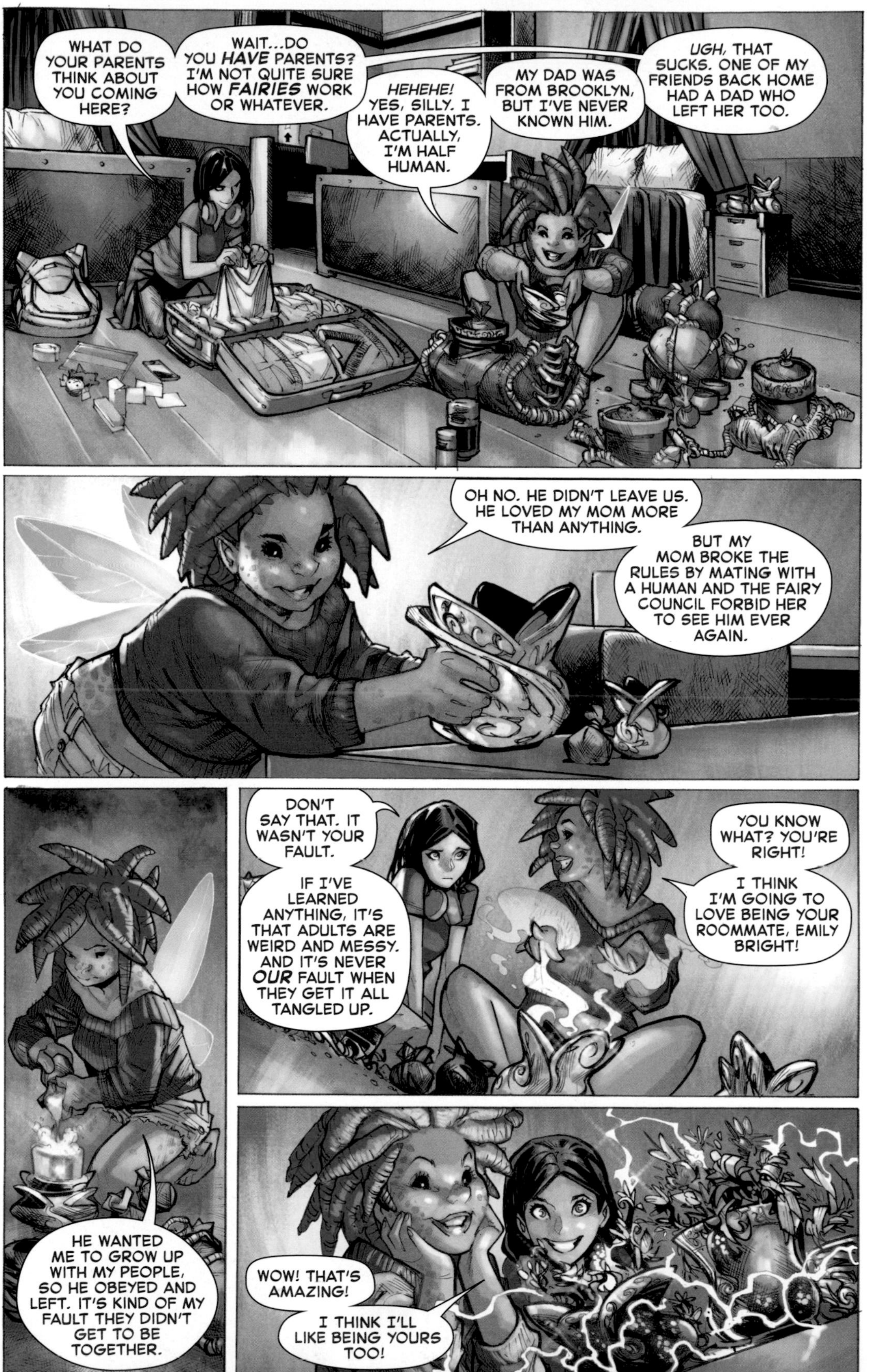
WHAT DO YOUR PARENTS THINK ABOUT YOU COMING HERE?
WAIT...DO YOU HAVE PARENTS? I'M NOT QUITE SURE HOW FAIRIES WORK OR WHATEVER.
HEHEHE! YES, SILLY. I HAVE PARENTS. ACTUALLY, I'M HALF HUMAN.
MY DAD WAS FROM BROOKLYN, BUT I'VE NEVER KNOWN HIM.
UGH, THAT SUCKS. ONE OF MY FRIENDS BACK HOME HAD A DAD WHO LEFT HER TOO.
OH NO. HE DIDN'T LEAVE US. HE LOVED MY MOM MORE THAN ANYTHING.
BUT MY MOM BROKE THE RULES BY MATING WITH A HUMAN AND THE FAIRY COUNCIL FORBID HER TO SEE HIM EVER AGAIN.
HE WANTED ME TO GROW UP WITH MY PEOPLE, SO HE OBEYED AND LEFT. IT'S KIND OF MY FAULT THEY DIDN'T GET TO BE TOGETHER.
DON'T SAY THAT. IT WASN'T YOUR FAULT.
IF I'VE LEARNED ANYTHING, IT'S THAT ADULTS ARE WEIRD AND MESSY. AND IT'S NEVER OUR FAULT WHEN THEY GET IT ALL TANGLED UP.
YOU KNOW WHAT? YOU'RE RIGHT!
I THINK I'M GOING TO LOVE BEING YOUR ROOMMATE, EMILY BRIGHT!
WOW! THAT'S AMAZING!
I THINK I'LL LIKE BEING YOURS TOO!

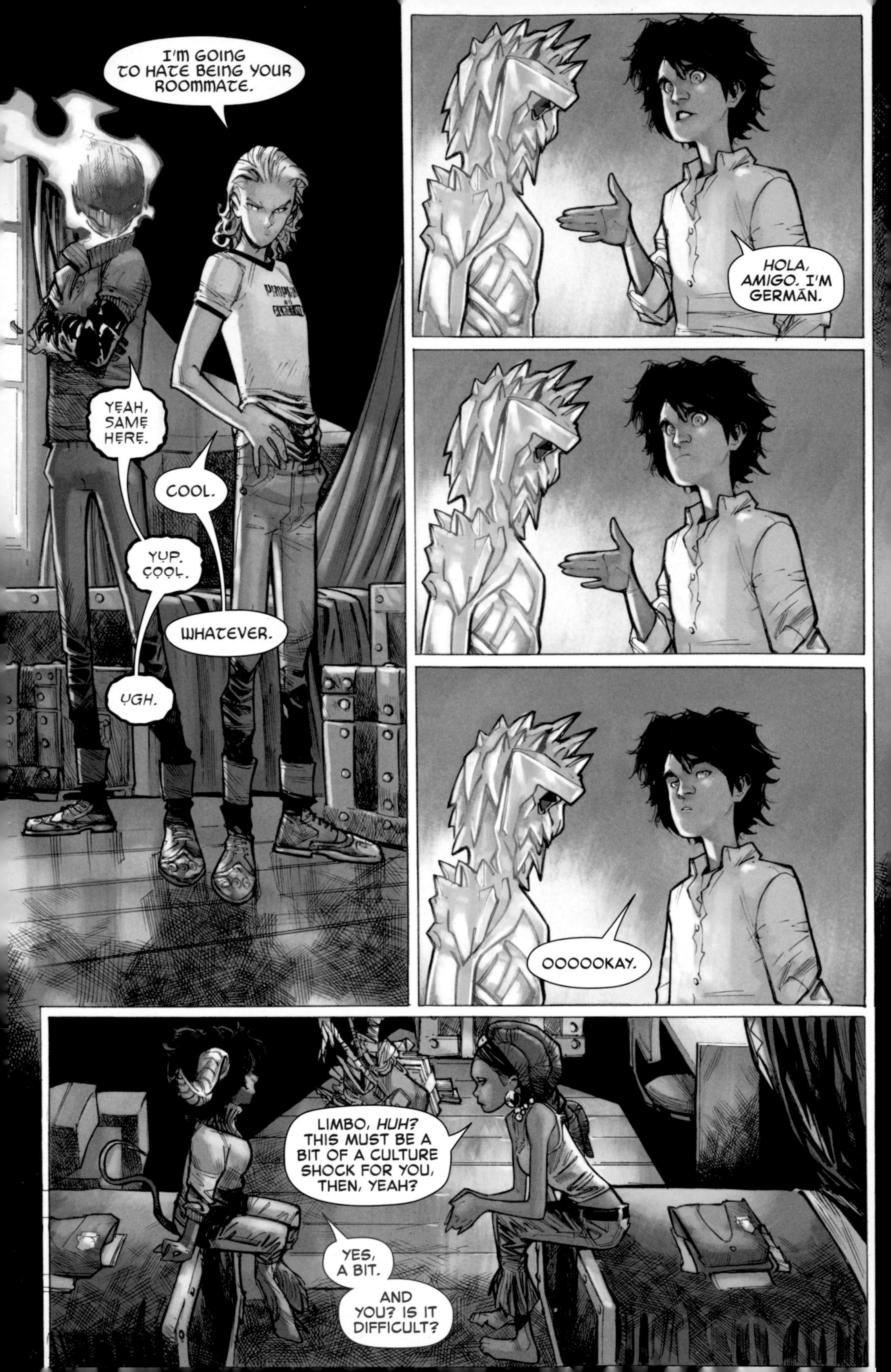
I'M GOING TO HATE BEING YOUR ROOMMATE.
YEAH, SAME HERE.
COOL.
YUP. COOL.
WHATEVER.
UGH.
HOLA, AMIGO. I'M GERMÁN.
OOOOOKAY.
LIMBO, *HUH*? THIS MUST BE A BIT OF A CULTURE SHOCK FOR YOU, THEN, YEAH?
YES, A BIT.
AND YOU? IS IT DIFFICULT?

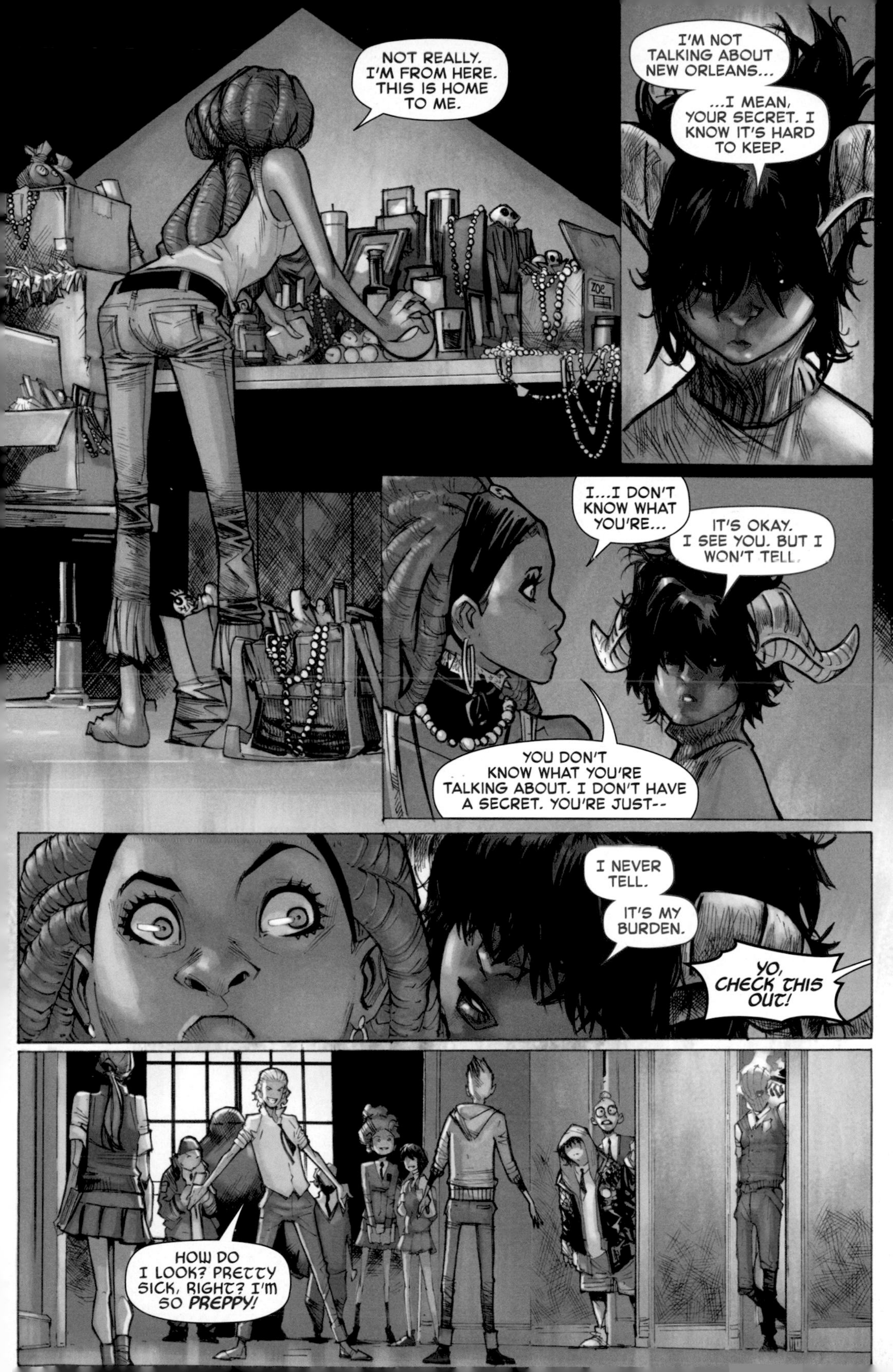
NOT REALLY. I'M FROM HERE. THIS IS HOME TO ME.
I'M NOT TALKING ABOUT NEW ORLEANS...
...I MEAN, YOUR SECRET. I KNOW IT'S HARD TO KEEP.
ZOE
I...I DON'T KNOW WHAT YOU'RE...
IT'S OKAY. I SEE YOU. BUT I WON'T TELL.
YOU DON'T KNOW WHAT YOU'RE TALKING ABOUT. I DON'T HAVE A SECRET. YOU'RE JUST--
I NEVER TELL.
IT'S MY BURDEN.
YO, CHECK THIS OUT!
HOW DO I LOOK? PRETTY SICK, RIGHT? I'M SO PREPPY!

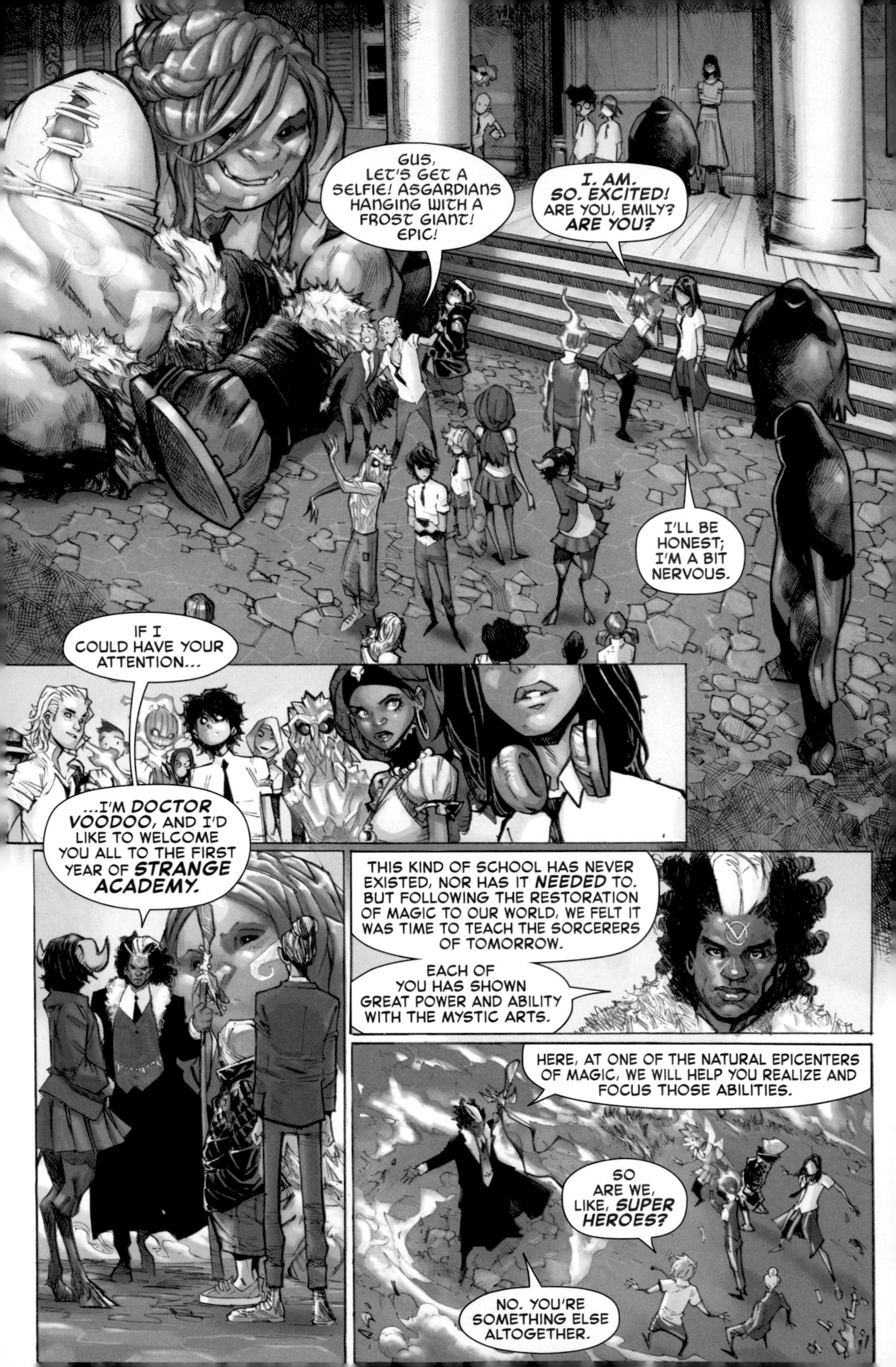
GUS, LET'S GET A SELFIE! ASGARDIANS HANGING WITH A FROST GIANT! EPIC!
I. AM. SO. EXCITED! ARE YOU, EMILY? ARE YOU?
I'LL BE HONEST; I'M A BIT NERVOUS.
IF I COULD HAVE YOUR ATTENTION...
...I'M DOCTOR VOODOO, AND I'D LIKE TO WELCOME YOU ALL TO THE FIRST YEAR OF STRANGE ACADEMY.
THIS KIND OF SCHOOL HAS NEVER EXISTED, NOR HAS IT NEEDED TO. BUT FOLLOWING THE RESTORATION OF MAGIC TO OUR WORLD, WE FELT IT WAS TIME TO TEACH THE SORCERERS OF TOMORROW.
EACH OF YOU HAS SHOWN GREAT POWER AND ABILITY WITH THE MYSTIC ARTS.
HERE, AT ONE OF THE NATURAL EPICENTERS OF MAGIC, WE WILL HELP YOU REALIZE AND FOCUS THOSE ABILITIES.
SO ARE WE, LIKE, SUPER HEROES?
NO. YOU'RE SOMETHING ELSE ALTOGETHER.

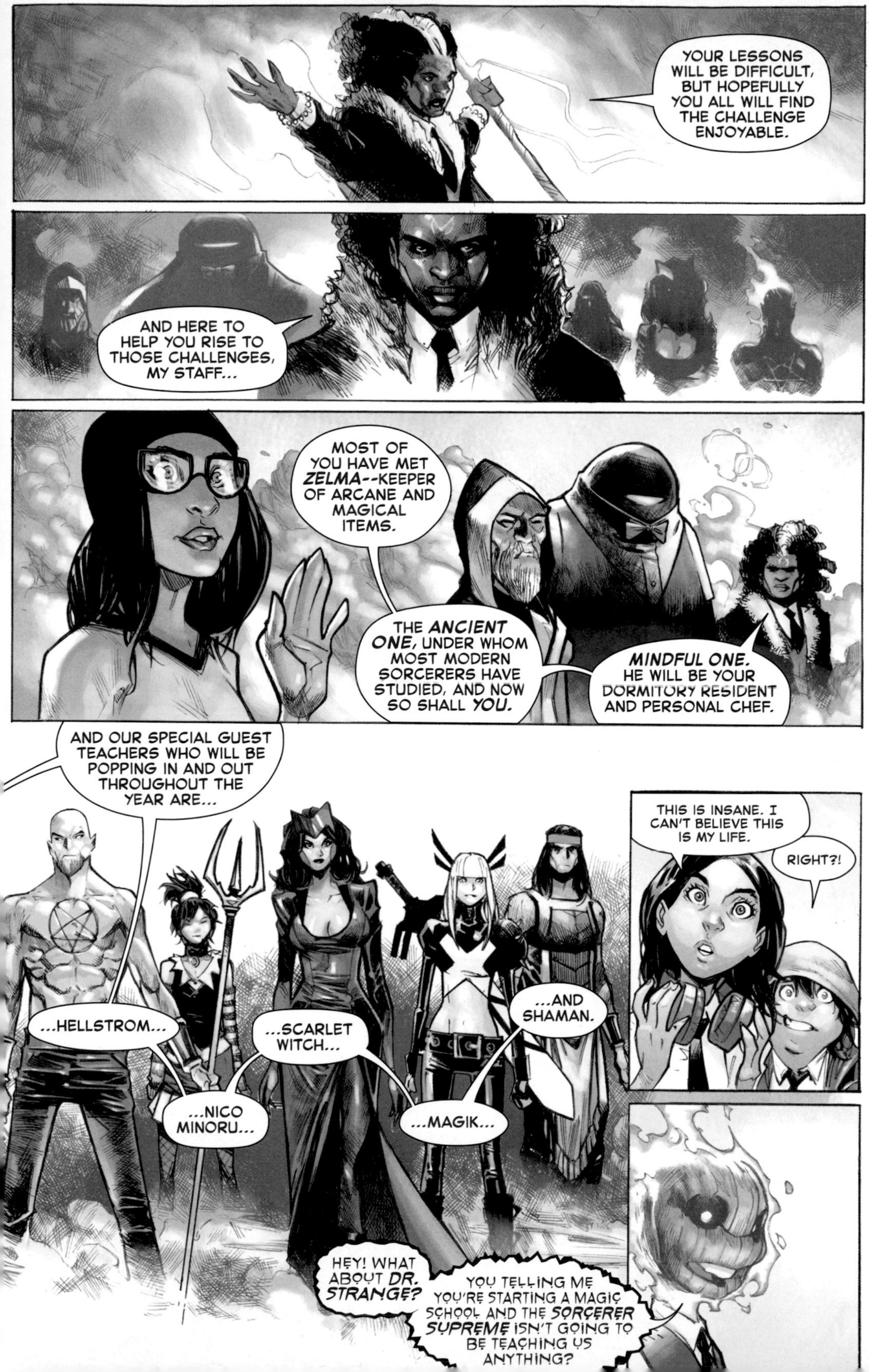
YOUR LESSONS WILL BE DIFFICULT, BUT HOPEFULLY YOU ALL WILL FIND THE CHALLENGE ENJOYABLE.
AND HERE TO HELP YOU RISE TO THOSE CHALLENGES, MY STAFF...
MOST OF YOU HAVE MET ZELMA--KEEPER OF ARCANE AND MAGICAL ITEMS.
THE ANCIENT ONE, UNDER WHOM MOST MODERN SORCERERS HAVE STUDIED, AND NOW SO SHALL YOU.
MINDFUL ONE. HE WILL BE YOUR DORMITORY RESIDENT AND PERSONAL CHEF.
AND OUR SPECIAL GUEST TEACHERS WHO WILL BE POPPING IN AND OUT THROUGHOUT THE YEAR ARE...
...HELLSTROM...
...NICO MINORU...
...SCARLET WITCH...
...MAGIK...
...AND SHAMAN.
THIS IS INSANE. I CAN'T BELIEVE THIS IS MY LIFE.
RIGHT?!
HEY! WHAT ABOUT DR. STRANGE?
YOU TELLING ME YOU'RE STARTING A MAGIC SCHOOL AND THE SORCERER SUPREME ISN'T GOING TO BE TEACHING US ANYTHING?

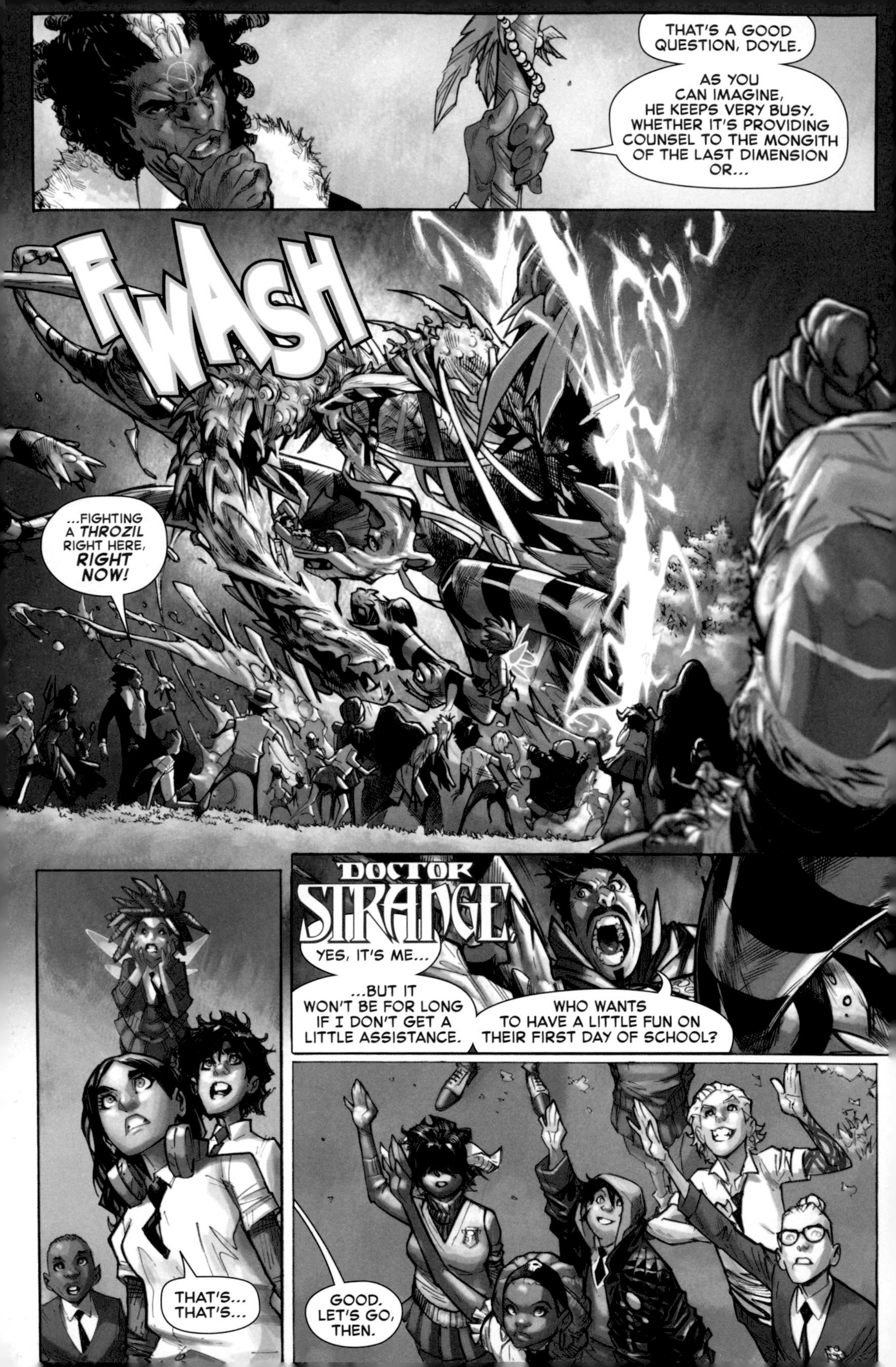

THAT'S A GOOD QUESTION, DOYLE.
AS YOU CAN IMAGINE, HE KEEPS VERY BUSY. WHETHER IT'S PROVIDING COUNSEL TO THE MONGITH OF THE LAST DIMENSION OR...
FWASH
...FIGHTING A THROZIL RIGHT HERE, RIGHT NOW!
DOCTOR STRANGE
YES, IT'S ME...
...BUT IT WON'T BE FOR LONG IF I DON'T GET A LITTLE ASSISTANCE.
WHO WANTS TO HAVE A LITTLE FUN ON THEIR FIRST DAY OF SCHOOL?
THAT'S... THAT'S...
GOOD. LET'S GO, THEN.

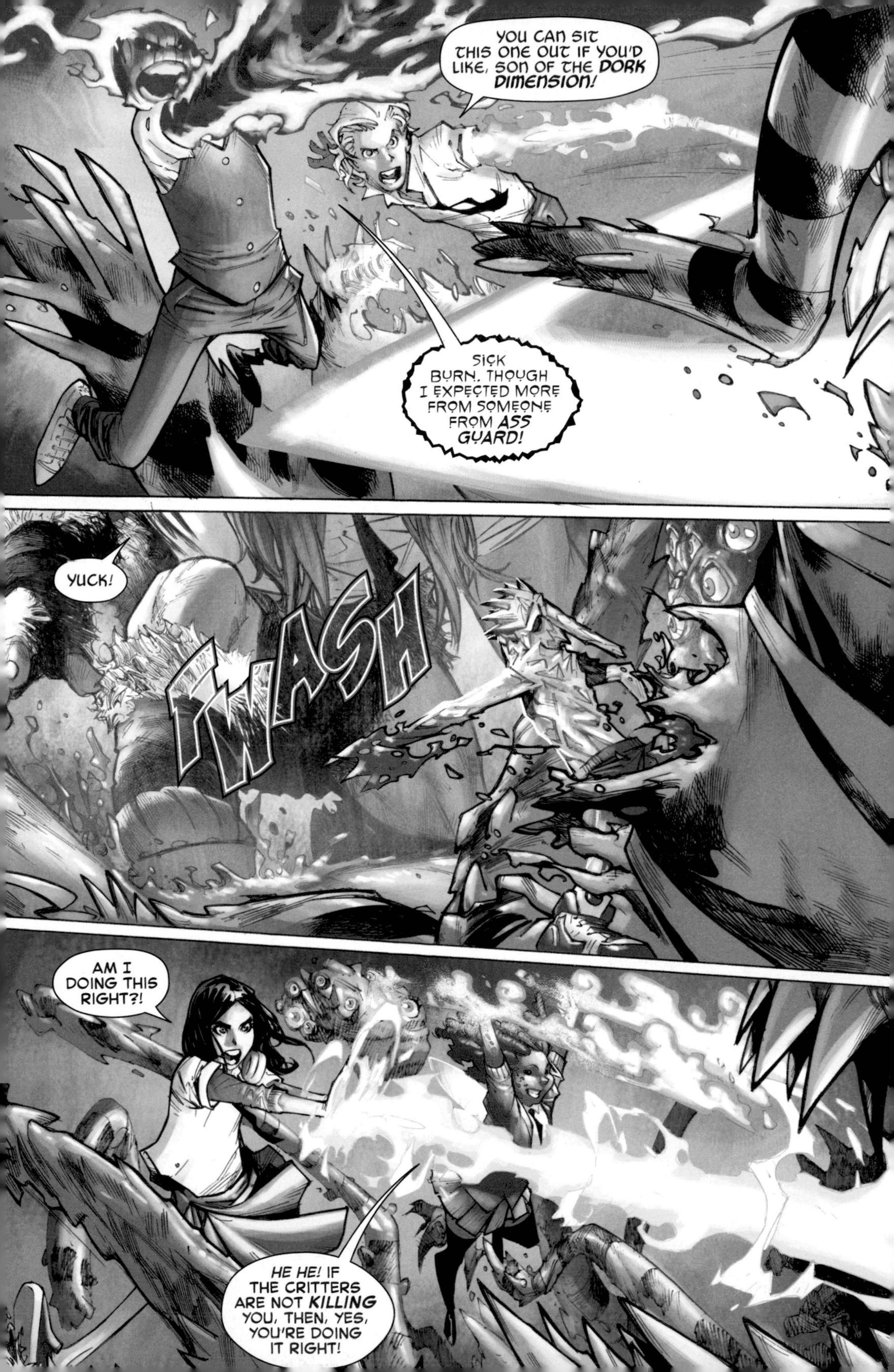
YOU CAN SIT THIS ONE OUT IF YOU'D LIKE, SON OF THE DORK DIMENSION!
SICK BURN. THOUGH I EXPECTED MORE FROM SOMEONE FROM ASS GUARD!
YUCK!
FWASH
AM I DOING THIS RIGHT?!
HE HE! IF THE CRITTERS ARE NOT KILLING YOU, THEN, YES, YOU'RE DOING IT RIGHT!

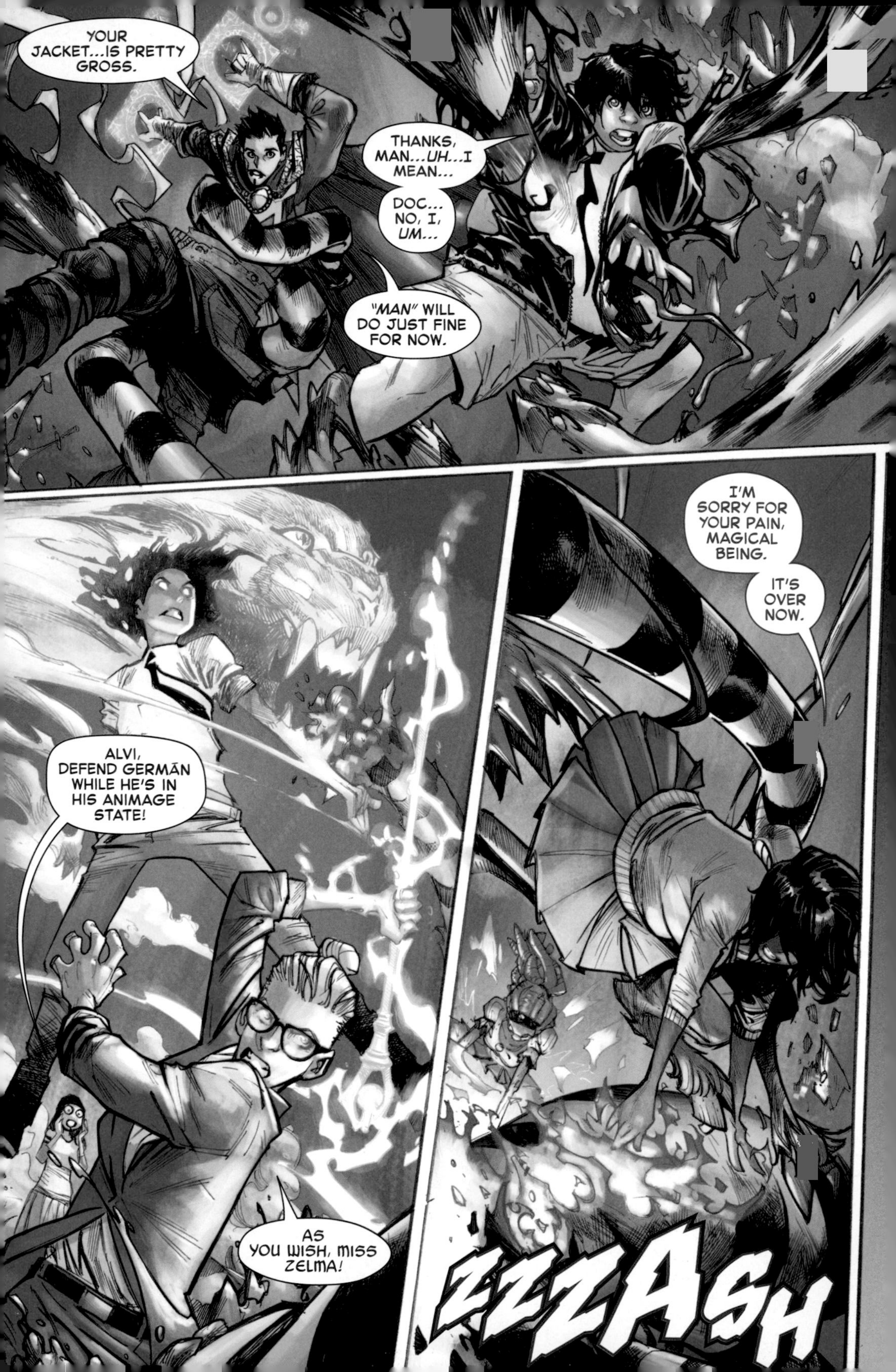
YOUR JACKET...IS PRETTY GROSS.
THANKS, MAN...UH...I MEAN...
DOC... NO, I, UM...
"MAN" WILL DO JUST FINE FOR NOW.
ALVI, DEFEND GERMĀN WHILE HE'S IN HIS ANIMAGE STATE!
AS YOU WISH, MISS ZELMA!
I'M SORRY FOR YOUR PAIN, MAGICAL BEING.
IT'S OVER NOW.
ZZZASH

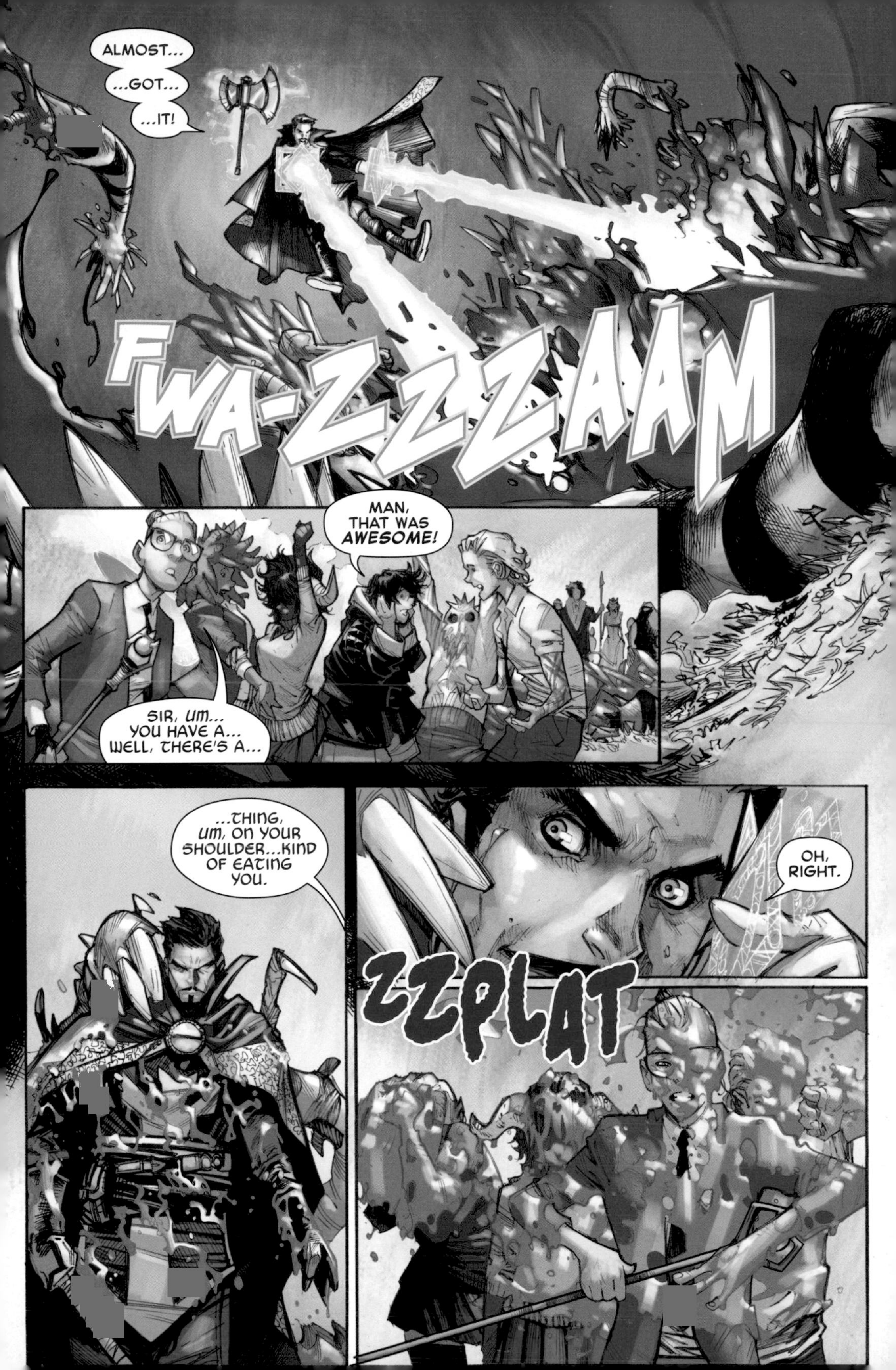
ALMOST...
...GOT...
...IT!
FWA-ZZZZAAAM
MAN, THAT WAS AWESOME!
SIR, UM... YOU HAVE A... WELL, THERE'S A...
...THING, UM, ON YOUR SHOULDER...KIND OF EATING YOU.
OH, RIGHT.
ZZPLAT

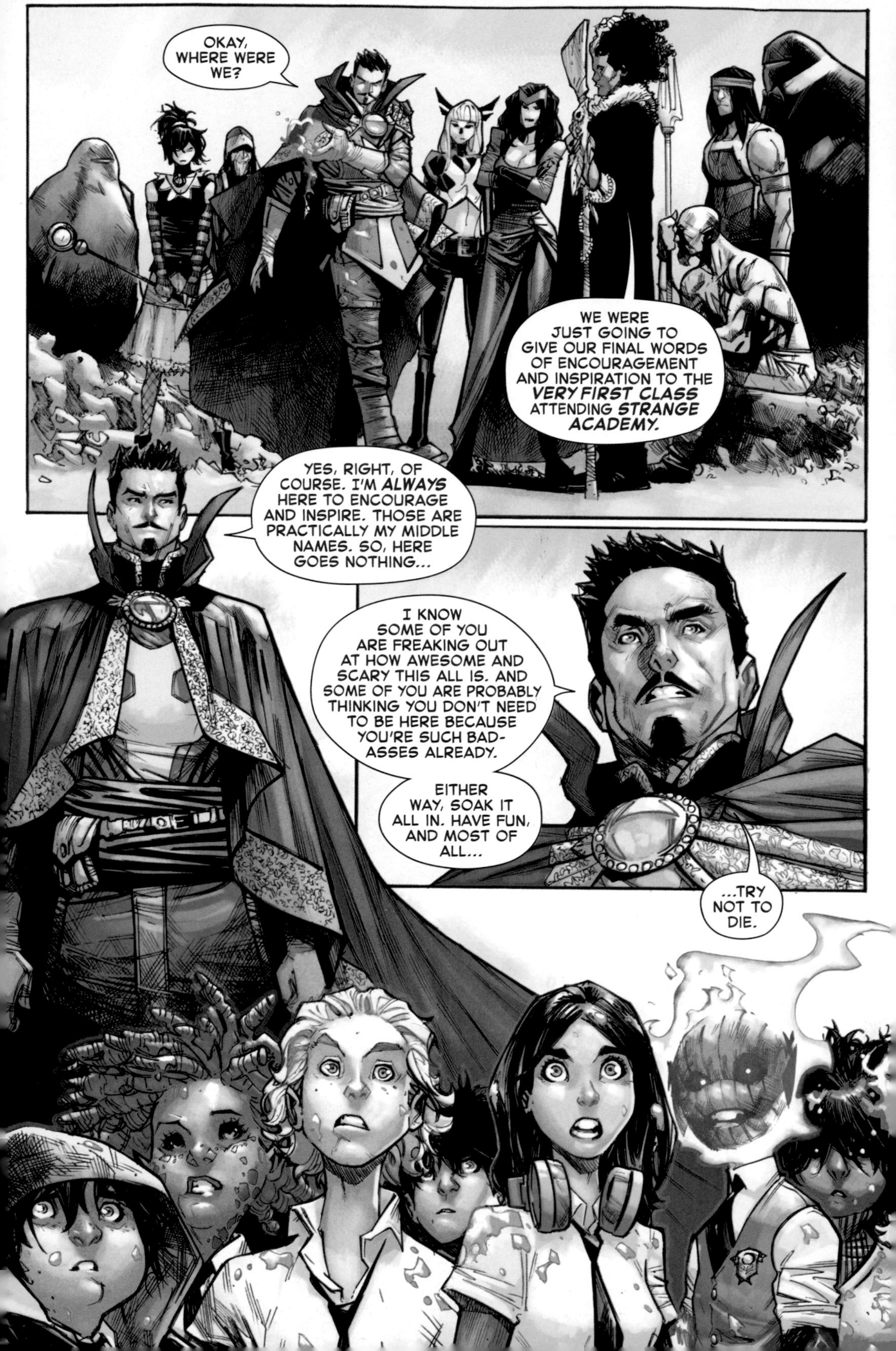
OKAY, WHERE WERE WE?
WE WERE JUST GOING TO GIVE OUR FINAL WORDS OF ENCOURAGEMENT AND INSPIRATION TO THE VERY FIRST CLASS ATTENDING STRANGE ACADEMY.
YES, RIGHT, OF COURSE. I'M ALWAYS HERE TO ENCOURAGE AND INSPIRE. THOSE ARE PRACTICALLY MY MIDDLE NAMES. SO, HERE GOES NOTHING...
I KNOW SOME OF YOU ARE FREAKING OUT AT HOW AWESOME AND SCARY THIS ALL IS. AND SOME OF YOU ARE PROBABLY THINKING YOU DON'T NEED TO BE HERE BECAUSE YOU'RE SUCH BAD-ASSES ALREADY.
EITHER WAY, SOAK IT ALL IN. HAVE FUN, AND MOST OF ALL...
...TRY NOT TO DIE.

STRANGE
ACADEMY
APPLICATION

Do YOU think you're worthy of one day becoming the SORCERER SUPREME? An acolyte of the occult? A master of the mystic arts? A local of New Orleans?

Tell us below what makes YOU a prime candidate for enrollment in STRANGE ACADEMY!

NAME: _____   **ADDRESS:** _____

ALIAS: _____   _____

FIRST EXPERIENCE WITH MAGIC:

_____

_____

GREATEST WEAKNESS:

_____

_____

NOTABLE MAGIC FEAT:

_____

_____

If Dormammu is levitating a quarter 30 centimeters above your desk, and you cast a deflection spell correctly, how many rabbits should appear?

_____

_____

If an astral projection is moving at 90 kilometers per minute toward the edge of the Earth's atmosphere, how long would it take to reach the blue area of the Moon?

_____

_____

COMPARISONS:

DOCTOR STRANGE IS TO NIDAVELLIR AS ICE CRYSTALS ARE TO _____

If you would like to see your responses printed in a future publication of **STRANGE ACADEMY**, please mark your applications **"OKAY TO PRINT"** and send via virtual mail to: **SPIDEYOFFICE@MARVEL.COM.**

Or remove this page and send through means of physical mail to:
STRANGE ACADEMY APPLICATION
C/O MARVEL ENTERTAINMENT LLC
1290 AVENUE OF THE AMERICAS
NEW YORK, NEW YORK 10104

2

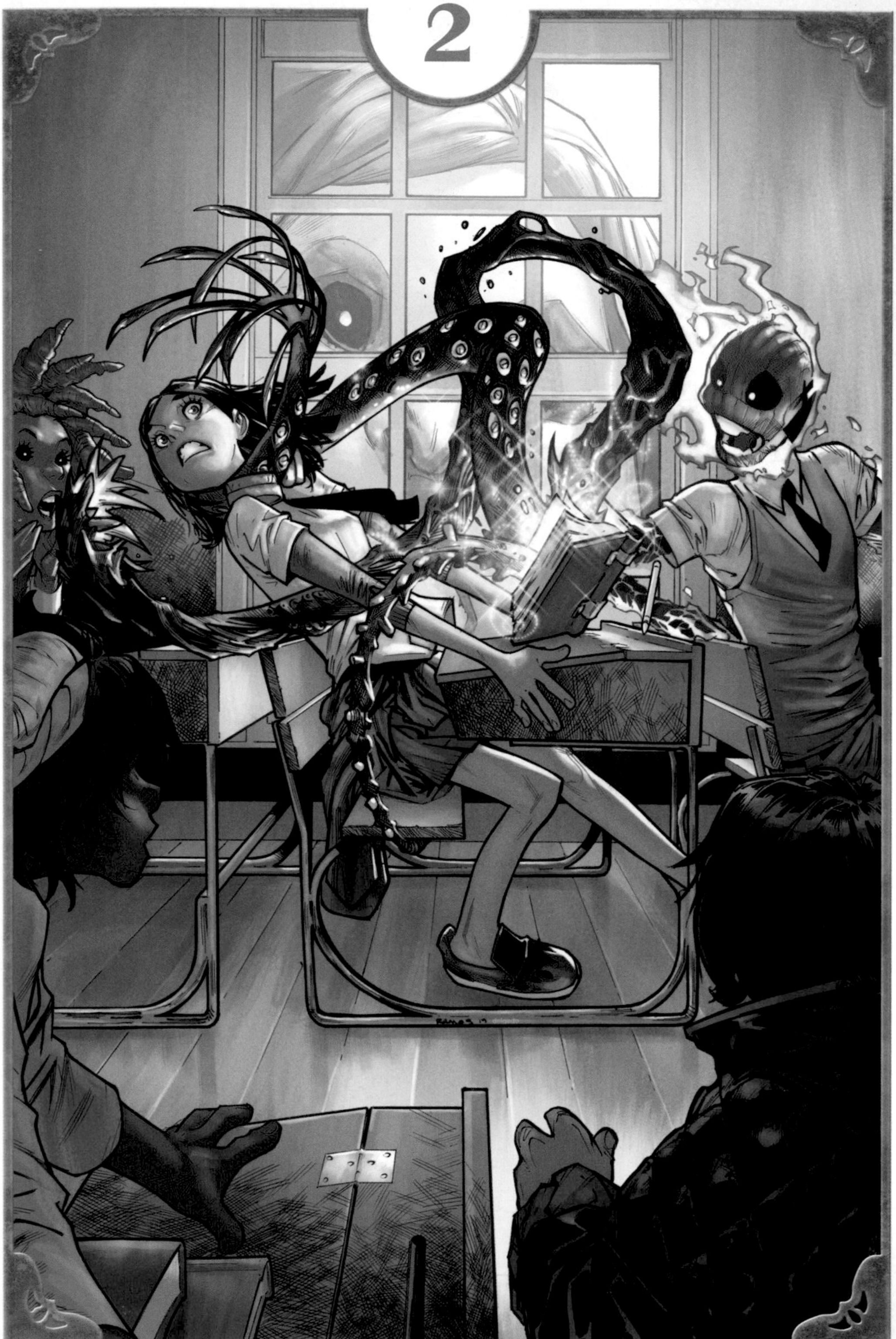

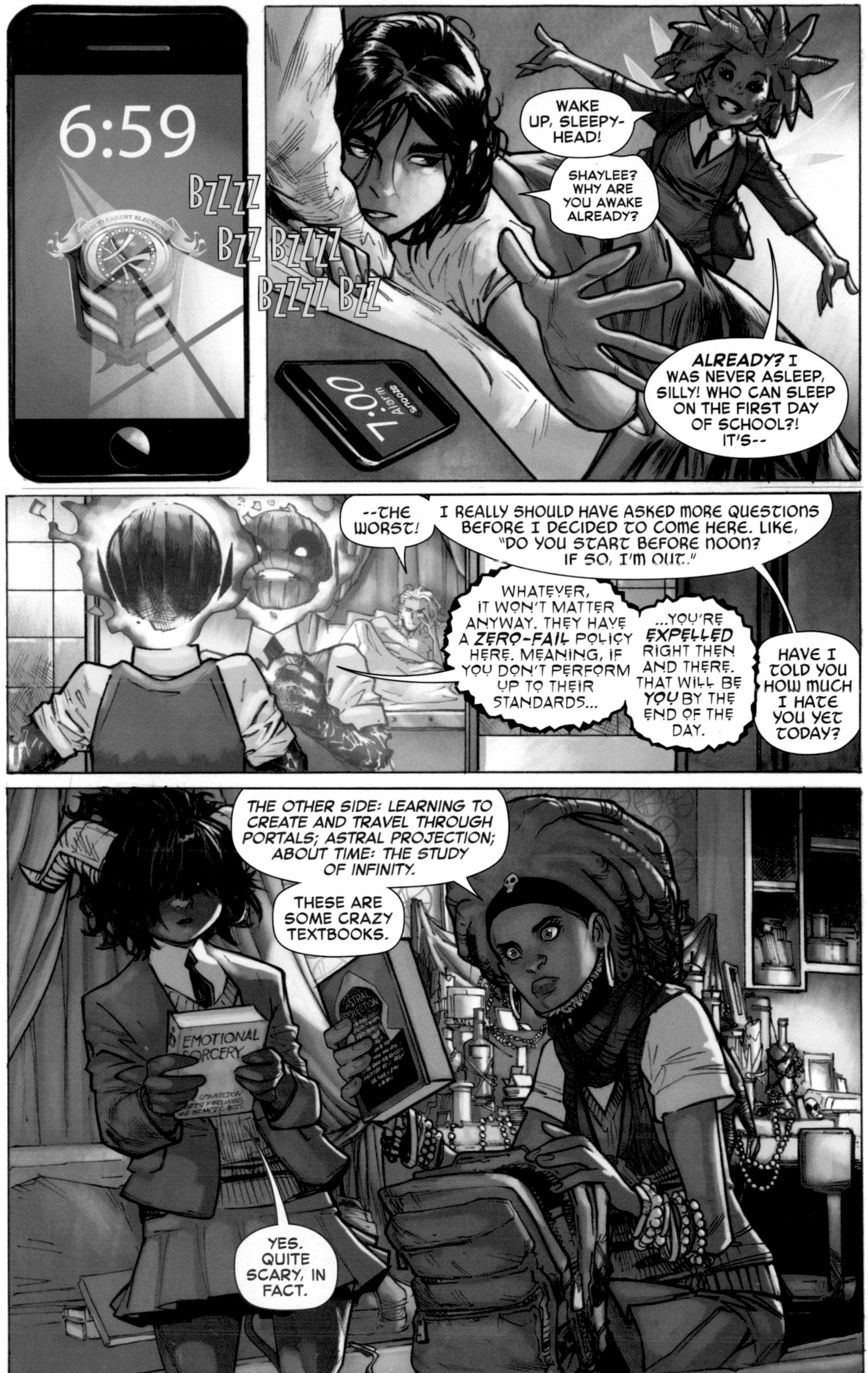
6:59
BZZZZ
BZZ BZZZZ
BZZZZ BZZ
7:00
Alarm
snooze
WAKE UP, SLEEPY-HEAD!
SHAYLEE? WHY ARE YOU AWAKE ALREADY?
ALREADY? I WAS NEVER ASLEEP, SILLY! WHO CAN SLEEP ON THE FIRST DAY OF SCHOOL?! IT'S--
--THE WORST!
I REALLY SHOULD HAVE ASKED MORE QUESTIONS BEFORE I DECIDED TO COME HERE. LIKE, "DO YOU START BEFORE NOON? IF SO, I'M OUT."
WHATEVER, IT WON'T MATTER ANYWAY. THEY HAVE A ZERO-FAIL POLICY HERE. MEANING, IF YOU DON'T PERFORM UP TO THEIR STANDARDS...
...YOU'RE EXPELLED RIGHT THEN AND THERE. THAT WILL BE YOU BY THE END OF THE DAY.
HAVE I TOLD YOU HOW MUCH I HATE YOU YET TODAY?
THE OTHER SIDE: LEARNING TO CREATE AND TRAVEL THROUGH PORTALS; ASTRAL PROJECTION; ABOUT TIME: THE STUDY OF INFINITY.
THESE ARE SOME CRAZY TEXTBOOKS.
EMOTIONAL SORCERY
ASTRAL PROJECTION
YES. QUITE SCARY, IN FACT.

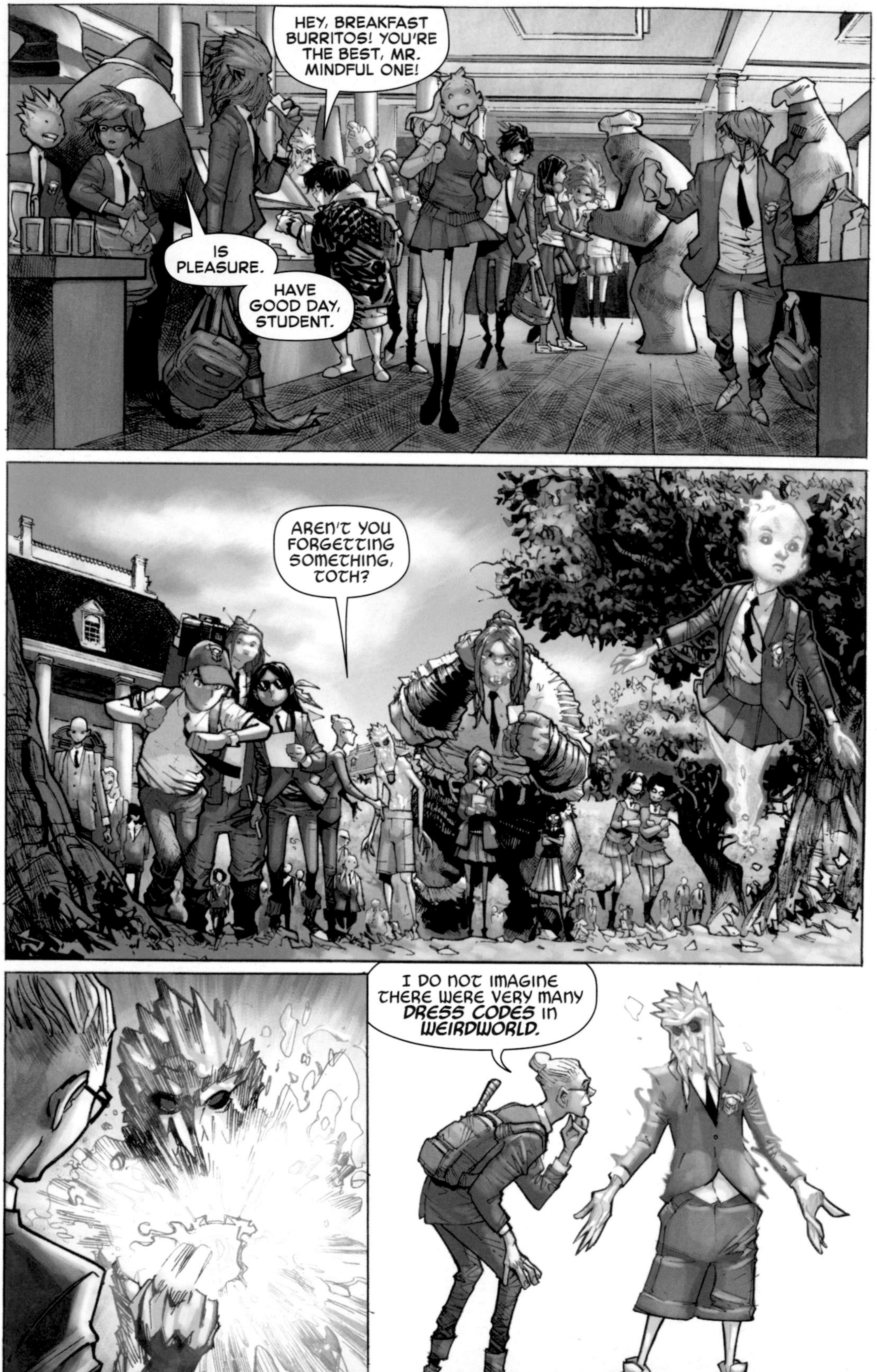
HEY, BREAKFAST BURRITOS! YOU'RE THE BEST, MR. MINDFUL ONE!
IS PLEASURE.
HAVE GOOD DAY, STUDENT.
AREN'T YOU FORGETTING SOMETHING, TOTH?
I DO NOT IMAGINE THERE WERE VERY MANY DRESS CODES IN WEIRDWORLD.

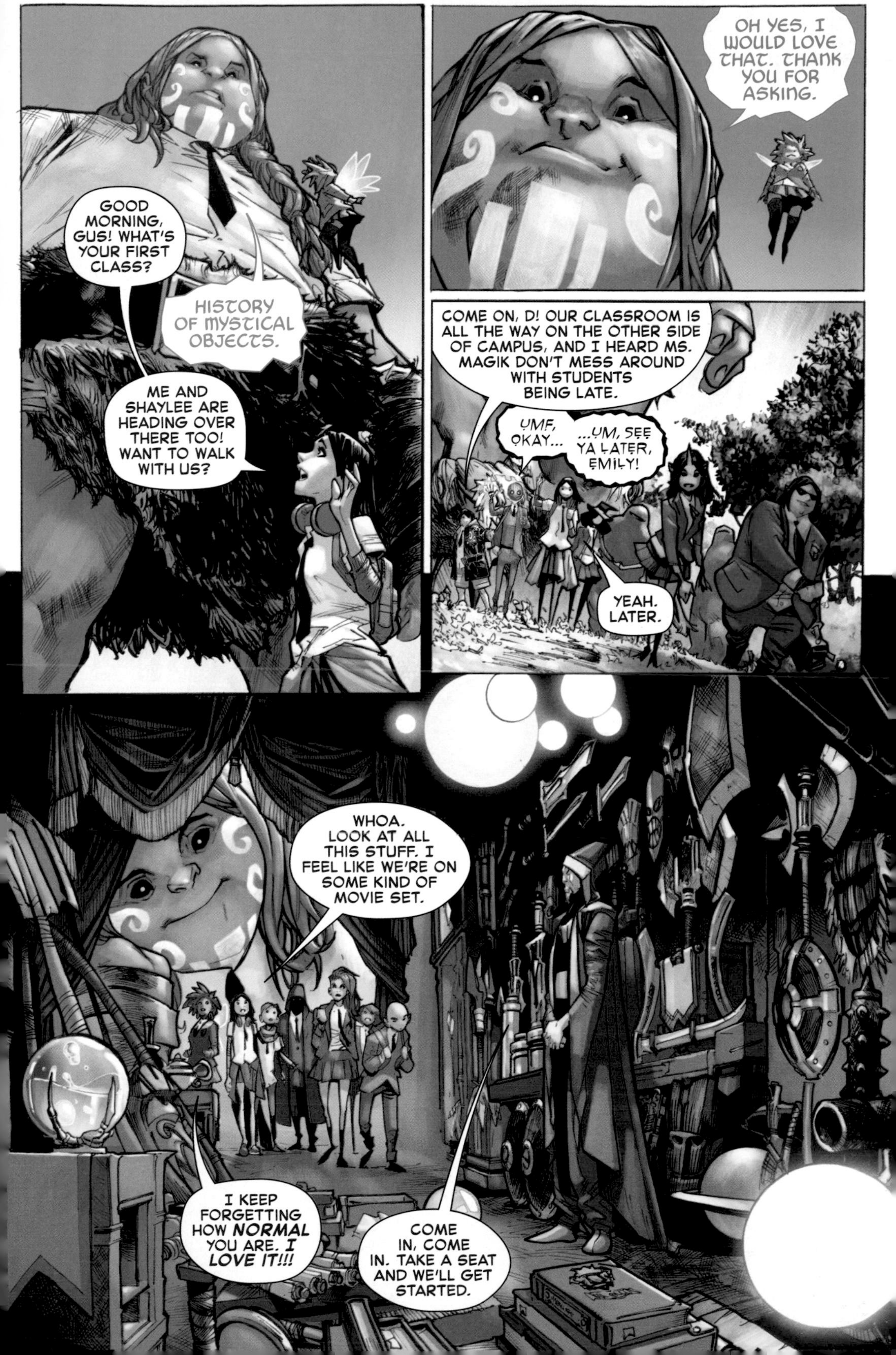
GOOD MORNING, GUS! WHAT'S YOUR FIRST CLASS?
HISTORY OF MYSTICAL OBJECTS.
ME AND SHAYLEE ARE HEADING OVER THERE TOO! WANT TO WALK WITH US?
OH YES, I WOULD LOVE THAT. THANK YOU FOR ASKING.
COME ON, D! OUR CLASSROOM IS ALL THE WAY ON THE OTHER SIDE OF CAMPUS, AND I HEARD MS. MAGIK DON'T MESS AROUND WITH STUDENTS BEING LATE.
UMF, OKAY...
...UM, SEE YA LATER, EMILY!
YEAH. LATER.
WHOA. LOOK AT ALL THIS STUFF. I FEEL LIKE WE'RE ON SOME KIND OF MOVIE SET.
I KEEP FORGETTING HOW NORMAL YOU ARE. I LOVE IT!!!
COME IN, COME IN. TAKE A SEAT AND WE'LL GET STARTED.

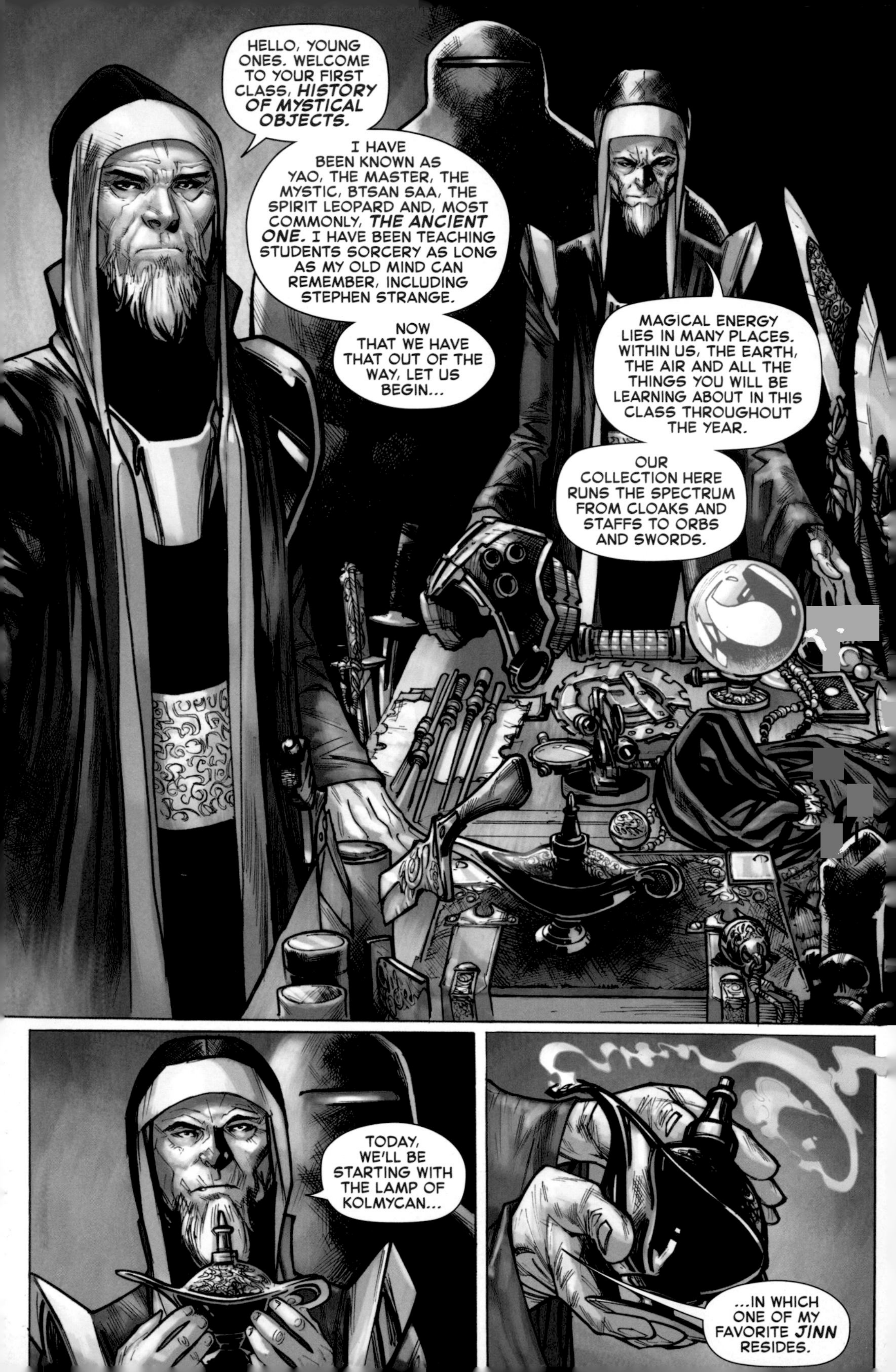
HELLO, YOUNG ONES. WELCOME TO YOUR FIRST CLASS, HISTORY OF MYSTICAL OBJECTS.
I HAVE BEEN KNOWN AS YAO, THE MASTER, THE MYSTIC, BTSAN SAA, THE SPIRIT LEOPARD AND, MOST COMMONLY, THE ANCIENT ONE. I HAVE BEEN TEACHING STUDENTS SORCERY AS LONG AS MY OLD MIND CAN REMEMBER, INCLUDING STEPHEN STRANGE.
NOW THAT WE HAVE THAT OUT OF THE WAY, LET US BEGIN...
MAGICAL ENERGY LIES IN MANY PLACES. WITHIN US, THE EARTH, THE AIR AND ALL THE THINGS YOU WILL BE LEARNING ABOUT IN THIS CLASS THROUGHOUT THE YEAR.
OUR COLLECTION HERE RUNS THE SPECTRUM FROM CLOAKS AND STAFFS TO ORBS AND SWORDS.
TODAY, WE'LL BE STARTING WITH THE LAMP OF KOLMYCAN...
...IN WHICH ONE OF MY FAVORITE JINN RESIDES.

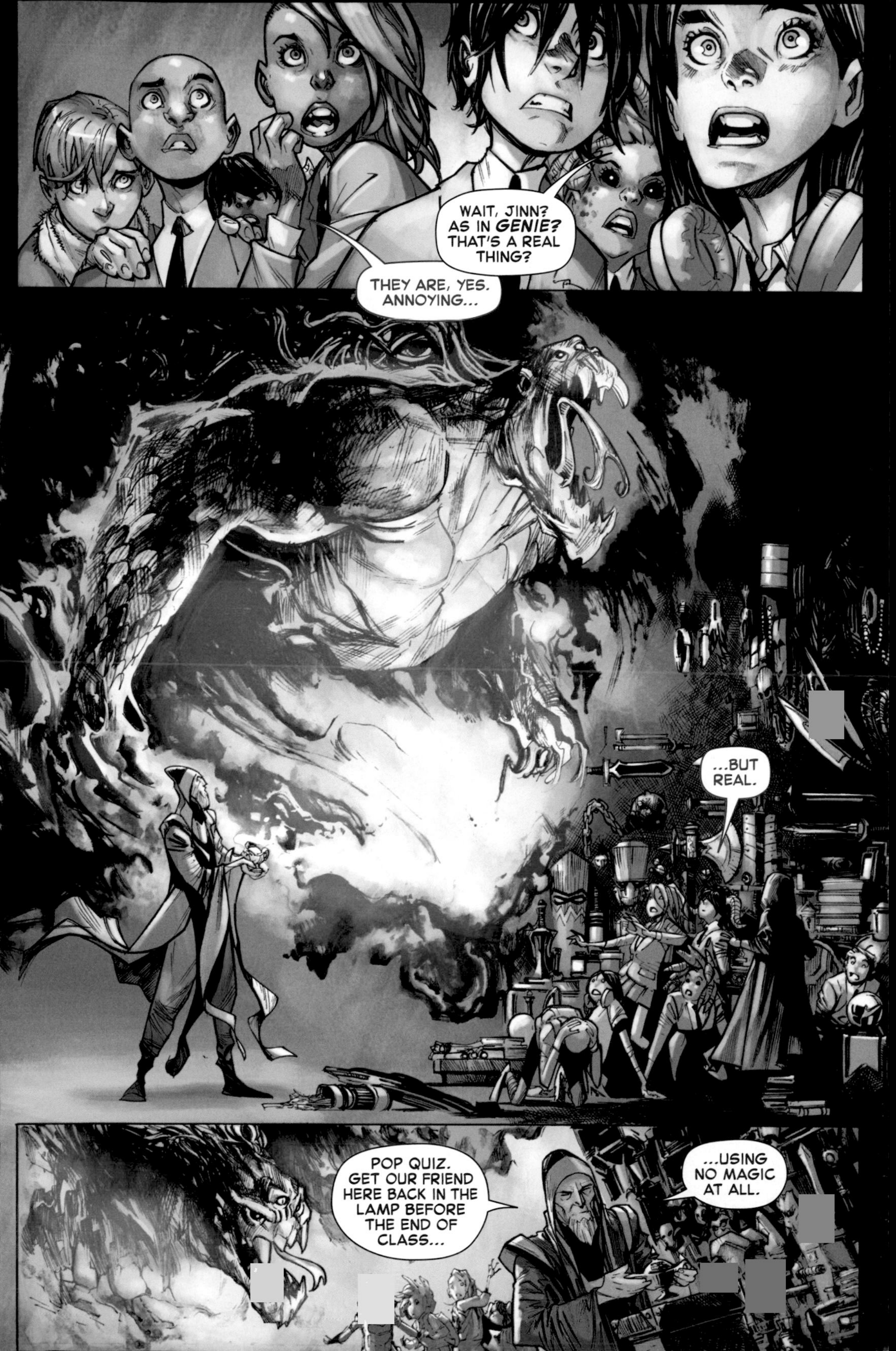

WAIT, JINN? AS IN *GENIE?* THAT'S A REAL THING?
THEY ARE, YES. ANNOYING...
...BUT REAL.
POP QUIZ. GET OUR FRIEND HERE BACK IN THE LAMP BEFORE THE END OF CLASS...
...USING NO MAGIC AT ALL.

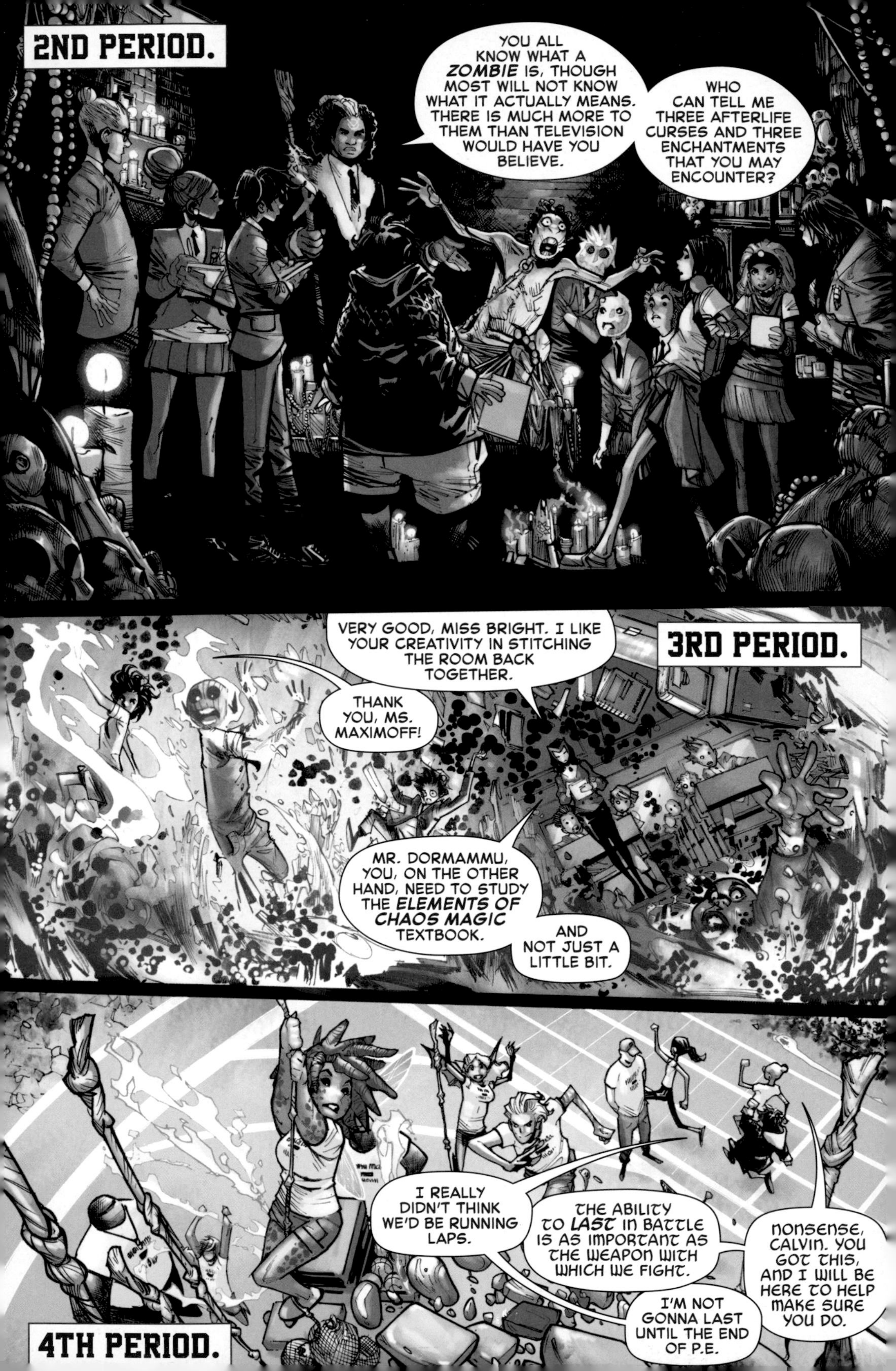
2ND PERIOD.
YOU ALL KNOW WHAT A ZOMBIE IS, THOUGH MOST WILL NOT KNOW WHAT IT ACTUALLY MEANS. THERE IS MUCH MORE TO THEM THAN TELEVISION WOULD HAVE YOU BELIEVE.
WHO CAN TELL ME THREE AFTERLIFE CURSES AND THREE ENCHANTMENTS THAT YOU MAY ENCOUNTER?
3RD PERIOD.
VERY GOOD, MISS BRIGHT. I LIKE YOUR CREATIVITY IN STITCHING THE ROOM BACK TOGETHER.
THANK YOU, MS. MAXIMOFF!
MR. DORMAMMU, YOU, ON THE OTHER HAND, NEED TO STUDY THE ELEMENTS OF CHAOS MAGIC TEXTBOOK.
AND NOT JUST A LITTLE BIT.
4TH PERIOD.
I REALLY DIDN'T THINK WE'D BE RUNNING LAPS.
THE ABILITY TO LAST IN BATTLE IS AS IMPORTANT AS THE WEAPON WITH WHICH WE FIGHT.
I'M NOT GONNA LAST UNTIL THE END OF P.E.
NONSENSE, CALVIN. YOU GOT THIS, AND I WILL BE HERE TO HELP MAKE SURE YOU DO.

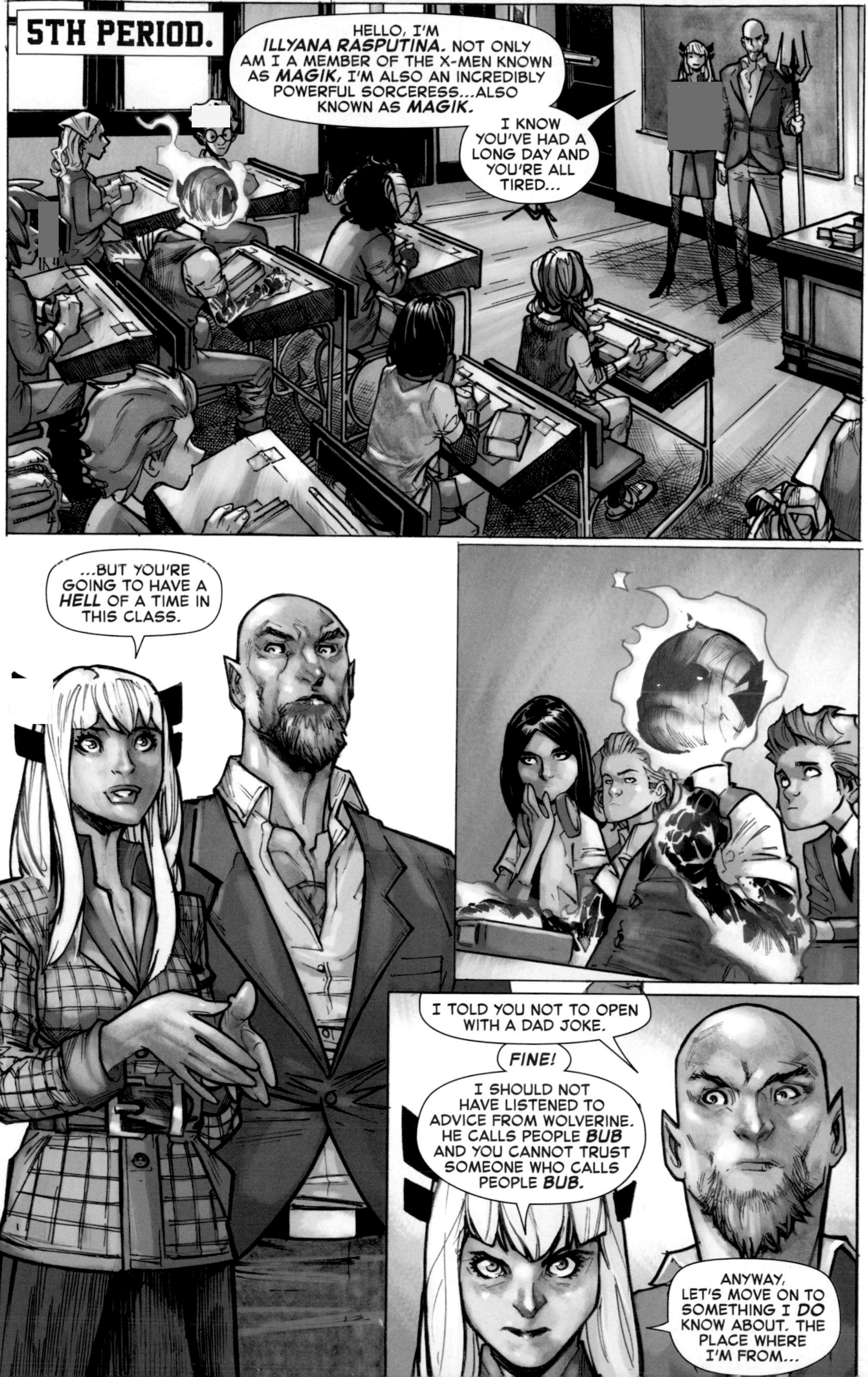
5TH PERIOD.
HELLO, I'M ILLYANA RASPUTINA. NOT ONLY AM I A MEMBER OF THE X-MEN KNOWN AS MAGIK, I'M ALSO AN INCREDIBLY POWERFUL SORCERESS...ALSO KNOWN AS MAGIK.
I KNOW YOU'VE HAD A LONG DAY AND YOU'RE ALL TIRED...
...BUT YOU'RE GOING TO HAVE A HELL OF A TIME IN THIS CLASS.
I TOLD YOU NOT TO OPEN WITH A DAD JOKE.
FINE!
I SHOULD NOT HAVE LISTENED TO ADVICE FROM WOLVERINE. HE CALLS PEOPLE BUB AND YOU CANNOT TRUST SOMEONE WHO CALLS PEOPLE BUB.
ANYWAY, LET'S MOVE ON TO SOMETHING I DO KNOW ABOUT. THE PLACE WHERE I'M FROM...

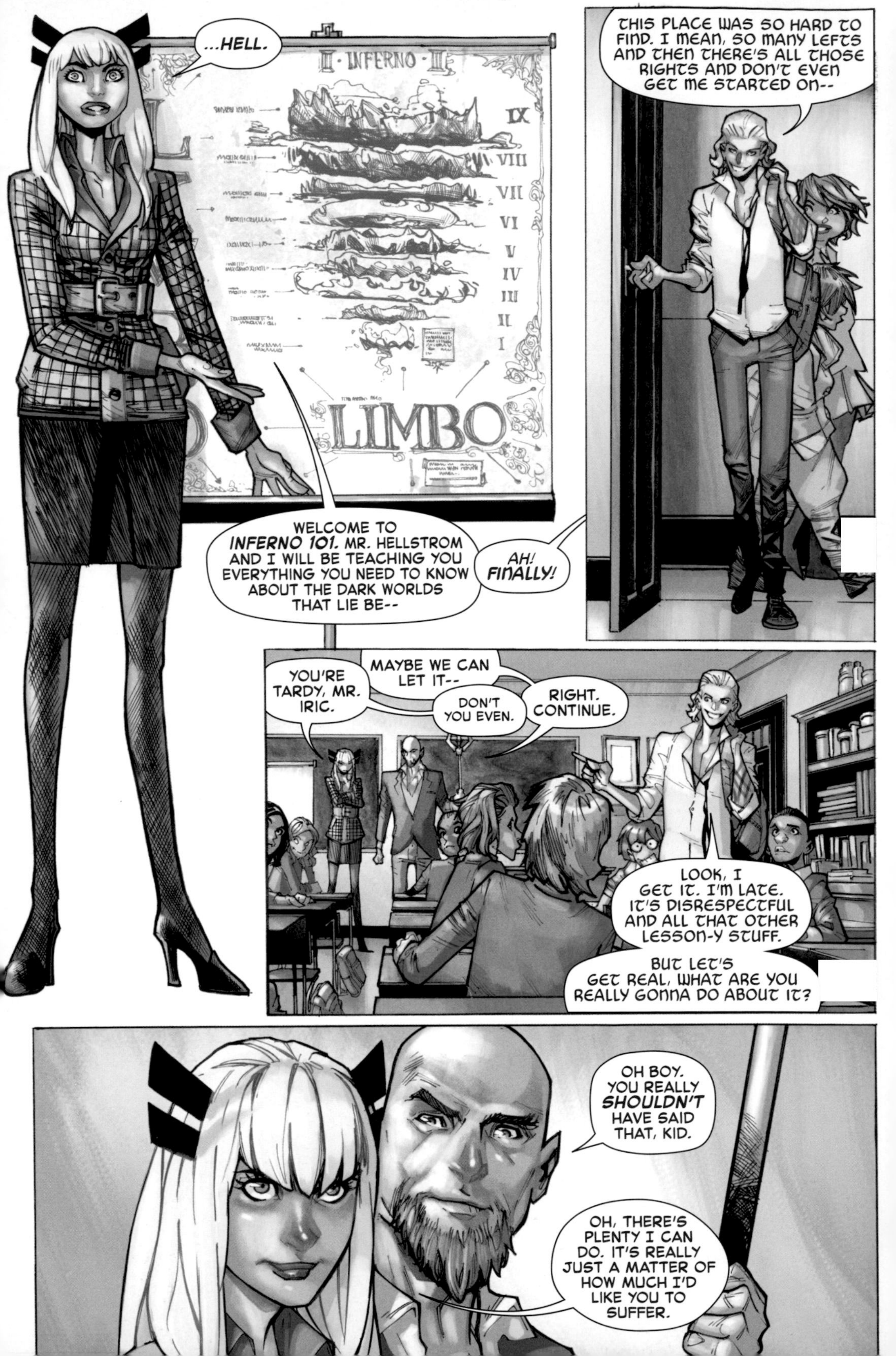
...HELL.
II · INFERNO · II
IX
VIII
VII
VI
V
IV
III
II
I
LIMBO
THIS PLACE WAS SO HARD TO FIND. I MEAN, SO MANY LEFTS AND THEN THERE'S ALL THOSE RIGHTS AND DON'T EVEN GET ME STARTED ON--
WELCOME TO *INFERNO 101.* MR. HELLSTROM AND I WILL BE TEACHING YOU EVERYTHING YOU NEED TO KNOW ABOUT THE DARK WORLDS THAT LIE BE--
AH! *FINALLY!*
YOU'RE TARDY, MR. IRIC.
MAYBE WE CAN LET IT--
DON'T YOU EVEN.
RIGHT. CONTINUE.
LOOK, I GET IT. I'M LATE. IT'S DISRESPECTFUL AND ALL THAT OTHER LESSON-Y STUFF.
BUT LET'S GET REAL, WHAT ARE YOU REALLY GONNA DO ABOUT IT?
OH BOY. YOU REALLY *SHOULDN'T* HAVE SAID THAT, KID.
OH, THERE'S PLENTY I CAN DO. IT'S REALLY JUST A MATTER OF HOW MUCH I'D LIKE YOU TO SUFFER.

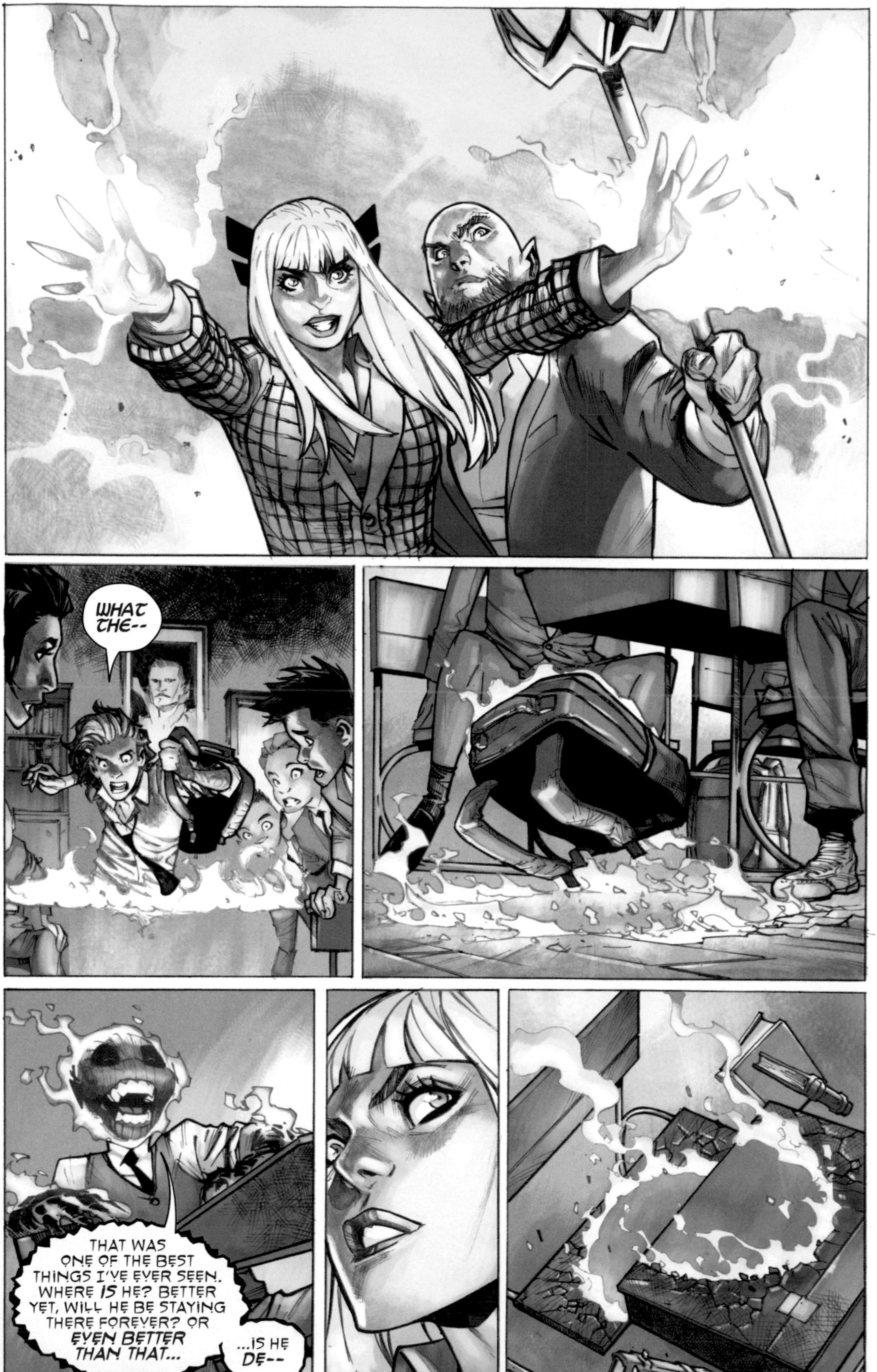
WHAT THE--
THAT WAS ONE OF THE BEST THINGS I'VE EVER SEEN. WHERE IS HE? BETTER YET, WILL HE BE STAYING THERE FOREVER? OR EVEN BETTER THAN THAT...
...IS HE DE--

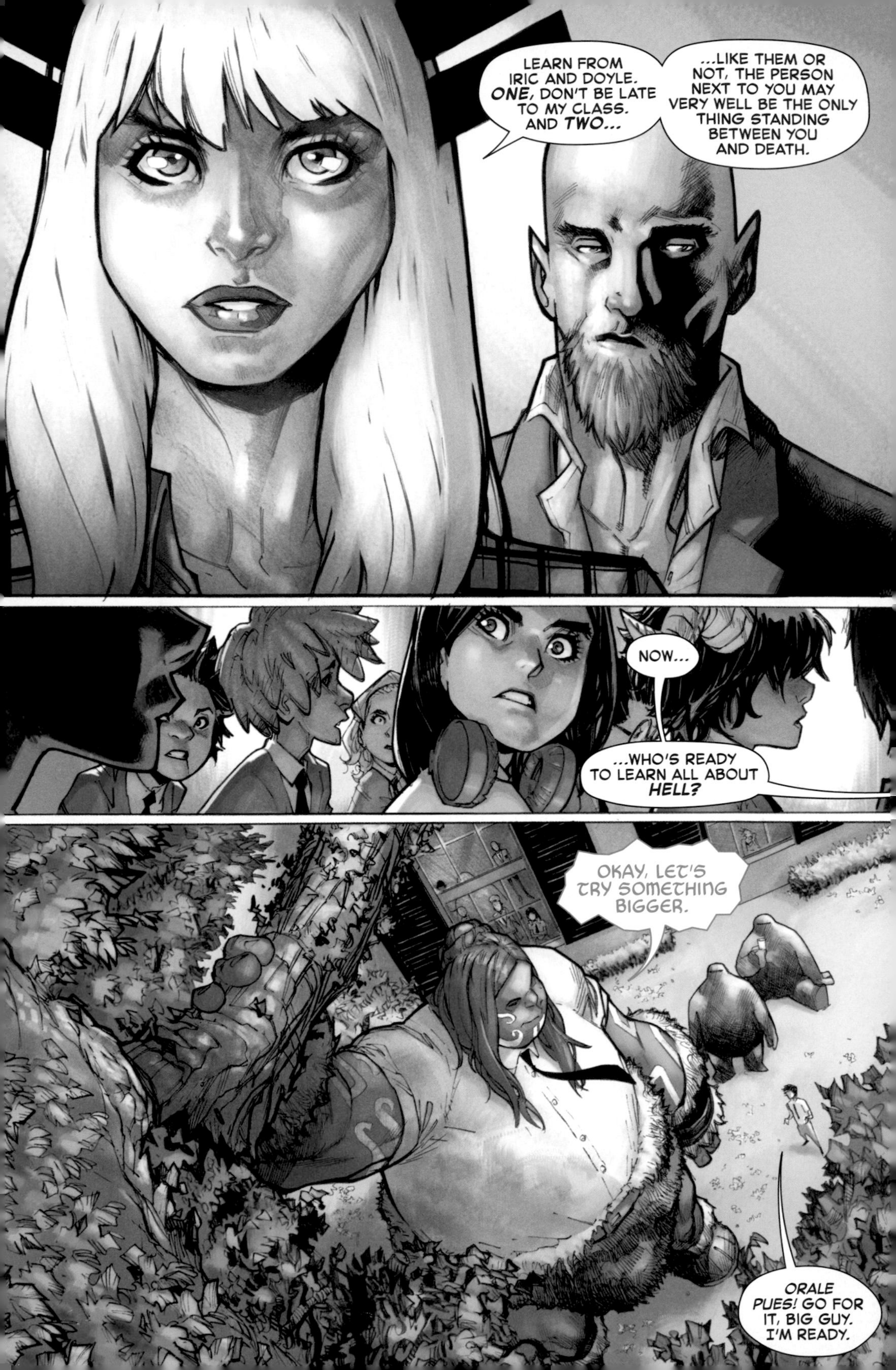

LEARN FROM IRIC AND DOYLE. ONE, DON'T BE LATE TO MY CLASS. AND TWO...
...LIKE THEM OR NOT, THE PERSON NEXT TO YOU MAY VERY WELL BE THE ONLY THING STANDING BETWEEN YOU AND DEATH.
NOW...
...WHO'S READY TO LEARN ALL ABOUT HELL?
OKAY, LET'S TRY SOMETHING BIGGER.
ORALE PUES! GO FOR IT, BIG GUY. I'M READY.

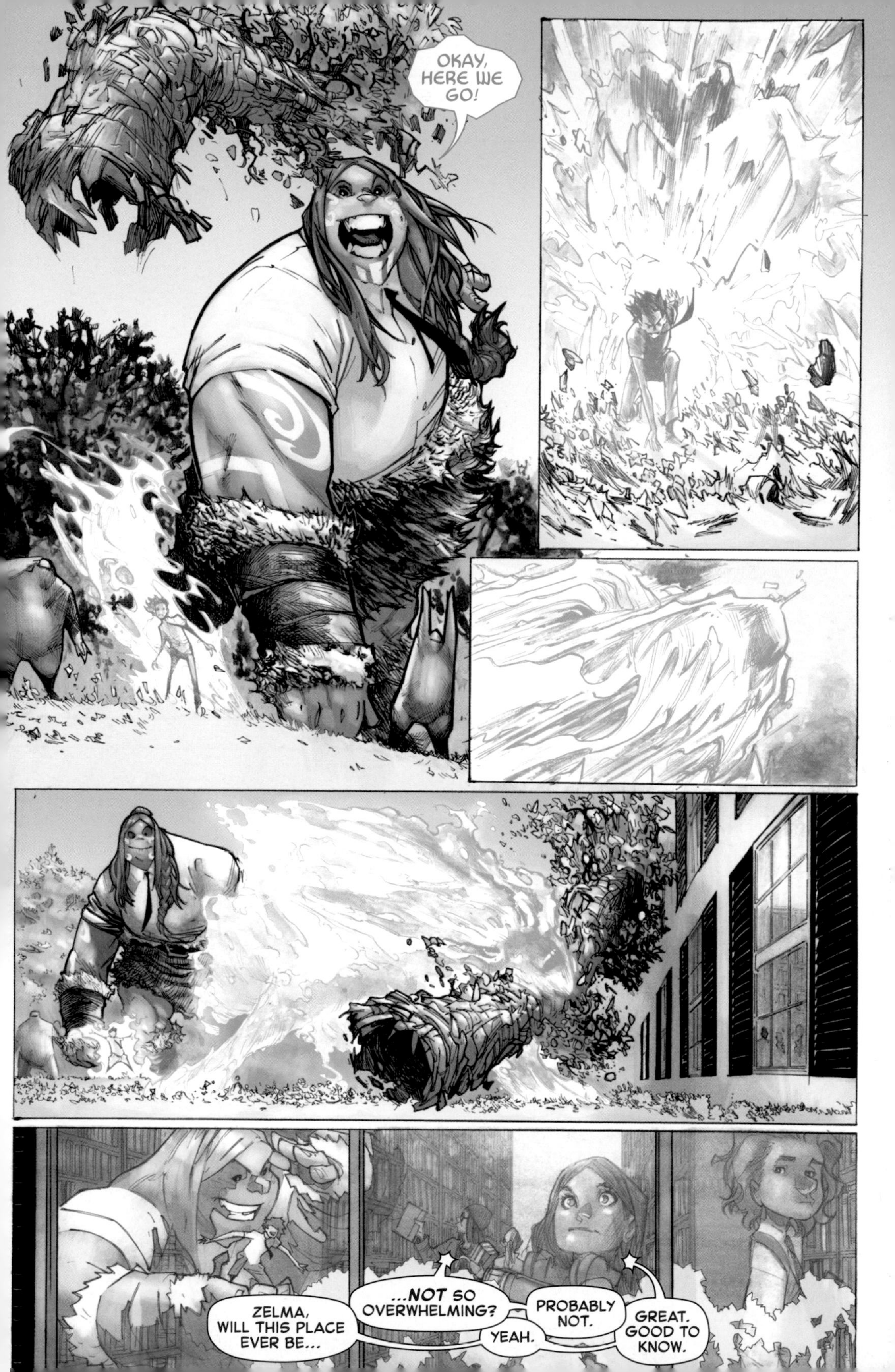
OKAY, HERE WE GO!
ZELMA, WILL THIS PLACE EVER BE...
...NOT SO OVERWHELMING?
YEAH.
PROBABLY NOT.
GREAT. GOOD TO KNOW.

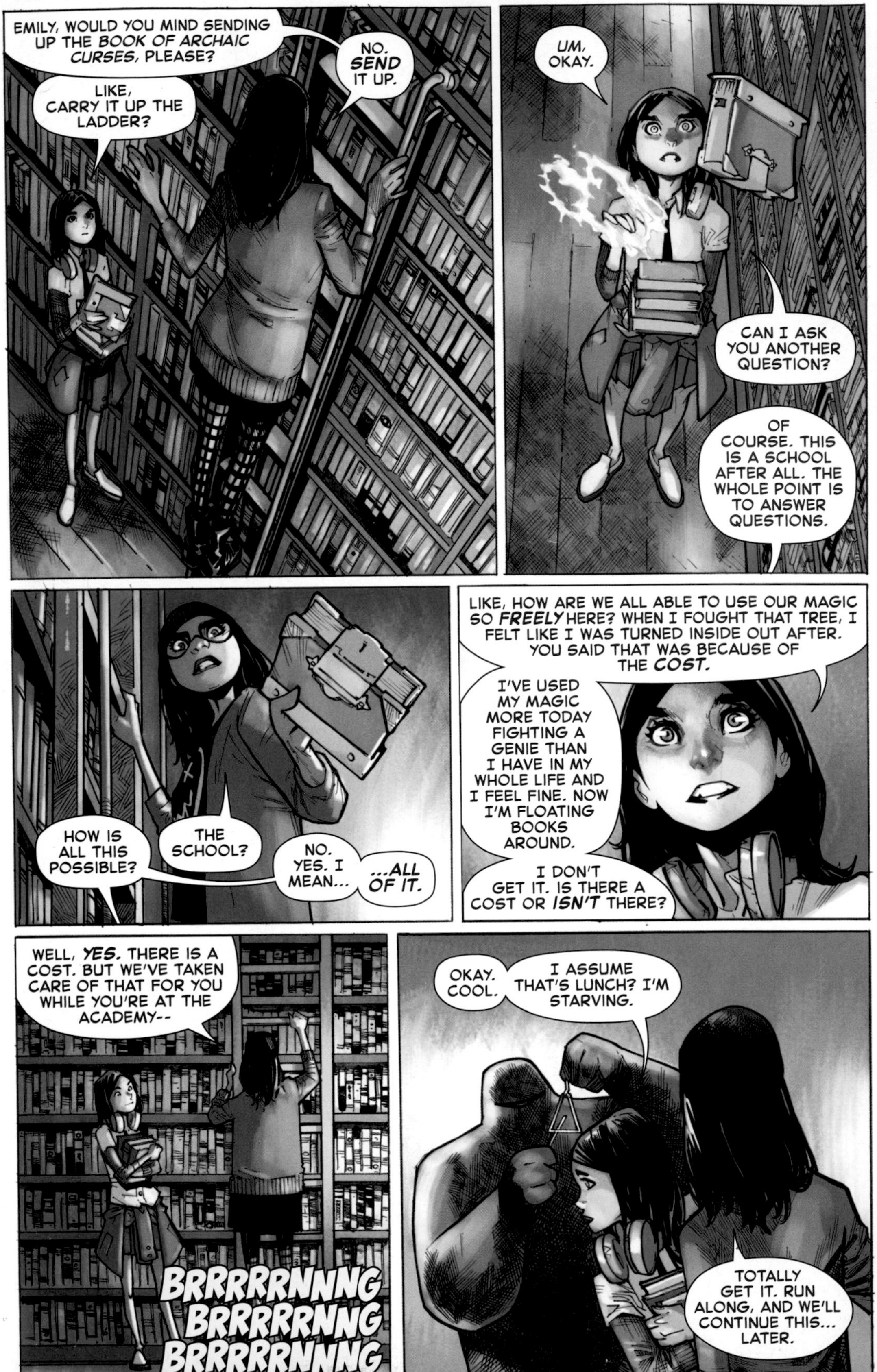
EMILY, WOULD YOU MIND SENDING UP THE BOOK OF ARCHAIC CURSES, PLEASE?
LIKE, CARRY IT UP THE LADDER?
NO. SEND IT UP.
UM, OKAY.
CAN I ASK YOU ANOTHER QUESTION?
OF COURSE. THIS IS A SCHOOL AFTER ALL. THE WHOLE POINT IS TO ANSWER QUESTIONS.
HOW IS ALL THIS POSSIBLE?
THE SCHOOL?
NO. YES. I MEAN...
...ALL OF IT.
LIKE, HOW ARE WE ALL ABLE TO USE OUR MAGIC SO FREELY HERE? WHEN I FOUGHT THAT TREE, I FELT LIKE I WAS TURNED INSIDE OUT AFTER. YOU SAID THAT WAS BECAUSE OF THE COST.
I'VE USED MY MAGIC MORE TODAY FIGHTING A GENIE THAN I HAVE IN MY WHOLE LIFE AND I FEEL FINE. NOW I'M FLOATING BOOKS AROUND.
I DON'T GET IT. IS THERE A COST OR ISN'T THERE?
WELL, YES. THERE IS A COST. BUT WE'VE TAKEN CARE OF THAT FOR YOU WHILE YOU'RE AT THE ACADEMY--
BRRRRRNNNG
BRRRRRNNG
BRRRRRNNNG
OKAY. COOL.
I ASSUME THAT'S LUNCH? I'M STARVING.
TOTALLY GET IT. RUN ALONG, AND WE'LL CONTINUE THIS... LATER.

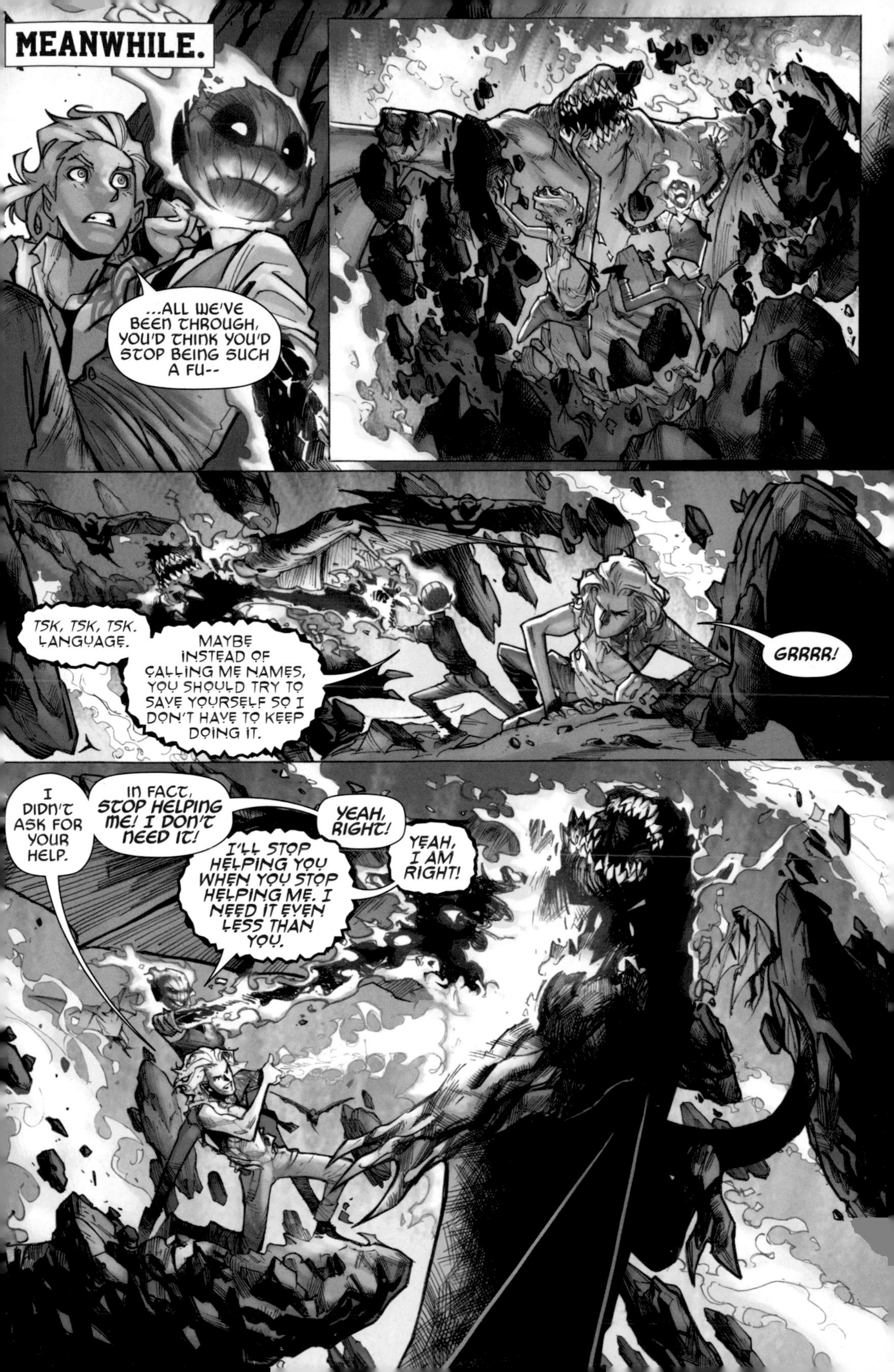
MEANWHILE.
...ALL WE'VE BEEN THROUGH, YOU'D THINK YOU'D STOP BEING SUCH A FU--
TSK, TSK, TSK. LANGUAGE.
MAYBE INSTEAD OF CALLING ME NAMES, YOU SHOULD TRY TO SAVE YOURSELF SO I DON'T HAVE TO KEEP DOING IT.
GRRRR!
I DIDN'T ASK FOR YOUR HELP.
IN FACT, STOP HELPING ME! I DON'T NEED IT!
YEAH, RIGHT!
I'LL STOP HELPING YOU WHEN YOU STOP HELPING ME. I NEED IT EVEN LESS THAN YOU.
YEAH, I AM RIGHT!

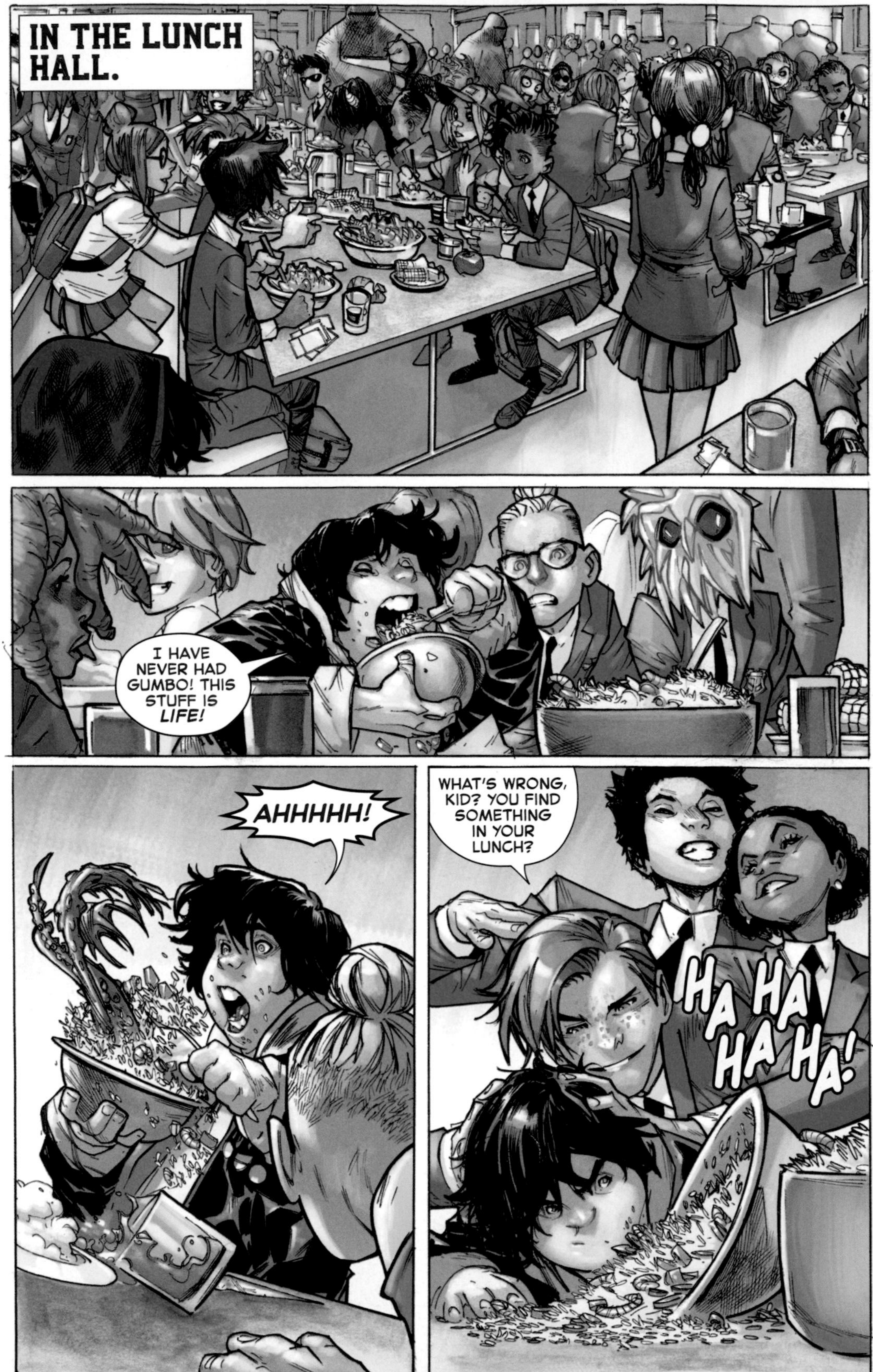
IN THE LUNCH HALL.
I HAVE NEVER HAD GUMBO! THIS STUFF IS *LIFE!*
AHHHHH!
WHAT'S WRONG, KID? YOU FIND SOMETHING IN YOUR LUNCH?
HA HA HA HA!

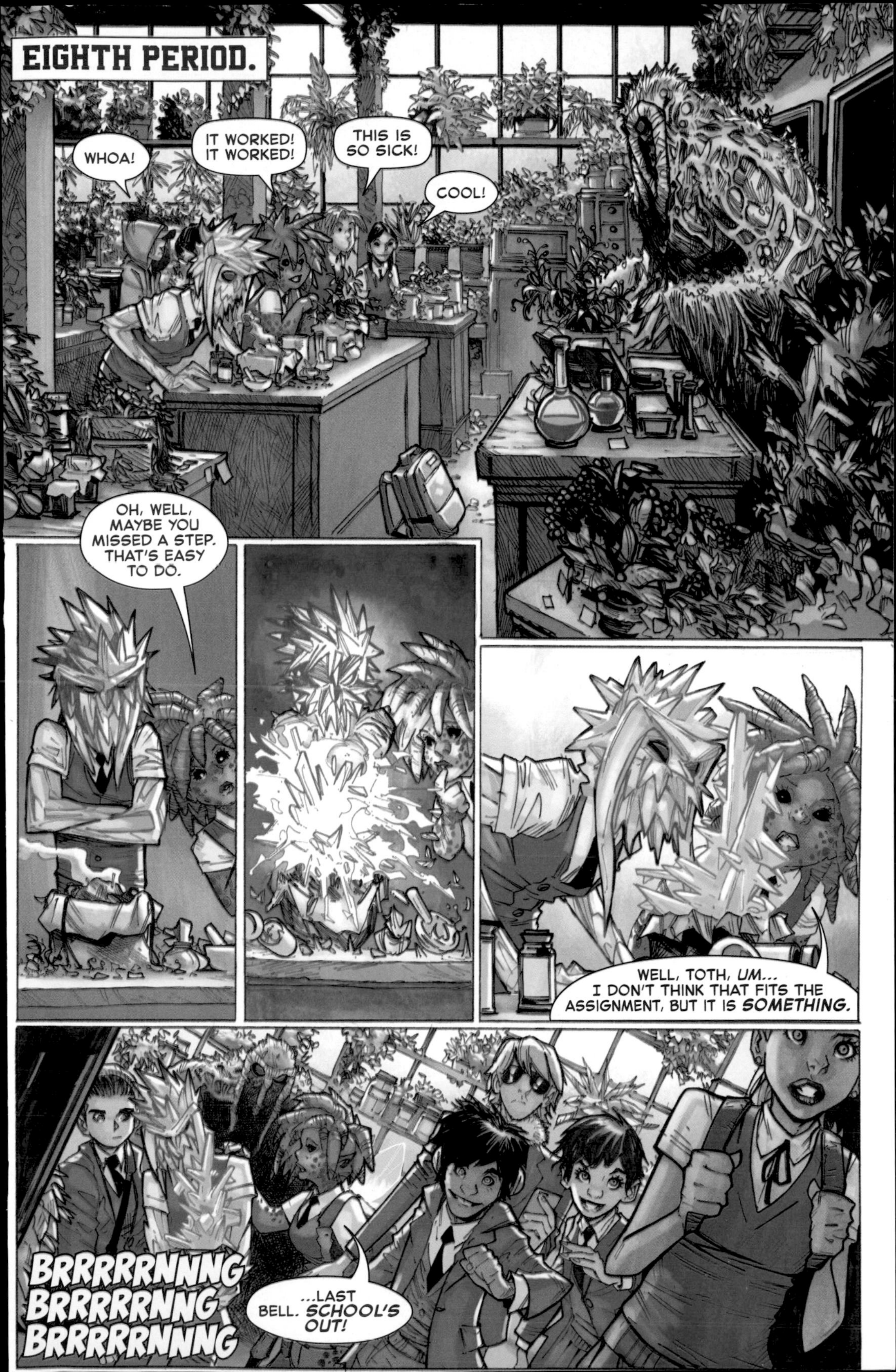
EIGHTH PERIOD.
WHOA!
IT WORKED! IT WORKED!
THIS IS SO SICK!
COOL!
OH, WELL, MAYBE YOU MISSED A STEP. THAT'S EASY TO DO.
WELL, TOTH, *UM*... I DON'T THINK THAT FITS THE ASSIGNMENT, BUT IT IS *SOMETHING.*
BRRRRRNNNG BRRRRRNNG BRRRRRNNNG
...LAST BELL. *SCHOOL'S OUT!*

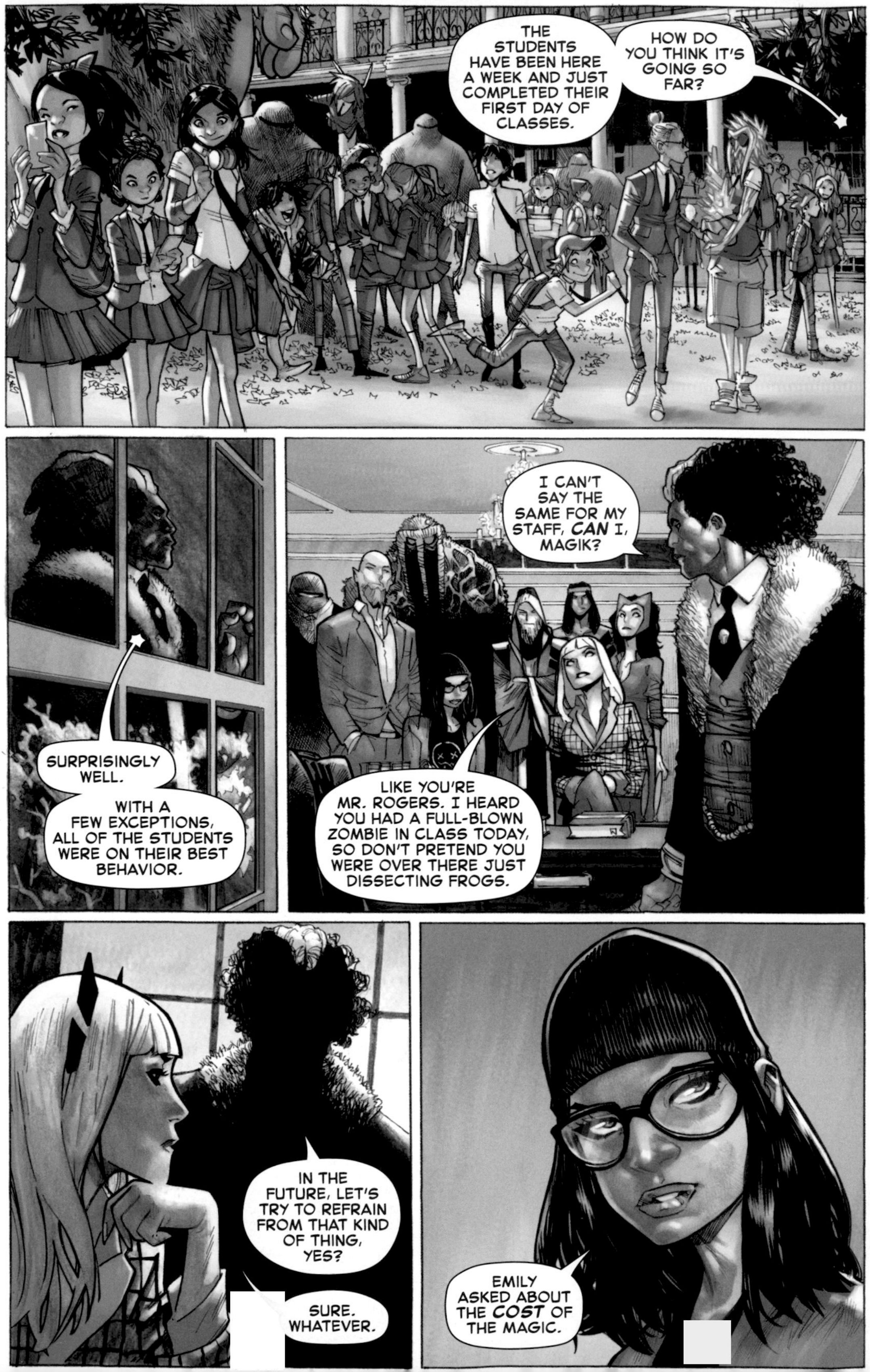
THE STUDENTS HAVE BEEN HERE A WEEK AND JUST COMPLETED THEIR FIRST DAY OF CLASSES.
HOW DO YOU THINK IT'S GOING SO FAR?
SURPRISINGLY WELL.
WITH A FEW EXCEPTIONS, ALL OF THE STUDENTS WERE ON THEIR BEST BEHAVIOR.
I CAN'T SAY THE SAME FOR MY STAFF, CAN I, MAGIK?
LIKE YOU'RE MR. ROGERS. I HEARD YOU HAD A FULL-BLOWN ZOMBIE IN CLASS TODAY, SO DON'T PRETEND YOU WERE OVER THERE JUST DISSECTING FROGS.
IN THE FUTURE, LET'S TRY TO REFRAIN FROM THAT KIND OF THING, YES?
SURE. WHATEVER.
EMILY ASKED ABOUT THE COST OF THE MAGIC.

WHAT DID YOU TELL HER?

YOU KNOW HOW I FEEL ABOUT THAT. AND HOW I FEEL ABOUT LYING TO THE STUDENTS.

SHE WON'T BE THE ONLY ONE TO ASK.

THAT WE TOOK CARE OF IT.

LIKE WE *DID*.

IF THAT'S ALL, THEN I WISH YOU ALL A GOOD EVENING.

I'M SO CONFUSED!

ABOUT WHAT?

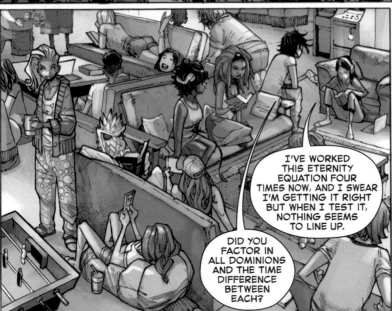

I'VE WORKED THIS ETERNITY EQUATION FOUR TIMES NOW, AND I SWEAR I'M GETTING IT RIGHT BUT WHEN I TEST IT, NOTHING SEEMS TO LINE UP.

DID YOU FACTOR IN ALL DOMINIONS AND THE TIME DIFFERENCE BETWEEN EACH?

UGH. AM I THE ONLY ONE WHO FEELS LIKE THEY DON'T BELONG HERE?

NOPE...

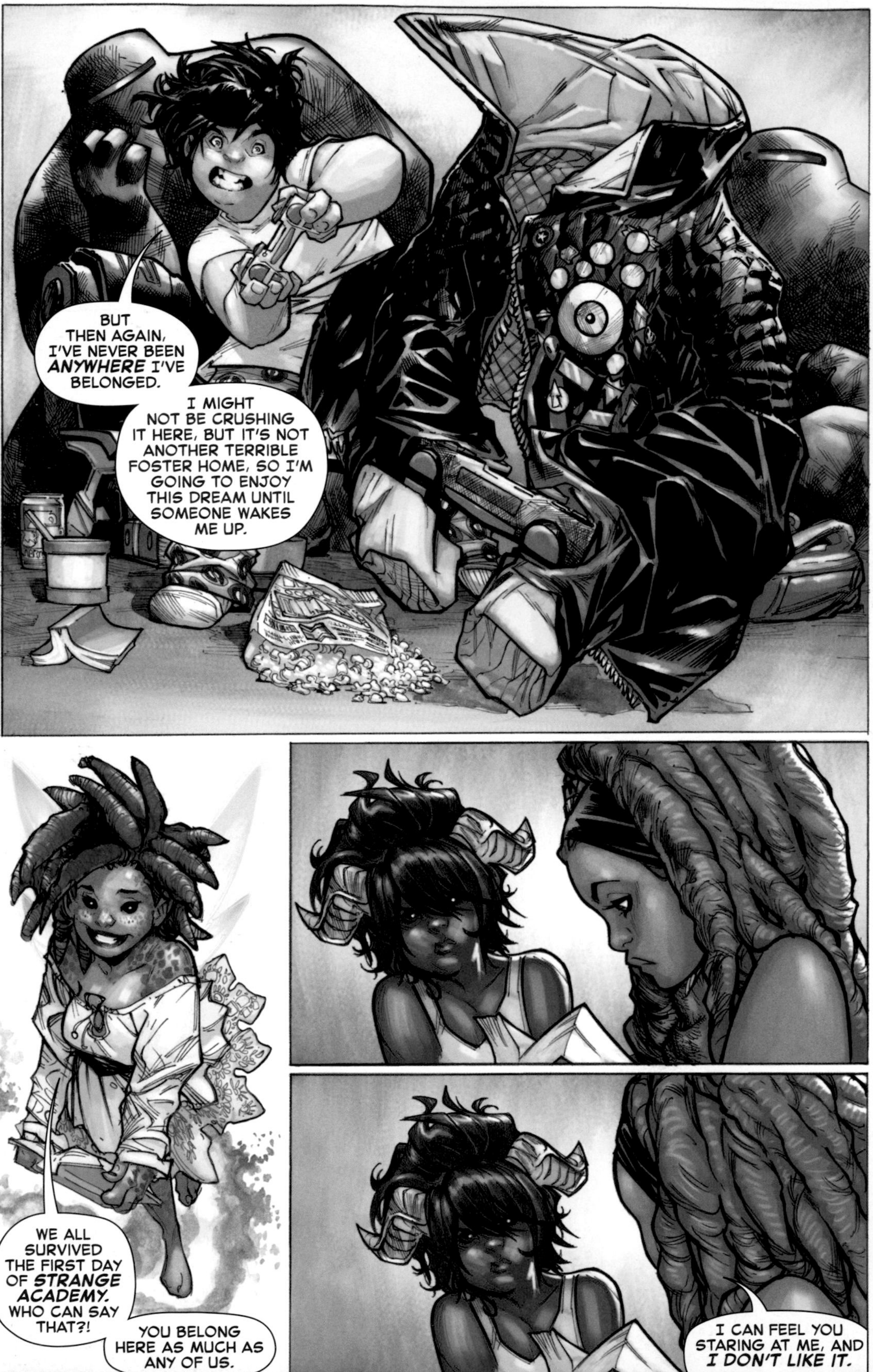
BUT THEN AGAIN, I'VE NEVER BEEN ***ANYWHERE*** I'VE BELONGED.
I MIGHT NOT BE CRUSHING IT HERE, BUT IT'S NOT ANOTHER TERRIBLE FOSTER HOME, SO I'M GOING TO ENJOY THIS DREAM UNTIL SOMEONE WAKES ME UP.
WE ALL SURVIVED THE FIRST DAY OF ***STRANGE ACADEMY.*** WHO CAN SAY THAT?!
YOU BELONG HERE AS MUCH AS ANY OF US.
I CAN FEEL YOU STARING AT ME, AND ***I DON'T LIKE IT.***

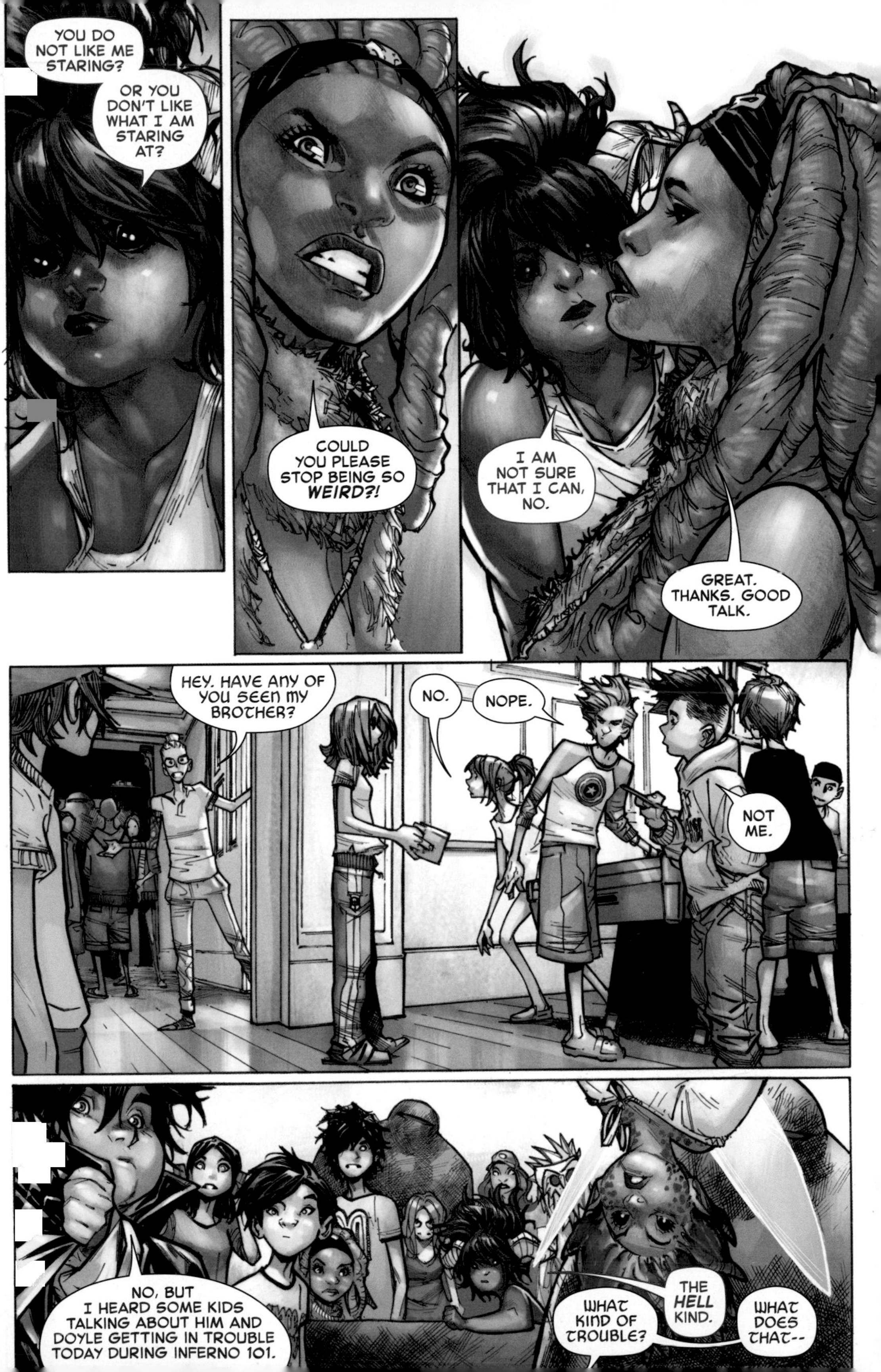
YOU DO NOT LIKE ME STARING?
OR YOU DON'T LIKE WHAT I AM STARING AT?
COULD YOU PLEASE STOP BEING SO *WEIRD?!*
I AM NOT SURE THAT I CAN, NO.
GREAT. THANKS. GOOD TALK.
HEY. HAVE ANY OF YOU SEEN MY BROTHER?
NO.
NOPE.
NOT ME.
NO, BUT I HEARD SOME KIDS TALKING ABOUT HIM AND DOYLE GETTING IN TROUBLE TODAY DURING INFERNO 101.
WHAT KIND OF TROUBLE?
THE *HELL* KIND.
WHAT DOES THAT--

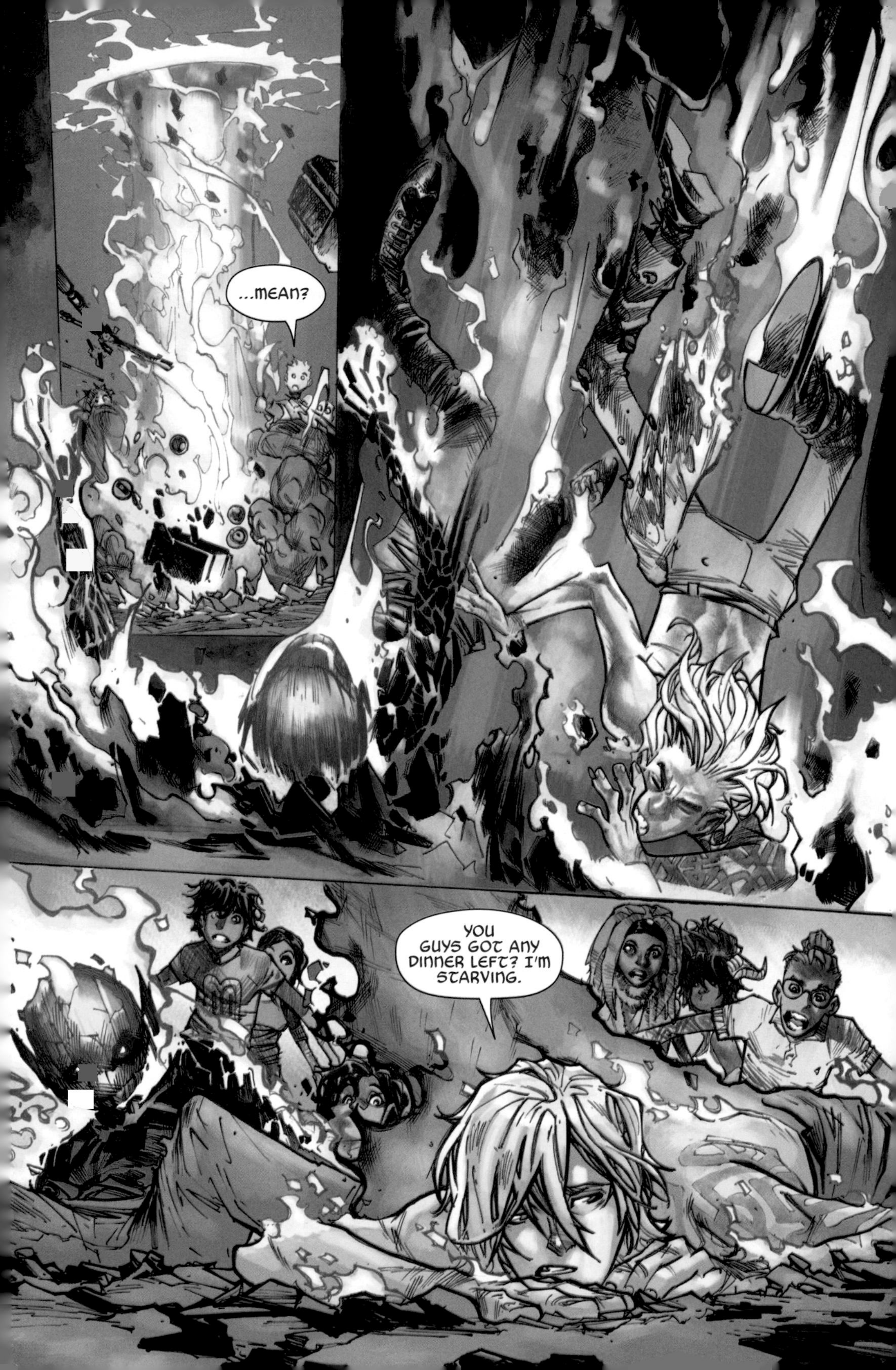
...MEAN?
YOU GUYS GOT ANY DINNER LEFT? I'M STARVING.

CLASS DESCRIPTIONS

HISTORY OF MAGICAL OBJECTS

What is the Wand of Watoomb? The Crystal of Kadavus? Tiboro's Coat? The answer to these questions may just save your life, so sign up for Professor Ancient One's course, which will give you a working knowledge of the 423 major magical artifacts from this and the 27 closest dimensions.

Instructor: Prof. Yao

ELEMENTS OF CHAOS MAGIC

Newton's Laws are basically Newton's Suggestions as all of physics bends to those who practice Chaos magic. Professor Maximoff is the foremost practitioner of the most volatile magic, and studying with her is the best way to avoid perishing at the hands of Dark Chaotitians.

Instructor: Adj. Prof. Wanda Maximoff

INTRODUCTION TO THE UNDEAD

The only thing that's certain is taxes, and sometimes what you thought was your last goodbye to Grandma isn't. Zombies are real and not to be trifled with. But don't think that TV and comic books have it right either. Zombies are a very particular sort of being, and you need to be ready to interact with them.

Instructor: Prof. Jericho Drumm

INFERNO 101

Love isn't officially a hell, but if it was you'd learn about it from Professors Rasputin & Hellstrom. There are several established hellscapes reachable from this Earth, and as you have a 98.4% chance of spending time in one, you better learn what you're in for. NOTE: Lateness isn't tolerated.

Instructor: Adj. Prof. Illyana Rasputina, Adj. Prof. Daimon Hellstrom

MAGICAL PLANTS AND THE CARE THEREOF

[Description not available until someone learns to communicate with Professor Man-Thing in a non-Fear language.]

Instructor: Adj. Prof. Man-Thing

GYM 1

A strong astral form necessitates a strong body, and Coach Taylor will get you there with calisthenics and some new magical devices.

Instructor: Coach Taylor

MATH 1

A project-based course in which students explore foundational principles of algebra and geometry to craft a mystical disguise. (Area of space displaced by magic proportionate to real mass compression, charisma trajectories, credibility decay and so on.)

Instructor: Adj. Prof. Rintrah

WORLD AND HEAVENLY HISTORY
(fulfills one Social Studies credit)

Studies ancient terrestrial civilizations beginning with Atlantis, Lemuria, Attilan, Mesopotamia and the valleys of the Nile, Indus, Yangtze and Yellow Rivers, and concluding in the postclassical age, concurrent with post-Sixth Day Celestial civilizations pre-rebellion through the Postdiluvian Equilibrium, and considering the effects of the Black Legion on the great man theory of history.

Instructor: Sister Sara of the Holy Sepulcher*

AP MICROECONOMICS
(fulfills 1 Social Studies credit)

Equivalent to an introductory-level college course in microeconomics, students will learn to think about the individual economic decision maker and get to know the forces and principles that influence their behavior, such as markets, policy, mala suerte, scarcity, cost, benefits, marginal analysis and *hechizo*.

Instructor: Señor Mágico

INFILTRATING MAGICALLY SECURED LOCATIONS

Discover a magical location? Something like...a...school? Learn how to successfully infiltrate and undermine the basic structure of said school.

Instructor: Prof. Emeritus Harkness

CREATIVE SPELL CASTING

Tap into your inner mage and learn to cast your own unique spells. Are you bursting with ideas and want to build your own spells but don't know where to start? Nico will show you how!

Prerequisite: Inferno 101

Instructor: Adj. Prof. Nico Minoru

ANATOMY 101

Learn the anatomy of over 1000 species from Earth to the far reaches of the galaxy and beyond even our reality!

Instructor: ~~Doctor Strange~~ ZELMA

ADVANCED ASTRAL PROJECTING

Put your astral projecting skills to the test by learning how to shift between realms and time!

Prerequisite: Astral Projection 101

Instructor: Prof. Yao

SANCTUM ECONOMICS

Everything starts at home. Learn how to protect and nurture your home and homelife. Chef Mindful One will provide easy-to-learn recipes for bountiful rejuvenation of your mystical skills. Also learn how to balance a checkbook.

Instructors: Adj. Prof. Wong & Mindful One

PREMED INTER-SPIRITUAL STUDIES

Learn how to perform medical work through spiritual means. Talk to your dead patients and see how you could have done better.

Instructor: Adj. Prof Shaman

Foreign Language

NECROMANCE LANGUAGES 100 - Adj. Prof. Dead Girl*

A prerequisite for Ghost Whispering 101, Vampiric Romanian 101, and Le Français du Loup-Garou 101

Course description forthcoming

*Check with your guidance counselor to confirm that you've mastered the art of maintaining homeostasis in our time-and-space-displaced classrooms.

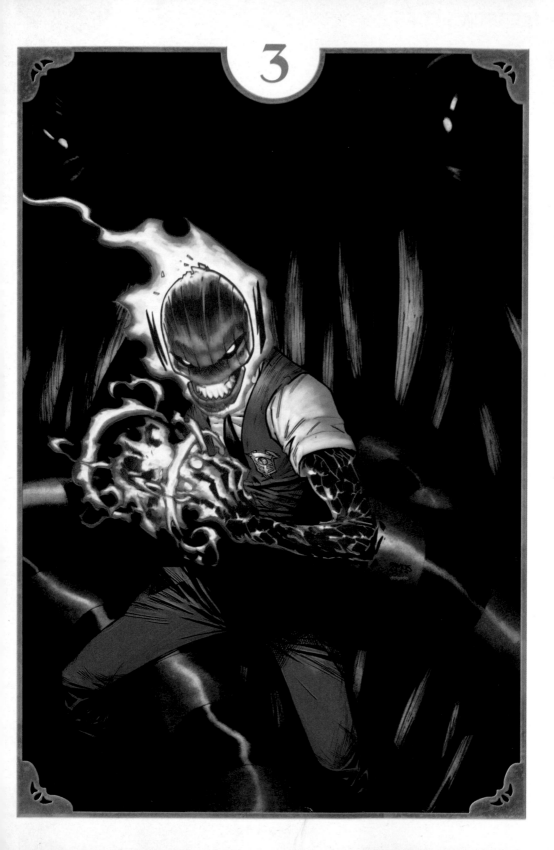

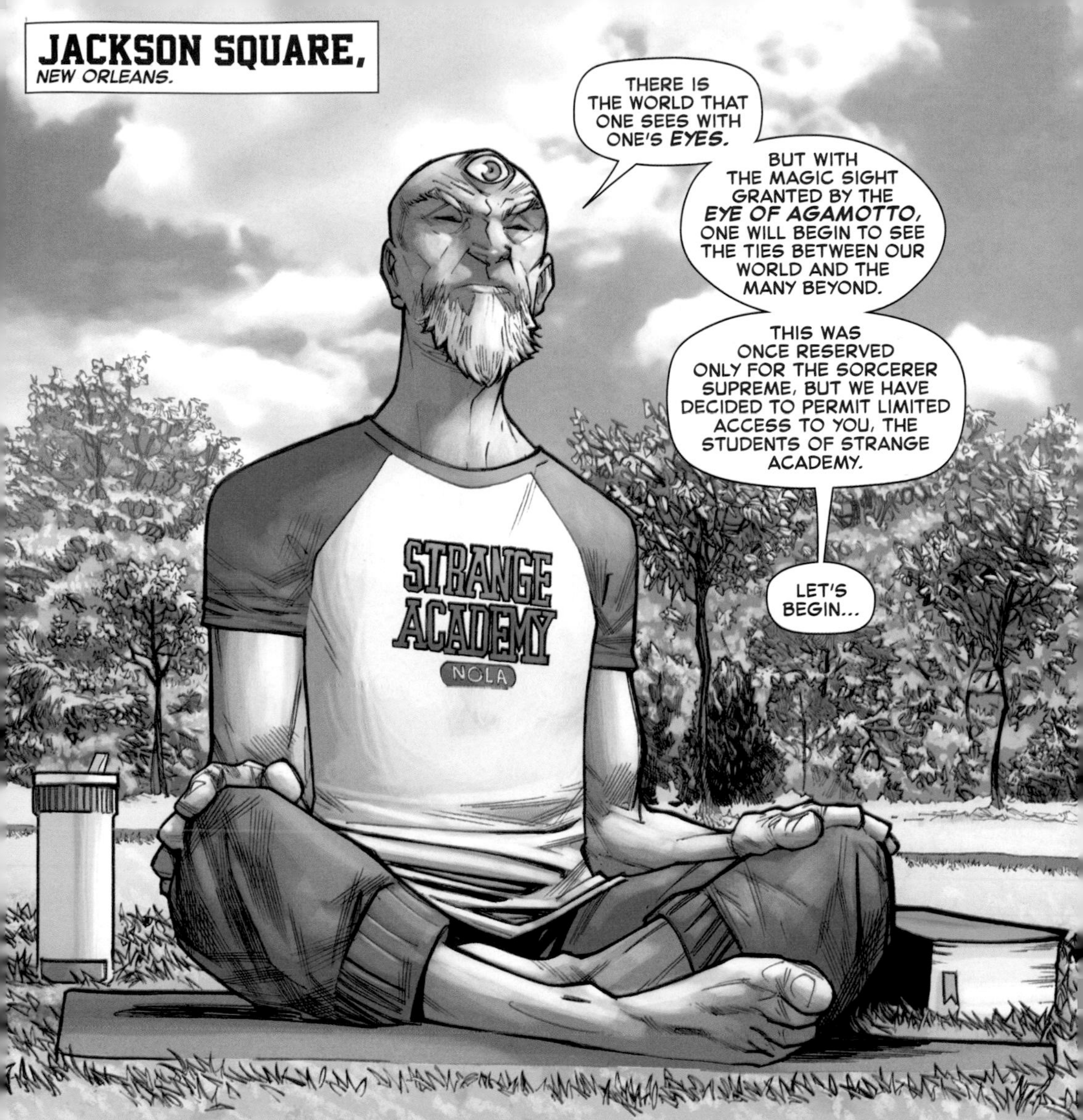
JACKSON SQUARE,
NEW ORLEANS.
THERE IS THE WORLD THAT ONE SEES WITH ONE'S *EYES.*
BUT WITH THE MAGIC SIGHT GRANTED BY THE *EYE OF AGAMOTTO,* ONE WILL BEGIN TO SEE THE TIES BETWEEN OUR WORLD AND THE MANY BEYOND.
THIS WAS ONCE RESERVED ONLY FOR THE SORCERER SUPREME, BUT WE HAVE DECIDED TO PERMIT LIMITED ACCESS TO YOU, THE STUDENTS OF STRANGE ACADEMY.
LET'S BEGIN...
STRANGE ACADEMY
NOLA

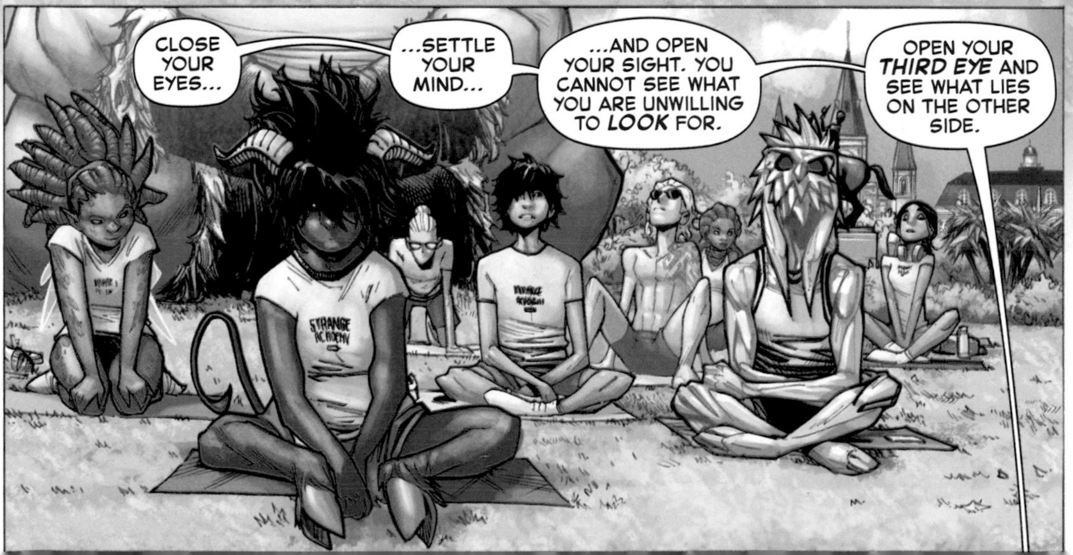
CLOSE YOUR EYES...
...SETTLE YOUR MIND...
...AND OPEN YOUR SIGHT. YOU CANNOT SEE WHAT YOU ARE UNWILLING TO *LOOK* FOR.
OPEN YOUR *THIRD EYE* AND SEE WHAT LIES ON THE OTHER SIDE.
STRANGE ACADEMY

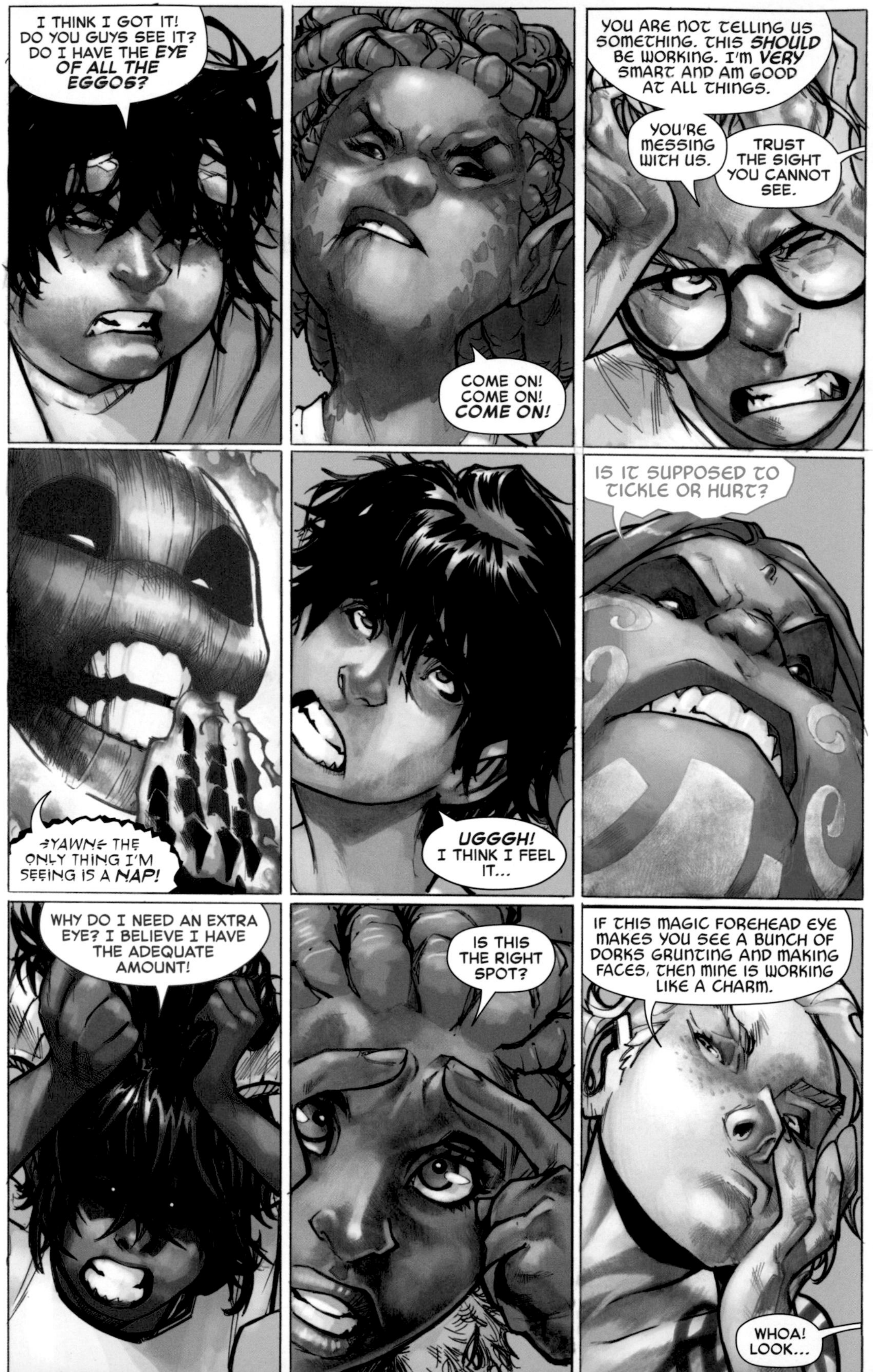
I THINK I GOT IT! DO YOU GUYS SEE IT? DO I HAVE THE EYE OF ALL THE EGGOS?
COME ON! COME ON! COME ON!
YOU ARE NOT TELLING US SOMETHING. THIS SHOULD BE WORKING. I'M VERY SMART AND AM GOOD AT ALL THINGS.
YOU'RE MESSING WITH US.
TRUST THE SIGHT YOU CANNOT SEE.
YAWN THE ONLY THING I'M SEEING IS A NAP!
UGGGH! I THINK I FEEL IT...
IS IT SUPPOSED TO TICKLE OR HURT?
WHY DO I NEED AN EXTRA EYE? I BELIEVE I HAVE THE ADEQUATE AMOUNT!
IS THIS THE RIGHT SPOT?
IF THIS MAGIC FOREHEAD EYE MAKES YOU SEE A BUNCH OF DORKS GRUNTING AND MAKING FACES, THEN MINE IS WORKING LIKE A CHARM.
WHOA! LOOK...

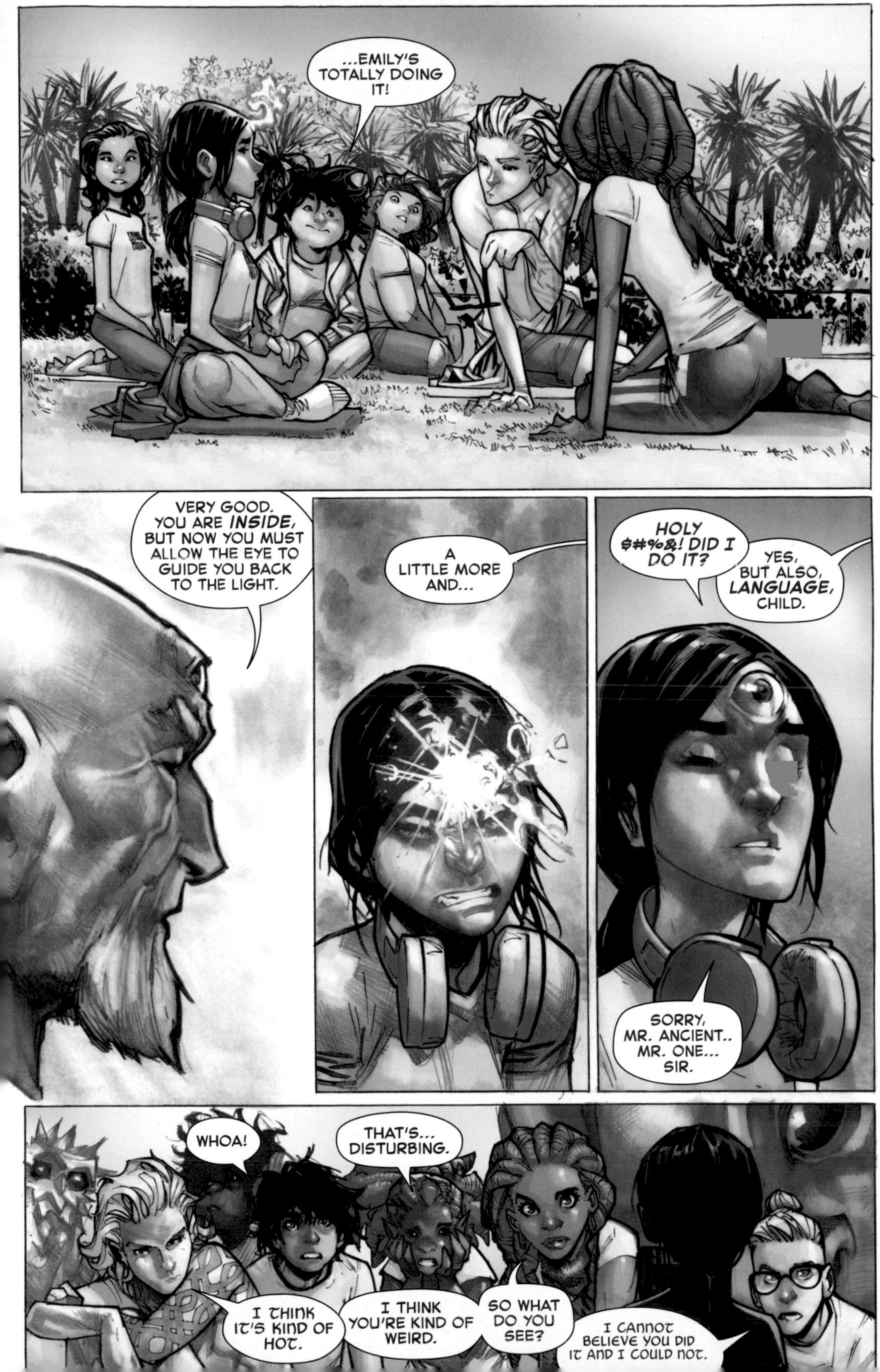
...EMILY'S TOTALLY DOING IT!
VERY GOOD. YOU ARE INSIDE, BUT NOW YOU MUST ALLOW THE EYE TO GUIDE YOU BACK TO THE LIGHT.
A LITTLE MORE AND...
HOLY $#%&! DID I DO IT?
YES, BUT ALSO, LANGUAGE, CHILD.
SORRY, MR. ANCIENT.. MR. ONE... SIR.
WHOA!
THAT'S... DISTURBING.
I THINK IT'S KIND OF HOT.
I THINK YOU'RE KIND OF WEIRD.
SO WHAT DO YOU SEE?
I CANNOT BELIEVE YOU DID IT AND I COULD NOT.

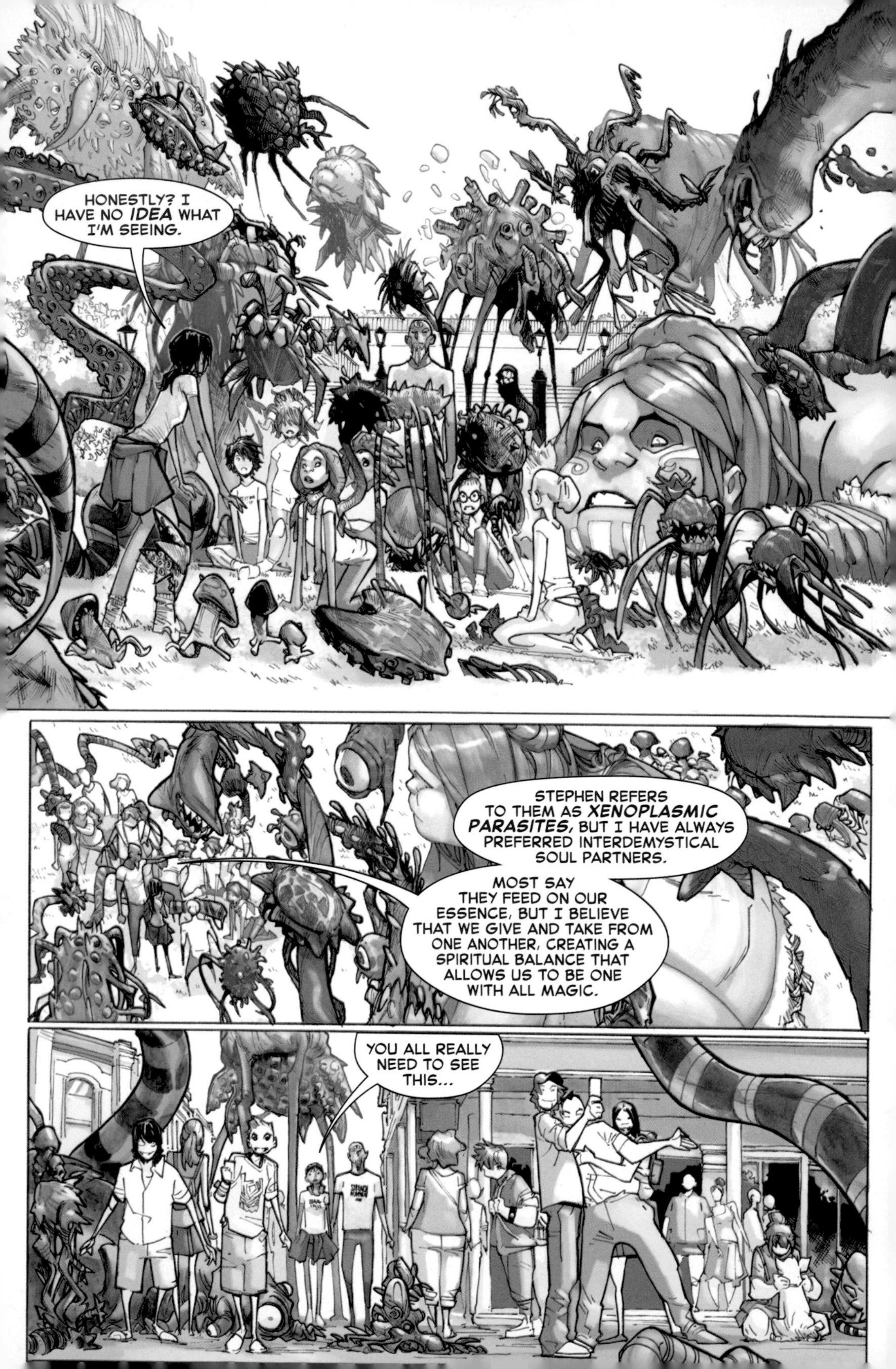
HONESTLY? I HAVE NO IDEA WHAT I'M SEEING.
STEPHEN REFERS TO THEM AS XENOPLASMIC PARASITES, BUT I HAVE ALWAYS PREFERRED INTERDEMYSTICAL SOUL PARTNERS.
MOST SAY THEY FEED ON OUR ESSENCE, BUT I BELIEVE THAT WE GIVE AND TAKE FROM ONE ANOTHER, CREATING A SPIRITUAL BALANCE THAT ALLOWS US TO BE ONE WITH ALL MAGIC.
YOU ALL REALLY NEED TO SEE THIS...

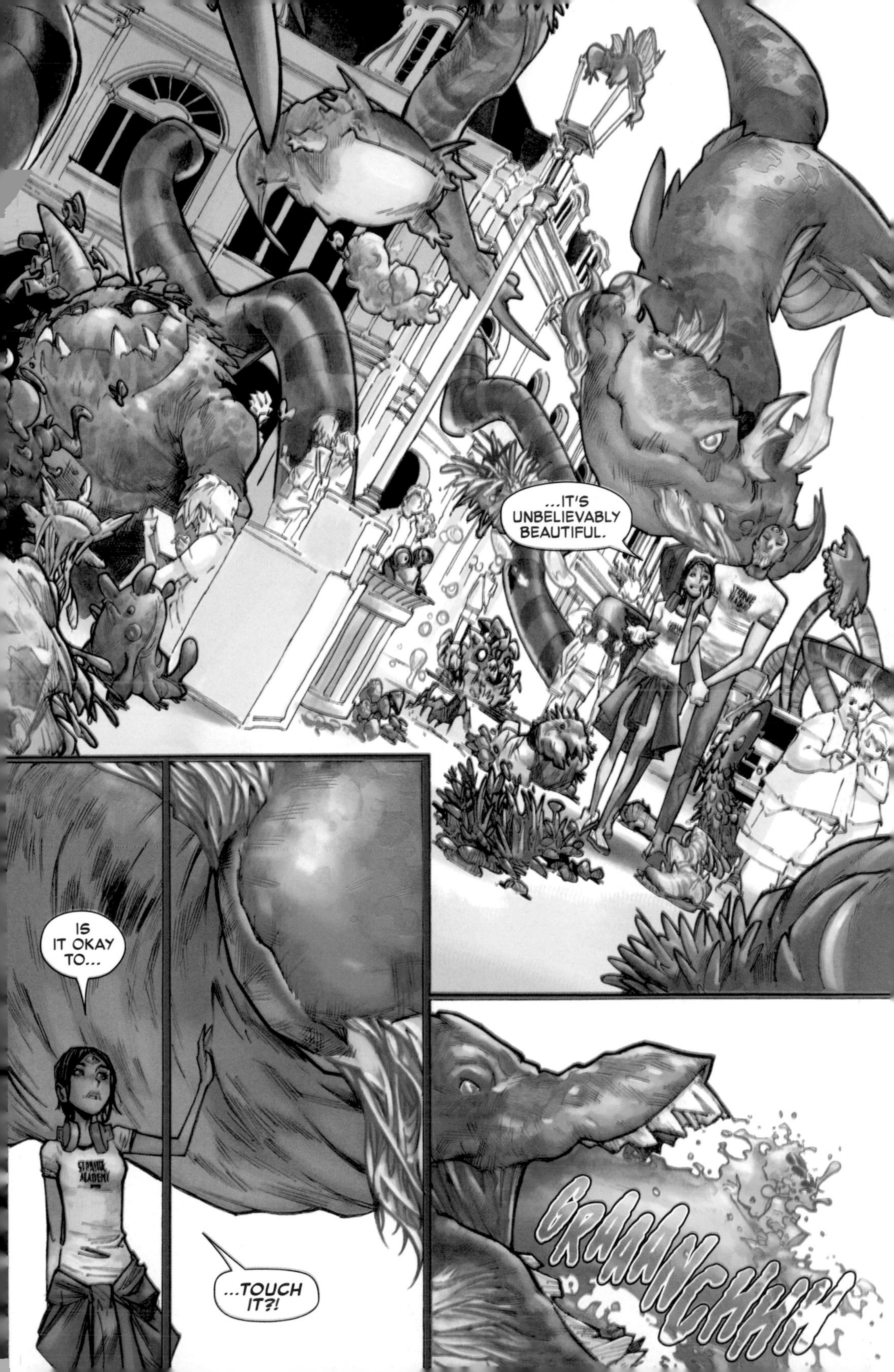
...IT'S UNBELIEVABLY BEAUTIFUL.
IS IT OKAY TO...
...TOUCH IT?!
GRAAAANCHHH!

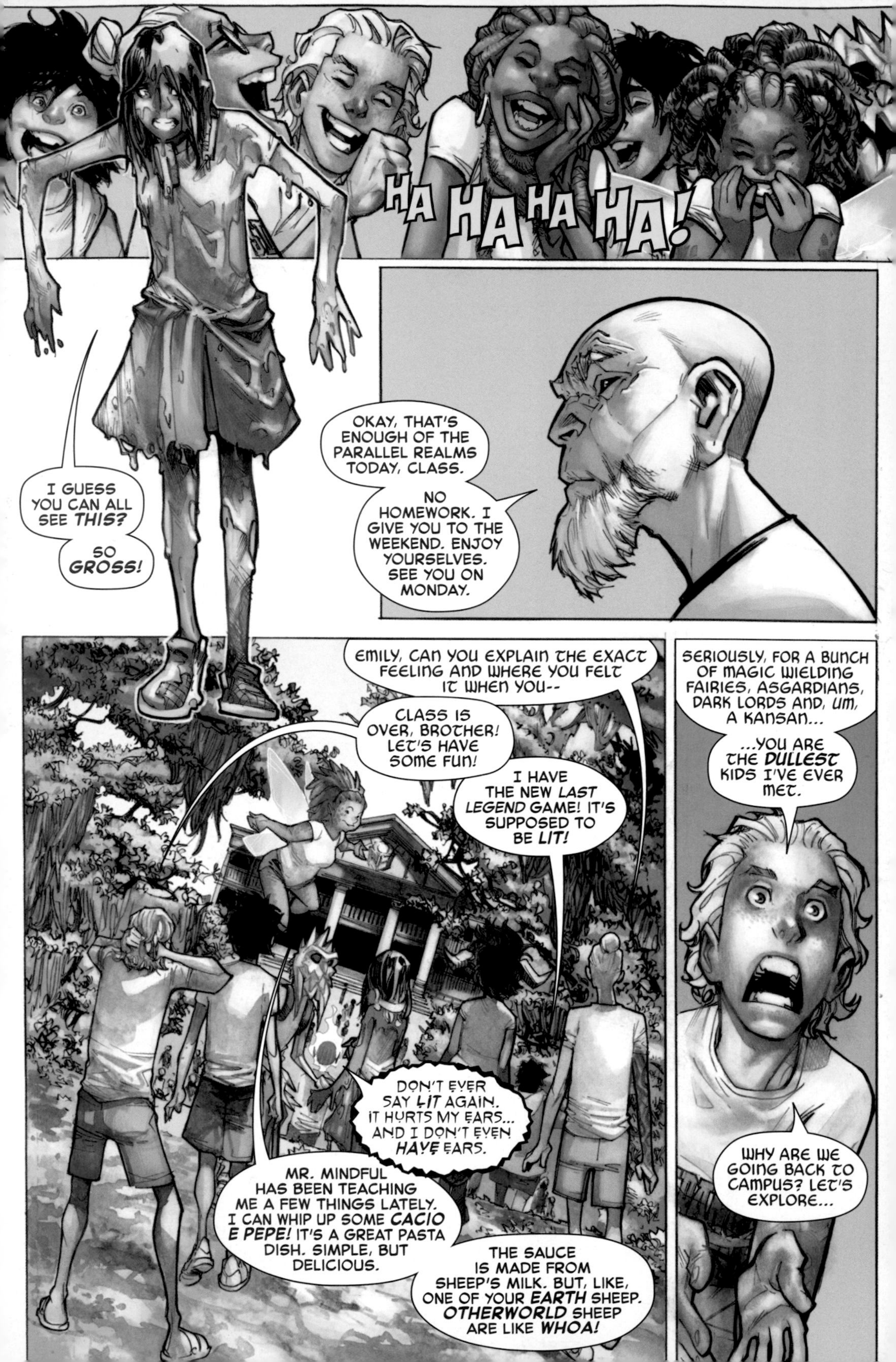
HA HA HA HA HA!
I GUESS YOU CAN ALL SEE THIS?
SO GROSS!
OKAY, THAT'S ENOUGH OF THE PARALLEL REALMS TODAY, CLASS.
NO HOMEWORK. I GIVE YOU TO THE WEEKEND. ENJOY YOURSELVES. SEE YOU ON MONDAY.
EMILY, CAN YOU EXPLAIN THE EXACT FEELING AND WHERE YOU FELT IT WHEN YOU--
CLASS IS OVER, BROTHER! LET'S HAVE SOME FUN!
I HAVE THE NEW LAST LEGEND GAME! IT'S SUPPOSED TO BE LIT!
DON'T EVER SAY LIT AGAIN. IT HURTS MY EARS... AND I DON'T EVEN HAVE EARS.
MR. MINDFUL HAS BEEN TEACHING ME A FEW THINGS LATELY. I CAN WHIP UP SOME CACIO E PEPE! IT'S A GREAT PASTA DISH. SIMPLE, BUT DELICIOUS.
THE SAUCE IS MADE FROM SHEEP'S MILK. BUT, LIKE, ONE OF YOUR EARTH SHEEP. OTHERWORLD SHEEP ARE LIKE WHOA!
SERIOUSLY, FOR A BUNCH OF MAGIC WIELDING FAIRIES, ASGARDIANS, DARK LORDS AND, UM, A KANSAN...
...YOU ARE THE DULLEST KIDS I'VE EVER MET.
WHY ARE WE GOING BACK TO CAMPUS? LET'S EXPLORE...

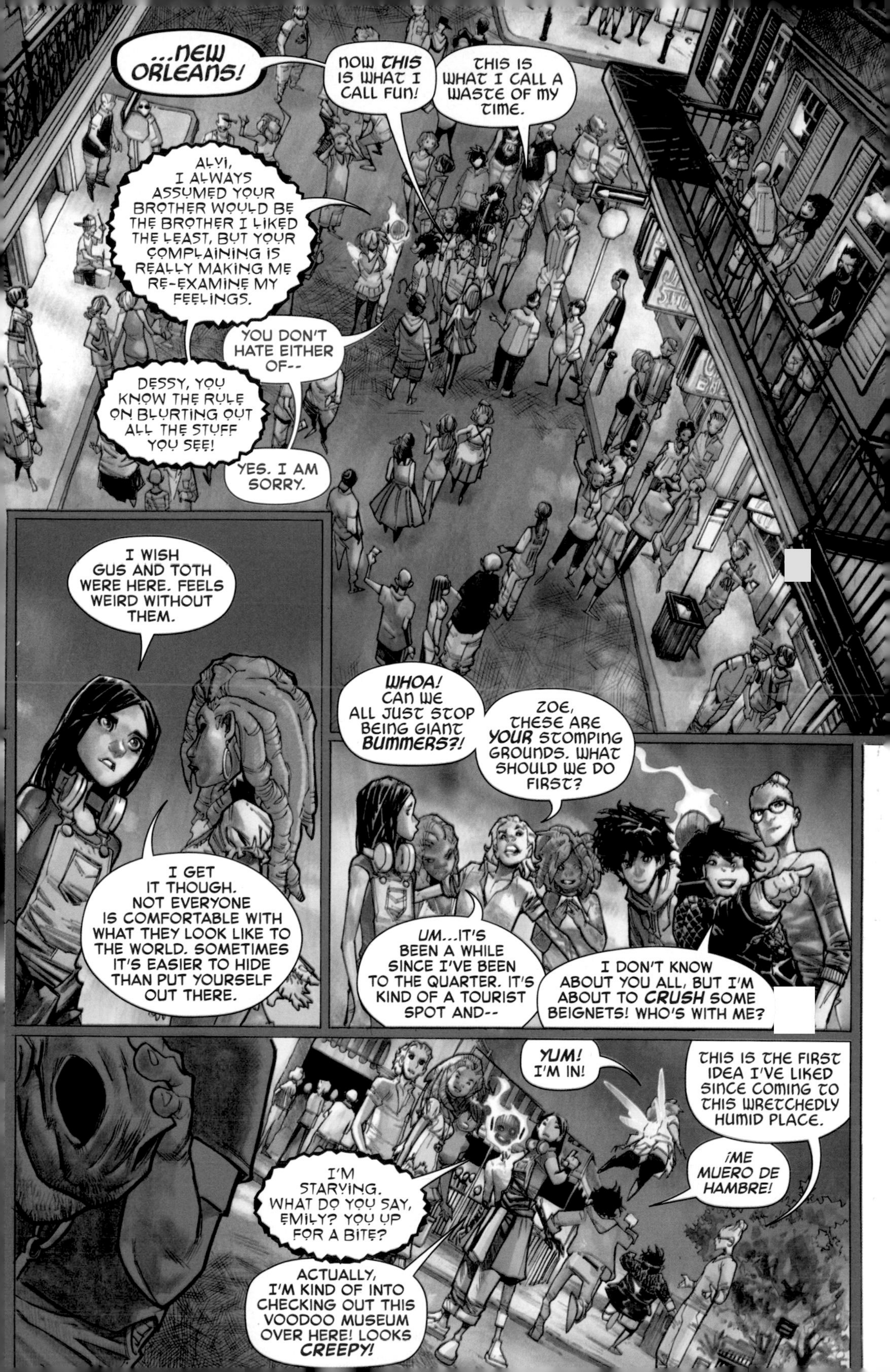
...NEW ORLEANS!
NOW THIS IS WHAT I CALL FUN!
THIS IS WHAT I CALL A WASTE OF MY TIME.
ALVI, I ALWAYS ASSUMED YOUR BROTHER WOULD BE THE BROTHER I LIKED THE LEAST, BUT YOUR COMPLAINING IS REALLY MAKING ME RE-EXAMINE MY FEELINGS.
YOU DON'T HATE EITHER OF--
DESSY, YOU KNOW THE RULE ON BLURTING OUT ALL THE STUFF YOU SEE!
YES. I AM SORRY.
I WISH GUS AND TOTH WERE HERE. FEELS WEIRD WITHOUT THEM.
I GET IT THOUGH. NOT EVERYONE IS COMFORTABLE WITH WHAT THEY LOOK LIKE TO THE WORLD. SOMETIMES IT'S EASIER TO HIDE THAN PUT YOURSELF OUT THERE.
WHOA! CAN WE ALL JUST STOP BEING GIANT BUMMERS?!
ZOE, THESE ARE YOUR STOMPING GROUNDS. WHAT SHOULD WE DO FIRST?
UM...IT'S BEEN A WHILE SINCE I'VE BEEN TO THE QUARTER. IT'S KIND OF A TOURIST SPOT AND--
I DON'T KNOW ABOUT YOU ALL, BUT I'M ABOUT TO CRUSH SOME BEIGNETS! WHO'S WITH ME?
YUM! I'M IN!
THIS IS THE FIRST IDEA I'VE LIKED SINCE COMING TO THIS WRETCHEDLY HUMID PLACE.
¡ME MUERO DE HAMBRE!
I'M STARVING. WHAT DO YOU SAY, EMILY? YOU UP FOR A BITE?
ACTUALLY, I'M KIND OF INTO CHECKING OUT THIS VOODOO MUSEUM OVER HERE! LOOKS CREEPY!

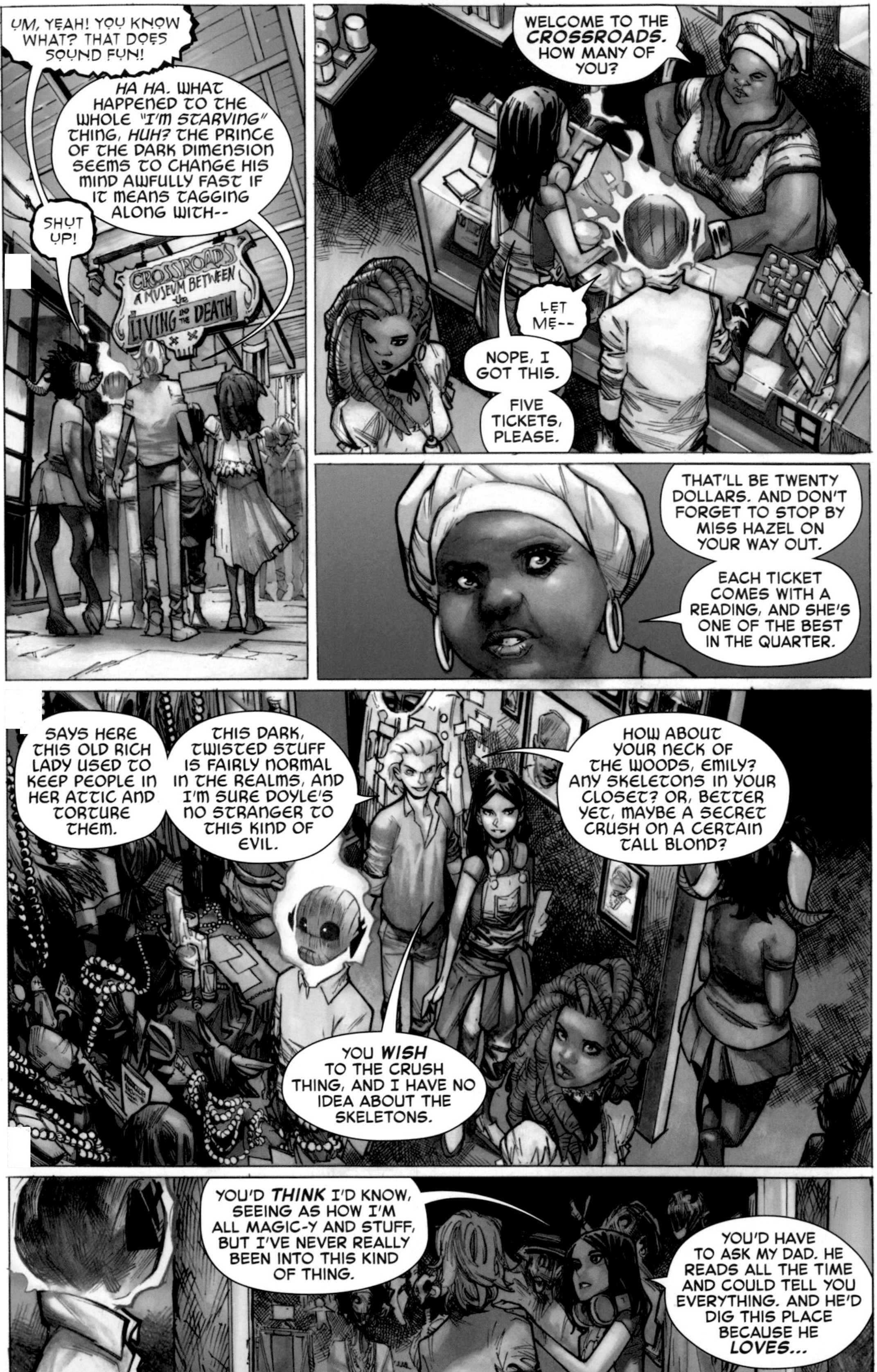

UM, YEAH! YOU KNOW WHAT? THAT DOES SOUND FUN!
HA HA. WHAT HAPPENED TO THE WHOLE "I'M STARVING" THING, HUH? THE PRINCE OF THE DARK DIMENSION SEEMS TO CHANGE HIS MIND AWFULLY FAST IF IT MEANS TAGGING ALONG WITH--
SHUT UP!
CROSSROADS A MUSEUM BETWEEN THE LIVING AND THE DEATH
WELCOME TO THE CROSSROADS. HOW MANY OF YOU?
LET ME--
NOPE, I GOT THIS.
FIVE TICKETS, PLEASE.
THAT'LL BE TWENTY DOLLARS. AND DON'T FORGET TO STOP BY MISS HAZEL ON YOUR WAY OUT.
EACH TICKET COMES WITH A READING, AND SHE'S ONE OF THE BEST IN THE QUARTER.
SAYS HERE THIS OLD RICH LADY USED TO KEEP PEOPLE IN HER ATTIC AND TORTURE THEM.
THIS DARK, TWISTED STUFF IS FAIRLY NORMAL IN THE REALMS, AND I'M SURE DOYLE'S NO STRANGER TO THIS KIND OF EVIL.
HOW ABOUT YOUR NECK OF THE WOODS, EMILY? ANY SKELETONS IN YOUR CLOSET? OR, BETTER YET, MAYBE A SECRET CRUSH ON A CERTAIN TALL BLOND?
YOU WISH TO THE CRUSH THING, AND I HAVE NO IDEA ABOUT THE SKELETONS.
YOU'D THINK I'D KNOW, SEEING AS HOW I'M ALL MAGIC-Y AND STUFF, BUT I'VE NEVER REALLY BEEN INTO THIS KIND OF THING.
YOU'D HAVE TO ASK MY DAD. HE READS ALL THE TIME AND COULD TELL YOU EVERYTHING. AND HE'D DIG THIS PLACE BECAUSE HE LOVES...

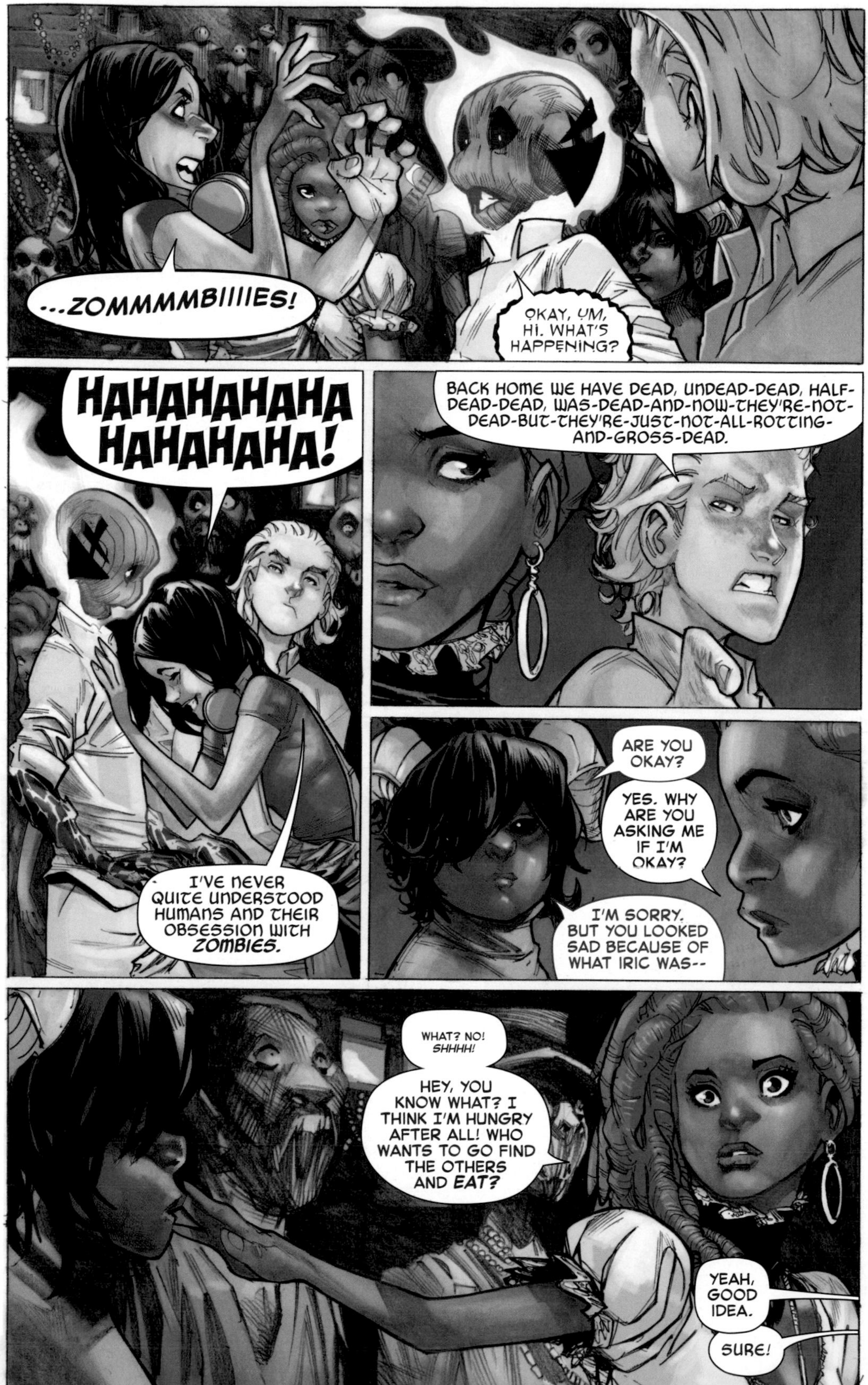
...ZOMMMMBIIIIES!
OKAY, UM, HI. WHAT'S HAPPENING?
HAHAHAHAHA HAHAHAHA!
I'VE NEVER QUITE UNDERSTOOD HUMANS AND THEIR OBSESSION WITH ZOMBIES.
BACK HOME WE HAVE DEAD, UNDEAD-DEAD, HALF-DEAD-DEAD, WAS-DEAD-AND-NOW-THEY'RE-NOT-DEAD-BUT-THEY'RE-JUST-NOT-ALL-ROTTING-AND-GROSS-DEAD.
ARE YOU OKAY?
YES. WHY ARE YOU ASKING ME IF I'M OKAY?
I'M SORRY. BUT YOU LOOKED SAD BECAUSE OF WHAT IRIC WAS--
WHAT? NO! SHHHH!
HEY, YOU KNOW WHAT? I THINK I'M HUNGRY AFTER ALL! WHO WANTS TO GO FIND THE OTHERS AND EAT?
YEAH, GOOD IDEA.
SURE!

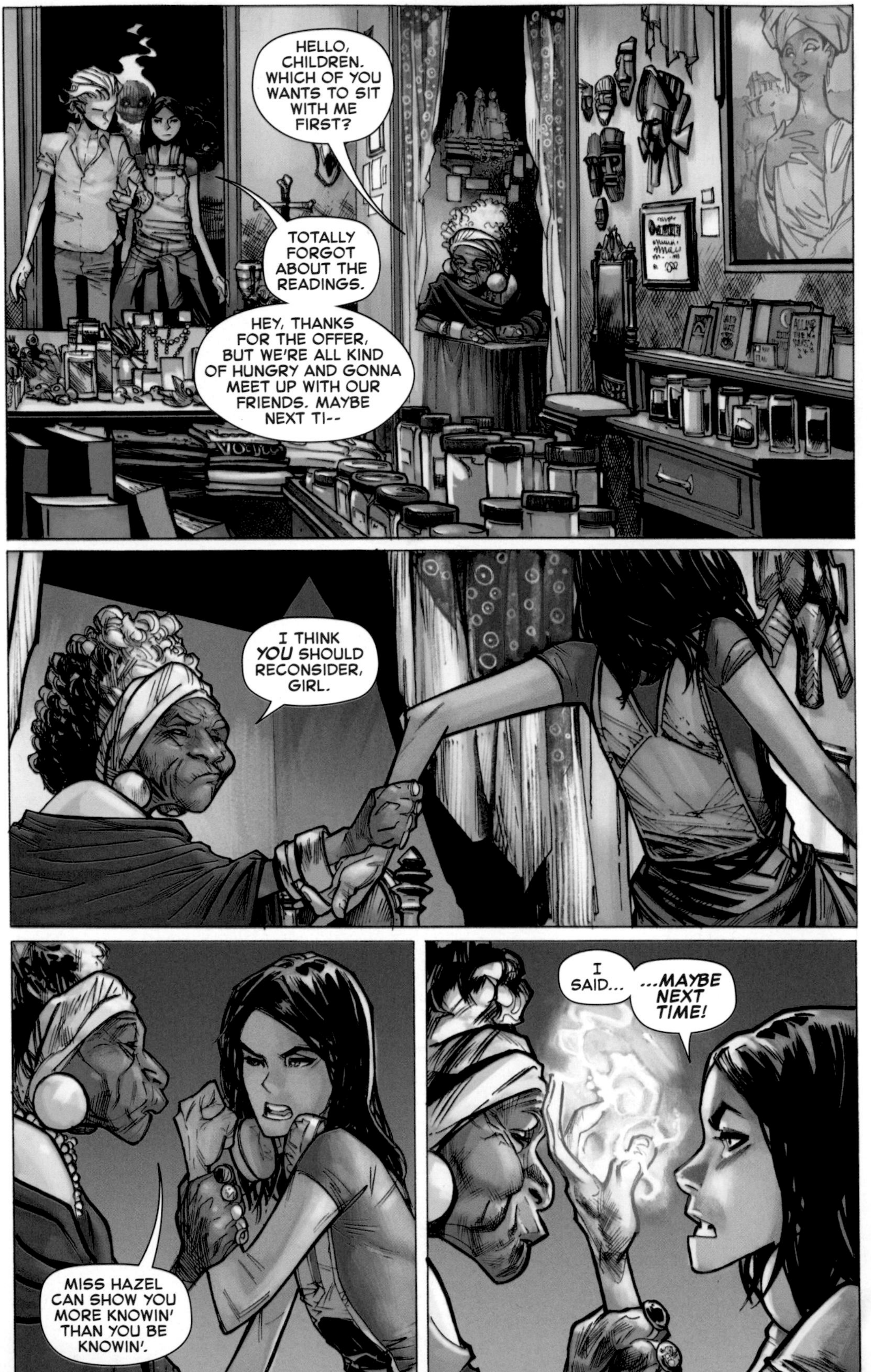
HELLO, CHILDREN. WHICH OF YOU WANTS TO SIT WITH ME FIRST?
TOTALLY FORGOT ABOUT THE READINGS.
HEY, THANKS FOR THE OFFER, BUT WE'RE ALL KIND OF HUNGRY AND GONNA MEET UP WITH OUR FRIENDS. MAYBE NEXT TI--
I THINK *YOU* SHOULD RECONSIDER, GIRL.
MISS HAZEL CAN SHOW YOU MORE KNOWIN' THAN YOU BE KNOWIN'.
I SAID...
...MAYBE NEXT TIME!

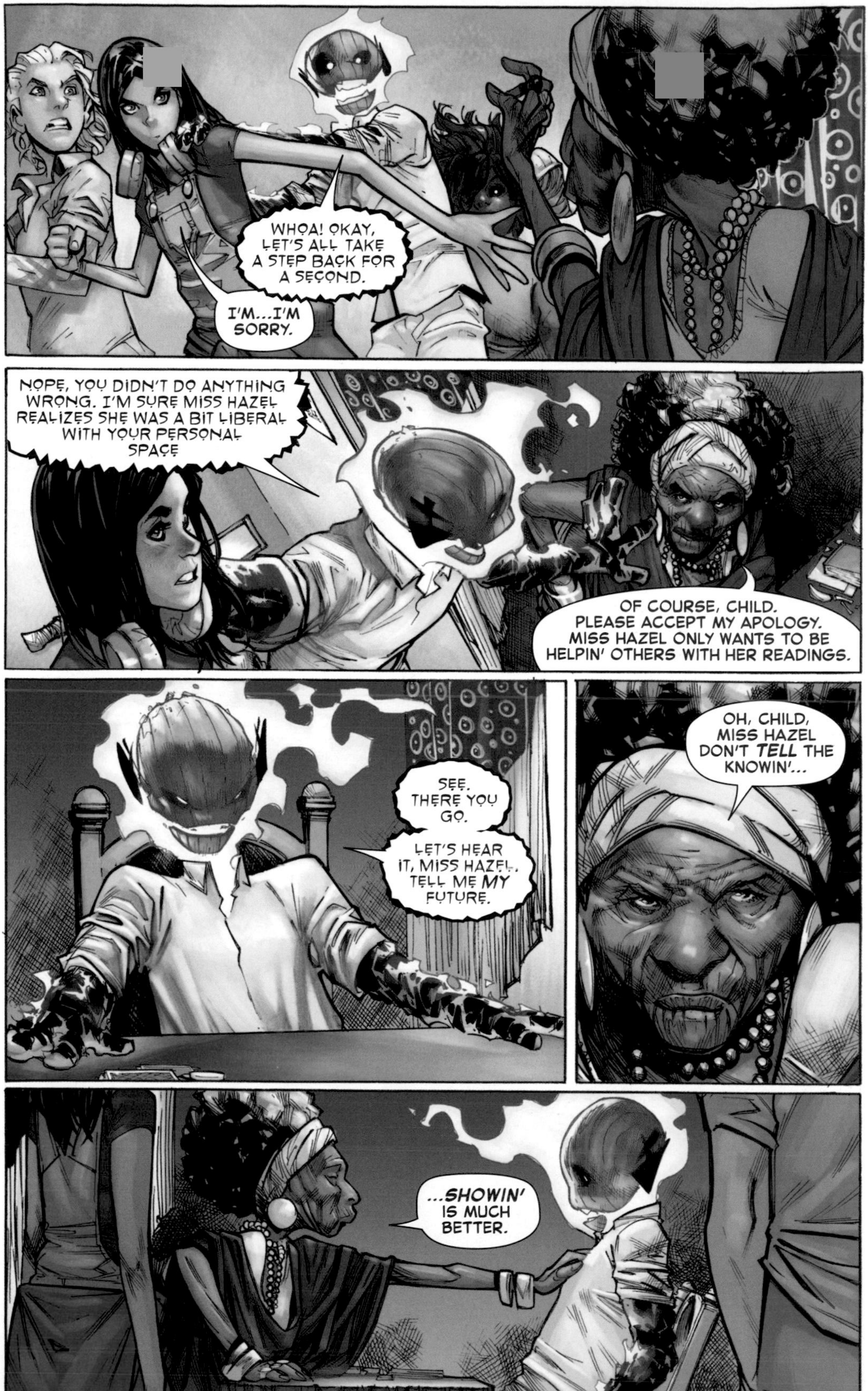
WHOA! OKAY, LET'S ALL TAKE A STEP BACK FOR A SECOND.
I'M...I'M SORRY.
NOPE, YOU DIDN'T DO ANYTHING WRONG. I'M SURE MISS HAZEL REALIZES SHE WAS A BIT LIBERAL WITH YOUR PERSONAL SPACE
OF COURSE, CHILD. PLEASE ACCEPT MY APOLOGY. MISS HAZEL ONLY WANTS TO BE HELPIN' OTHERS WITH HER READINGS.
SEE. THERE YOU GO.
LET'S HEAR IT, MISS HAZEL. TELL ME MY FUTURE.
OH, CHILD, MISS HAZEL DON'T TELL THE KNOWIN'...
...SHOWIN' IS MUCH BETTER.

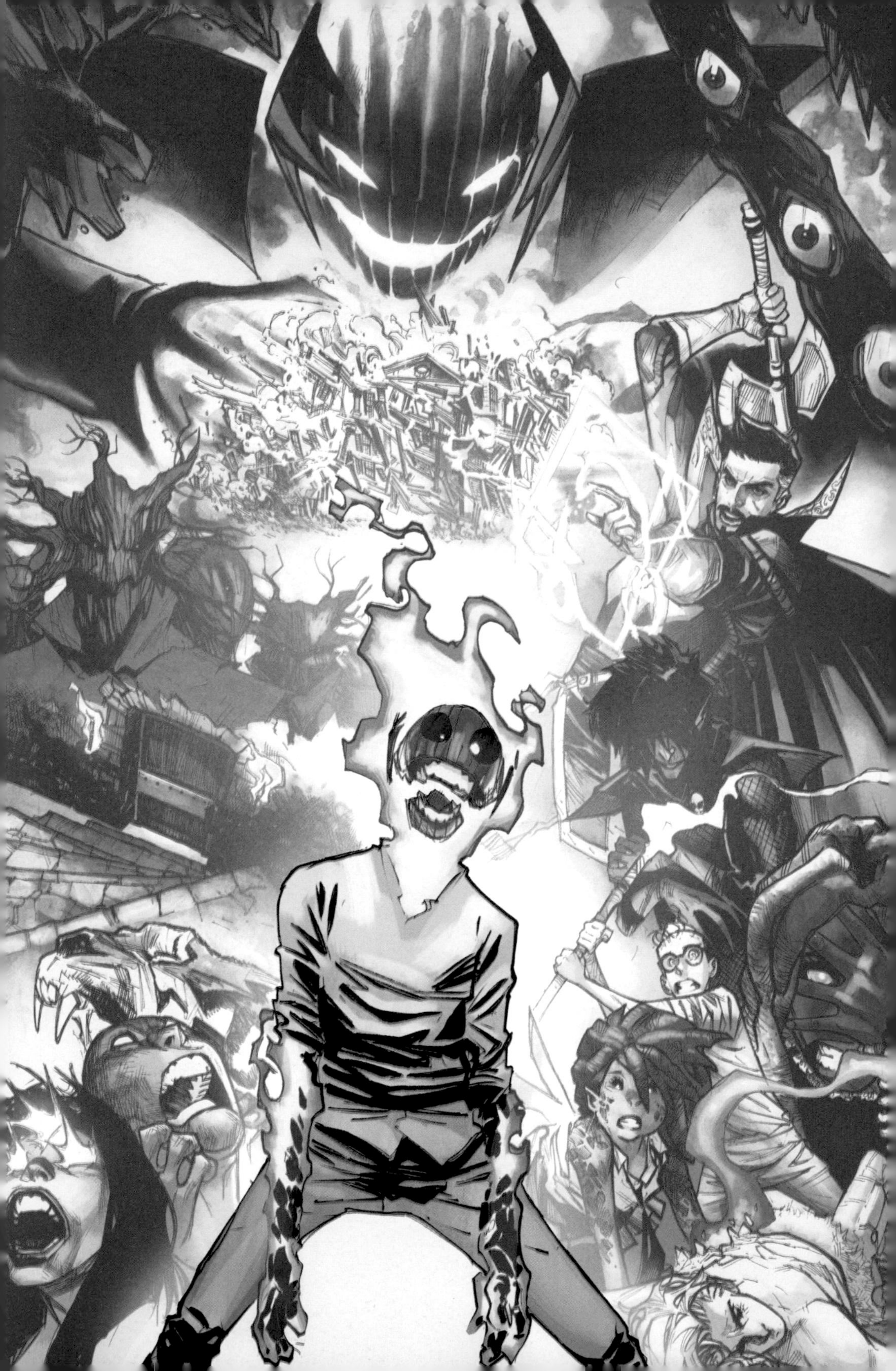

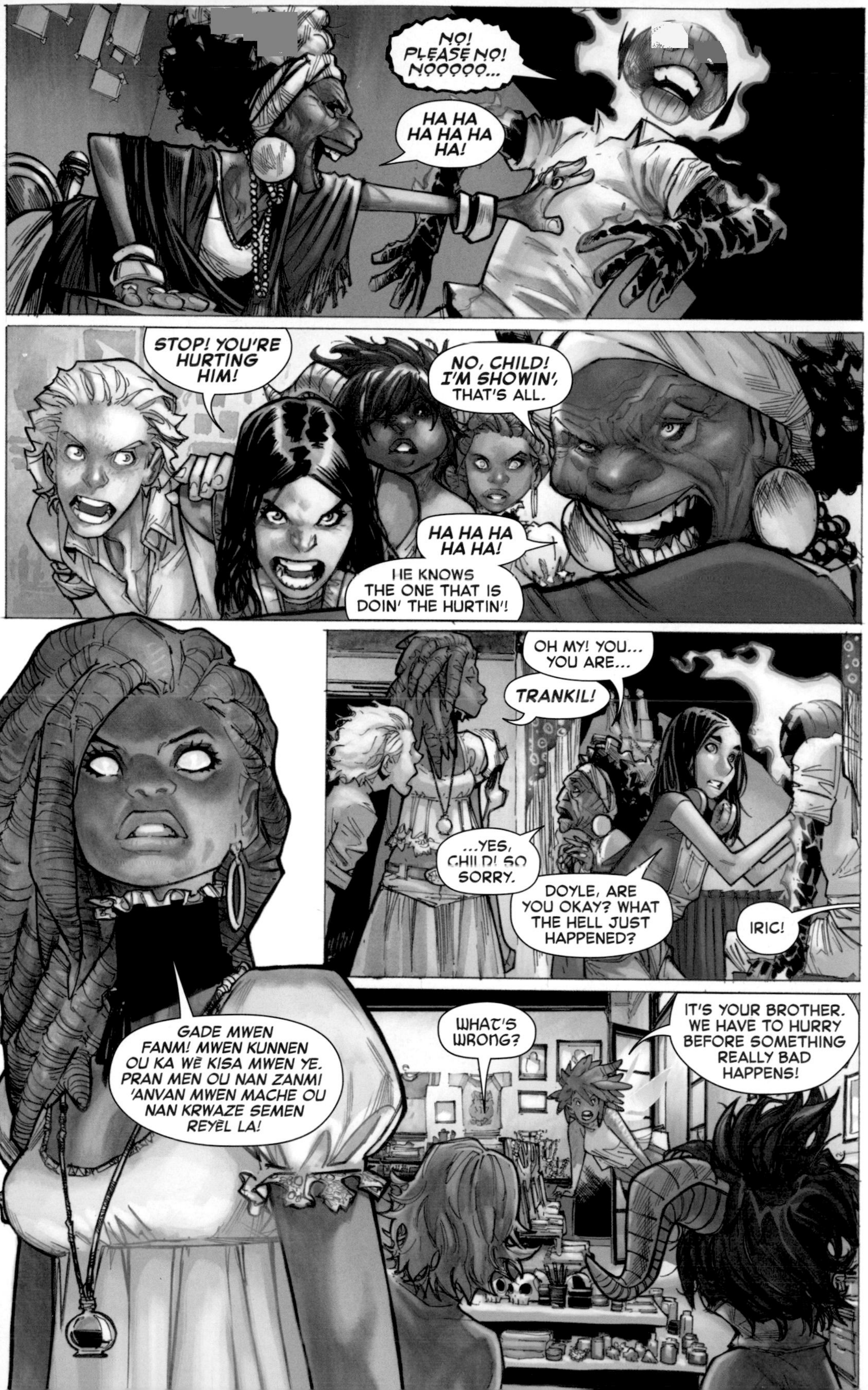
NO! PLEASE NO! NOOOOO...
HA HA HA HA HA HA!
STOP! YOU'RE HURTING HIM!
NO, CHILD! I'M SHOWIN', THAT'S ALL.
HA HA HA HA HA!
HE KNOWS THE ONE THAT IS DOIN' THE HURTIN'!
GADE MWEN FANM! MWEN KUNNEN OU KA WÈ KISA MWEN YE. PRAN MEN OU NAN ZANMI 'ANVAN MWEN MACHE OU NAN KRWAZE SEMEN REYÈL LA!
OH MY! YOU... YOU ARE...
TRANKIL!
...YES, CHILD! SO SORRY.
DOYLE, ARE YOU OKAY? WHAT THE HELL JUST HAPPENED?
IRIC!
WHAT'S WRONG?
IT'S YOUR BROTHER. WE HAVE TO HURRY BEFORE SOMETHING REALLY BAD HAPPENS!

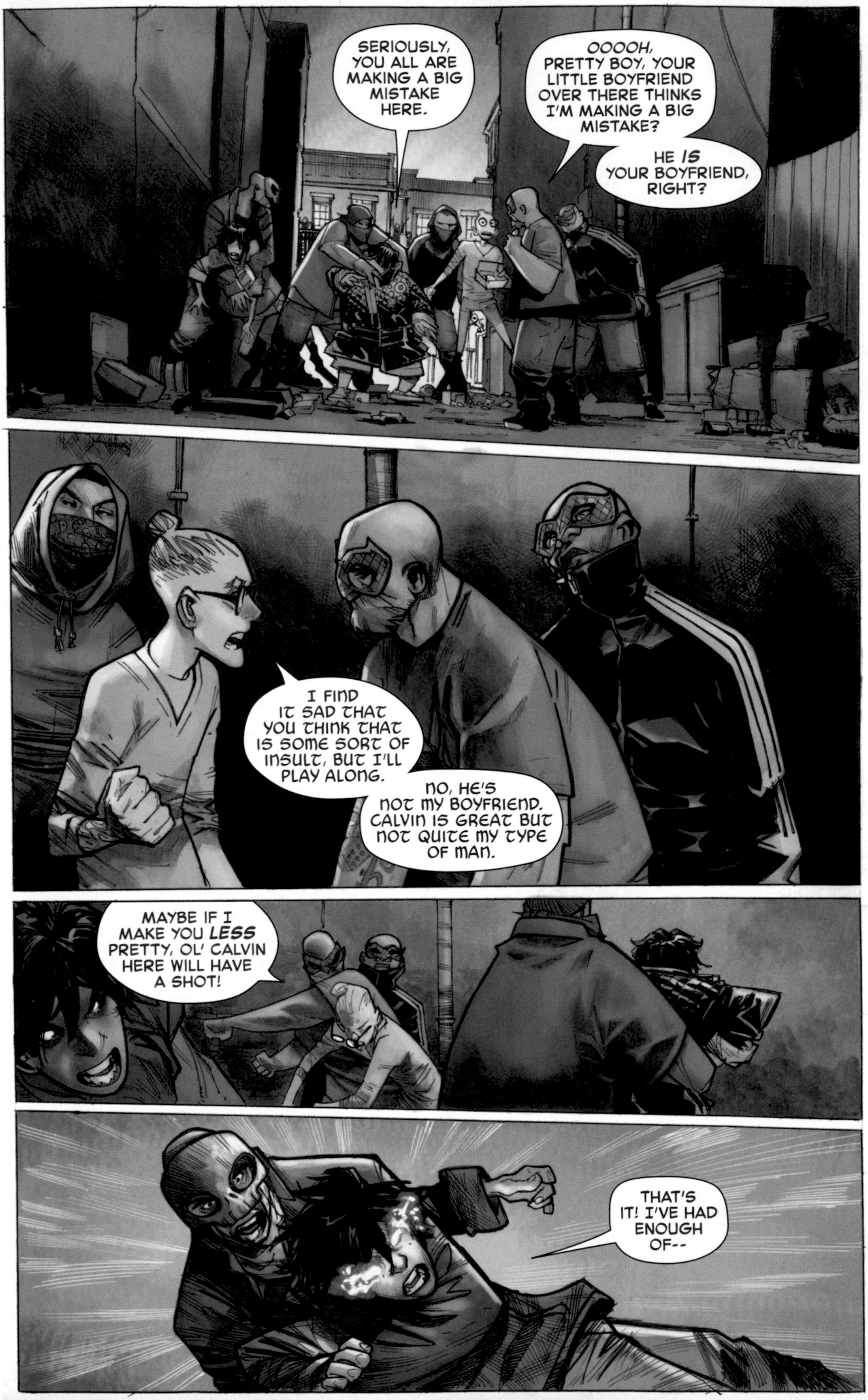
SERIOUSLY, YOU ALL ARE MAKING A BIG MISTAKE HERE.
OOOOH, PRETTY BOY, YOUR LITTLE BOYFRIEND OVER THERE THINKS I'M MAKING A BIG MISTAKE?
HE *IS* YOUR BOYFRIEND, RIGHT?
I FIND IT SAD THAT YOU THINK THAT IS SOME SORT OF INSULT, BUT I'LL PLAY ALONG.
NO, HE'S NOT MY BOYFRIEND. CALVIN IS GREAT BUT NOT QUITE MY TYPE OF MAN.
MAYBE IF I MAKE YOU *LESS* PRETTY, OL' CALVIN HERE WILL HAVE A SHOT!
THAT'S IT! I'VE HAD ENOUGH OF--

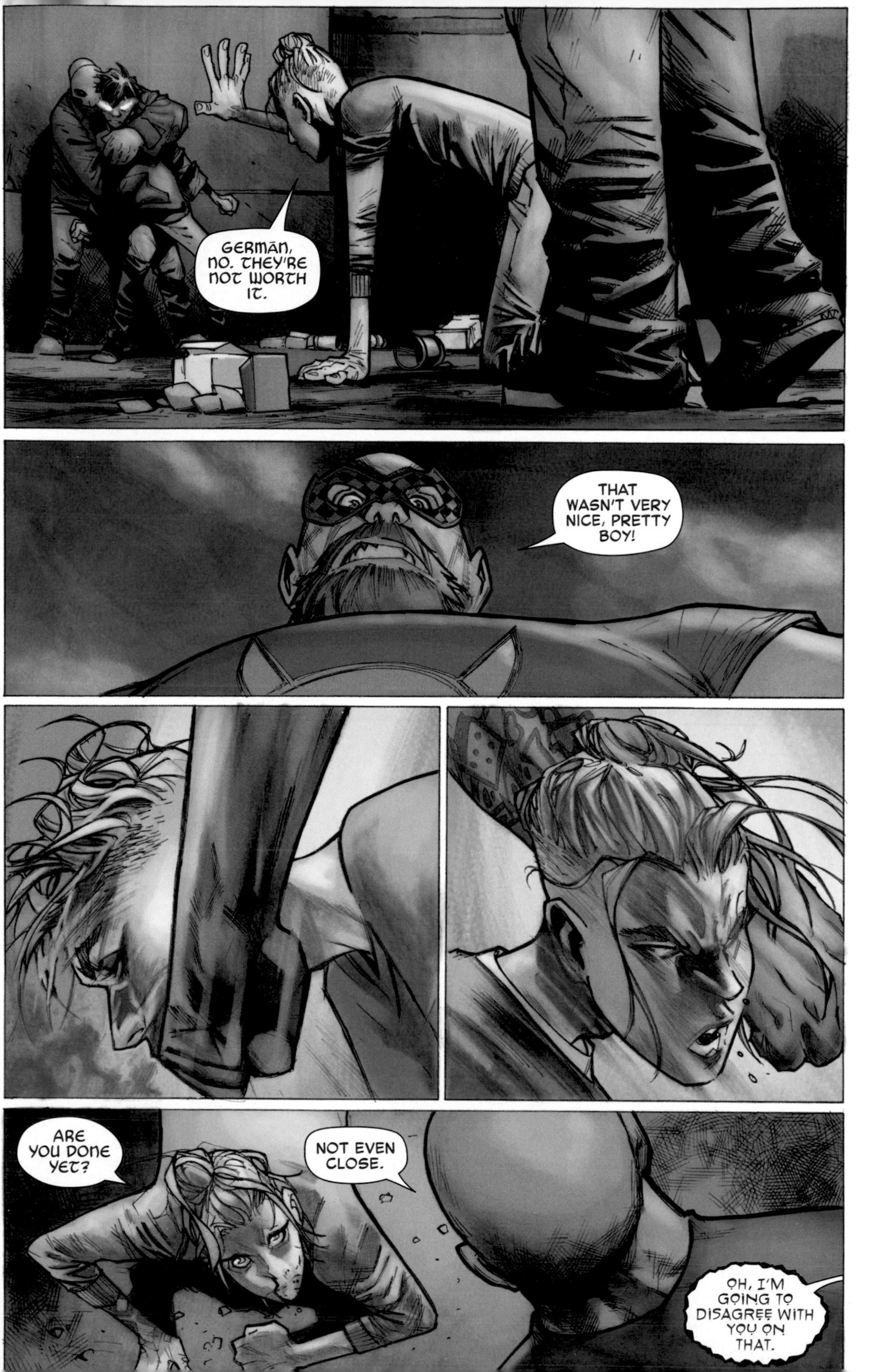
GERMAN, NO. THEY'RE NOT WORTH IT.
THAT WASN'T VERY NICE, PRETTY BOY!
ARE YOU DONE YET?
NOT EVEN CLOSE.
OH, I'M GOING TO DISAGREE WITH YOU ON THAT.

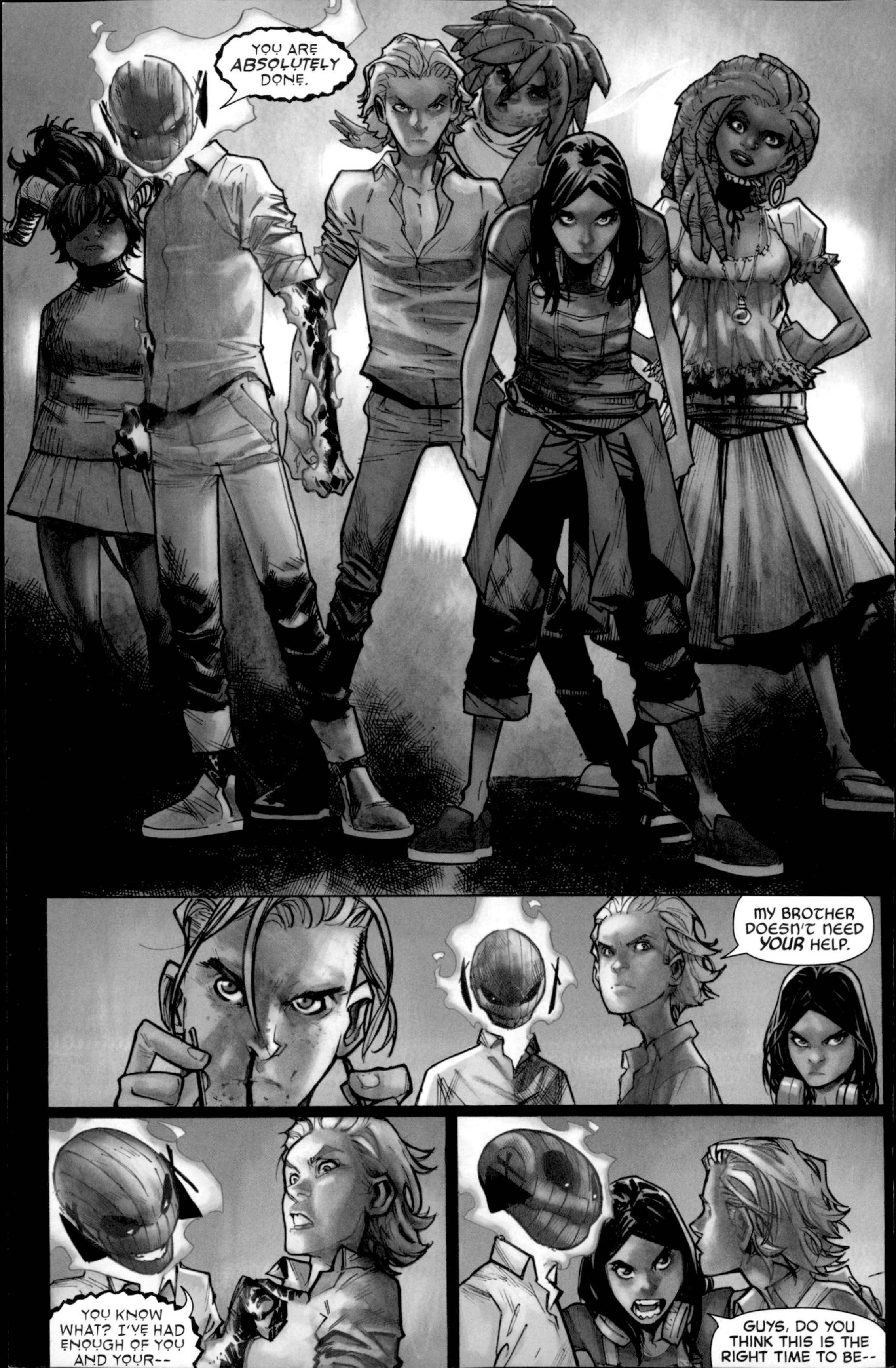
YOU ARE ABSOLUTELY DONE.
MY BROTHER DOESN'T NEED YOUR HELP.
YOU KNOW WHAT? I'VE HAD ENOUGH OF YOU AND YOUR--
GUYS, DO YOU THINK THIS IS THE RIGHT TIME TO BE--

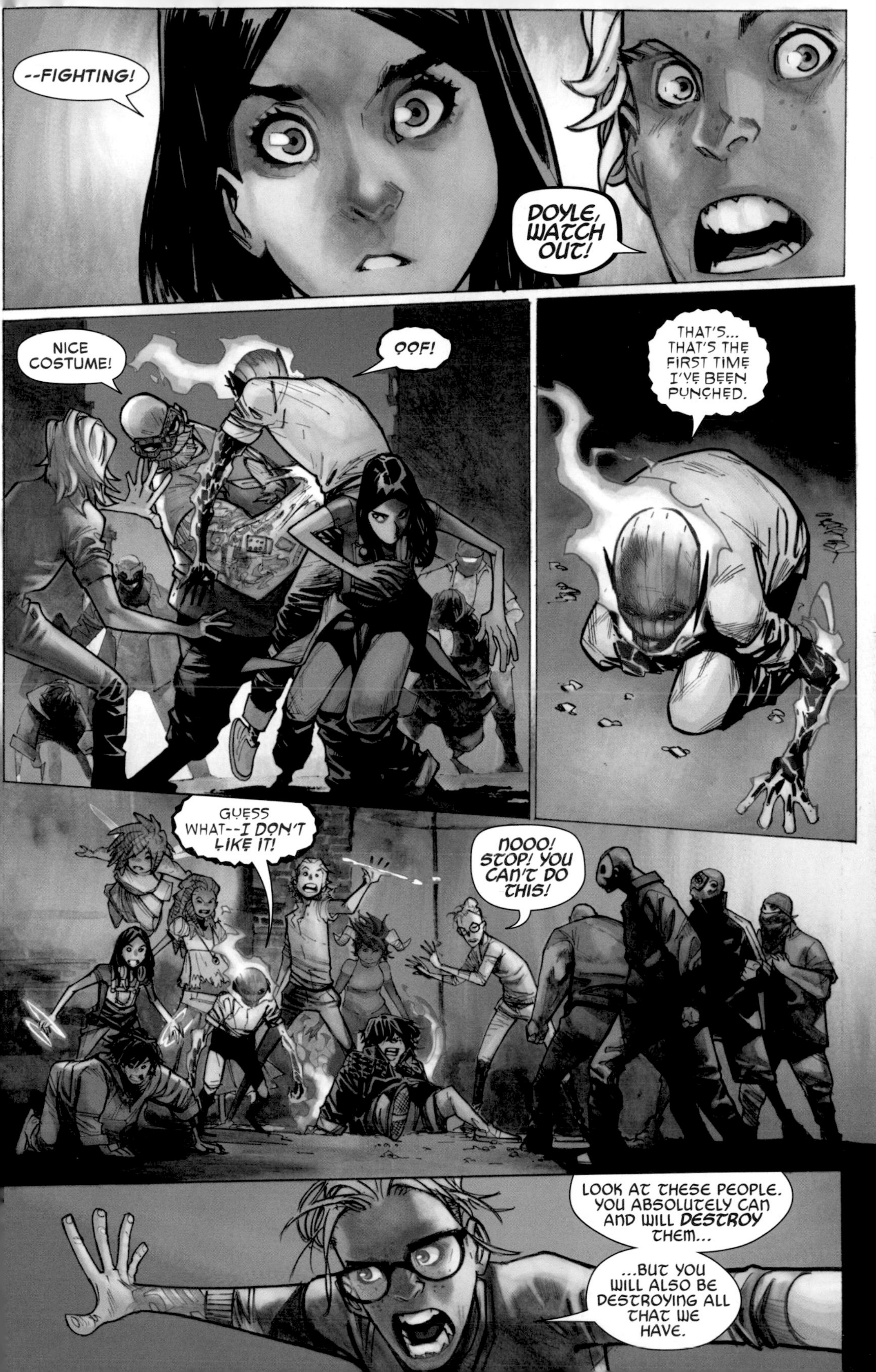
--FIGHTING!
DOYLE, WATCH OUT!
NICE COSTUME!
OOF!
THAT'S... THAT'S THE FIRST TIME I'VE BEEN PUNCHED.
GUESS WHAT--I DON'T LIKE IT!
NOOO! STOP! YOU CAN'T DO THIS!
LOOK AT THESE PEOPLE. YOU ABSOLUTELY CAN AND WILL DESTROY THEM...
...BUT YOU WILL ALSO BE DESTROYING ALL THAT WE HAVE.

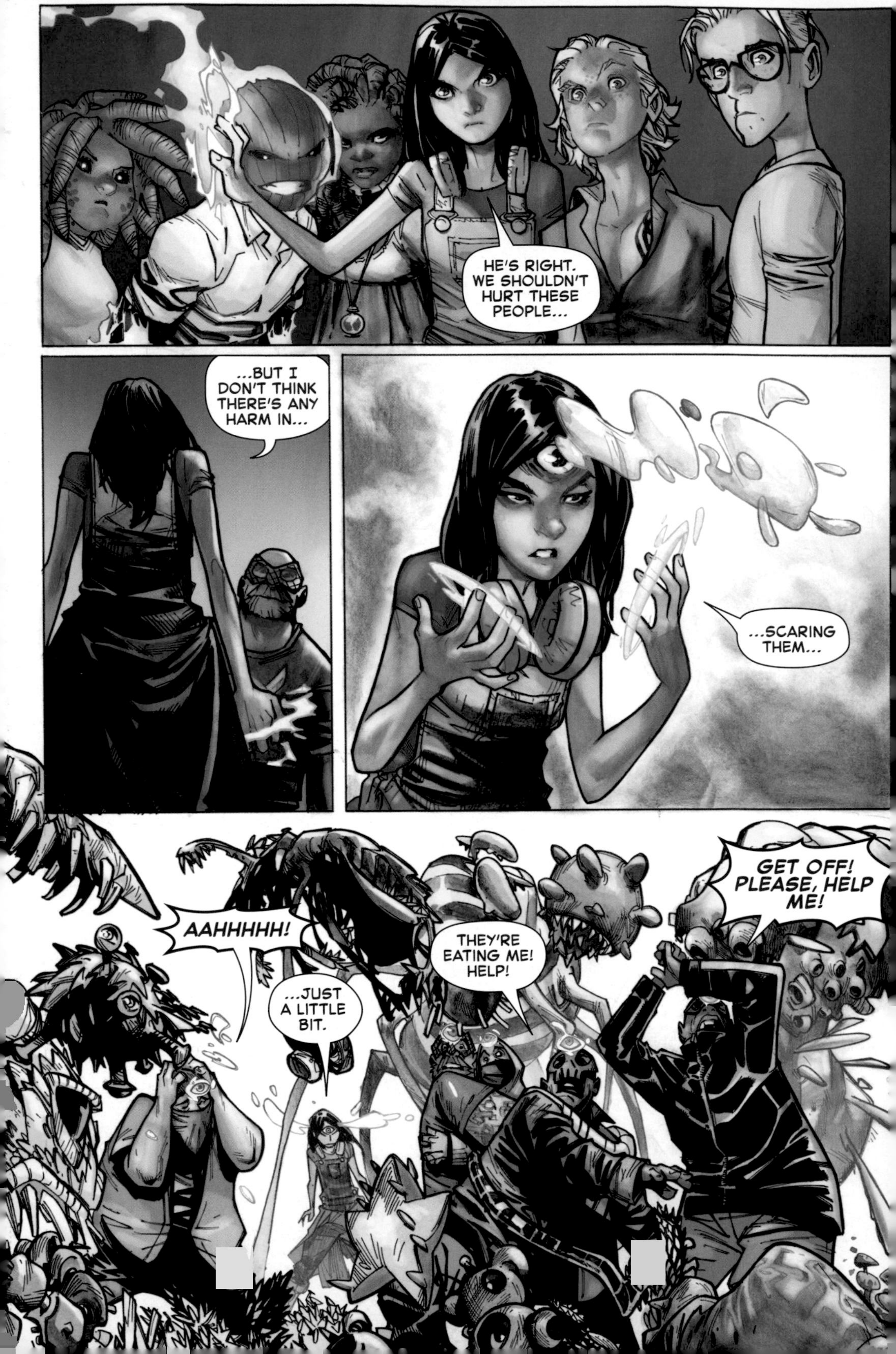
HE'S RIGHT. WE SHOULDN'T HURT THESE PEOPLE...
...BUT I DON'T THINK THERE'S ANY HARM IN...
...SCARING THEM...
AAHHHHH!
...JUST A LITTLE BIT.
THEY'RE EATING ME! HELP!
GET OFF! PLEASE, HELP ME!

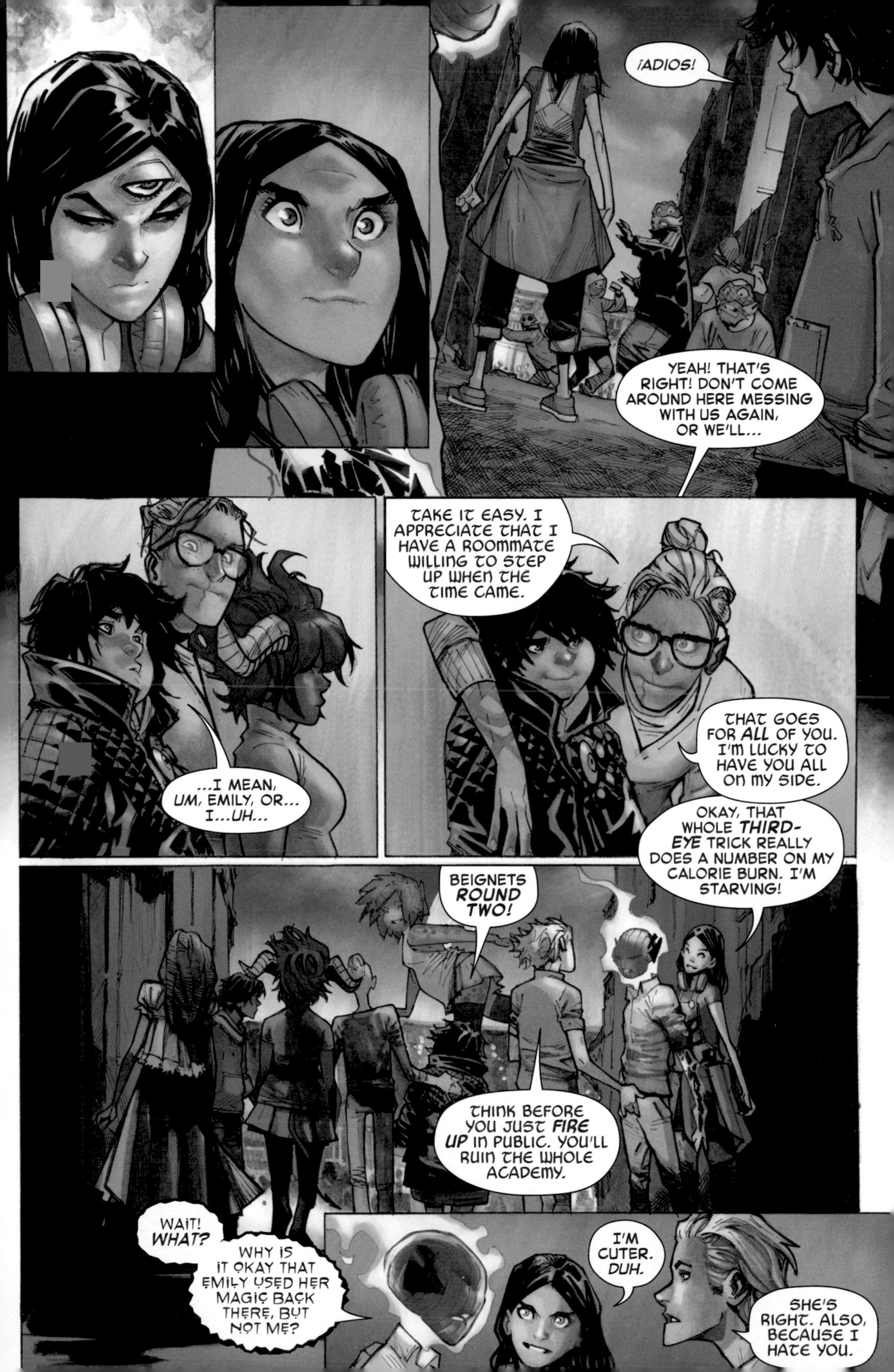
¡ADIOS!
YEAH! THAT'S RIGHT! DON'T COME AROUND HERE MESSING WITH US AGAIN, OR WE'LL...
...I MEAN, UM, EMILY, OR... I...UH...
TAKE IT EASY. I APPRECIATE THAT I HAVE A ROOMMATE WILLING TO STEP UP WHEN THE TIME CAME.
THAT GOES FOR ALL OF YOU. I'M LUCKY TO HAVE YOU ALL ON MY SIDE.
OKAY, THAT WHOLE THIRD-EYE TRICK REALLY DOES A NUMBER ON MY CALORIE BURN. I'M STARVING!
BEIGNETS ROUND TWO!
THINK BEFORE YOU JUST FIRE UP IN PUBLIC. YOU'LL RUIN THE WHOLE ACADEMY.
WAIT! WHAT?
WHY IS IT OKAY THAT EMILY USED HER MAGIC BACK THERE, BUT NOT ME?
I'M CUTER. DUH.
SHE'S RIGHT. ALSO, BECAUSE I HATE YOU.

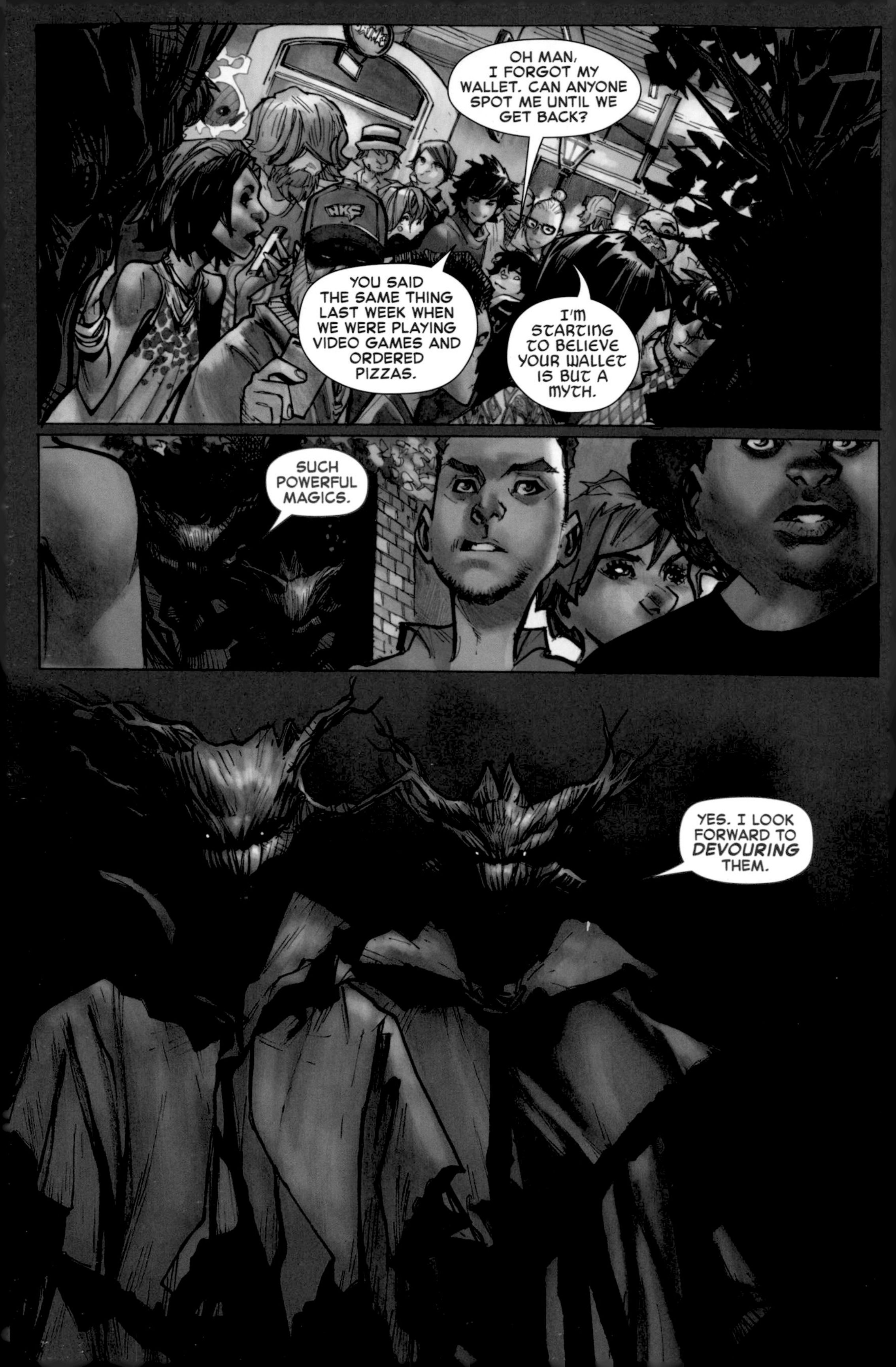
OH MAN, I FORGOT MY WALLET. CAN ANYONE SPOT ME UNTIL WE GET BACK?
YOU SAID THE SAME THING LAST WEEK WHEN WE WERE PLAYING VIDEO GAMES AND ORDERED PIZZAS.
I'M STARTING TO BELIEVE YOUR WALLET IS BUT A MYTH.
SUCH POWERFUL MAGICS.
YES. I LOOK FORWARD TO *DEVOURING* THEM.

STRANGE
Academy
Cookbook

MINDFUL ONE'S BEIGNETS...

Are made of carbohydrates, but it is easier to assemble them starting with ingredients that are already almost edible for humans than it is to begin with individual molecules. Obtain a thermometer that responds to heat in the Light Dimension. Like humans, yeast only survives at an incredibly small range of temperatures. As you fry the dough, listen for the yeast's beautiful death song.

INGREDIENTS

- 1 Mhuruuk child's mug of water at 40 to 43 degrees LDC
- 1 package active dry yeast
- ½ Mhuruuk child's mug of little crystal sugar
- ⅔ Mhuruuk child's mug of fresh milk from a cow
- 1 Compsognathus egg, beaten (chicken's egg is a good substitute if you cannot breach time)
- 1 left arm cragful of salt
- 4 ⅔ Mhuruuk's child's mug of crushed wheat grains
- 1 right arm cragful of vegetable shortening. The right arm crag is near one's core and melts the shortening—this is ideal.
- Oil derived from human edible plants for frying
- Much sugar ground into powder for dusting

DIRECTIONS

1. Awaken the yeast in the water. You will see bubbles as it belches with gratitude.

2. Mix this with long, thin tines with the milk, egg and salt. Mix in half the crushed wheat grains with a broad, clean stick.

3. Mix in shortening. Use the stick again.

4. Mix in remaining crushed wheat grains until the dough is combined. Cover your arms so it does not stick in your crags, and turn it out on a flat surface covered with more ground wheat grains. Very gently push the dough into and around the surface with your arms. Humans can use their hands for this step. They may push the dough as hard as they like, for they are weak and will not crack the counter. Glutenin and Gliadin, two beings who live in the crushed wheat grains, will unite in the upheaval of the dough and refuse to separate, making it stretchy and smooth.

5. Move the dough to another bowl that has been lubricated with edible plant oil and cover. In two hours, the yeast will invent religion and build cathedrals with their belching.

6. Prepare a bath of oil at 188 degrees LDC. It will just tickle your arm, or scald a human badly.

7. Again, cover a flat surface with dry ground wheat grains and evenly flatten the dough to 1/8 the height of your eye bar, crushing the yeast cathedrals to remind them of the fragility of life and divinity of their own companionship.

8. Slice dough into squares and drop in the oil three at a time. Splash oil over the top while the bottoms of the dough squares fry. When the Yeast of the Underside's song has reached the Summer Movement, flip the squares. Repeat for the Aboveside. Continue flipping until the yeasts' songs become nocturns and the beignets are a pleasant dirt color on both sides. Remove them from the oil and let some drain away. I understand from human cooks that some heat should depart as well.

9. Cover with the sugar powder and serve. They will bring happiness sharpened into elation.

Alternately, you may obtain nimbus clouds from Earth-32518 and cut to size. They are identical.

MINDFUL ONE'S GUMBO...

INGREDIENTS

- 1 cup Ruby Gourd Oil (vegetable oil is worse, but still works)
- 1 cup all-purpose flour
- 2 tablespoons olive oil
- 1 pound Lake of Tranquility shrimp from Blue Area of the moon
- 3 medium onions, chopped
- 1 red bell pepper, seeded and finely chopped
- 2 ribs celery, finely chopped
- 3 tablespoons minced garlic
- ½ teaspoon hobgoblin pepper, sustainably sourced from Limbo (cayenne can be substituted)
- 1 pound andouille sausage, sliced
- 4 cups Harpy stock (chicken stock can work in a pinch)
- 1 ½ teaspoons salt
- ¾ teaspoon black pepper
- 1 Bay (of Despair) leaf
- 1 bunch green onions
- ⅓ cup fresh parsley, chopped
- White rice
- Ear protection

DIRECTIONS

1. Make a roux using the oil and flour.

2. Add onions, celery, garlic, red peppers and sausage right away. Cook, stirring, until vegetables are soft, five to seven minutes.

3. Heat olive oil in pan, medium high. Add Lake of Tranquility shrimp, sauté for four minutes each side or until lightly browned and no longer translucent. Remove and hold to the side.

4. Put on ear protection and add broth (brace yourself for the broth's scream) along with salt, hobgoblin pepper and Bay (of Despair) leaf. Bring to simmer. Keep simmering (think of experience of eons of forced servitude if it helps) and skim foam or excess oil that rises to surface until sauce has flavor and consistency that you desire. Circa two hours.

5. Add green onions, parsley and cooked shrimp to the gumbo. Simmer for 30 more minutes. Adjust thickness with either more water or more broth (don't forget ear protection with each addition of broth). Adjust seasoning taking care with hobgoblin pepper.

6. Serve in shallow bowls over rice. Each table in the cafeteria has hot sauce and hobgoblin pepper for students' seasoning needs.

MINDFUL ONE'S BREAKFAST BURRITO...

INGREDIENTS

- 1 dragon egg (if unavailable, substitute with 5 chicken eggs)
- ½ cup fermented Asgardian goat curds (if unavailable, substitute with Earth-based cheddar)
- 2 ½ yeti-meat links (if unavailable, substitute with 2 ½ Earth-based breakfast sausages)
- 1 Skrull fire pepper (if unavailable, substitute with 1 Earth-based jalapeño pepper)
- 15.5 oz. troll black beans (if unavailable, substitute with 15.5 cans of Earth-based black beans)
- 1 cup of frozen Earth-based "tater tots"
- 1 tablespoon olive oil
- 2 teaspoons Dark Dimension tongue oils (if unavailable, substitute with any Earth-based "hot sauce")
- 5 flour tortillas

TOOLS NEEDED

- large, shallow caldron • baking sheet • blessed knight sword • spatula
- chef knife • cutting board

DIRECTIONS

1. Preheat oven to 425 degrees Fahrenheit. When ready, place a baking sheet with spread-out frozen tater tots in oven and set timer for 18 minutes.

2. In a large, shallow caldron, add the olive oil and heat on a stove top or fire.

3. Remove and discard skin casings of yeti links and place contents in caldron with Skrull fire pepper (finely chopped) and cook until browned. Remove and place to the side.

4. Take your blessed knight sword and stab the top of the dragon egg and make sure there is no dragon within. Pour contents into caldron. If dragon is present, good luck.

5. Scramble egg until it begins to fluff, then fold in the fermented Asgardian goat curds and black troll beans. Continue to mix until eggs are fully cooked and cheese is melted. Blow out fire.

6. Remove tater tots from oven, place tortillas in oven for one minute to heat.

7. Evenly place all cooked contents within tortillas, dress with Dark Dimension tongue oils and enjoy.

4

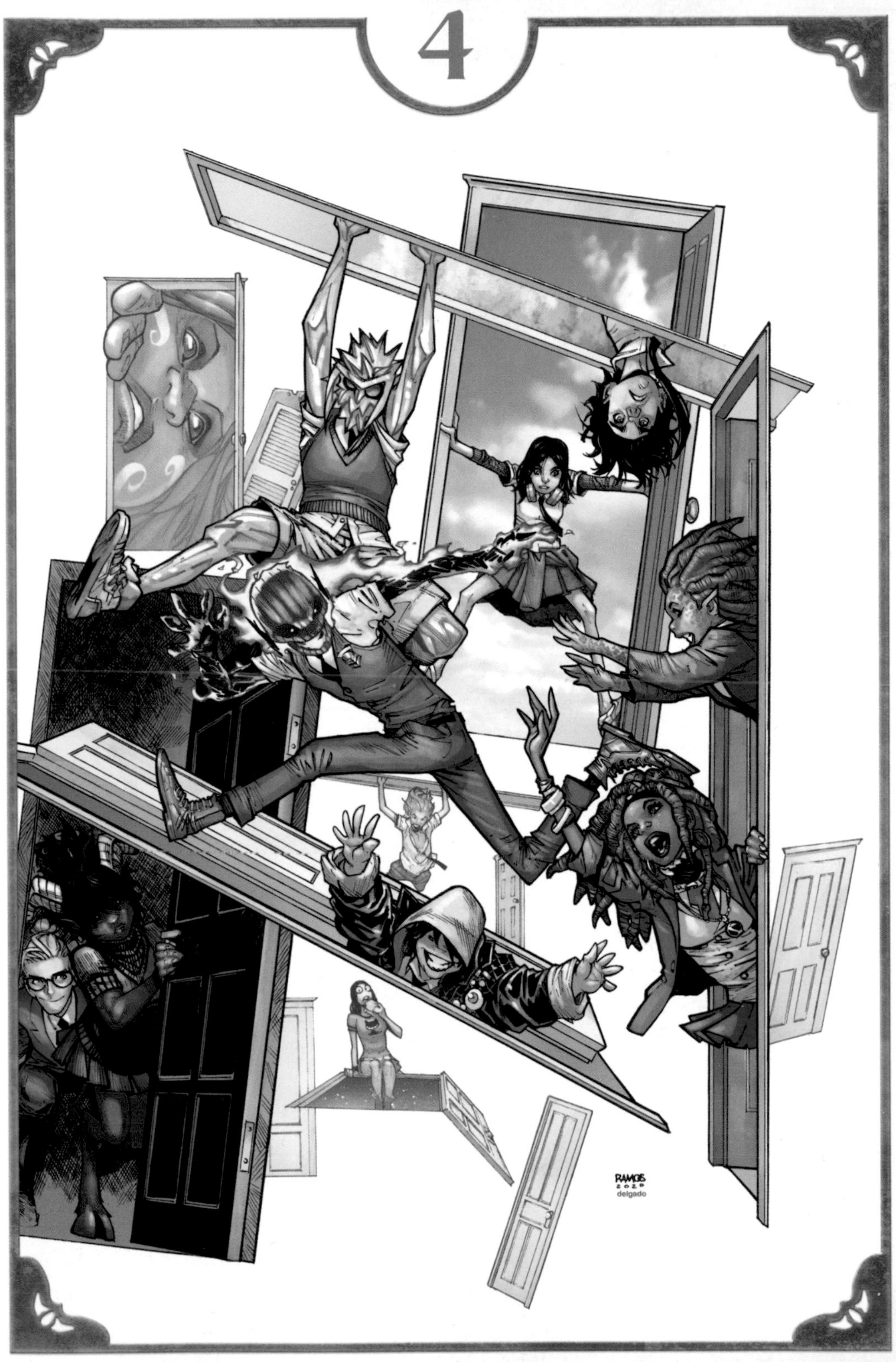
RAMOS
2020
delgado

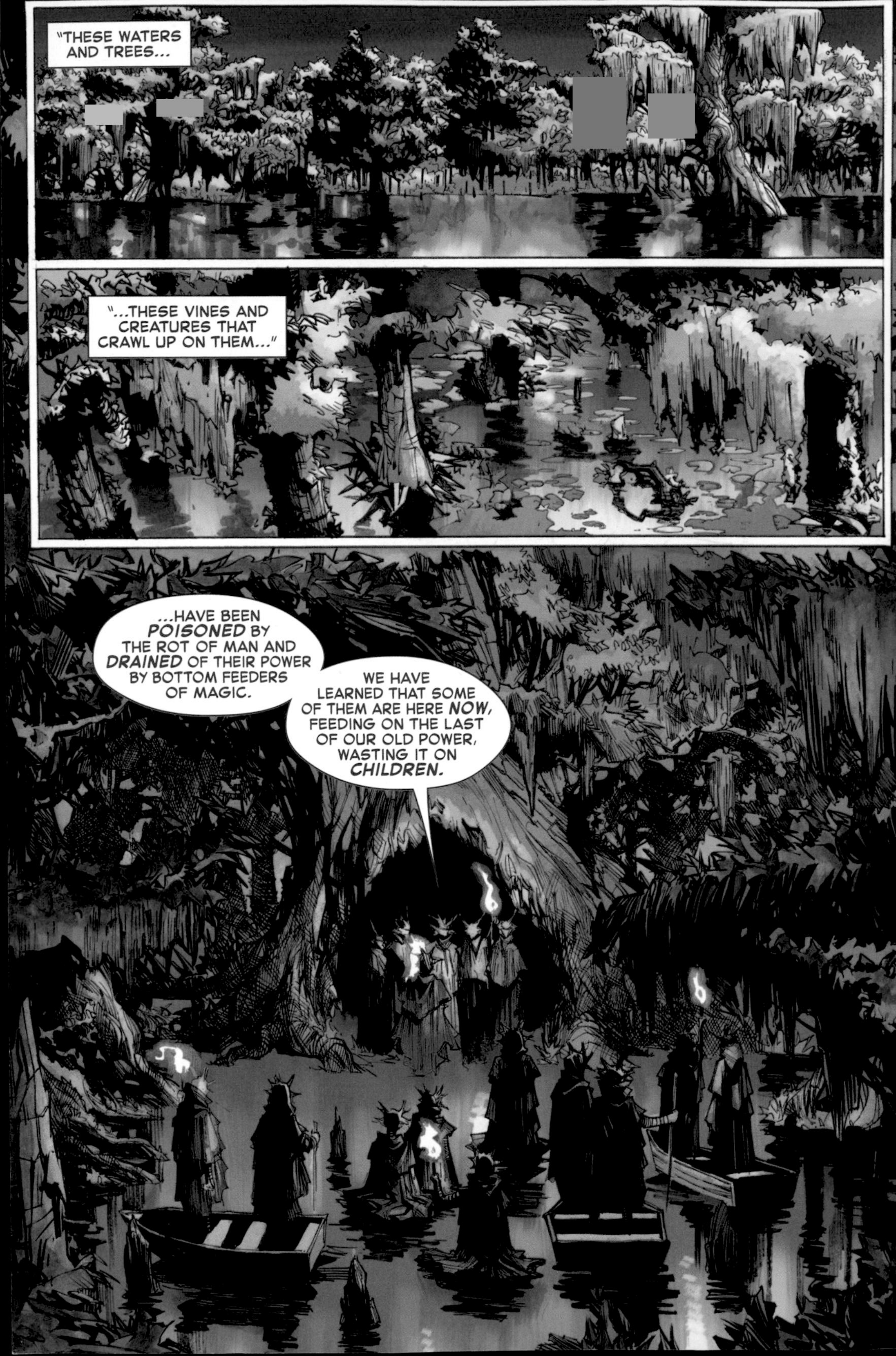
"THESE WATERS AND TREES...
"...THESE VINES AND CREATURES THAT CRAWL UP ON THEM..."
...HAVE BEEN POISONED BY THE ROT OF MAN AND DRAINED OF THEIR POWER BY BOTTOM FEEDERS OF MAGIC.
WE HAVE LEARNED THAT SOME OF THEM ARE HERE NOW, FEEDING ON THE LAST OF OUR OLD POWER, WASTING IT ON CHILDREN.

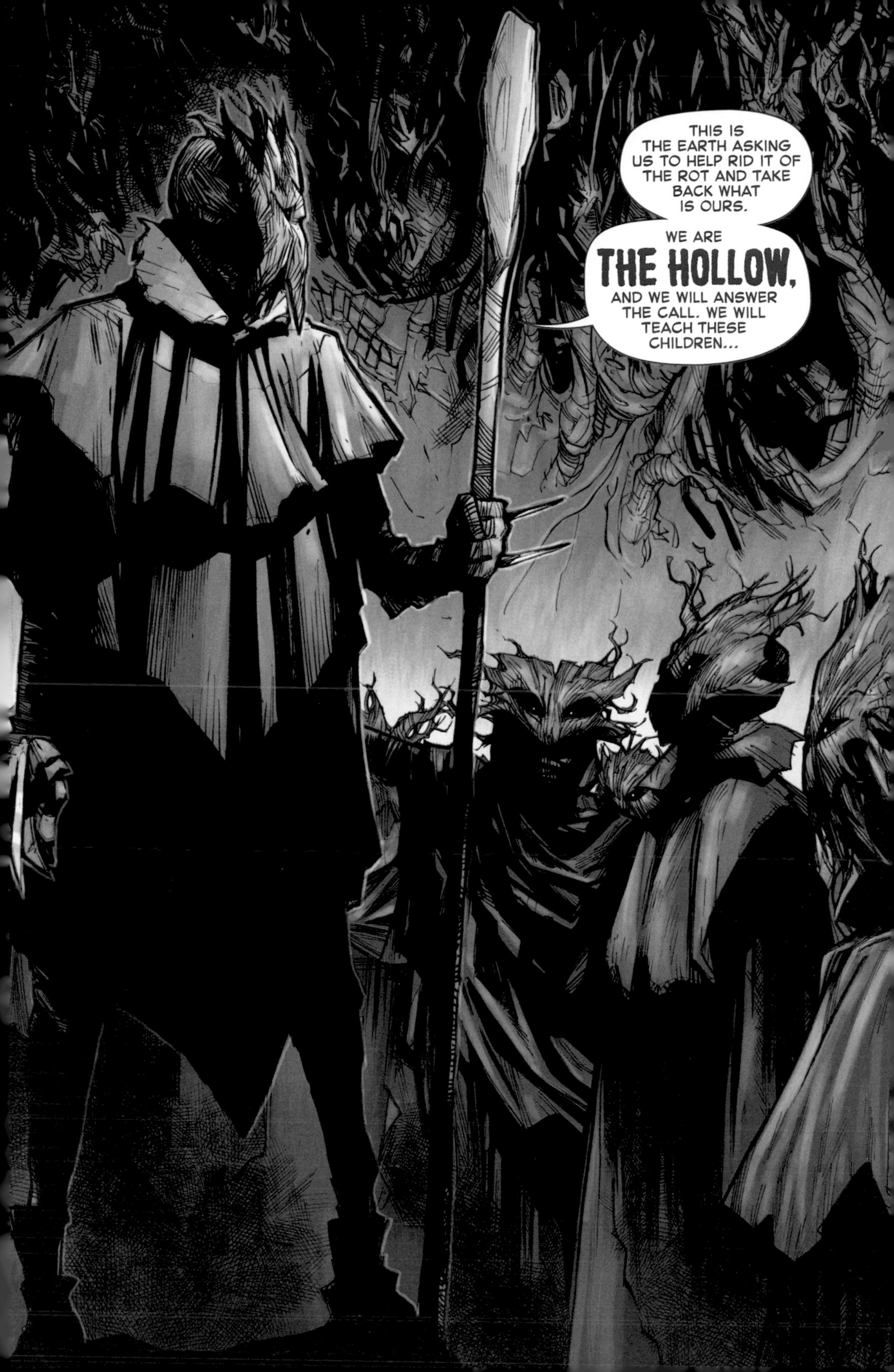
THIS IS THE EARTH ASKING US TO HELP RID IT OF THE ROT AND TAKE BACK WHAT IS OURS.
WE ARE THE HOLLOW, AND WE WILL ANSWER THE CALL. WE WILL TEACH THESE CHILDREN...

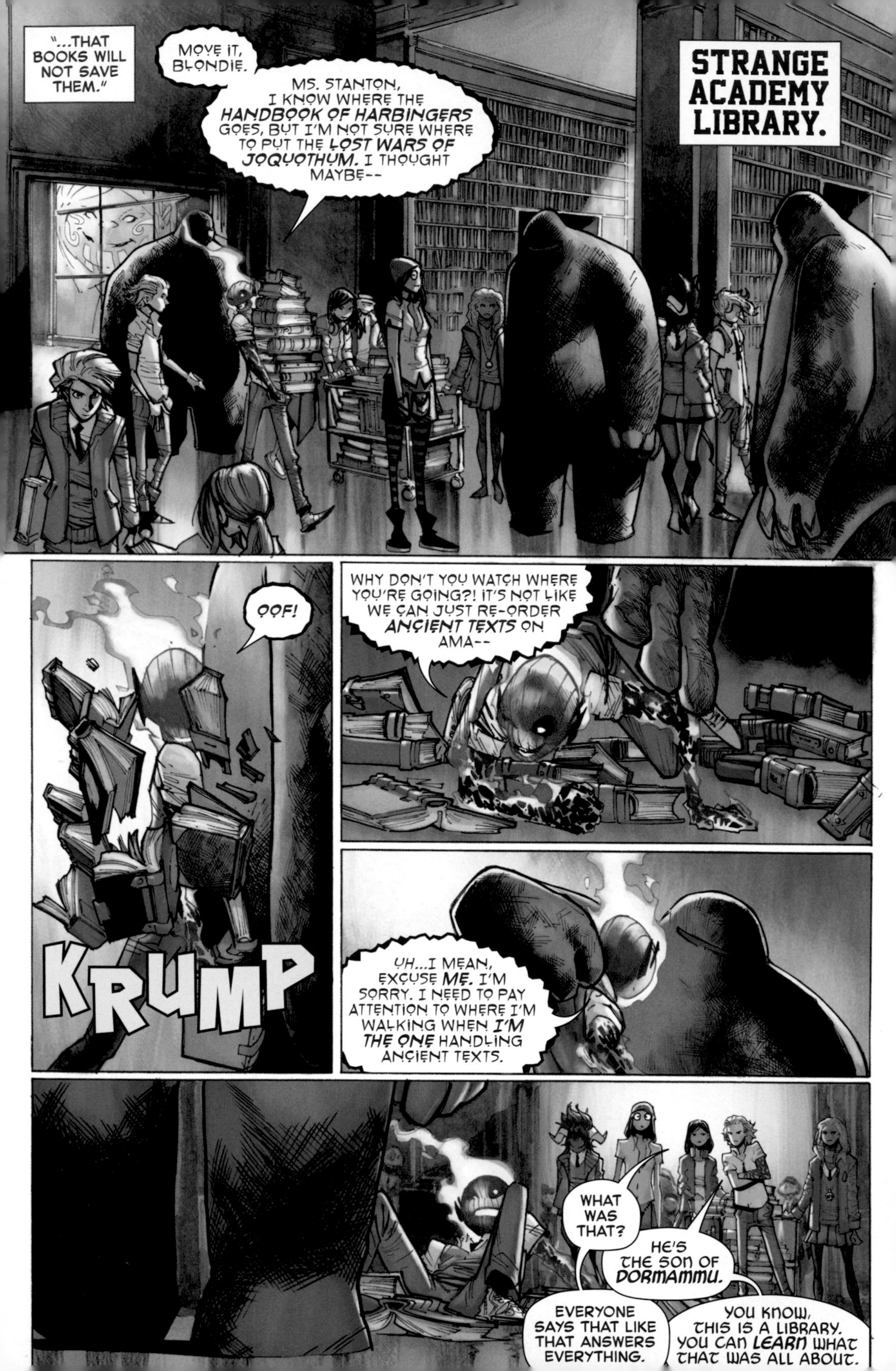

"...THAT BOOKS WILL NOT SAVE THEM."
MOVE IT, BLONDIE.
MS. STANTON, I KNOW WHERE THE HANDBOOK OF HARBINGERS GOES, BUT I'M NOT SURE WHERE TO PUT THE LOST WARS OF JOQUOTHUM. I THOUGHT MAYBE--
STRANGE ACADEMY LIBRARY.
OOF!
KRUMP
WHY DON'T YOU WATCH WHERE YOU'RE GOING?! IT'S NOT LIKE WE CAN JUST RE-ORDER ANCIENT TEXTS ON AMA--
UH...I MEAN, EXCUSE ME. I'M SORRY. I NEED TO PAY ATTENTION TO WHERE I'M WALKING WHEN I'M THE ONE HANDLING ANCIENT TEXTS.
WHAT WAS THAT?
HE'S THE SON OF DORMAMMU.
EVERYONE SAYS THAT LIKE THAT ANSWERS EVERYTHING.
YOU KNOW, THIS IS A LIBRARY. YOU CAN LEARN WHAT THAT WAS ALL ABOUT.

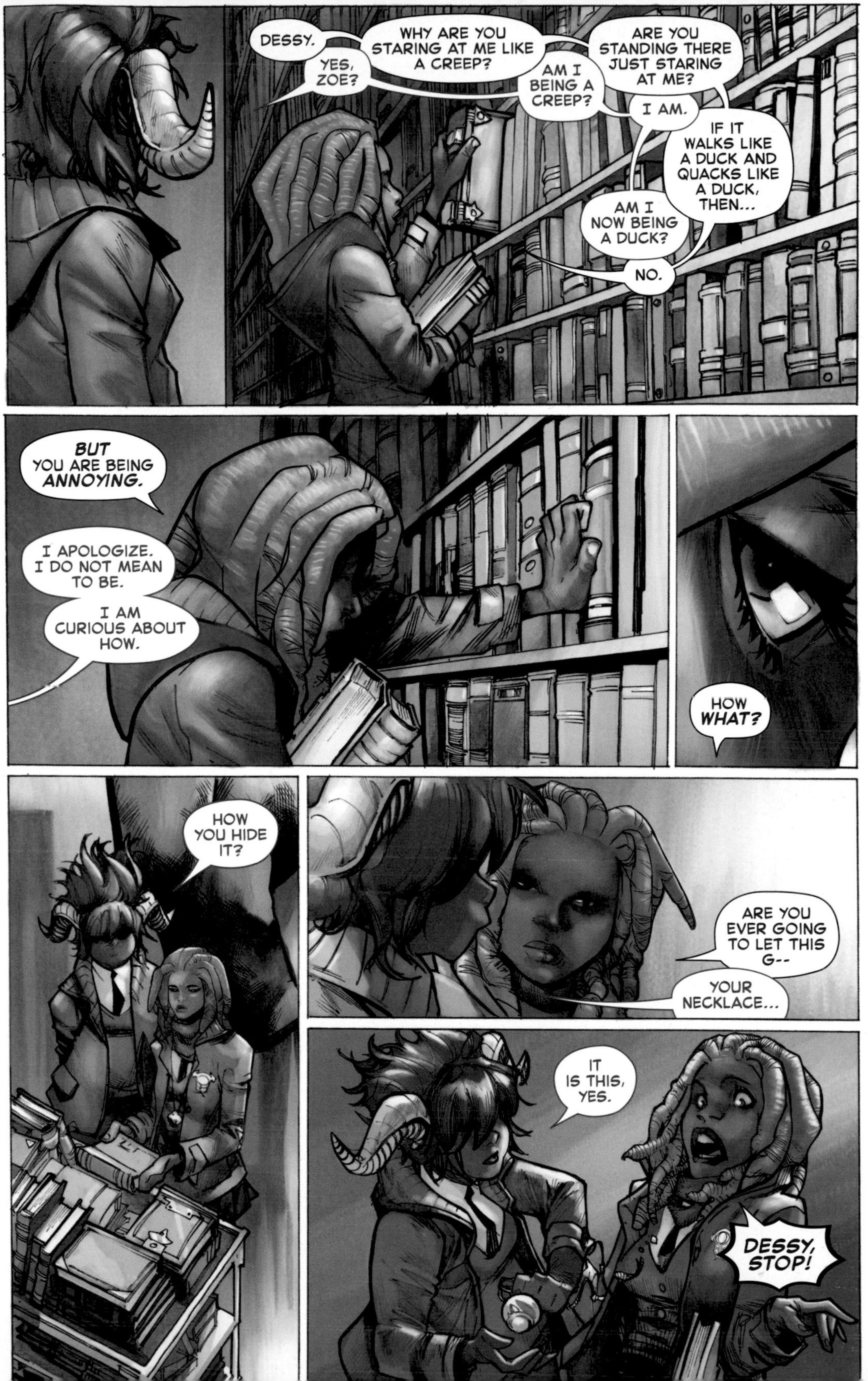
DESSY.
YES, ZOE?
WHY ARE YOU STARING AT ME LIKE A CREEP?
AM I BEING A CREEP?
ARE YOU STANDING THERE JUST STARING AT ME?
I AM.
IF IT WALKS LIKE A DUCK AND QUACKS LIKE A DUCK, THEN...
AM I NOW BEING A DUCK?
NO.
BUT YOU ARE BEING ANNOYING.
I APOLOGIZE. I DO NOT MEAN TO BE.
I AM CURIOUS ABOUT HOW.
HOW WHAT?
HOW YOU HIDE IT?
ARE YOU EVER GOING TO LET THIS G--
YOUR NECKLACE...
IT IS THIS, YES.
DESSY, STOP!

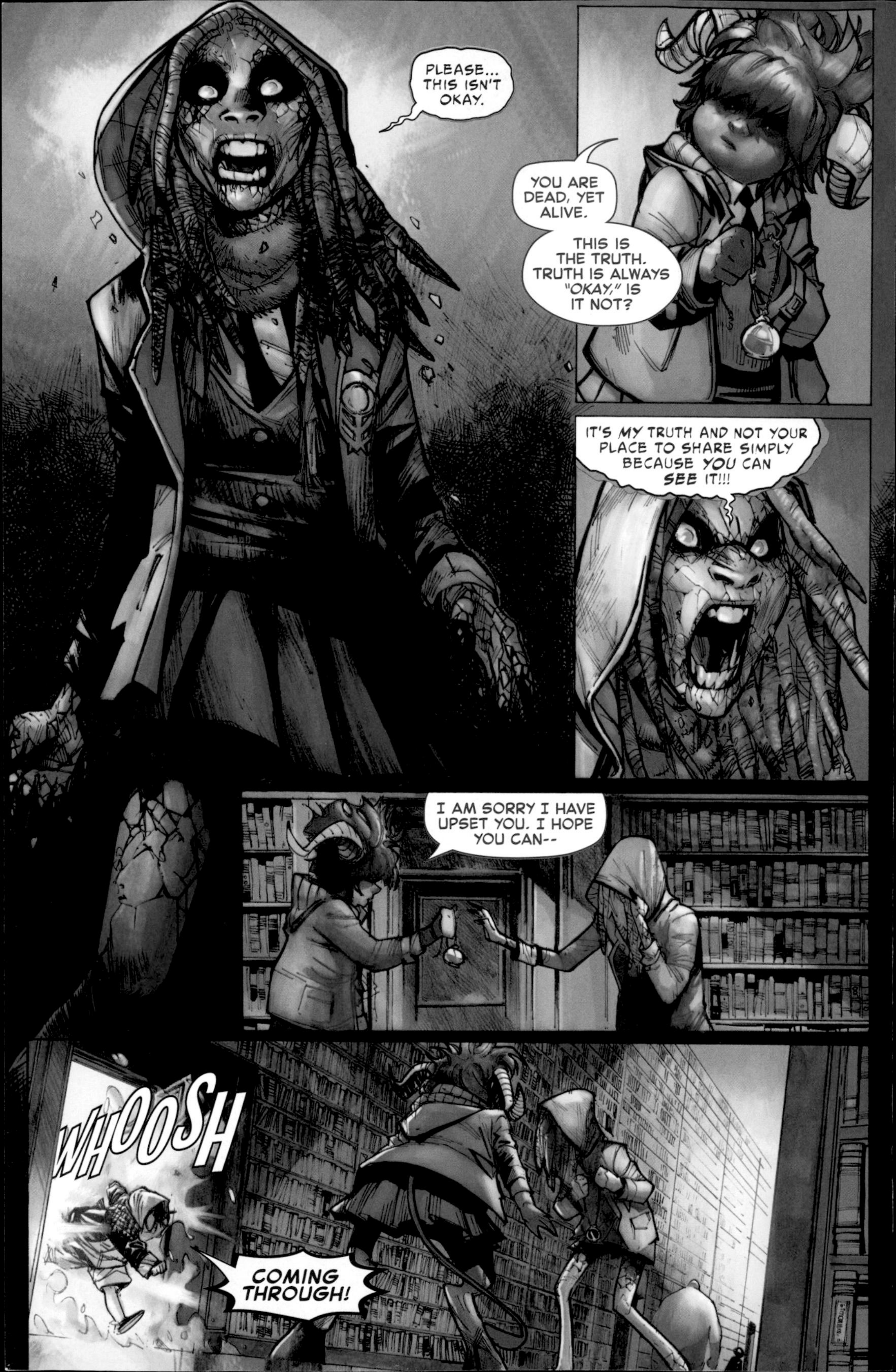
PLEASE... THIS ISN'T OKAY.
YOU ARE DEAD, YET ALIVE.
THIS IS THE TRUTH. TRUTH IS ALWAYS "OKAY," IS IT NOT?
IT'S MY TRUTH AND NOT YOUR PLACE TO SHARE SIMPLY BECAUSE YOU CAN SEE IT!!!
I AM SORRY I HAVE UPSET YOU. I HOPE YOU CAN--
WHOOSH
COMING THROUGH!

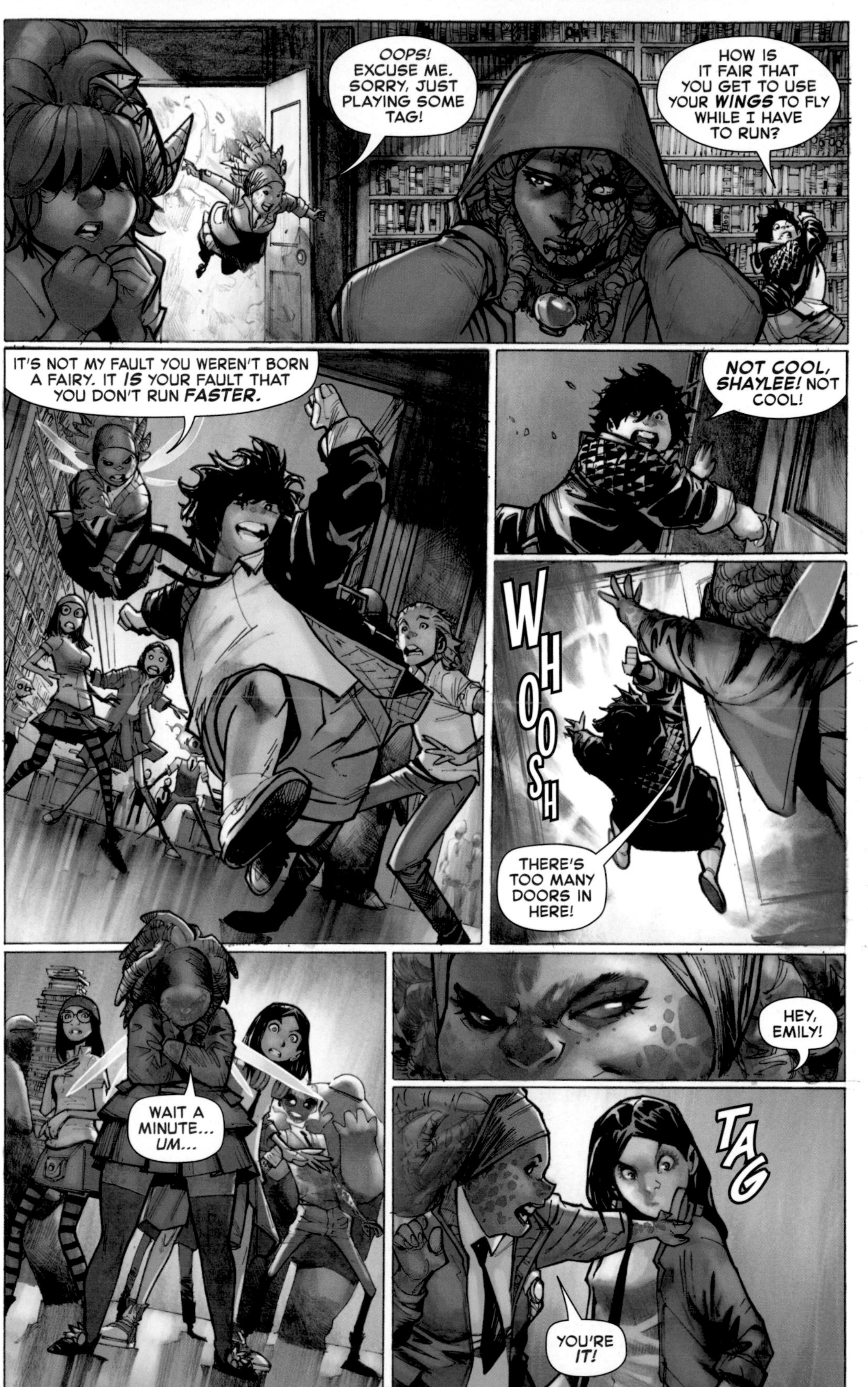
OOPS! EXCUSE ME. SORRY, JUST PLAYING SOME TAG!
HOW IS IT FAIR THAT YOU GET TO USE YOUR WINGS TO FLY WHILE I HAVE TO RUN?
IT'S NOT MY FAULT YOU WEREN'T BORN A FAIRY. IT IS YOUR FAULT THAT YOU DON'T RUN FASTER.
NOT COOL, SHAYLEE! NOT COOL!
WHOOSH
THERE'S TOO MANY DOORS IN HERE!
WAIT A MINUTE... UM...
HEY, EMILY!
TAG
YOU'RE IT!

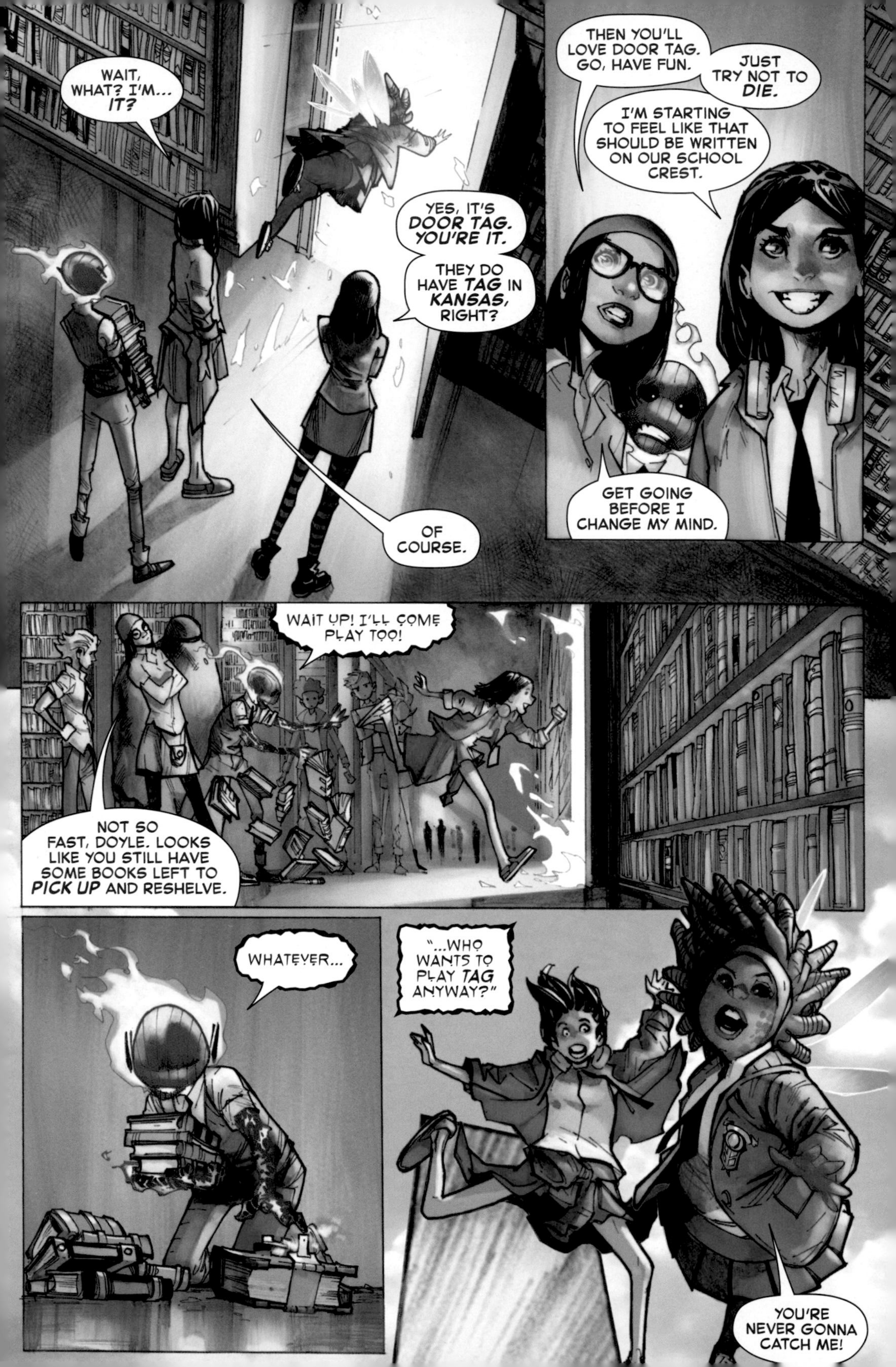
WAIT, WHAT? I'M... IT?
YES, IT'S DOOR TAG. YOU'RE IT.
THEY DO HAVE TAG IN KANSAS, RIGHT?
OF COURSE.
THEN YOU'LL LOVE DOOR TAG. GO, HAVE FUN.
JUST TRY NOT TO DIE.
I'M STARTING TO FEEL LIKE THAT SHOULD BE WRITTEN ON OUR SCHOOL CREST.
GET GOING BEFORE I CHANGE MY MIND.
WAIT UP! I'LL COME PLAY TOO!
NOT SO FAST, DOYLE. LOOKS LIKE YOU STILL HAVE SOME BOOKS LEFT TO PICK UP AND RESHELVE.
WHATEVER...
"...WHO WANTS TO PLAY TAG ANYWAY?"
YOU'RE NEVER GONNA CATCH ME!

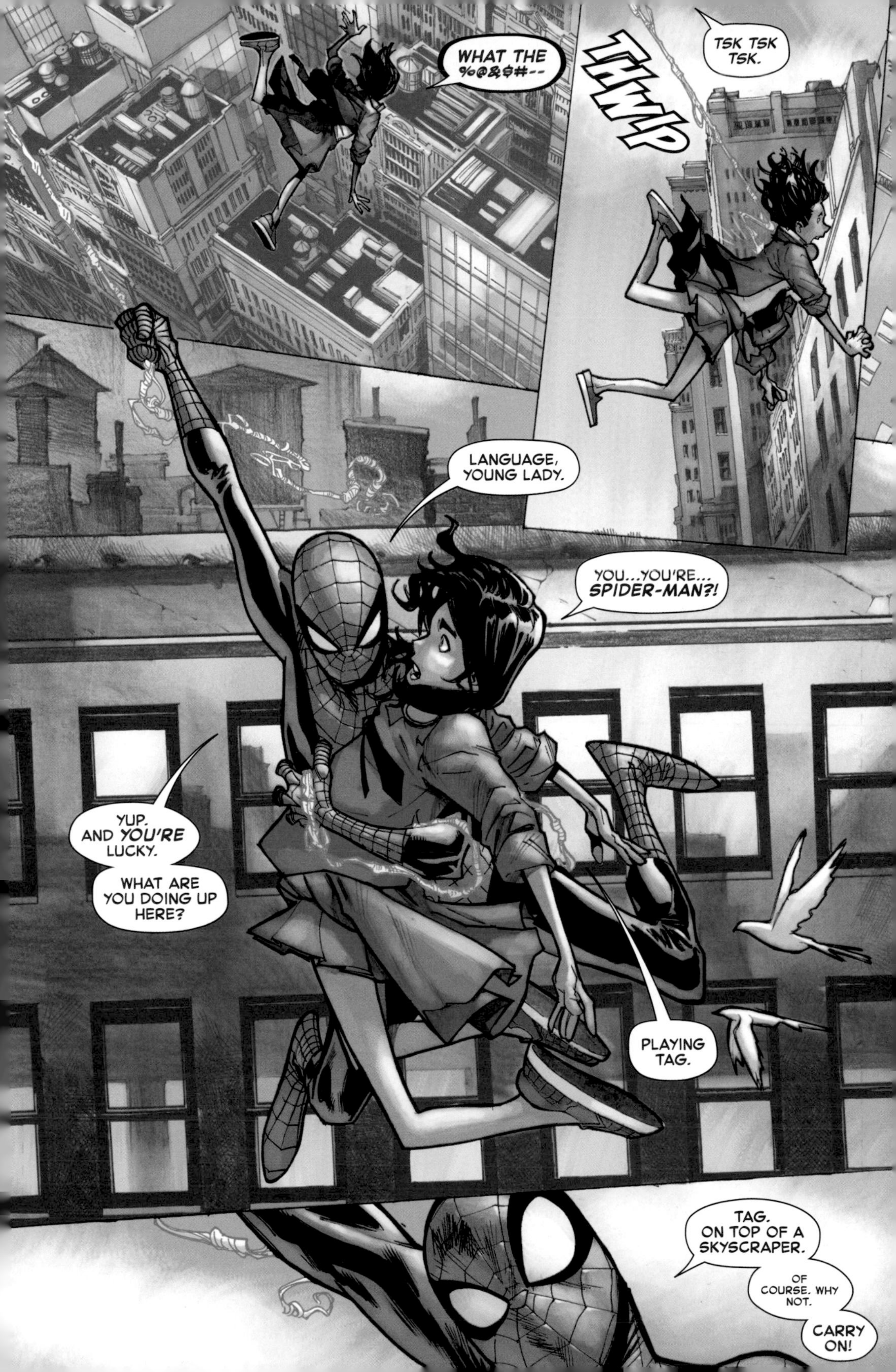
WHAT THE %@&$#--
THWIP
TSK TSK TSK.
LANGUAGE, YOUNG LADY.
YOU...YOU'RE... SPIDER-MAN?!
YUP. AND YOU'RE LUCKY.
WHAT ARE YOU DOING UP HERE?
PLAYING TAG.
TAG. ON TOP OF A SKYSCRAPER.
OF COURSE. WHY NOT.
CARRY ON!

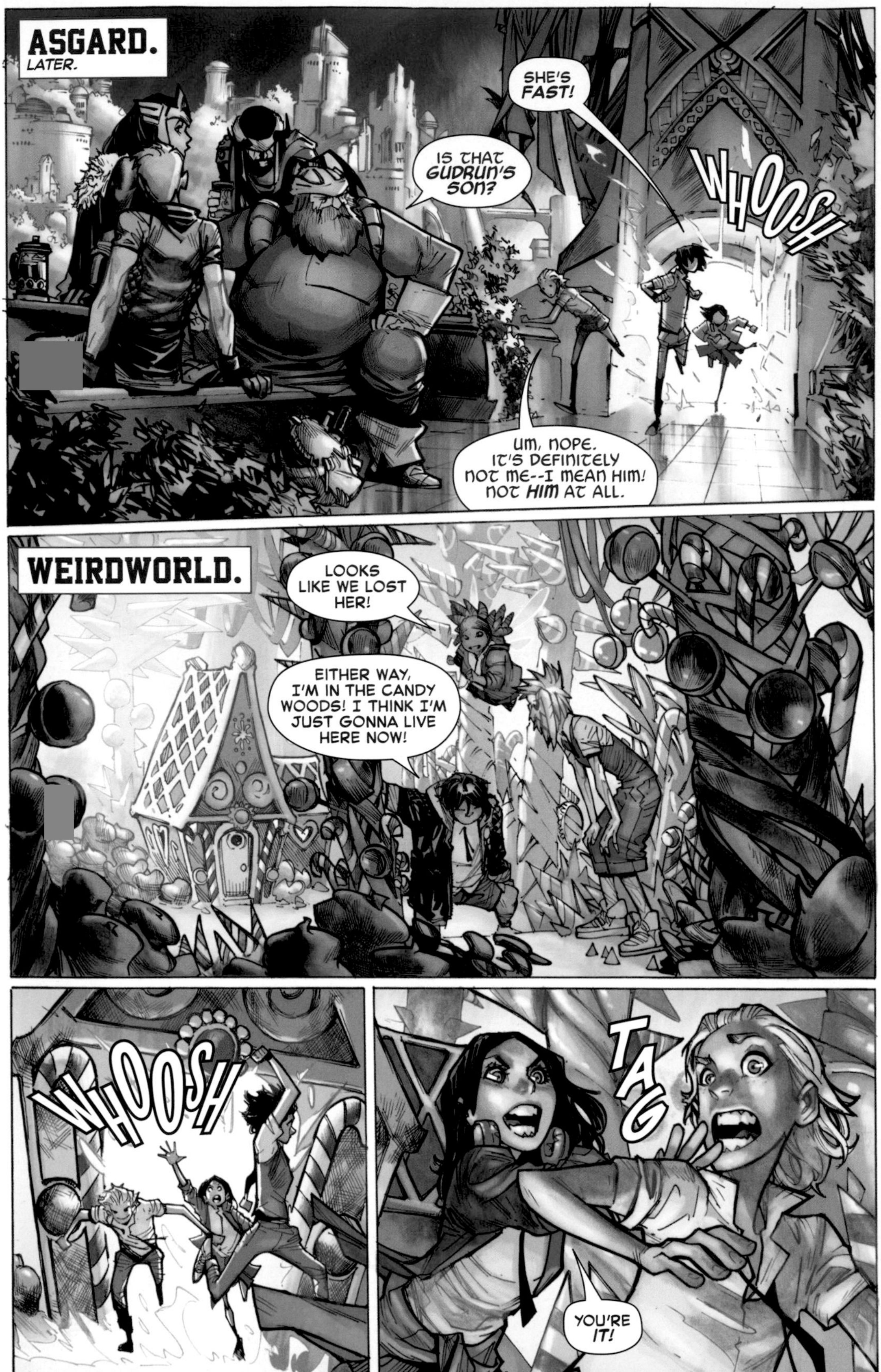
ASGARD.
LATER.
SHE'S FAST!
IS THAT GUDRUN'S SON?
WHOOSH
UM, NOPE. IT'S DEFINITELY NOT ME--I MEAN HIM! NOT HIM AT ALL.
WEIRDWORLD.
LOOKS LIKE WE LOST HER!
EITHER WAY, I'M IN THE CANDY WOODS! I THINK I'M JUST GONNA LIVE HERE NOW!
WHOOSH
TAG
YOU'RE IT!

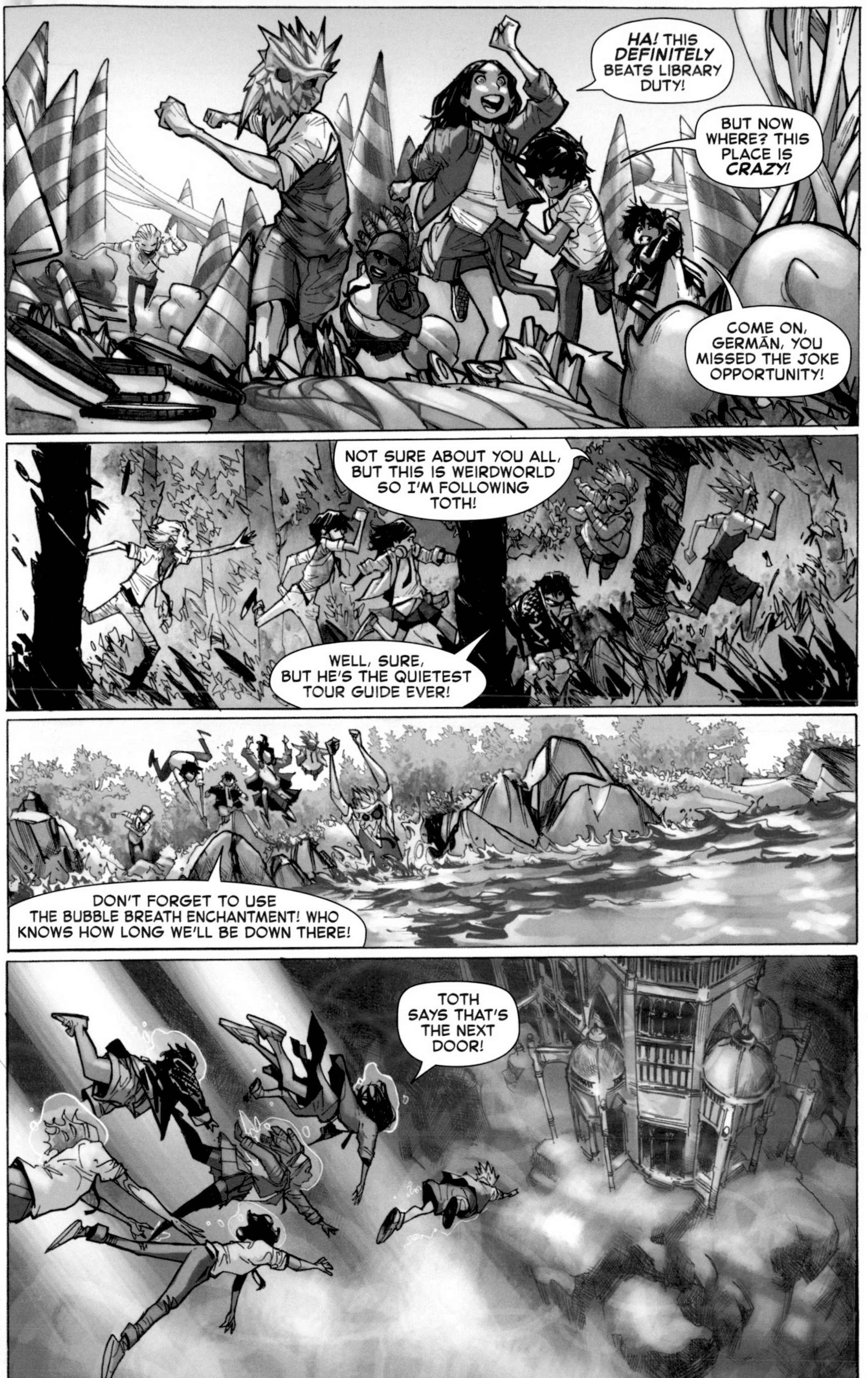
HA! THIS DEFINITELY BEATS LIBRARY DUTY!
BUT NOW WHERE? THIS PLACE IS CRAZY!
COME ON, GERMÁN, YOU MISSED THE JOKE OPPORTUNITY!
NOT SURE ABOUT YOU ALL, BUT THIS IS WEIRDWORLD SO I'M FOLLOWING TOTH!
WELL, SURE, BUT HE'S THE QUIETEST TOUR GUIDE EVER!
DON'T FORGET TO USE THE BUBBLE BREATH ENCHANTMENT! WHO KNOWS HOW LONG WE'LL BE DOWN THERE!
TOTH SAYS THAT'S THE NEXT DOOR!

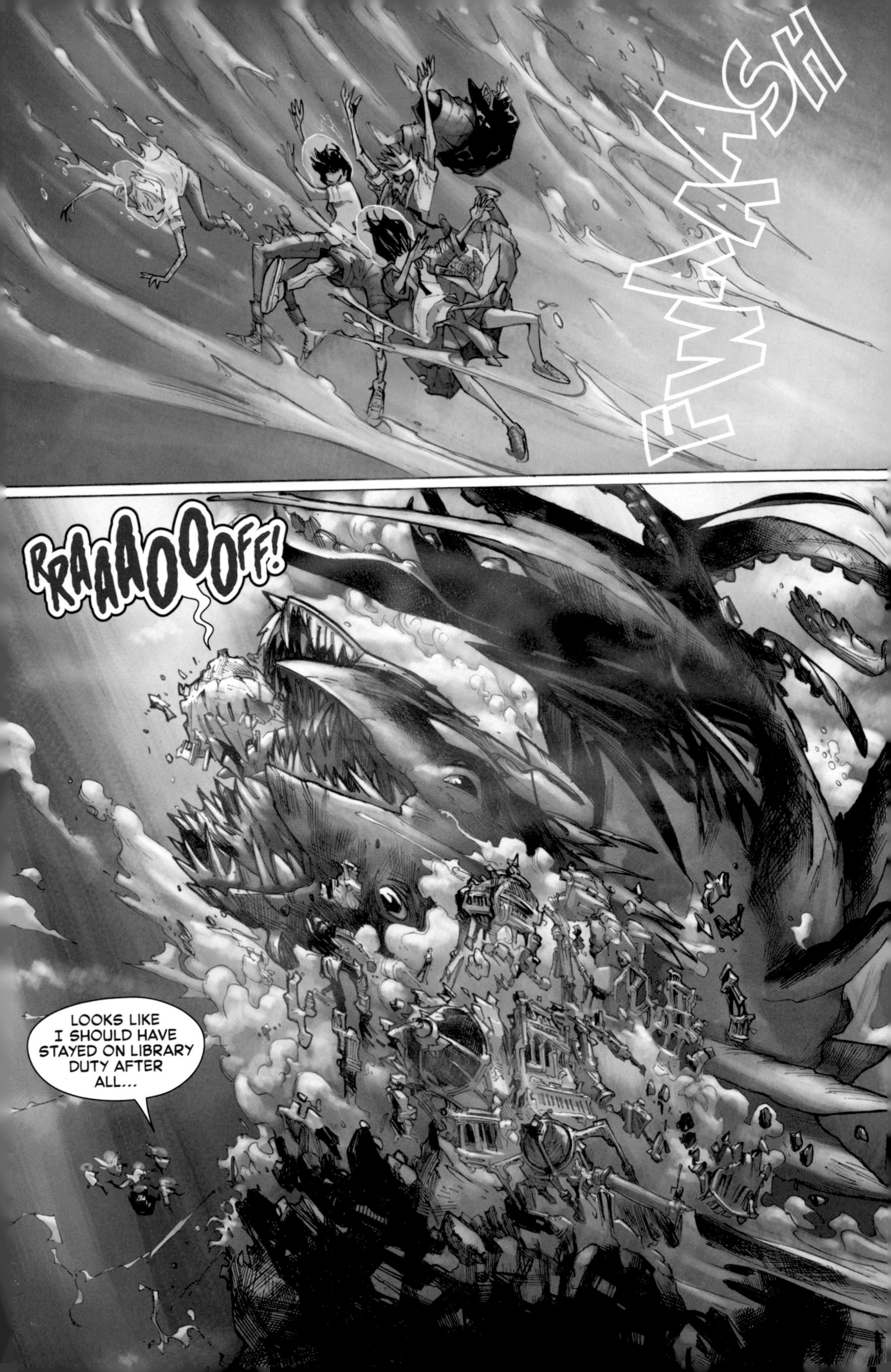
FWAASH
RRAAAOOOFF!
LOOKS LIKE I SHOULD HAVE STAYED ON LIBRARY DUTY AFTER ALL...

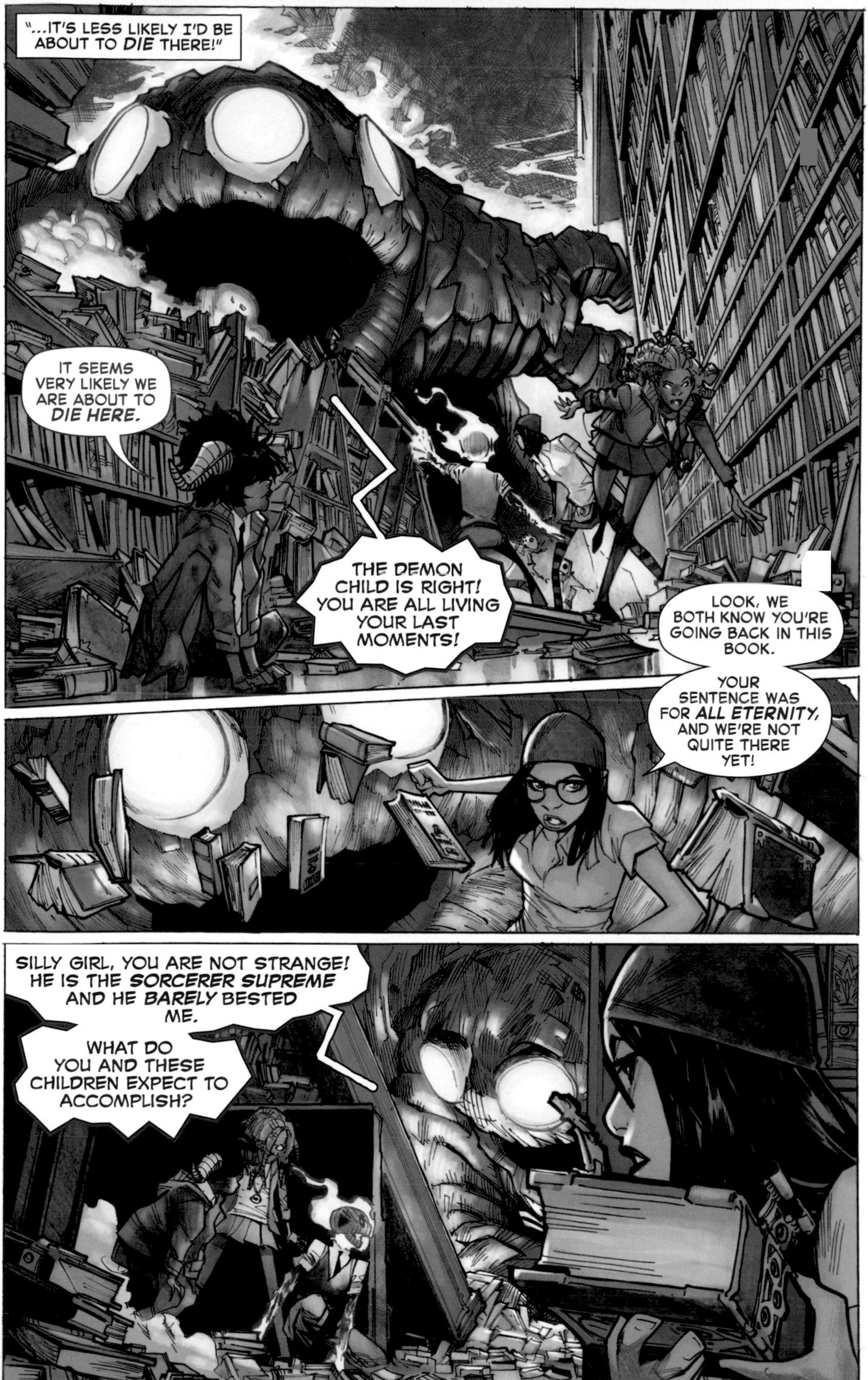
"...IT'S LESS LIKELY I'D BE ABOUT TO *DIE* THERE!"
IT SEEMS VERY LIKELY WE ARE ABOUT TO *DIE HERE.*
THE DEMON CHILD IS RIGHT! YOU ARE ALL LIVING YOUR LAST MOMENTS!
LOOK, WE BOTH KNOW YOU'RE GOING BACK IN THIS BOOK.
YOUR SENTENCE WAS FOR *ALL ETERNITY,* AND WE'RE NOT QUITE THERE YET!
SILLY GIRL, YOU ARE NOT STRANGE! HE IS THE *SORCERER SUPREME* AND HE *BARELY* BESTED ME.
WHAT DO YOU AND THESE CHILDREN EXPECT TO ACCOMPLISH?

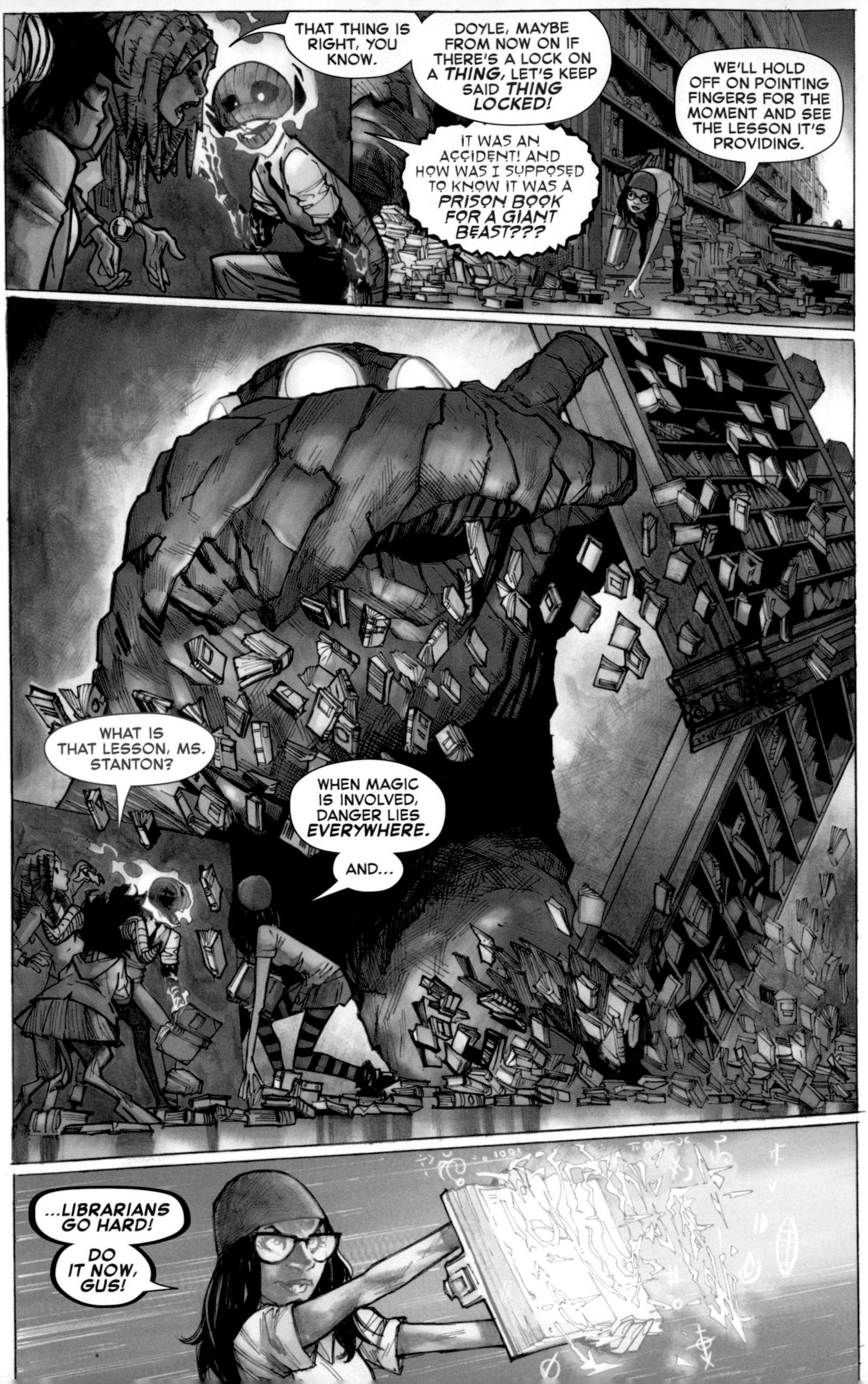
THAT THING IS RIGHT, YOU KNOW.
DOYLE, MAYBE FROM NOW ON IF THERE'S A LOCK ON A THING, LET'S KEEP SAID THING LOCKED!
IT WAS AN ACCIDENT! AND HOW WAS I SUPPOSED TO KNOW IT WAS A PRISON BOOK FOR A GIANT BEAST???
WE'LL HOLD OFF ON POINTING FINGERS FOR THE MOMENT AND SEE THE LESSON IT'S PROVIDING.
WHAT IS THAT LESSON, MS. STANTON?
WHEN MAGIC IS INVOLVED, DANGER LIES EVERYWHERE.
AND...
...LIBRARIANS GO HARD!
DO IT NOW, GUS!

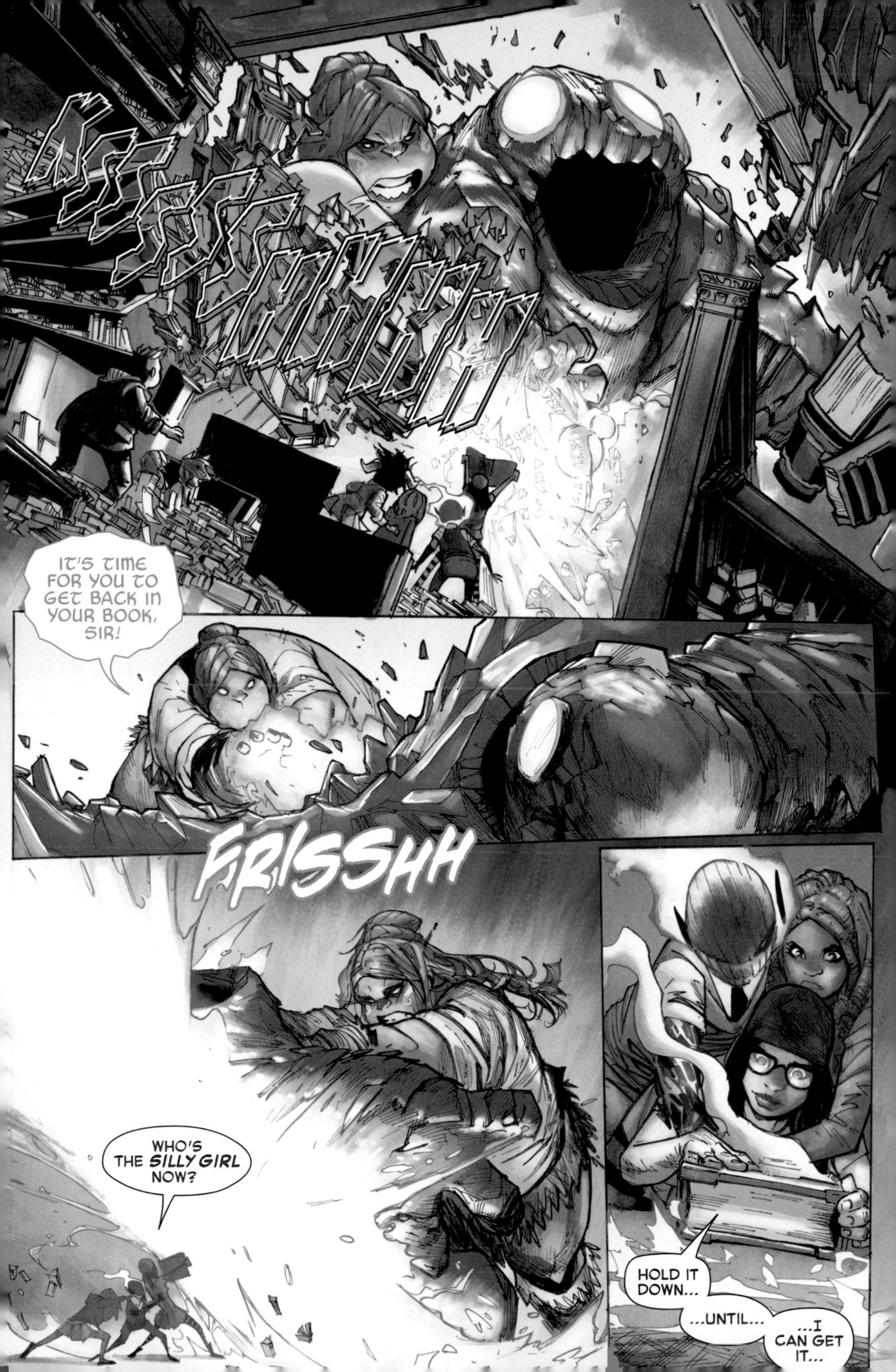
KSSSSHUUUUCH
IT'S TIME FOR YOU TO GET BACK IN YOUR BOOK, SIR!
FRISSHH
WHO'S THE SILLY GIRL NOW?
HOLD IT DOWN...
...UNTIL...
...I CAN GET IT...

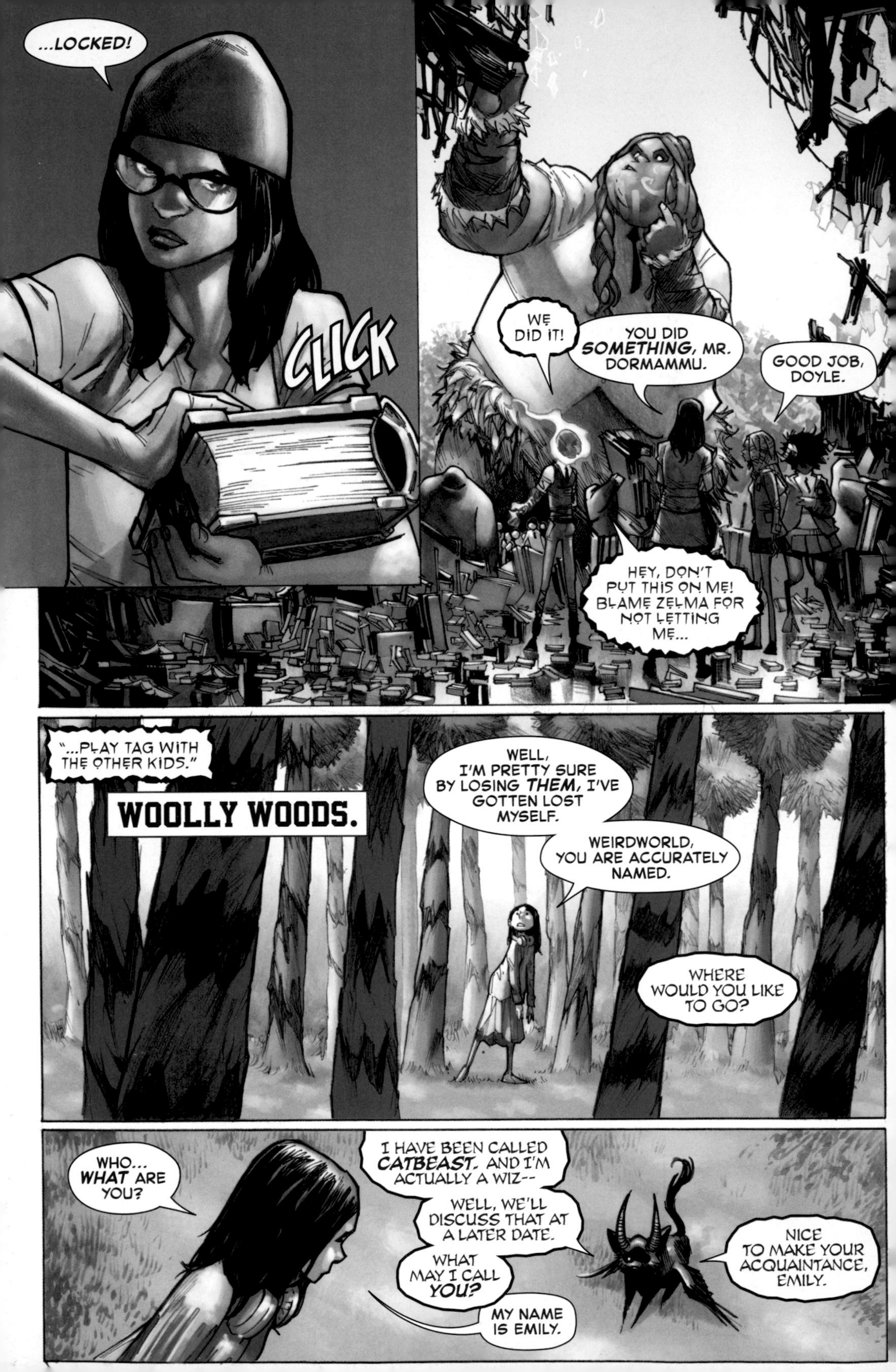
...LOCKED!
CLICK
WE DID IT!
YOU DID SOMETHING, MR. DORMAMMU.
GOOD JOB, DOYLE.
HEY, DON'T PUT THIS ON ME! BLAME ZELMA FOR NOT LETTING ME...
"...PLAY TAG WITH THE OTHER KIDS."
WOOLLY WOODS.
WELL, I'M PRETTY SURE BY LOSING THEM, I'VE GOTTEN LOST MYSELF.
WEIRDWORLD, YOU ARE ACCURATELY NAMED.
WHERE WOULD YOU LIKE TO GO?
WHO... WHAT ARE YOU?
I HAVE BEEN CALLED CATBEAST. AND I'M ACTUALLY A WIZ--
WELL, WE'LL DISCUSS THAT AT A LATER DATE.
WHAT MAY I CALL YOU?
MY NAME IS EMILY.
NICE TO MAKE YOUR ACQUAINTANCE, EMILY.

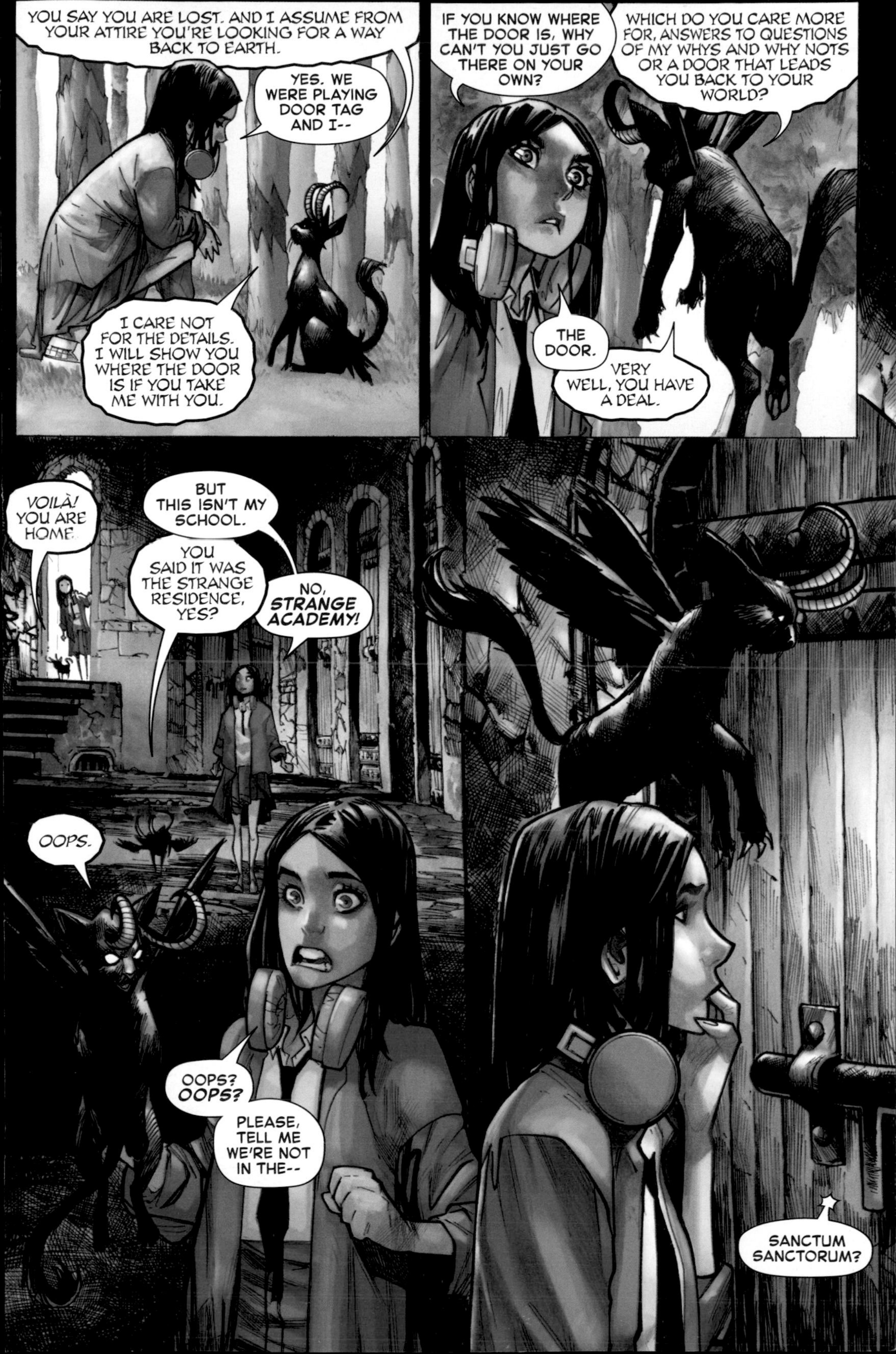
YOU SAY YOU ARE LOST. AND I ASSUME FROM YOUR ATTIRE YOU'RE LOOKING FOR A WAY BACK TO EARTH.
YES. WE WERE PLAYING DOOR TAG AND I--
I CARE NOT FOR THE DETAILS. I WILL SHOW YOU WHERE THE DOOR IS IF YOU TAKE ME WITH YOU.
IF YOU KNOW WHERE THE DOOR IS, WHY CAN'T YOU JUST GO THERE ON YOUR OWN?
WHICH DO YOU CARE MORE FOR, ANSWERS TO QUESTIONS OF MY WHYS AND WHY NOTS OR A DOOR THAT LEADS YOU BACK TO YOUR WORLD?
THE DOOR.
VERY WELL, YOU HAVE A DEAL.
VOILÀ! YOU ARE HOME.
BUT THIS ISN'T MY SCHOOL.
YOU SAID IT WAS THE STRANGE RESIDENCE, YES?
NO, ***STRANGE ACADEMY!***
OOPS.
OOPS? ***OOPS?***
PLEASE, TELL ME WE'RE NOT IN THE--
SANCTUM SANCTORUM?

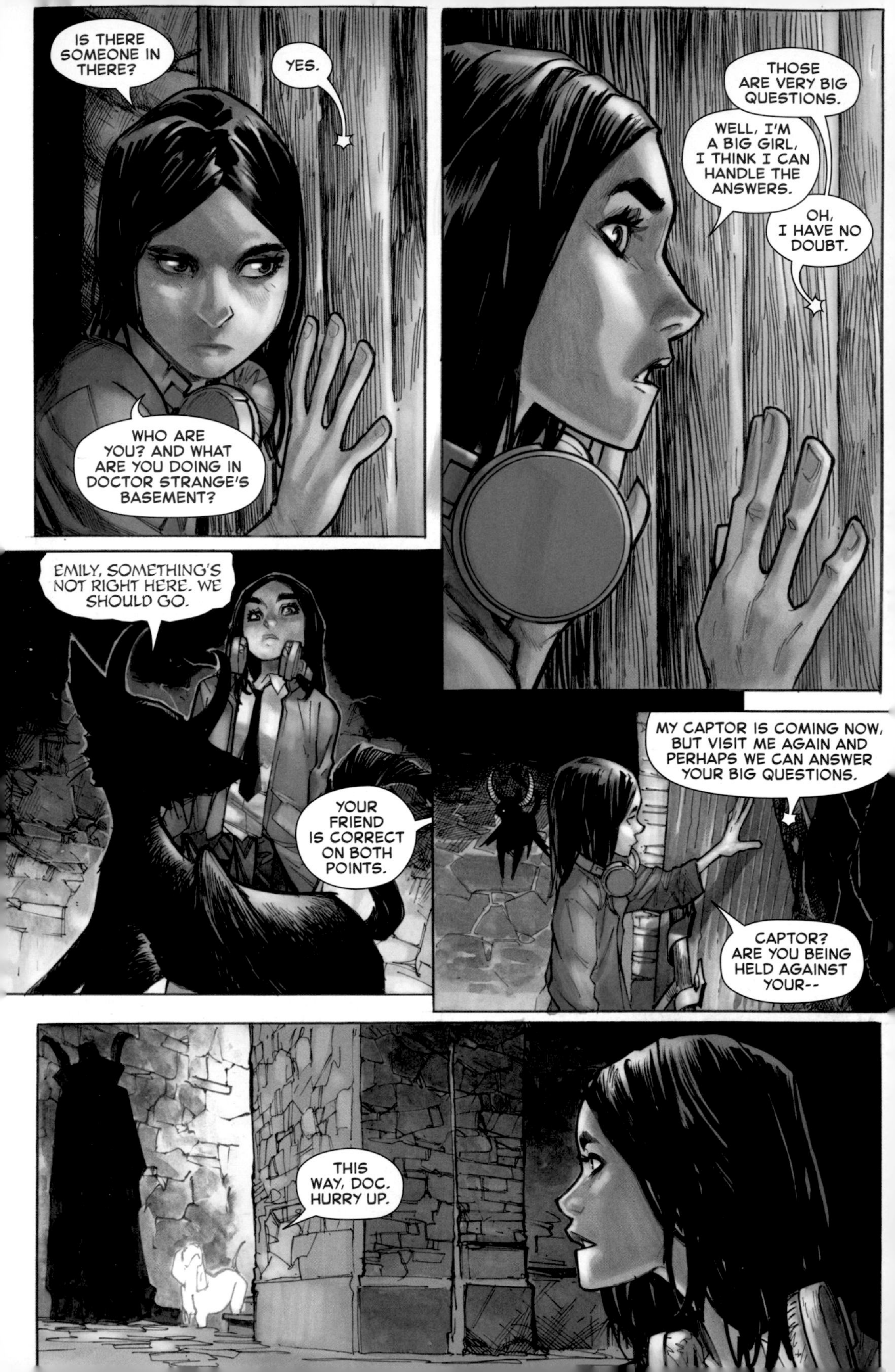
IS THERE SOMEONE IN THERE?
YES.
WHO ARE YOU? AND WHAT ARE YOU DOING IN DOCTOR STRANGE'S BASEMENT?
THOSE ARE VERY BIG QUESTIONS.
WELL, I'M A BIG GIRL, I THINK I CAN HANDLE THE ANSWERS.
OH, I HAVE NO DOUBT.
EMILY, SOMETHING'S NOT RIGHT HERE. WE SHOULD GO.
YOUR FRIEND IS CORRECT ON BOTH POINTS.
MY CAPTOR IS COMING NOW, BUT VISIT ME AGAIN AND PERHAPS WE CAN ANSWER YOUR BIG QUESTIONS.
CAPTOR? ARE YOU BEING HELD AGAINST YOUR--
THIS WAY, DOC. HURRY UP.

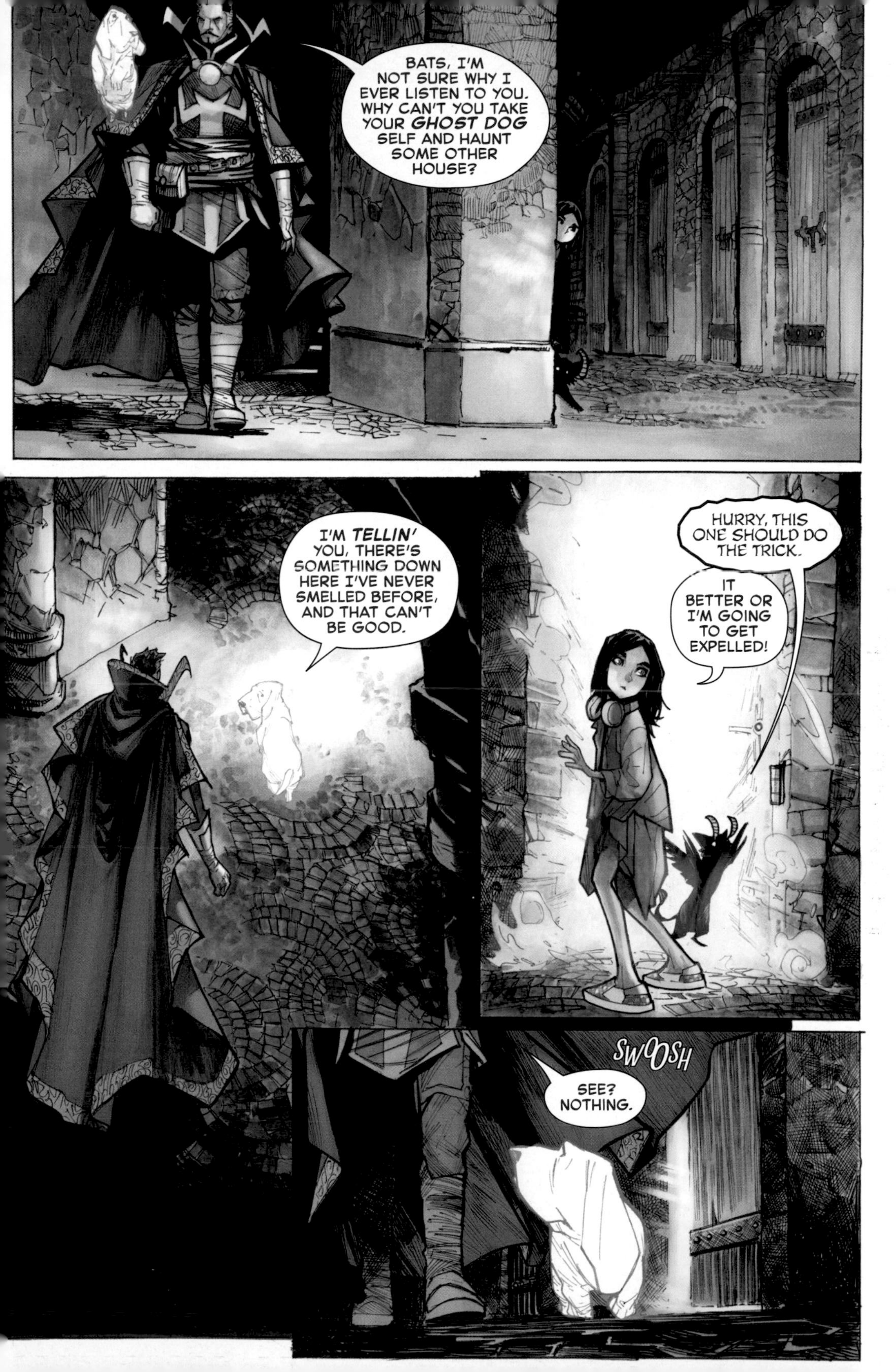
BATS, I'M NOT SURE WHY I EVER LISTEN TO YOU. WHY CAN'T YOU TAKE YOUR **GHOST DOG** SELF AND HAUNT SOME OTHER HOUSE?
I'M **TELLIN'** YOU, THERE'S SOMETHING DOWN HERE I'VE NEVER SMELLED BEFORE, AND THAT CAN'T BE GOOD.
HURRY, THIS ONE SHOULD DO THE TRICK.
IT BETTER OR I'M GOING TO GET EXPELLED!
SWOOSH
SEE? NOTHING.

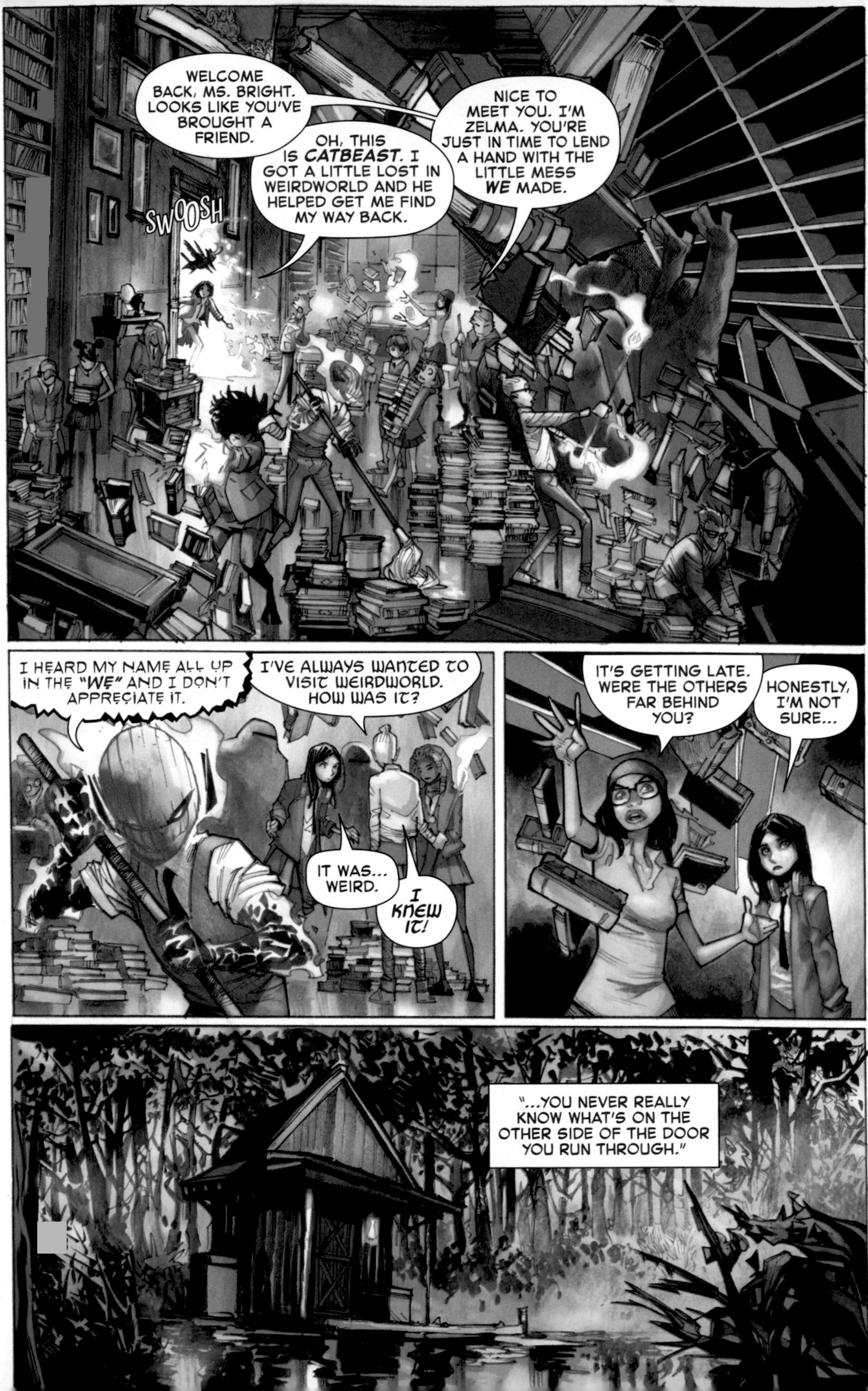
WELCOME BACK, MS. BRIGHT. LOOKS LIKE YOU'VE BROUGHT A FRIEND.
OH, THIS IS CATBEAST. I GOT A LITTLE LOST IN WEIRDWORLD AND HE HELPED GET ME FIND MY WAY BACK.
NICE TO MEET YOU. I'M ZELMA. YOU'RE JUST IN TIME TO LEND A HAND WITH THE LITTLE MESS WE MADE.
SWOOSH
I HEARD MY NAME ALL UP IN THE "WE" AND I DON'T APPRECIATE IT.
I'VE ALWAYS WANTED TO VISIT WEIRDWORLD. HOW WAS IT?
IT WAS... WEIRD.
I KNEW IT!
IT'S GETTING LATE. WERE THE OTHERS FAR BEHIND YOU?
HONESTLY, I'M NOT SURE...
"...YOU NEVER REALLY KNOW WHAT'S ON THE OTHER SIDE OF THE DOOR YOU RUN THROUGH."

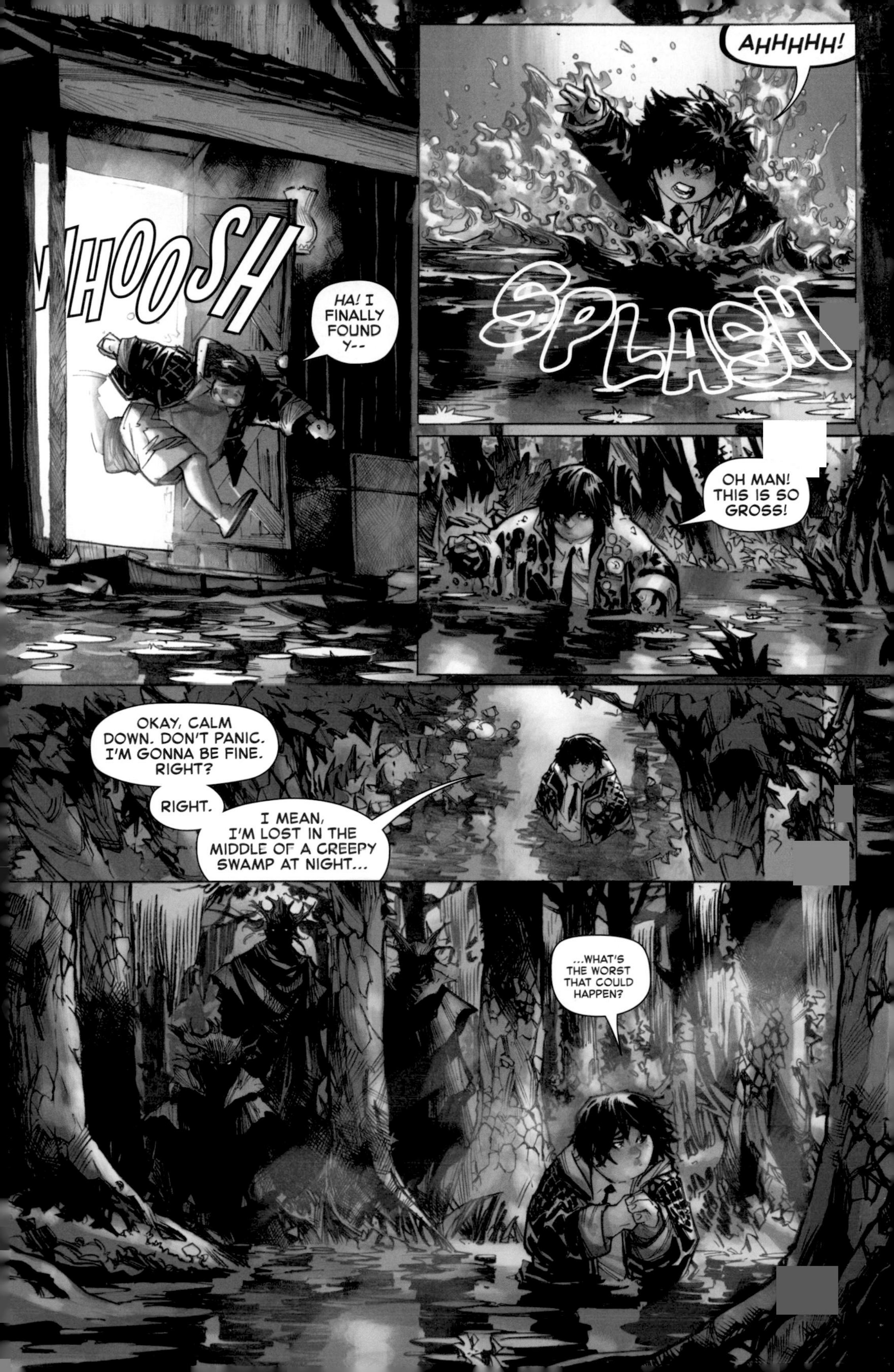
WHOOSH
HA! I FINALLY FOUND Y--
AHHHHH!
SPLASH
OH MAN! THIS IS SO GROSS!
OKAY, CALM DOWN. DON'T PANIC. I'M GONNA BE FINE. RIGHT?
RIGHT.
I MEAN, I'M LOST IN THE MIDDLE OF A CREEPY SWAMP AT NIGHT...
...WHAT'S THE WORST THAT COULD HAPPEN?

STRANGE Academy

PERMISSION SLIP

For the upcoming field trip to Asgard!
—Dr. Voodoo

I _____ , the parent/guardian of _____ , give permission for my child to attend _____

(trip of the week).

I understand that personal injury may occur from any of the following:

-Burns from dragon's breath, hellfire, hel fire, napalm, liquid dragon's oil, ice, Asgardian lightning, bubbling or mildly warm cauldrons

-Mind erasure from Dark Dimension inhabitants (including other students' parents), mutant sorcerers, demons, or Purple Men/Children

-Partial or permanent mind swap by magical or technological means, including, but not limited to: Jean Grey, Roxxon Techno-Sorcerors, Starktech, Morgan Le Fey or any of the Le Feyniacs, Baintronics Mindtrader 2020, any Beyond Corp. product

-Soul removal by traditional or new age means

-Troll rash

-Removal of any one (1), some, or all physical organs

-Death by drowning, burning, crushing, stretching, dropping, flying, climbing, running, falling, freezing, impaling, astral projecting, or entering/exiting any realms

-Death by Death

-Side-effects of resurrection from aforementioned death

By signing this form, I waive any rights to sue Doctor Stephen Strange, the Strange Academy, and any of its staff and employees for any harm that may come to my child by any of the situations listed above, or any added situations after signing, depending on the severity of the injury.

This slip only covers this one (1) trip.

I agree, and consent, to all of the above statements, even under psychic influence.

_____ (Parent/Guardian's Signature)

_____ Date

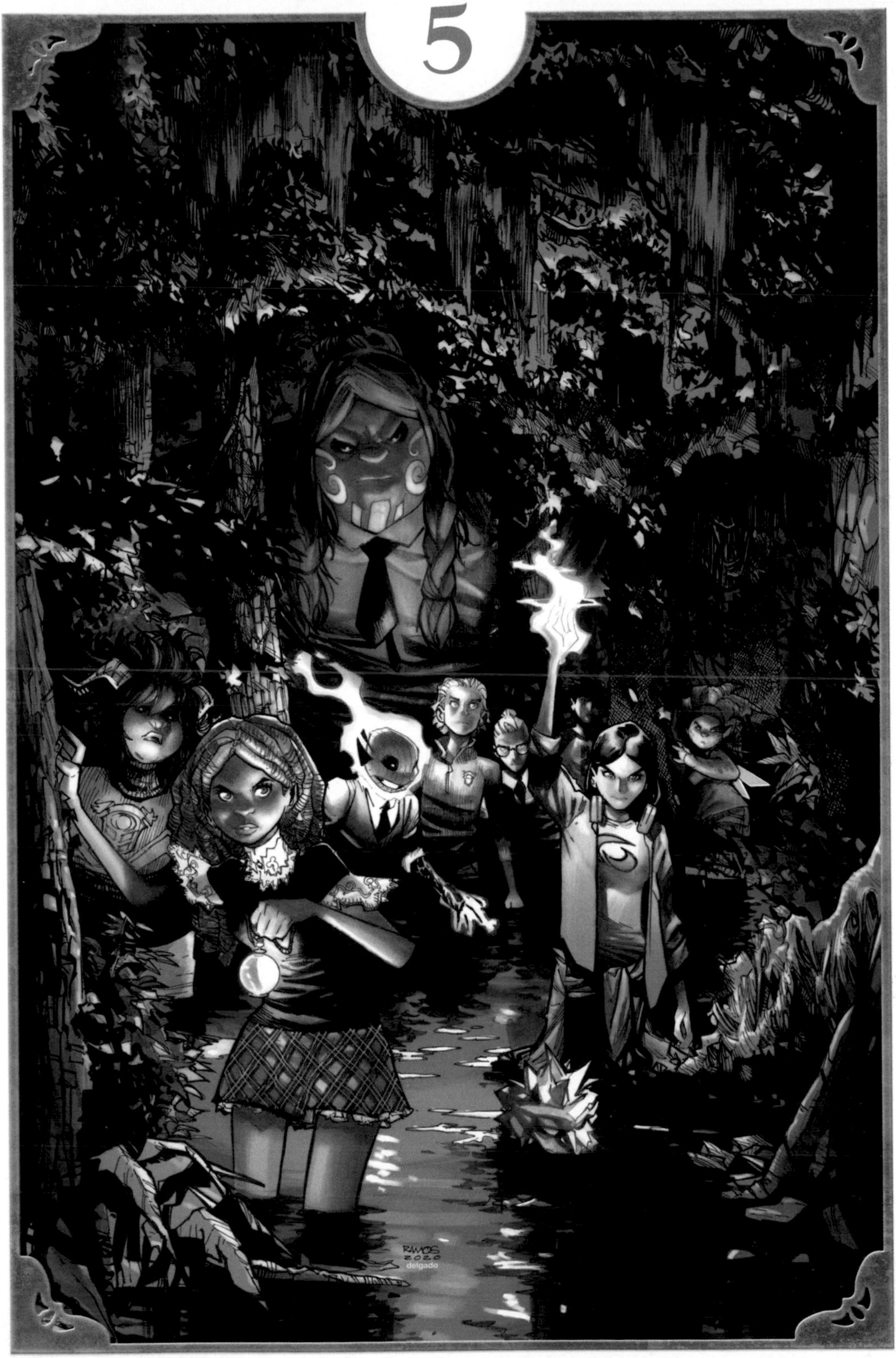
5
RAMOS
2020
delgado

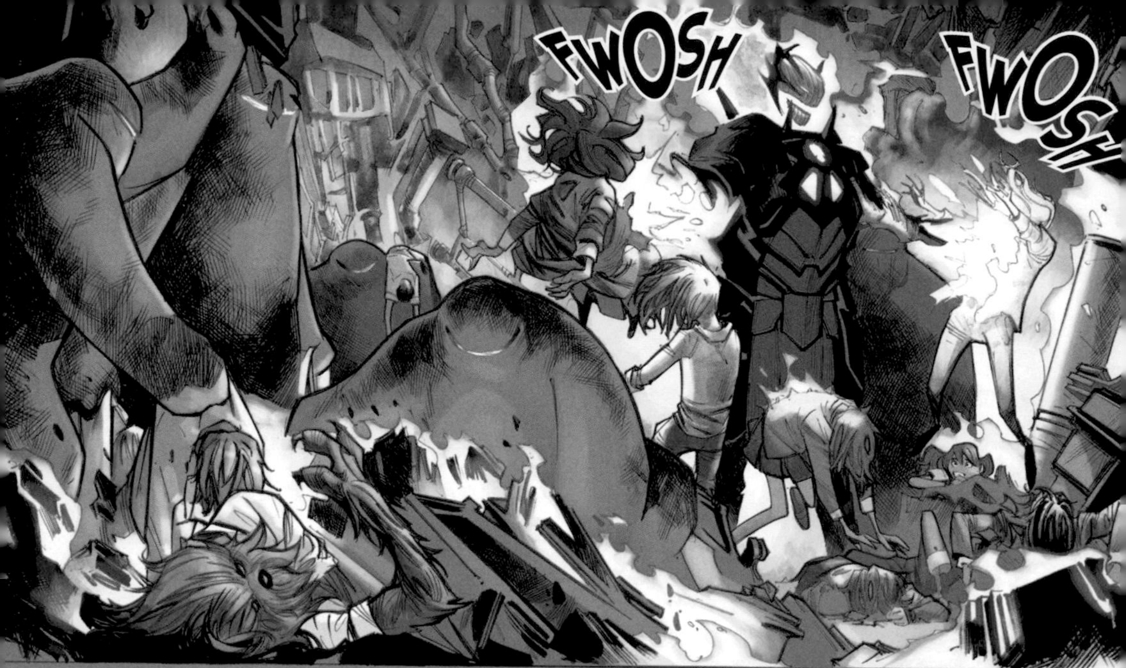
FWOSH
FWOSH

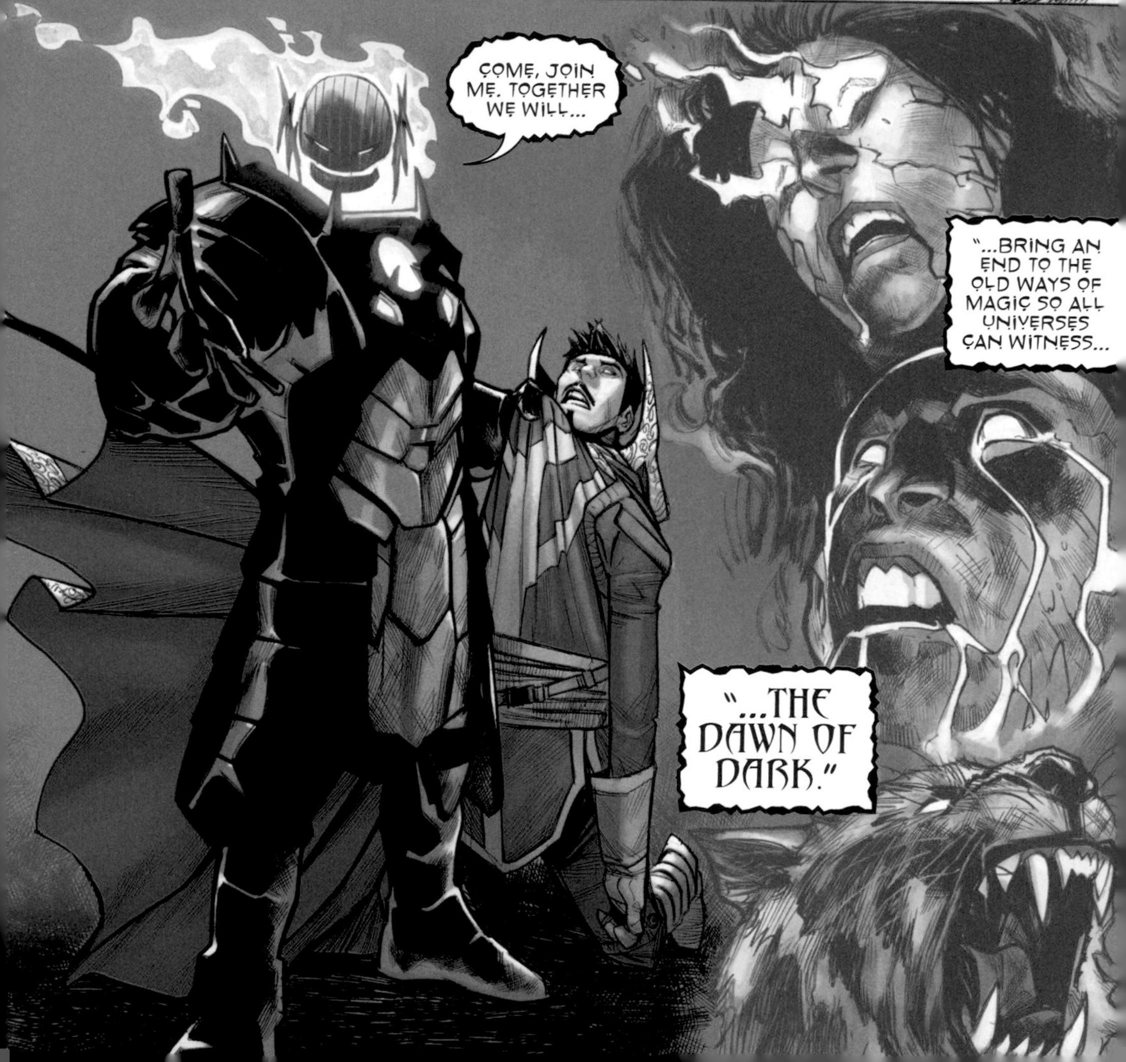
COME, JOIN ME. TOGETHER WE WILL...
"...BRING AN END TO THE OLD WAYS OF MAGIC SO ALL UNIVERSES CAN WITNESS...
"...THE DAWN OF DARK."

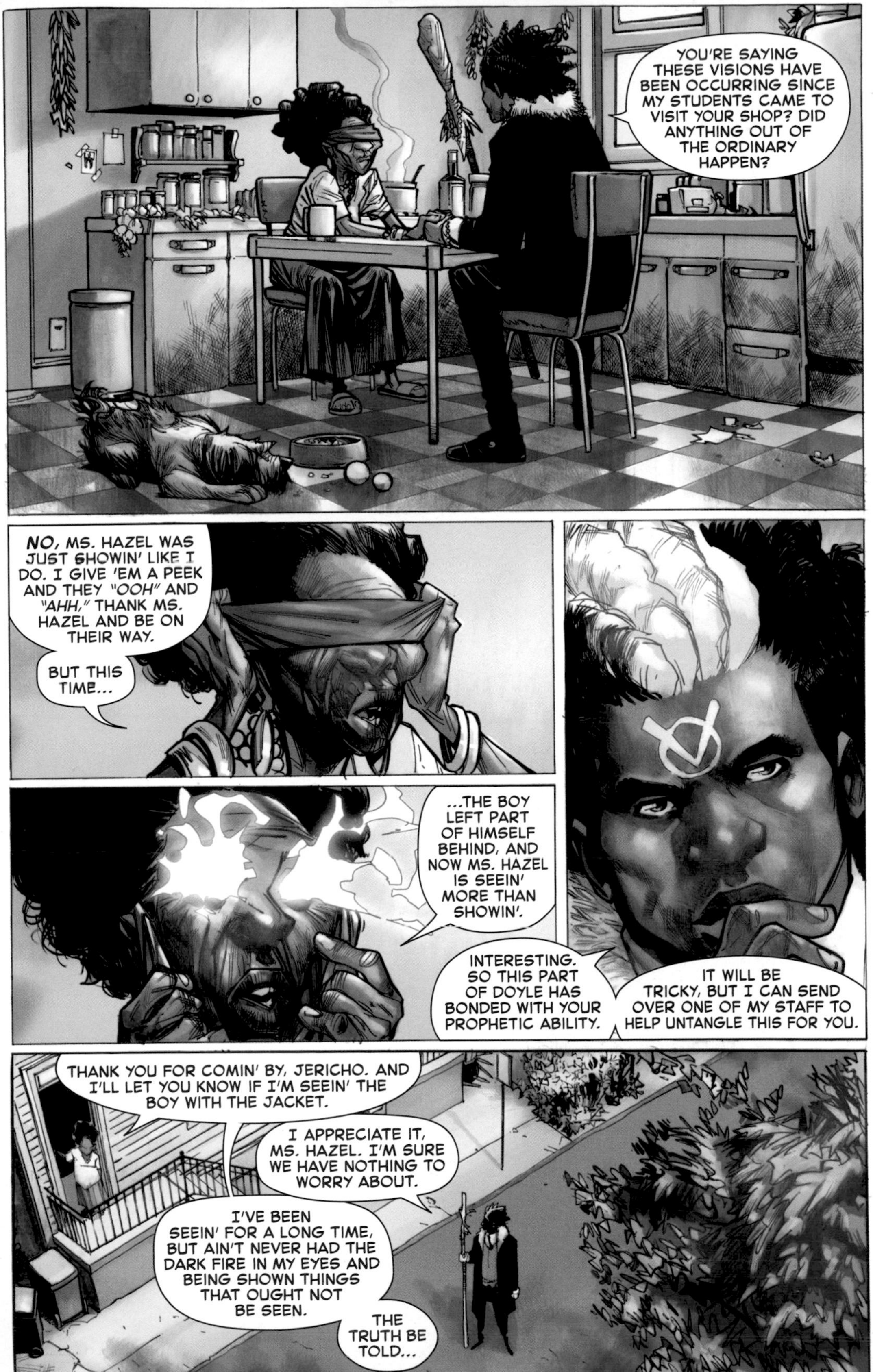
YOU'RE SAYING THESE VISIONS HAVE BEEN OCCURRING SINCE MY STUDENTS CAME TO VISIT YOUR SHOP? DID ANYTHING OUT OF THE ORDINARY HAPPEN?
NO, MS. HAZEL WAS JUST SHOWIN' LIKE I DO. I GIVE 'EM A PEEK AND THEY "OOH" AND "AHH," THANK MS. HAZEL AND BE ON THEIR WAY.
BUT THIS TIME...
...THE BOY LEFT PART OF HIMSELF BEHIND, AND NOW MS. HAZEL IS SEEIN' MORE THAN SHOWIN'.
INTERESTING. SO THIS PART OF DOYLE HAS BONDED WITH YOUR PROPHETIC ABILITY.
IT WILL BE TRICKY, BUT I CAN SEND OVER ONE OF MY STAFF TO HELP UNTANGLE THIS FOR YOU.
THANK YOU FOR COMIN' BY, JERICHO. AND I'LL LET YOU KNOW IF I'M SEEIN' THE BOY WITH THE JACKET.
I APPRECIATE IT, MS. HAZEL. I'M SURE WE HAVE NOTHING TO WORRY ABOUT.
I'VE BEEN SEEIN' FOR A LONG TIME, BUT AIN'T NEVER HAD THE DARK FIRE IN MY EYES AND BEING SHOWN THINGS THAT OUGHT NOT BE SEEN.
THE TRUTH BE TOLD...

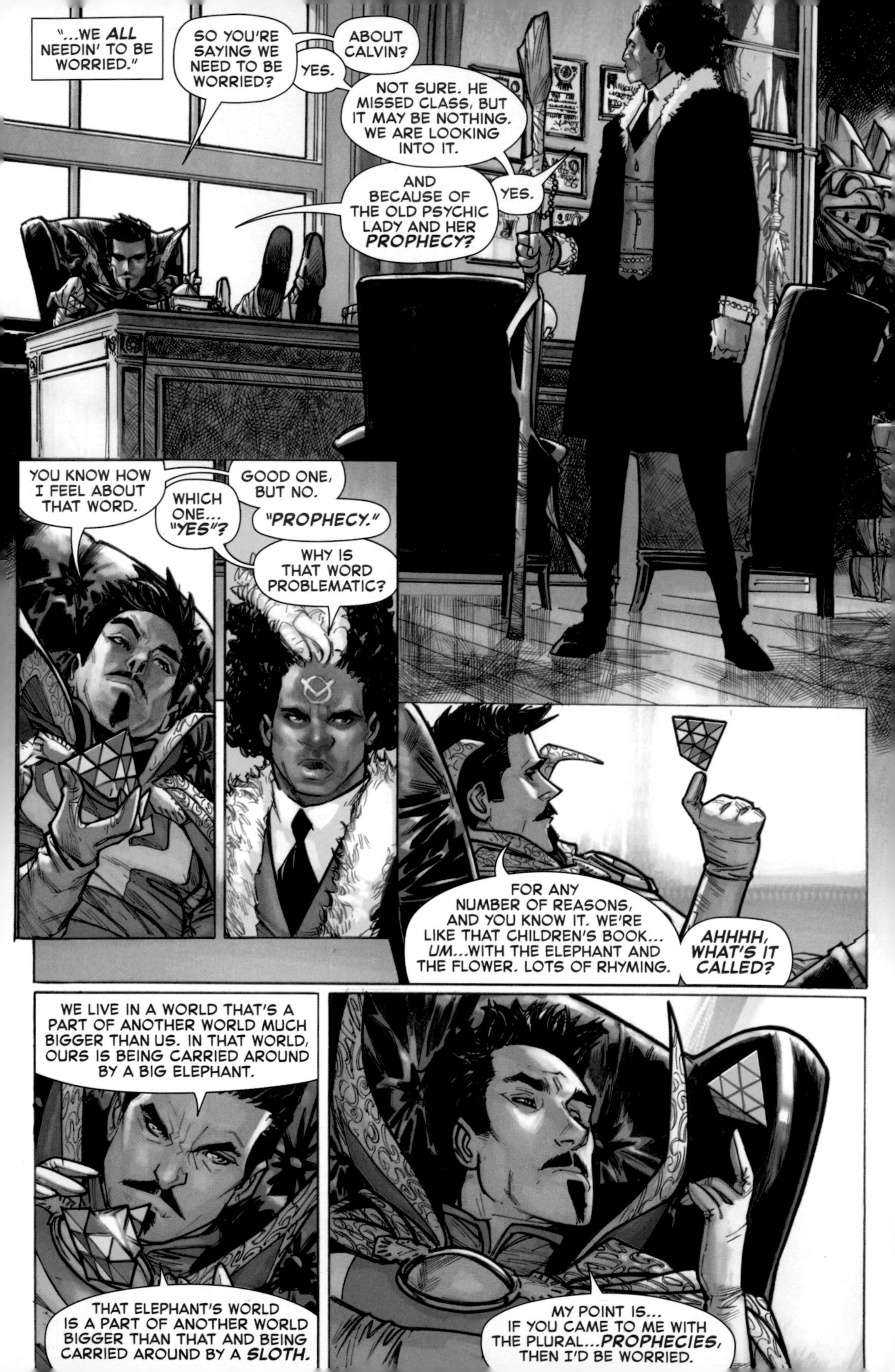
"...WE ALL NEEDIN' TO BE WORRIED."
SO YOU'RE SAYING WE NEED TO BE WORRIED?
ABOUT CALVIN?
YES.
NOT SURE. HE MISSED CLASS, BUT IT MAY BE NOTHING. WE ARE LOOKING INTO IT.
AND BECAUSE OF THE OLD PSYCHIC LADY AND HER PROPHECY?
YES.
YOU KNOW HOW I FEEL ABOUT THAT WORD.
WHICH ONE... "YES"?
GOOD ONE, BUT NO.
"PROPHECY."
WHY IS THAT WORD PROBLEMATIC?
FOR ANY NUMBER OF REASONS, AND YOU KNOW IT. WE'RE LIKE THAT CHILDREN'S BOOK... UM...WITH THE ELEPHANT AND THE FLOWER. LOTS OF RHYMING.
AHHHH, WHAT'S IT CALLED?
WE LIVE IN A WORLD THAT'S A PART OF ANOTHER WORLD MUCH BIGGER THAN US. IN THAT WORLD, OURS IS BEING CARRIED AROUND BY A BIG ELEPHANT.
THAT ELEPHANT'S WORLD IS A PART OF ANOTHER WORLD BIGGER THAN THAT AND BEING CARRIED AROUND BY A SLOTH.
MY POINT IS... IF YOU CAME TO ME WITH THE PLURAL...PROPHECIES, THEN I'D BE WORRIED.

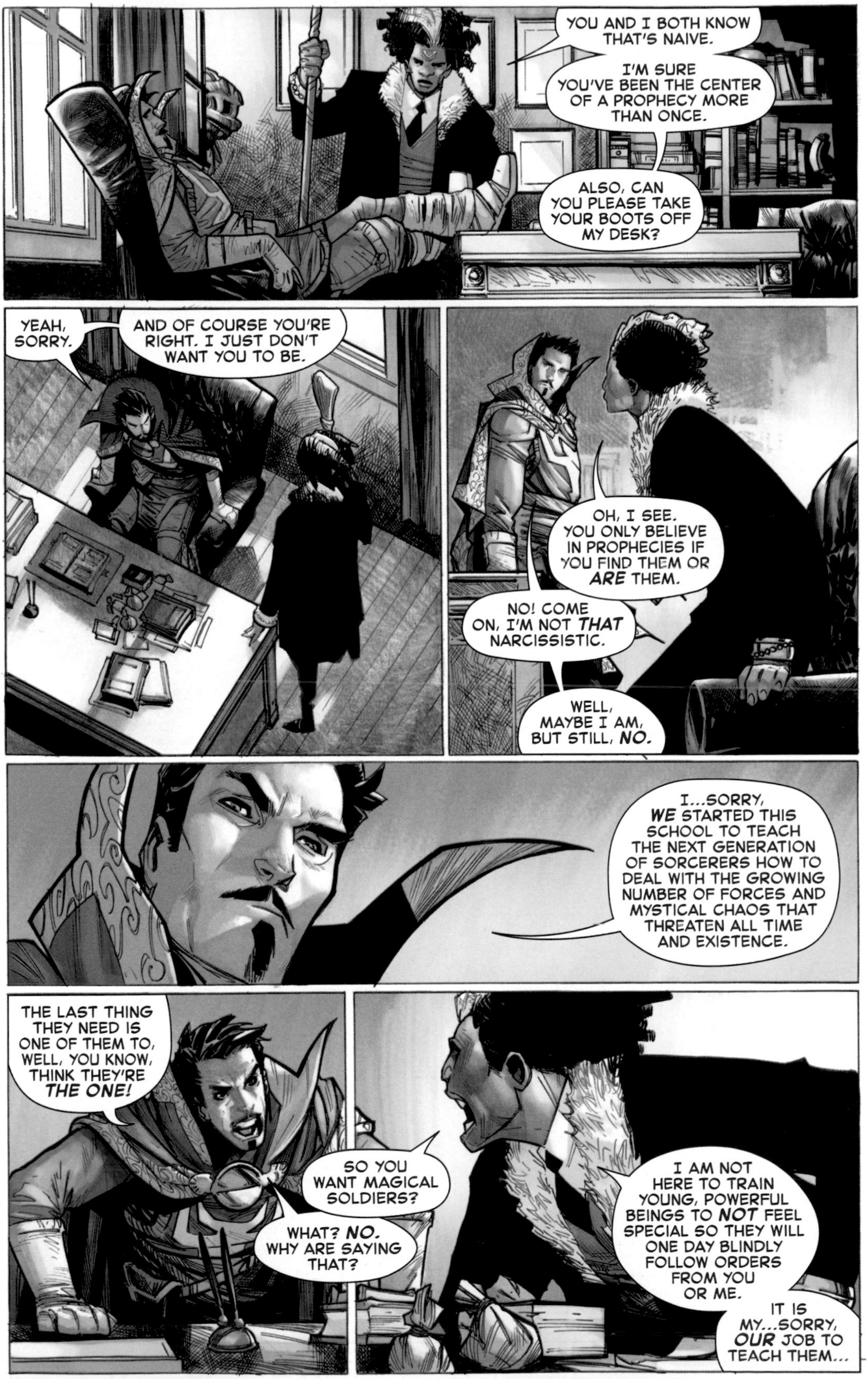
YOU AND I BOTH KNOW THAT'S NAIVE.
I'M SURE YOU'VE BEEN THE CENTER OF A PROPHECY MORE THAN ONCE.
ALSO, CAN YOU PLEASE TAKE YOUR BOOTS OFF MY DESK?
YEAH, SORRY.
AND OF COURSE YOU'RE RIGHT. I JUST DON'T WANT YOU TO BE.
OH, I SEE. YOU ONLY BELIEVE IN PROPHECIES IF YOU FIND THEM OR ARE THEM.
NO! COME ON, I'M NOT THAT NARCISSISTIC.
WELL, MAYBE I AM, BUT STILL, NO.
I...SORRY, WE STARTED THIS SCHOOL TO TEACH THE NEXT GENERATION OF SORCERERS HOW TO DEAL WITH THE GROWING NUMBER OF FORCES AND MYSTICAL CHAOS THAT THREATEN ALL TIME AND EXISTENCE.
THE LAST THING THEY NEED IS ONE OF THEM TO, WELL, YOU KNOW, THINK THEY'RE THE ONE!
SO YOU WANT MAGICAL SOLDIERS?
WHAT? NO. WHY ARE SAYING THAT?
I AM NOT HERE TO TRAIN YOUNG, POWERFUL BEINGS TO NOT FEEL SPECIAL SO THEY WILL ONE DAY BLINDLY FOLLOW ORDERS FROM YOU OR ME.
IT IS MY...SORRY, OUR JOB TO TEACH THEM...

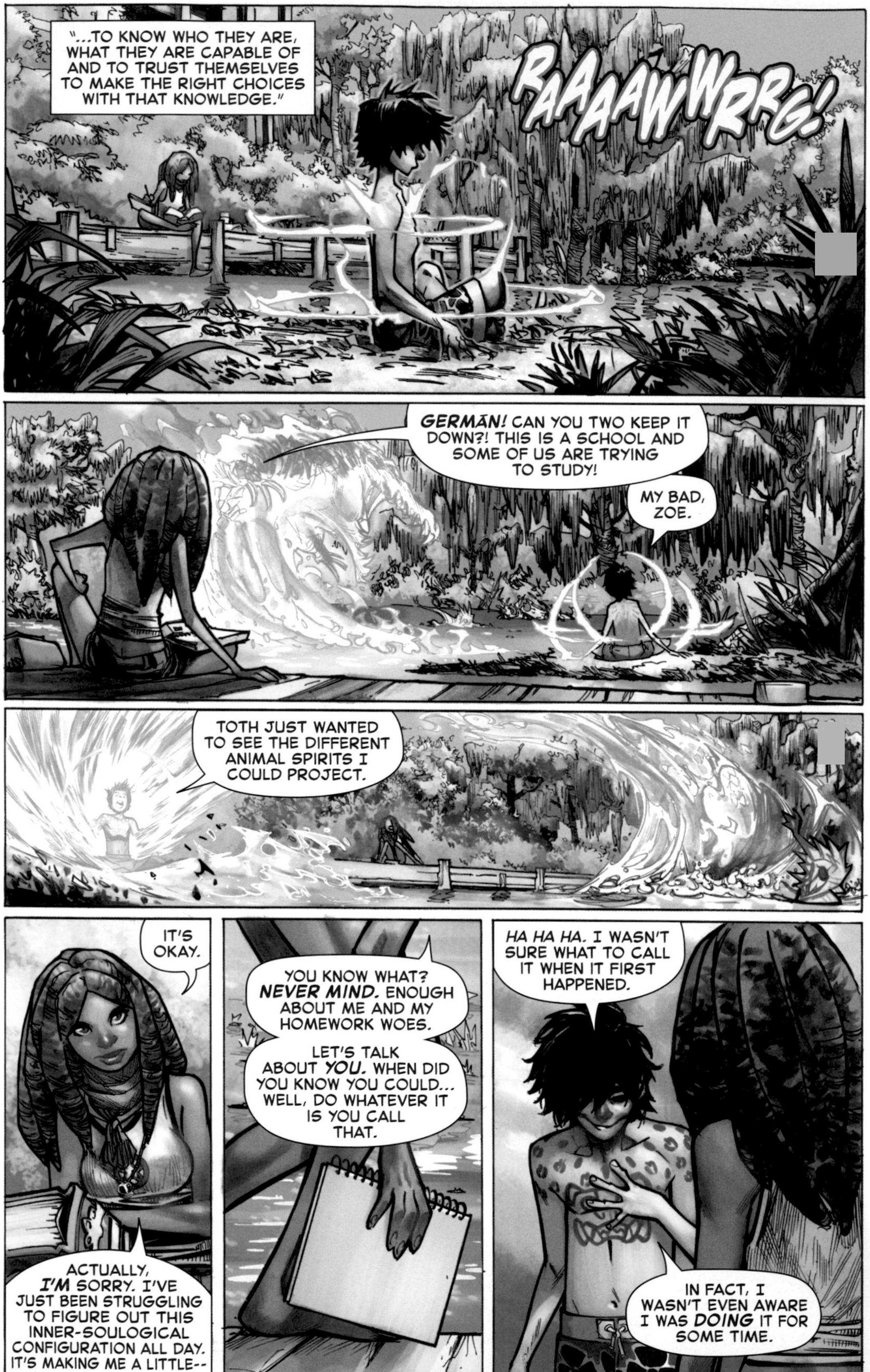
"...TO KNOW WHO THEY ARE, WHAT THEY ARE CAPABLE OF AND TO TRUST THEMSELVES TO MAKE THE RIGHT CHOICES WITH THAT KNOWLEDGE."
RAAAAWRRG!
GERMĀN! CAN YOU TWO KEEP IT DOWN?! THIS IS A SCHOOL AND SOME OF US ARE TRYING TO STUDY!
MY BAD, ZOE.
TOTH JUST WANTED TO SEE THE DIFFERENT ANIMAL SPIRITS I COULD PROJECT.
IT'S OKAY.
ACTUALLY, I'M SORRY. I'VE JUST BEEN STRUGGLING TO FIGURE OUT THIS INNER-SOULOGICAL CONFIGURATION ALL DAY. IT'S MAKING ME A LITTLE--
YOU KNOW WHAT? NEVER MIND. ENOUGH ABOUT ME AND MY HOMEWORK WOES.
LET'S TALK ABOUT YOU. WHEN DID YOU KNOW YOU COULD... WELL, DO WHATEVER IT IS YOU CALL THAT.
HA HA HA. I WASN'T SURE WHAT TO CALL IT WHEN IT FIRST HAPPENED.
IN FACT, I WASN'T EVEN AWARE I WAS DOING IT FOR SOME TIME.

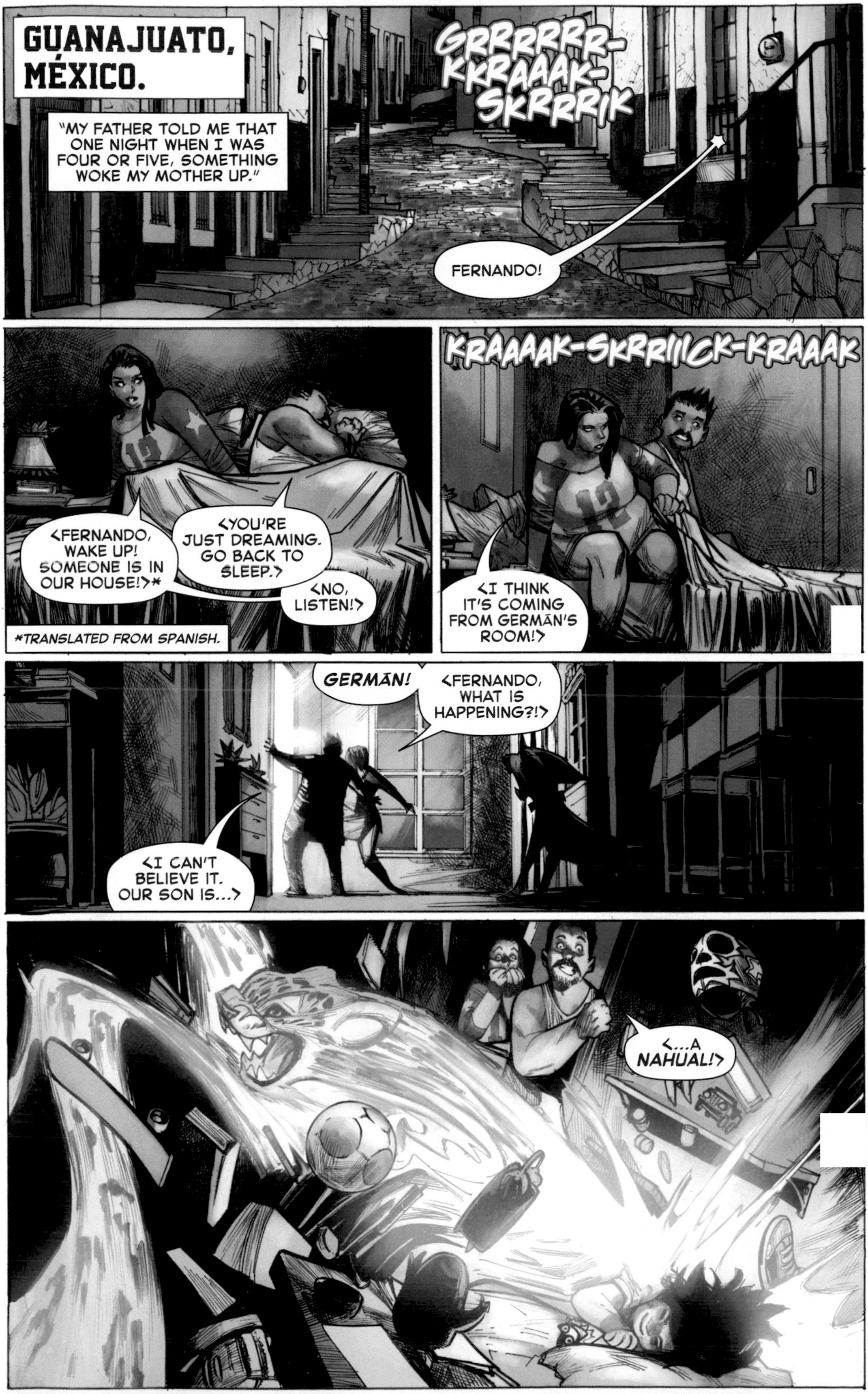
GUANAJUATO, MÉXICO.
"MY FATHER TOLD ME THAT ONE NIGHT WHEN I WAS FOUR OR FIVE, SOMETHING WOKE MY MOTHER UP."
GRRRRRR-KKRAAAK-SKRRRIK
FERNANDO!
<FERNANDO, WAKE UP! SOMEONE IS IN OUR HOUSE!>*
<YOU'RE JUST DREAMING. GO BACK TO SLEEP.>
<NO, LISTEN!>
*TRANSLATED FROM SPANISH.
KRAAAAK-SKRRIIICK-KRAAAK
<I THINK IT'S COMING FROM GERMĀN'S ROOM!>
GERMĀN!
<FERNANDO, WHAT IS HAPPENING?!>
<I CAN'T BELIEVE IT. OUR SON IS...>
<...A NAHUAL!>

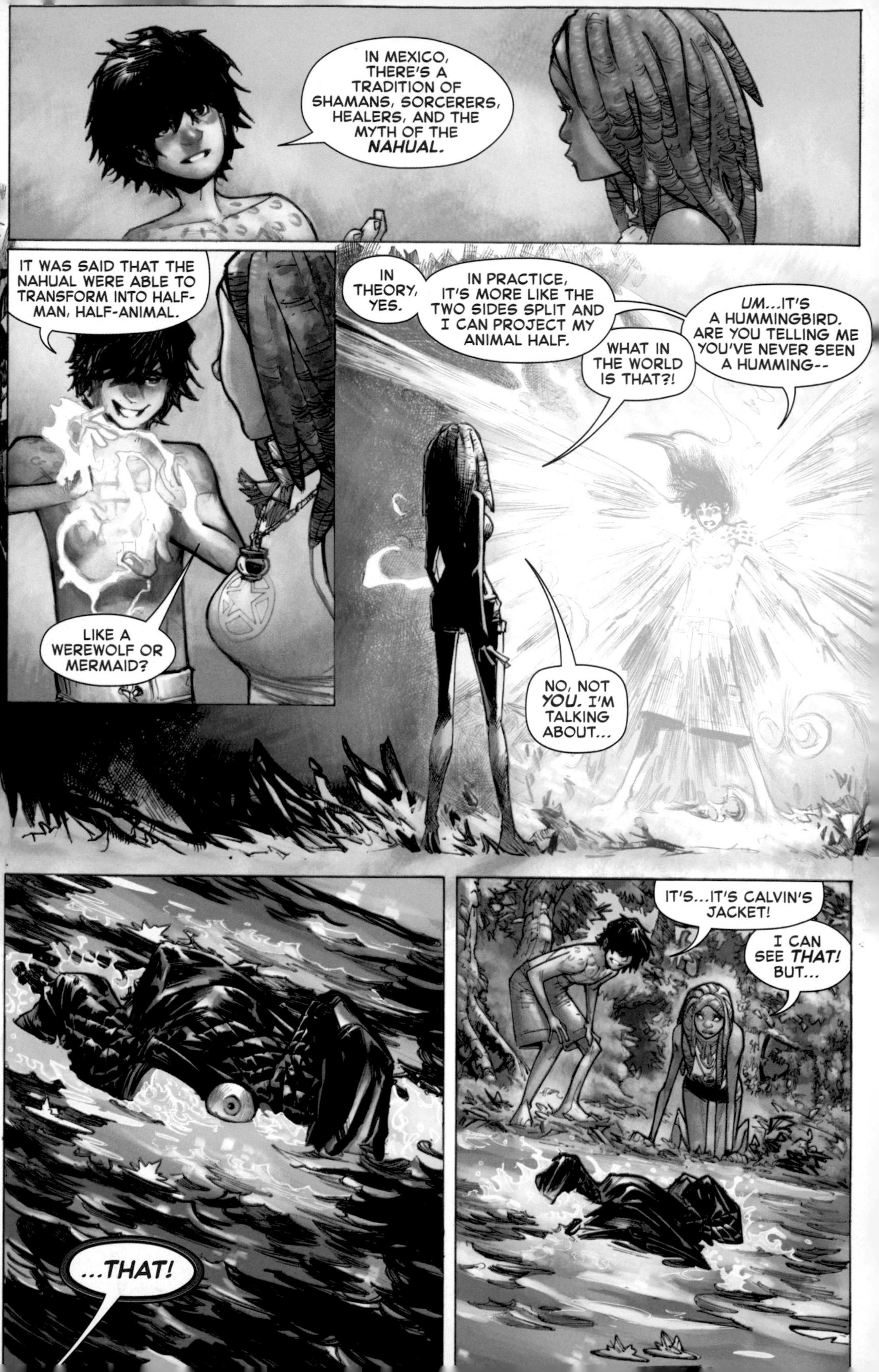
IN MEXICO, THERE'S A TRADITION OF SHAMANS, SORCERERS, HEALERS, AND THE MYTH OF THE *NAHUAL.*
IT WAS SAID THAT THE NAHUAL WERE ABLE TO TRANSFORM INTO HALF-MAN, HALF-ANIMAL.
LIKE A WEREWOLF OR MERMAID?
IN THEORY, YES.
IN PRACTICE, IT'S MORE LIKE THE TWO SIDES SPLIT AND I CAN PROJECT MY ANIMAL HALF.
WHAT IN THE WORLD IS THAT?!
UM...IT'S A HUMMINGBIRD. ARE YOU TELLING ME YOU'VE NEVER SEEN A HUMMING--
NO, NOT *YOU.* I'M TALKING ABOUT...
...THAT!
IT'S...IT'S CALVIN'S JACKET!
I CAN SEE *THAT!* BUT...

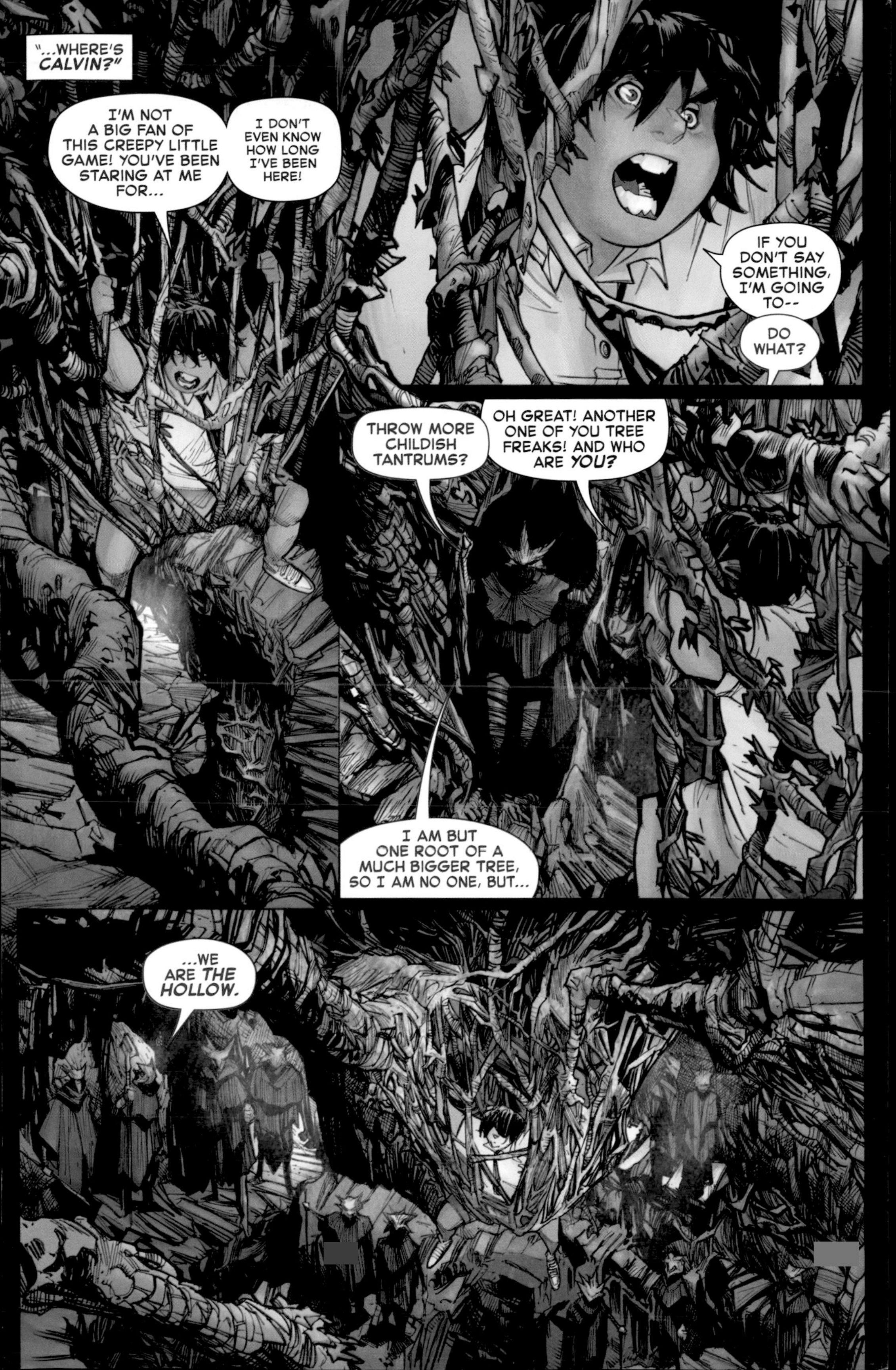
"...WHERE'S CALVIN?"
I'M NOT A BIG FAN OF THIS CREEPY LITTLE GAME! YOU'VE BEEN STARING AT ME FOR...
I DON'T EVEN KNOW HOW LONG I'VE BEEN HERE!
IF YOU DON'T SAY SOMETHING, I'M GOING TO--
DO WHAT?
THROW MORE CHILDISH TANTRUMS?
OH GREAT! ANOTHER ONE OF YOU TREE FREAKS! AND WHO ARE YOU?
I AM BUT ONE ROOT OF A MUCH BIGGER TREE, SO I AM NO ONE, BUT...
...WE ARE THE HOLLOW.

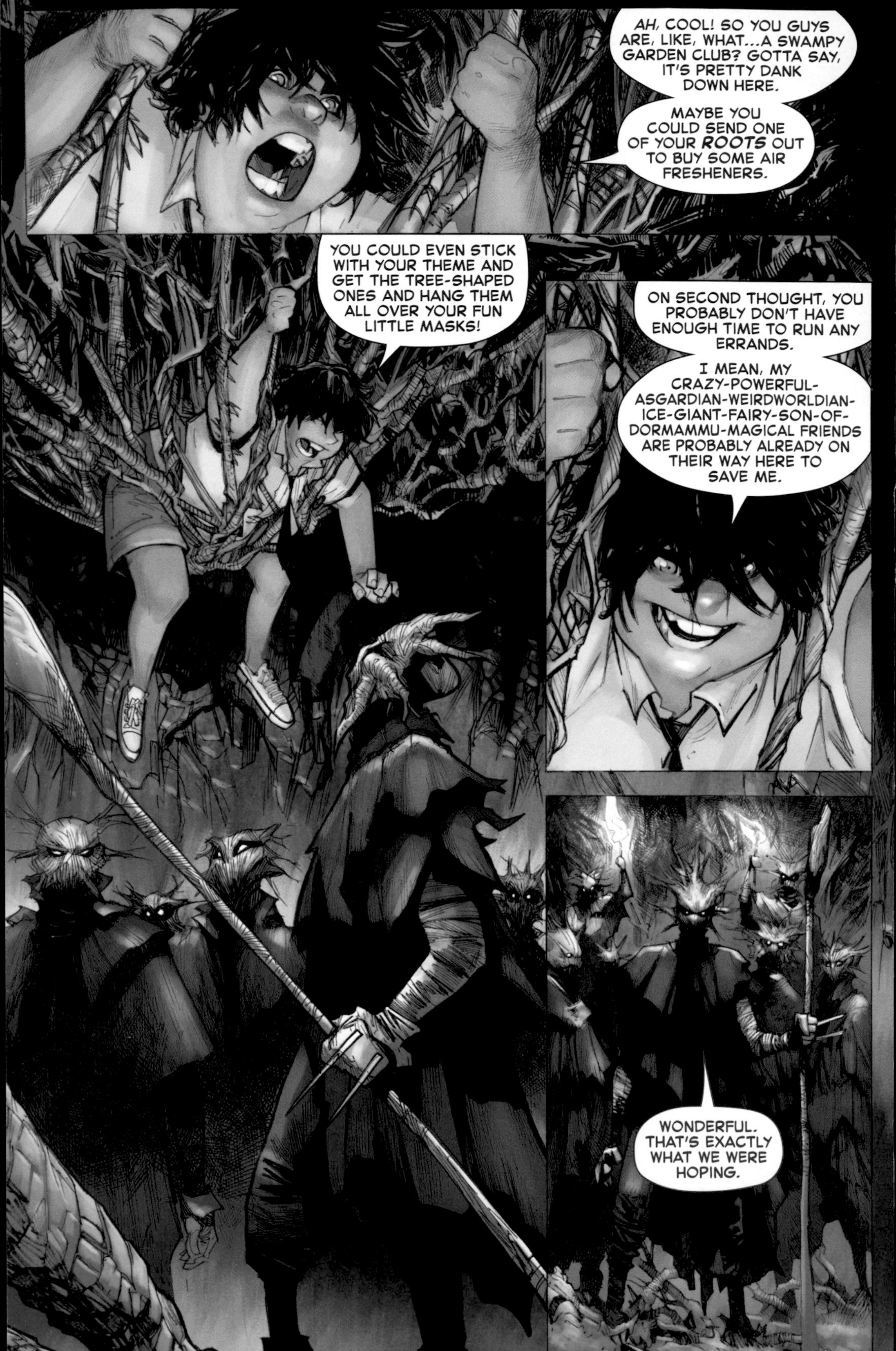
AH, COOL! SO YOU GUYS ARE, LIKE, WHAT...A SWAMPY GARDEN CLUB? GOTTA SAY, IT'S PRETTY DANK DOWN HERE.
MAYBE YOU COULD SEND ONE OF YOUR *ROOTS* OUT TO BUY SOME AIR FRESHENERS.
YOU COULD EVEN STICK WITH YOUR THEME AND GET THE TREE-SHAPED ONES AND HANG THEM ALL OVER YOUR FUN LITTLE MASKS!
ON SECOND THOUGHT, YOU PROBABLY DON'T HAVE ENOUGH TIME TO RUN ANY ERRANDS.
I MEAN, MY CRAZY-POWERFUL-ASGARDIAN-WEIRDWORLDIAN-ICE-GIANT-FAIRY-SON-OF-DORMAMMU-MAGICAL FRIENDS ARE PROBABLY ALREADY ON THEIR WAY HERE TO SAVE ME.
WONDERFUL. THAT'S EXACTLY WHAT WE WERE HOPING.

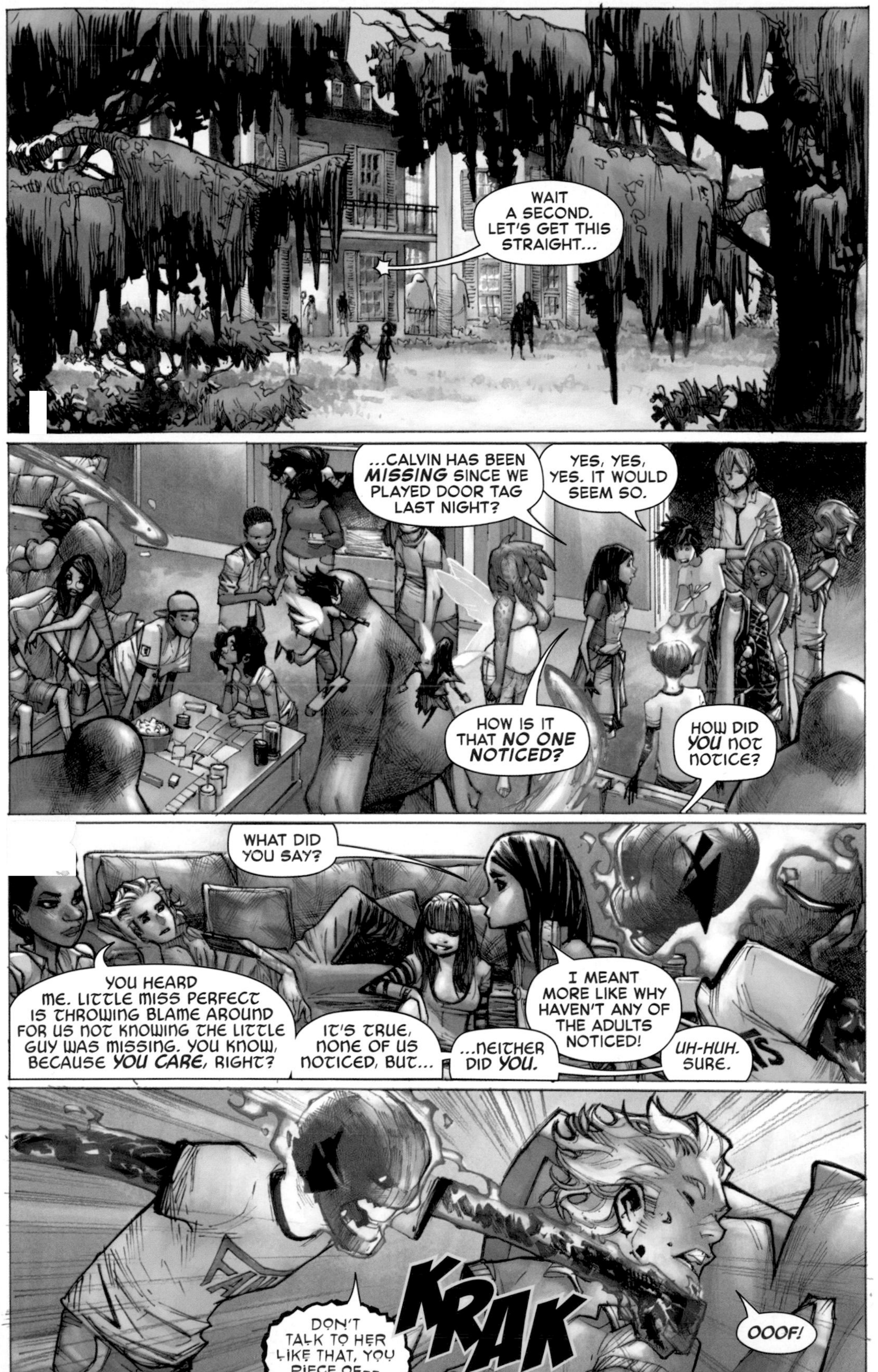
WAIT A SECOND. LET'S GET THIS STRAIGHT...
...CALVIN HAS BEEN MISSING SINCE WE PLAYED DOOR TAG LAST NIGHT?
YES, YES, YES. IT WOULD SEEM SO.
HOW IS IT THAT NO ONE NOTICED?
HOW DID YOU NOT NOTICE?
WHAT DID YOU SAY?
YOU HEARD ME. LITTLE MISS PERFECT IS THROWING BLAME AROUND FOR US NOT KNOWING THE LITTLE GUY WAS MISSING. YOU KNOW, BECAUSE YOU CARE, RIGHT?
IT'S TRUE, NONE OF US NOTICED, BUT...
...NEITHER DID YOU.
I MEANT MORE LIKE WHY HAVEN'T ANY OF THE ADULTS NOTICED!
UH-HUH. SURE.
DON'T TALK TO HER LIKE THAT, YOU PIECE OF--
KRAK
OOOF!

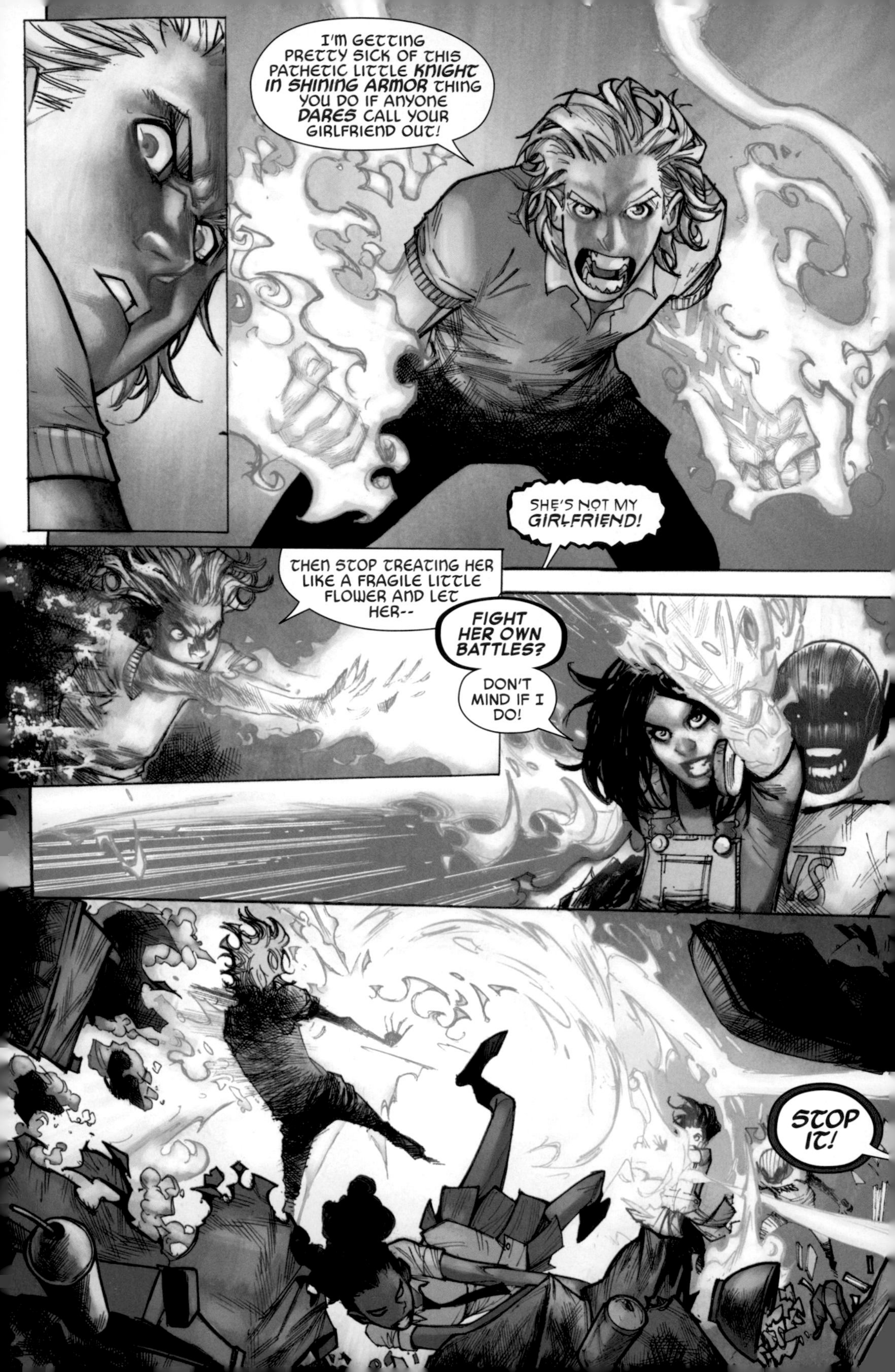

I'M GETTING PRETTY SICK OF THIS PATHETIC LITTLE KNIGHT IN SHINING ARMOR THING YOU DO IF ANYONE DARES CALL YOUR GIRLFRIEND OUT!
SHE'S NOT MY GIRLFRIEND!
THEN STOP TREATING HER LIKE A FRAGILE LITTLE FLOWER AND LET HER--
FIGHT HER OWN BATTLES?
DON'T MIND IF I DO!
STOP IT!

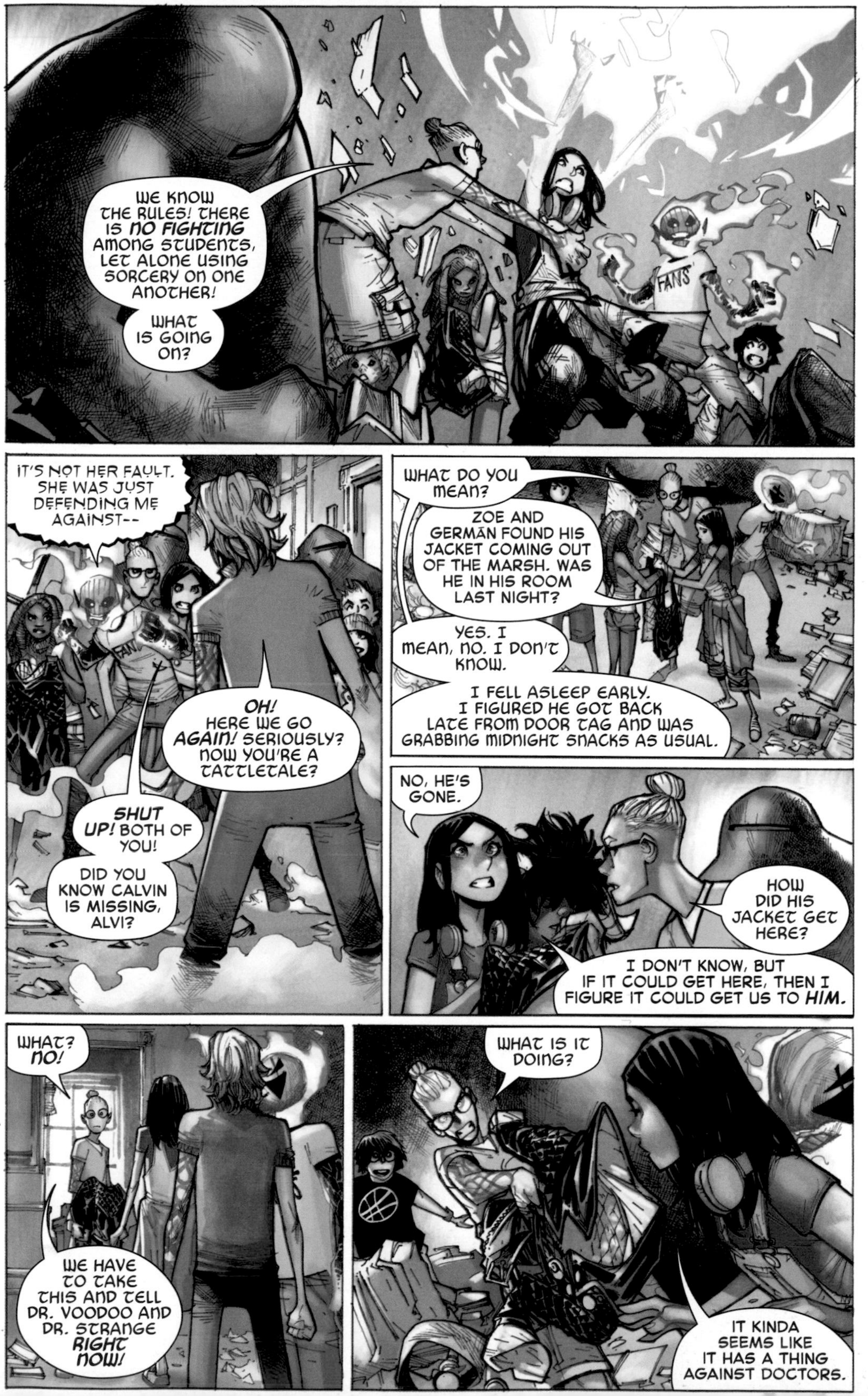
WE KNOW THE RULES! THERE IS NO FIGHTING AMONG STUDENTS, LET ALONE USING SORCERY ON ONE ANOTHER!
WHAT IS GOING ON?
FANS
IT'S NOT HER FAULT. SHE WAS JUST DEFENDING ME AGAINST--
OH! HERE WE GO AGAIN! SERIOUSLY? NOW YOU'RE A TATTLETALE?
SHUT UP! BOTH OF YOU!
DID YOU KNOW CALVIN IS MISSING, ALVI?
WHAT DO YOU MEAN?
ZOE AND GERMÁN FOUND HIS JACKET COMING OUT OF THE MARSH. WAS HE IN HIS ROOM LAST NIGHT?
YES. I MEAN, NO. I DON'T KNOW.
I FELL ASLEEP EARLY. I FIGURED HE GOT BACK LATE FROM DOOR TAG AND WAS GRABBING MIDNIGHT SNACKS AS USUAL.
NO, HE'S GONE.
HOW DID HIS JACKET GET HERE?
I DON'T KNOW, BUT IF IT COULD GET HERE, THEN I FIGURE IT COULD GET US TO HIM.
WHAT? NO!
WE HAVE TO TAKE THIS AND TELL DR. VOODOO AND DR. STRANGE RIGHT NOW!
WHAT IS IT DOING?
IT KINDA SEEMS LIKE IT HAS A THING AGAINST DOCTORS.

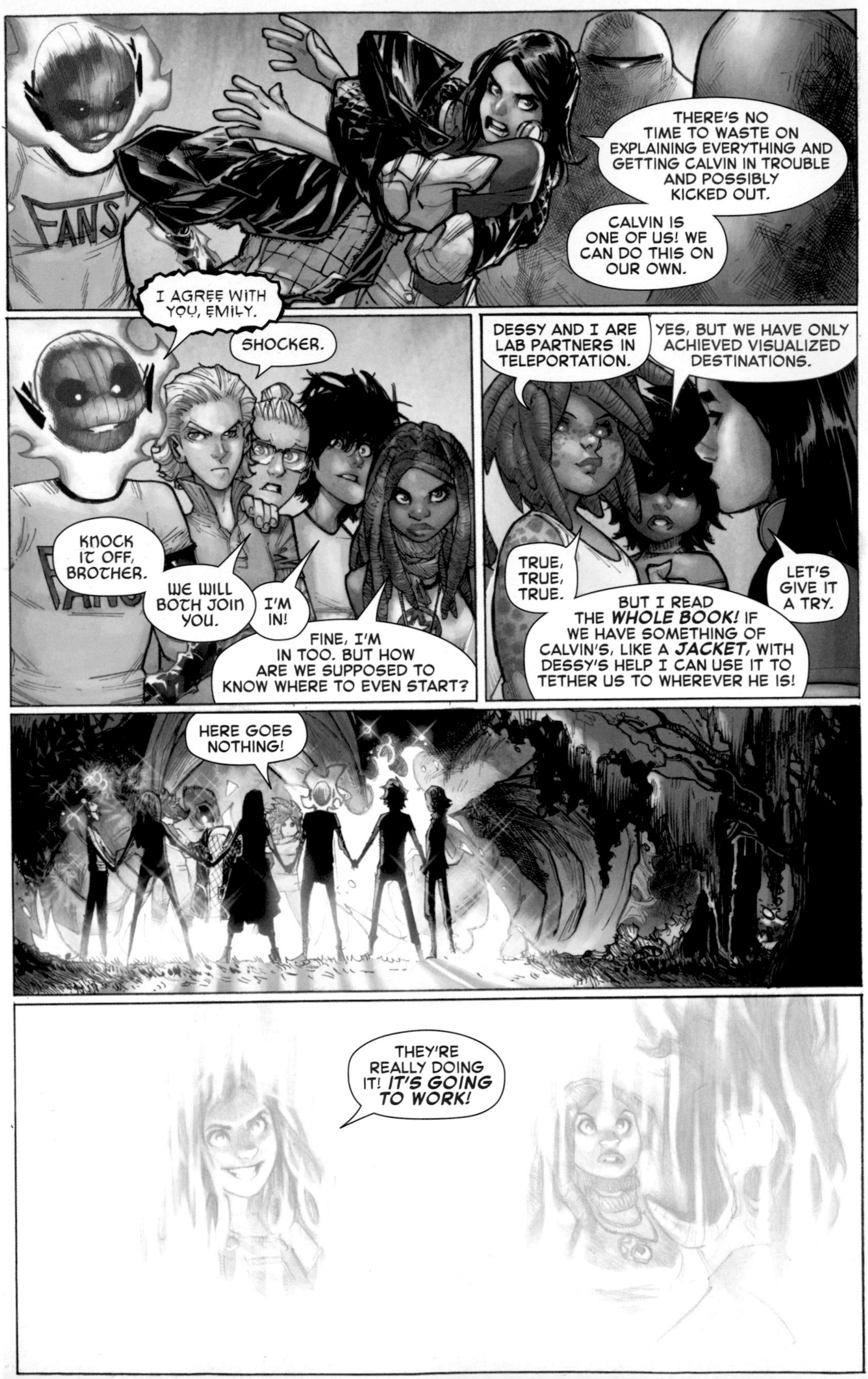
THERE'S NO TIME TO WASTE ON EXPLAINING EVERYTHING AND GETTING CALVIN IN TROUBLE AND POSSIBLY KICKED OUT.
CALVIN IS ONE OF US! WE CAN DO THIS ON OUR OWN.
I AGREE WITH YOU, EMILY.
SHOCKER.
KNOCK IT OFF, BROTHER.
WE WILL BOTH JOIN YOU.
I'M IN!
FINE, I'M IN TOO. BUT HOW ARE WE SUPPOSED TO KNOW WHERE TO EVEN START?
DESSY AND I ARE LAB PARTNERS IN TELEPORTATION.
YES, BUT WE HAVE ONLY ACHIEVED VISUALIZED DESTINATIONS.
TRUE, TRUE, TRUE.
BUT I READ THE *WHOLE BOOK!* IF WE HAVE SOMETHING OF CALVIN'S, LIKE A *JACKET,* WITH DESSY'S HELP I CAN USE IT TO TETHER US TO WHEREVER HE IS!
LET'S GIVE IT A TRY.
HERE GOES NOTHING!
THEY'RE REALLY DOING IT! *IT'S GOING TO WORK!*

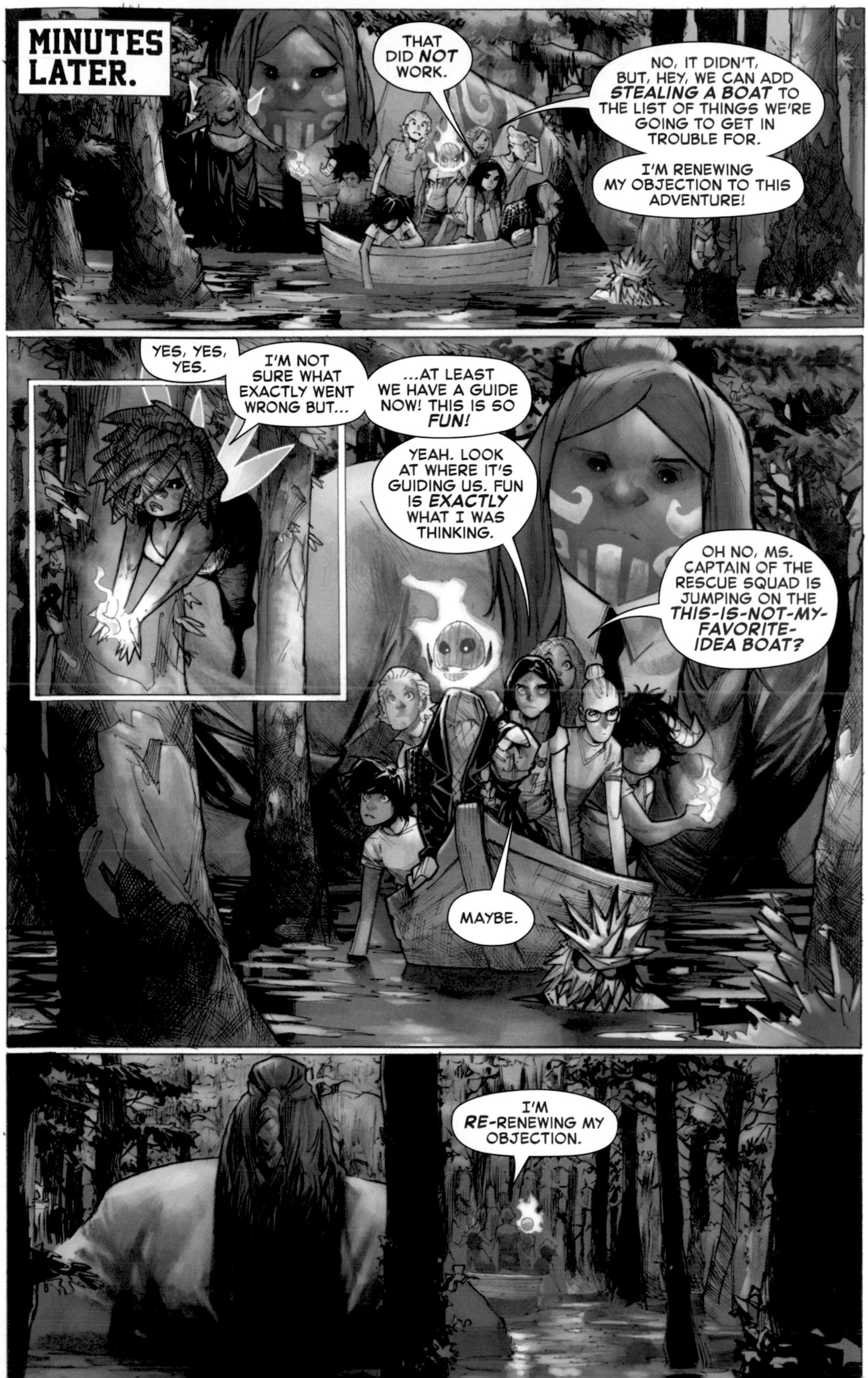
MINUTES LATER.
THAT DID NOT WORK.
NO, IT DIDN'T, BUT, HEY, WE CAN ADD STEALING A BOAT TO THE LIST OF THINGS WE'RE GOING TO GET IN TROUBLE FOR.
I'M RENEWING MY OBJECTION TO THIS ADVENTURE!
YES, YES, YES.
I'M NOT SURE WHAT EXACTLY WENT WRONG BUT...
...AT LEAST WE HAVE A GUIDE NOW! THIS IS SO FUN!
YEAH. LOOK AT WHERE IT'S GUIDING US. FUN IS EXACTLY WHAT I WAS THINKING.
OH NO, MS. CAPTAIN OF THE RESCUE SQUAD IS JUMPING ON THE THIS-IS-NOT-MY-FAVORITE-IDEA BOAT?
MAYBE.
I'M RE-RENEWING MY OBJECTION.

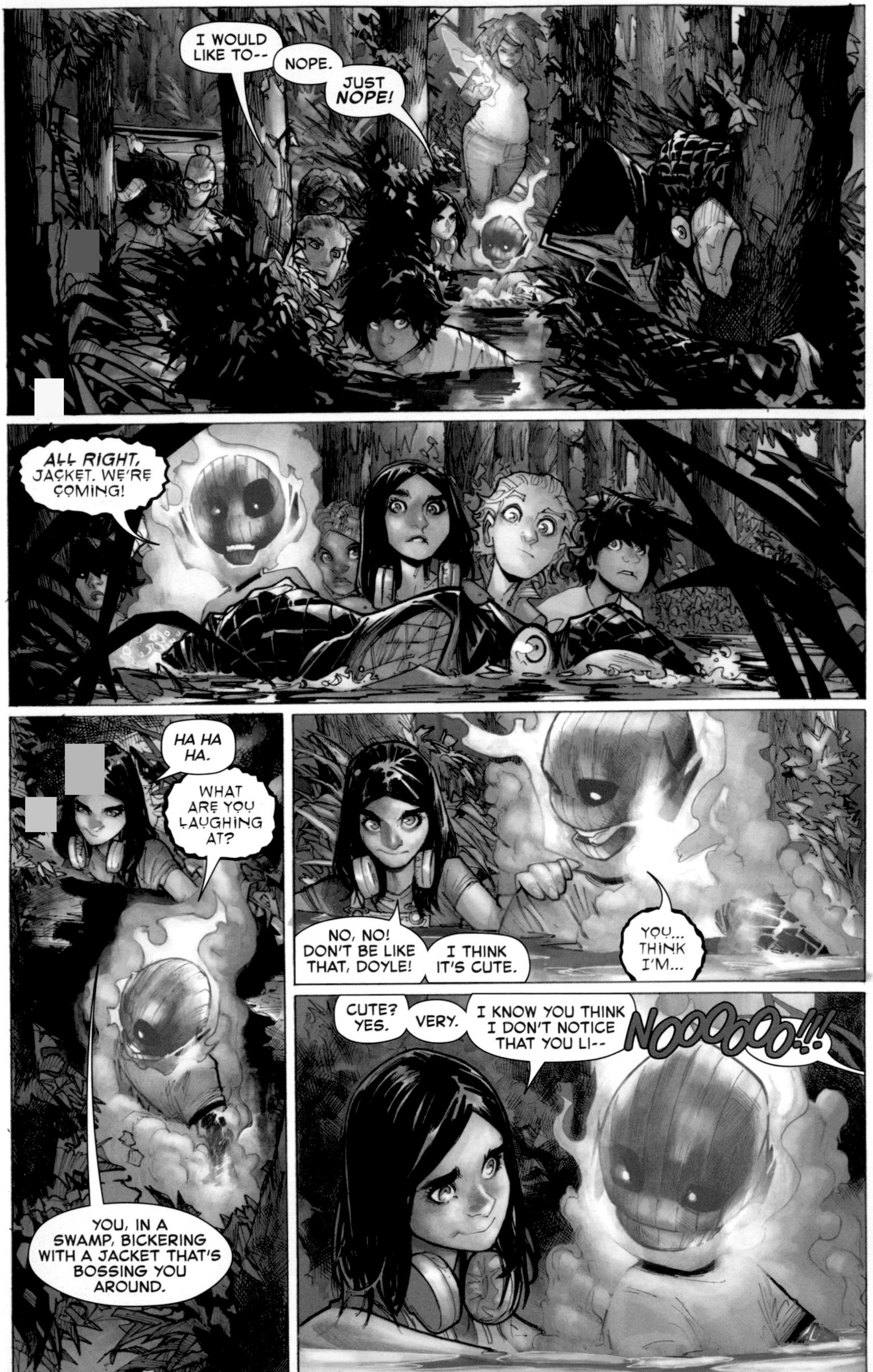
I WOULD LIKE TO--
NOPE.
JUST NOPE!
ALL RIGHT, JACKET. WE'RE COMING!
HA HA HA.
WHAT ARE YOU LAUGHING AT?
YOU, IN A SWAMP, BICKERING WITH A JACKET THAT'S BOSSING YOU AROUND.
NO, NO! DON'T BE LIKE THAT, DOYLE!
I THINK IT'S CUTE.
YOU... THINK I'M...
CUTE? YES.
VERY.
I KNOW YOU THINK I DON'T NOTICE THAT YOU LI--
NOOOOOOO!!!

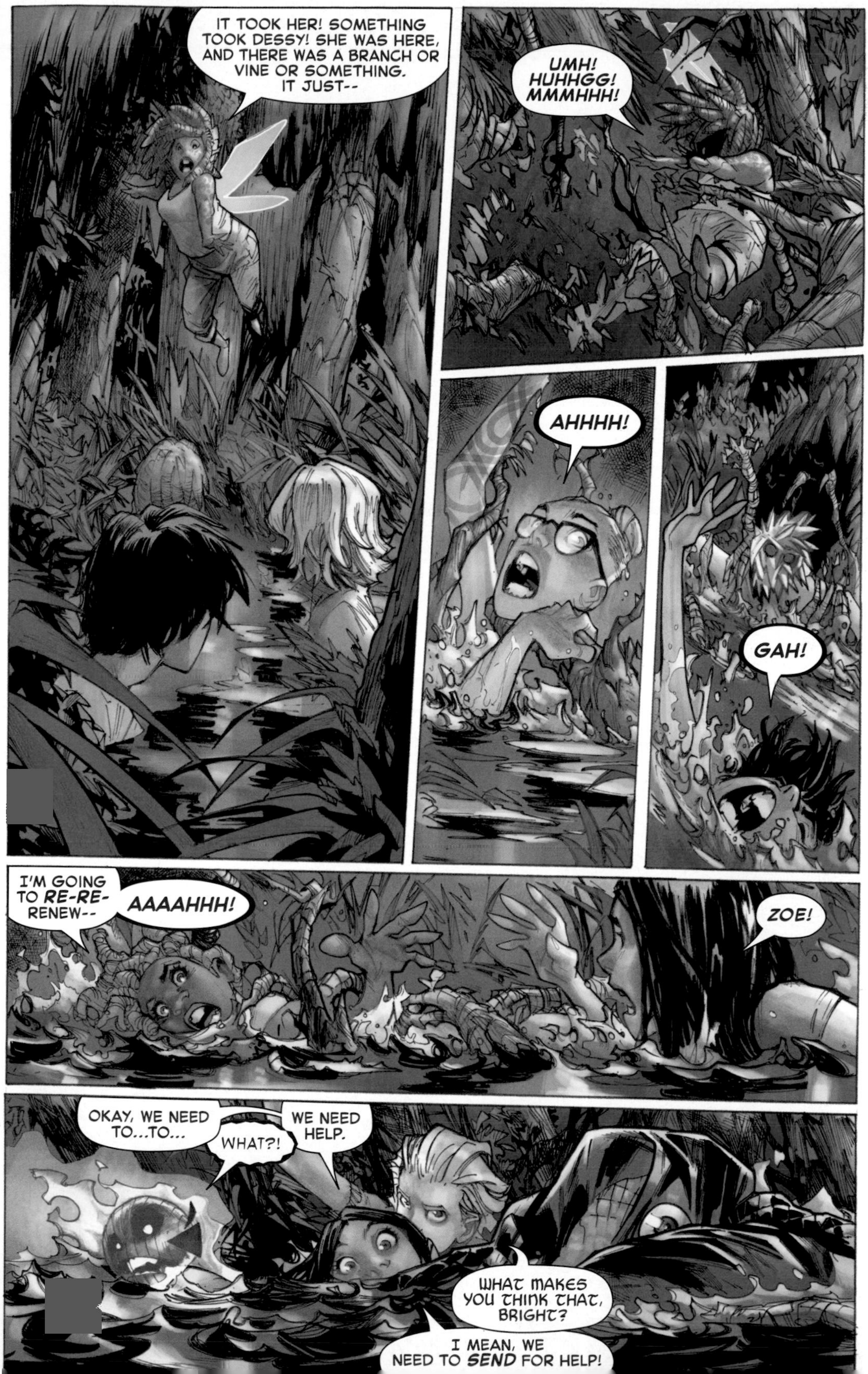
IT TOOK HER! SOMETHING TOOK DESSY! SHE WAS HERE, AND THERE WAS A BRANCH OR VINE OR SOMETHING. IT JUST--
UMH! HUHHGG! MMMHHH!
AHHHH!
GAH!
I'M GOING TO RE-RE-RENEW--
AAAAHHH!
ZOE!
OKAY, WE NEED TO...TO...
WHAT?!
WE NEED HELP.
WHAT MAKES YOU THINK THAT, BRIGHT?
I MEAN, WE NEED TO SEND FOR HELP!

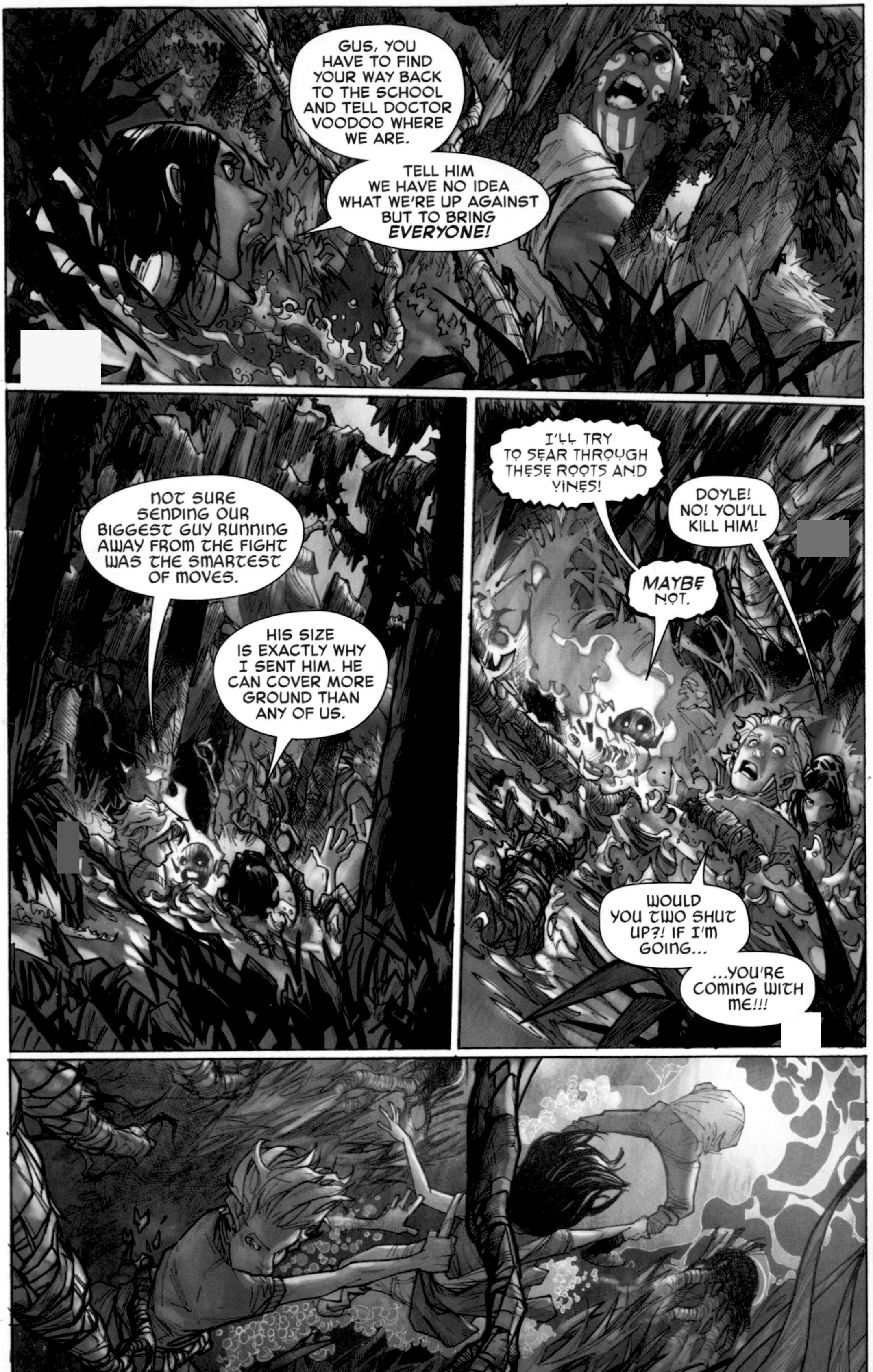
GUS, YOU HAVE TO FIND YOUR WAY BACK TO THE SCHOOL AND TELL DOCTOR VOODOO WHERE WE ARE.
TELL HIM WE HAVE NO IDEA WHAT WE'RE UP AGAINST BUT TO BRING *EVERYONE!*
NOT SURE SENDING OUR BIGGEST GUY RUNNING AWAY FROM THE FIGHT WAS THE SMARTEST OF MOVES.
HIS SIZE IS EXACTLY WHY I SENT HIM. HE CAN COVER MORE GROUND THAN ANY OF US.
I'LL TRY TO SEAR THROUGH THESE ROOTS AND VINES!
DOYLE! NO! YOU'LL KILL HIM!
MAYBE NOT.
WOULD YOU TWO SHUT UP?! IF I'M GOING...
...YOU'RE COMING WITH ME!!!

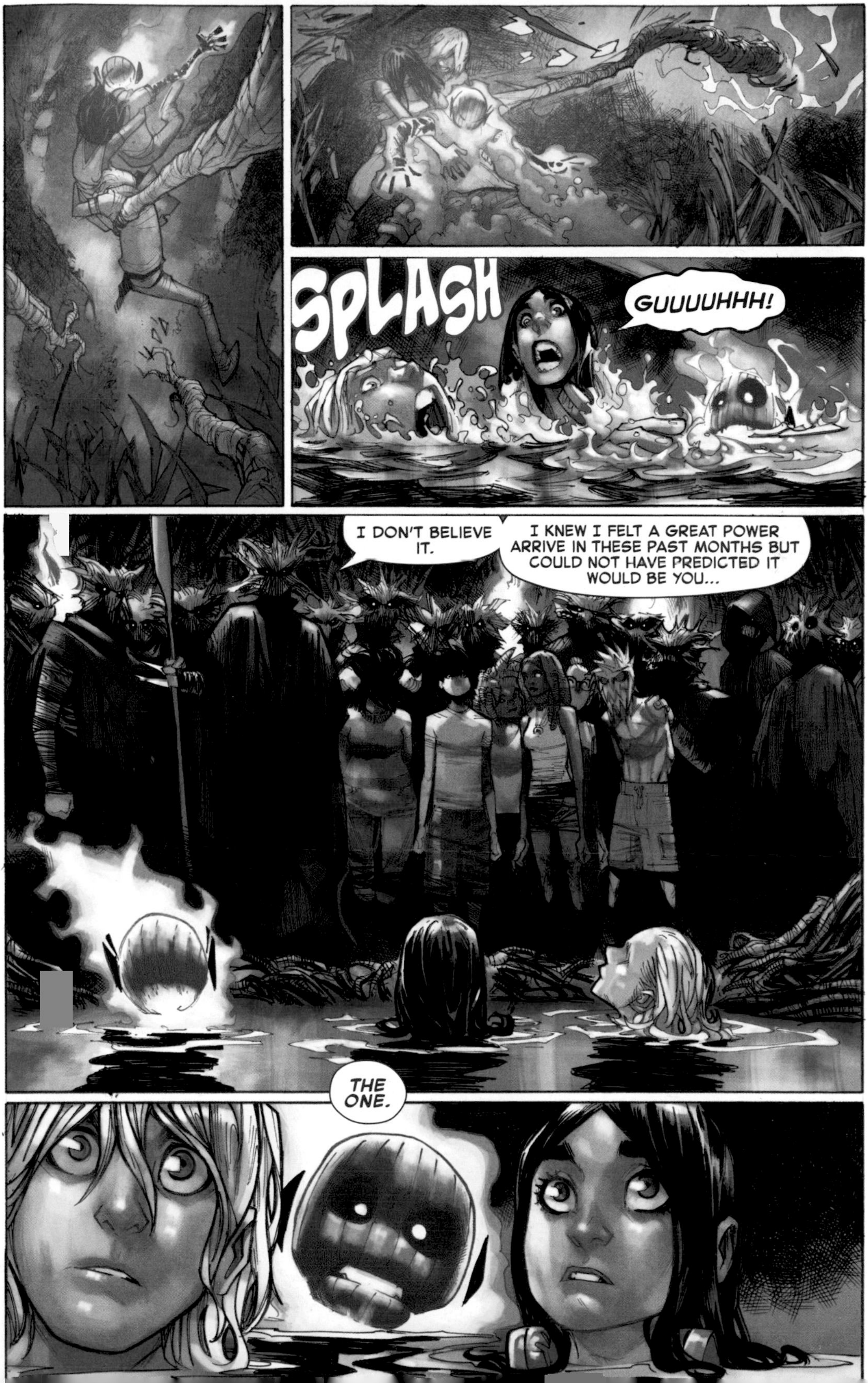
SPLASH
GUUUUHHH!
I DON'T BELIEVE IT.
I KNEW I FELT A GREAT POWER ARRIVE IN THESE PAST MONTHS BUT COULD NOT HAVE PREDICTED IT WOULD BE YOU...
THE ONE.

WHAT IS HE TALKING ABOUT?

I-- I DON'T KNOW.

HE'S SAYING THAT ONE OF US IS, YOU KNOW, *THE ONE.*

SAVIOR. HERO. DEFEATER OF ALL EVIL AND WHATNOT.

SO, ONE OF *US* IS *THE ONE?*

HA. MAYBE. MAYBE NOT. ASGARD HAS THREE *THE ONES* IN EVERY CASTLE IN THE REALM.

ᚦᚹᚠᚴᚺᚾᚴᚷᚺᚴᛗ ᛃᚾᚤᚥᛗᚤᛒᚠᚴᚱᛗ ᚤᚱᛗᚦ.

THEN WHY ARE THEY GETTING ALL CHANTY?

FOR TOO LONG THE HOLLOW HAS BEEN DEPRIVED OF THE NOURISHMENT WE NEED AND *DESERVE.* WE ARE EXCITED THAT WILL ALL CHANGE TONIGHT.

YEAH, I'M NOT SURE WHAT ANY OF THAT MEANT, BUT I DO FEEL LIKE NONE OF *US* ARE OKAY WITH IT.

WHO'S WITH ME?

YOU KNOW I AM.

SHOCKER.

BUT YES, ME TOO.

WHAT ABOUT YOU GUYS?

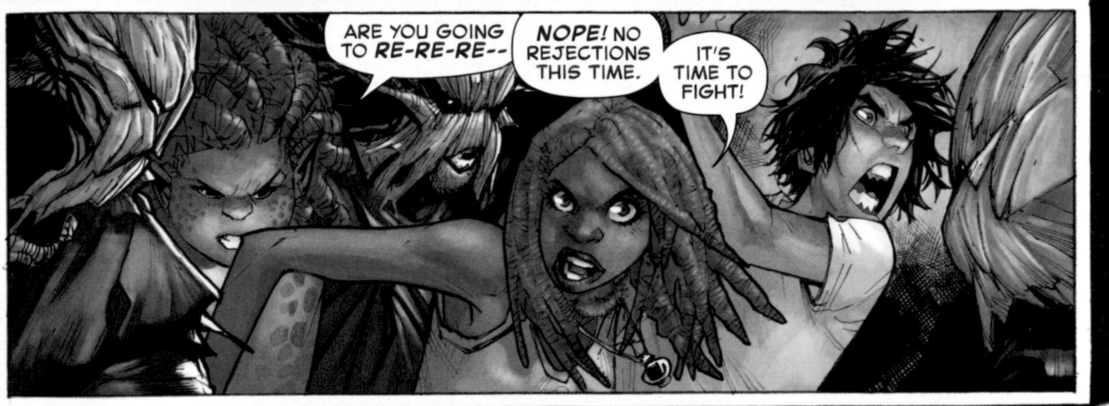
ARE YOU GOING TO RE-RE-RE--
NOPE! NO REJECTIONS THIS TIME.
IT'S TIME TO FIGHT!
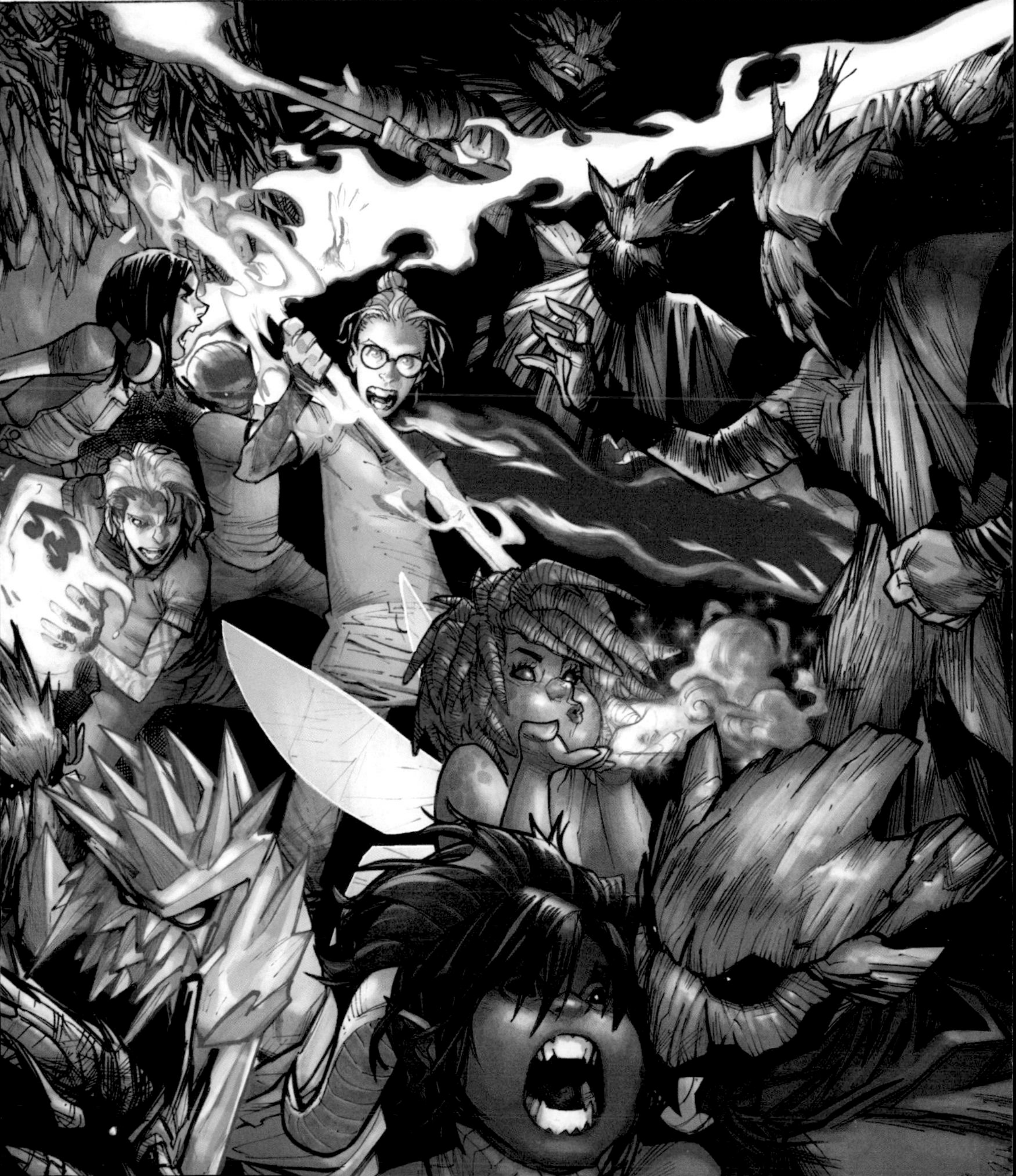

https://mail.strange-academy.com/mail.xm4.av16/#inbox

STRANGE Academy

New | Reply | Reply All | Forward | Trash

search

wmaximoff@strange-academy.com

Inbox (128)
Drafts
Deleted Items
EoCM
Avengers

Virtual Chat
Astral Chat

Doyle Dormammu	**My Dad and the Dark Dimension Report** Report Submission is available on the portal. Please note, this was uploaded past the due...	1:13 a.m. Fri
Iric "The Most Dashing Dude in...	**Asgardian Theory of Ragnarok Report** Report Submission is available on the portal.	11:58 p.m. Thu
Carol Danvers	**A-Force Assemble!** WANDA! We locked down a date for girls' night AND YOU BETTER NOT...	11:32 p.m. Thu
Zoe Laveau	**The Art of Magic in New Orleans Culture Report** Report Submission is available on the portal.	2:34 p.m. Thu
Pietro Maximoff	**(no subject)** Wandagivemeacallimmediatelydontdawdle (End Message)	12:01 p.m. Thu
Steven Rogers	**Avengers Reserve Member Training** Dear Wanda, I wanted to send you a personal reminder for this year's Annual Avengers...	12:01 p.m. Thu
GUSLAUG	**The Varying Degrees of Ice in Magic Report** Report Submission is available on the portal.	3:13 p.m. Wed
Iric "The Most Dashing Dude in...	**Submission Portal** Hey Prof, I still can't seem to find the submission portal you mentioned in class again today...	12:30 p.m. Wed
Henry McCoy	**Krakoa Beckons!** Dearest Wanda, Hank again. I know you're not TECHNICALLY a mutant, but I'd LOVE for you to try a Krakoa gate...	11:45 a.m. Wed
SA Portal	**REMINDER: Elements of Chaos Magic Today @ 12:30 p.m.** This an automated reminder for your upcoming class. If you need to cancel, please let...	11:30 a.m. Wed
Emily Bright	**Chaos Magic and the Impact on the Multiverse Report** Report Submission is available on the portal.	12:26 a.m. Wed
Magneto@krakoa.mut	**Quality Time** Wanda, I know I may not be your ACTUAL father, but I'd still love to catch up with you and Pietro...	12:25 a.m. Wed
ALVI	**Asgardian Philosophy of Ragnarok Report** Report Submission is available on the... portal.	12:14 a.m. Wed
Shaylee Moonpeddle	**Magic of Otherworld Report** Report Submission is available on the portal.	12:00 a.m. Wed

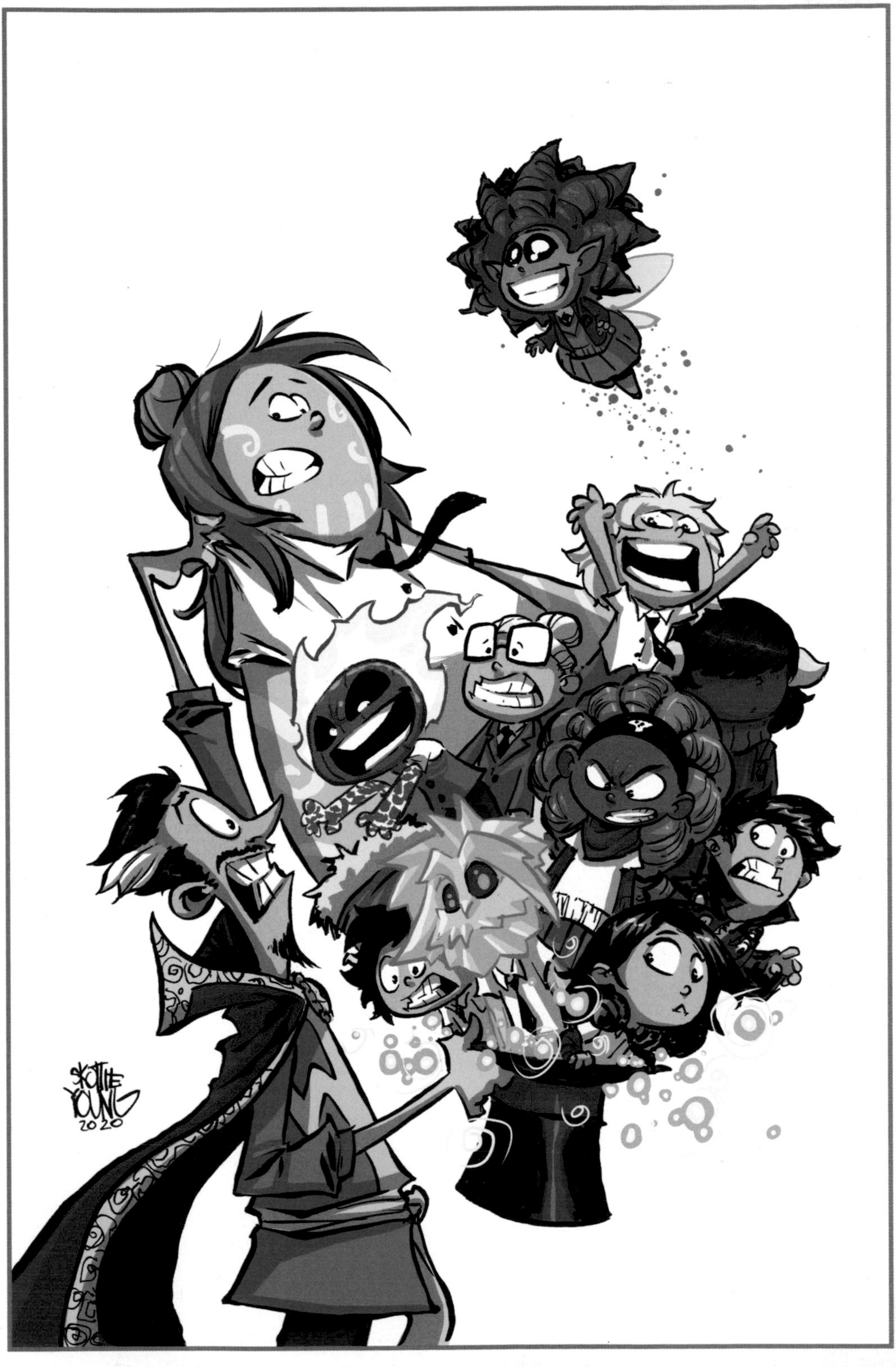
SKOTTIE YOUNG
2020

#1 VARIANT BY **Skottie Young**

6

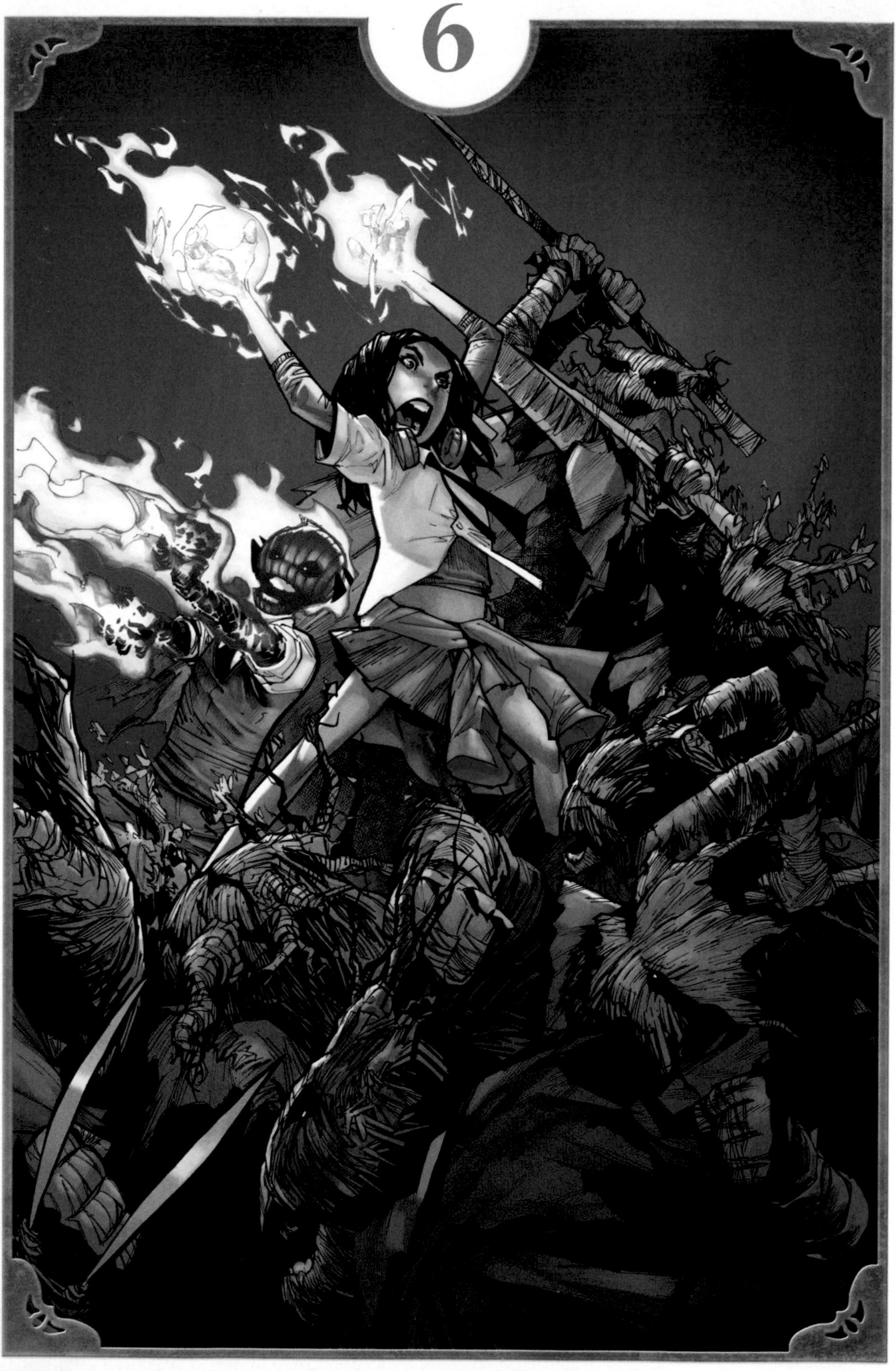

COVER ALL THREE OF YOUR EYES, ZELMA. I HAVE A FEELING THIS ONE IS GOING TO MAKE A BIT OF MESS.

ILLYANA, NO!

ᛋᚳᚱᚠᛗᚱᛁᚠᚦᚦᚱᛋᛗ ᛋᚢᚠᚱᚱᛋᚱᛗᚠ ᚠᛋᛦᚣᚢᛦᚠᚩ· ᛋᚢᚲᛒᚾᚱᚠᚾᛗᚲᛒᛦᛋᚠ ᚩᚱᛒᚢᛗᛋᚱᚢᚾᚠᚩ ᛋᚢᚦᚱᚲᚠᚾᛗᚠᛗ ᚩᚱᚳᚺᚱᛒᛞᚾᚺᛗᚩ ᚠᚪᚳᚱᛒᚾᛗᛗᛁᚱᛗ·

ᚺᚠᚠᚳᛁ ᚩᛦᚱᛁᚱᛋᚠᚳ· ᚺᚲᚩᚠᚾᚠᚩᛦᛏ ᚦᚠᚪᚳᛋᛦᚳ ᛋᚱᛈ·

ᚦᚱᚳᚱᚱᚠᚠ ᛒᚱᛗᚾᚠᚠᚠ ᛋᚠᚷᚾᚦ ᛗᛒᚠᚦᛁᚱᛒ· ᚩᚱᛗᛁ ᚳᛦᛒᚠ ᛋᛒᚾᚦᚱ·

ᛦᛋ ᚦᛦᚱᛒᛗᚱ·

UGH. THAT SMELLS DISGUSTING.

WHY WOULD YOU HAVE A *WHATEVER* THAT GROSS THING IS IN YOUR BAG???

BECAUSE IF WE'RE GOING TO FIND WHERE CALVIN WENT MISSING...

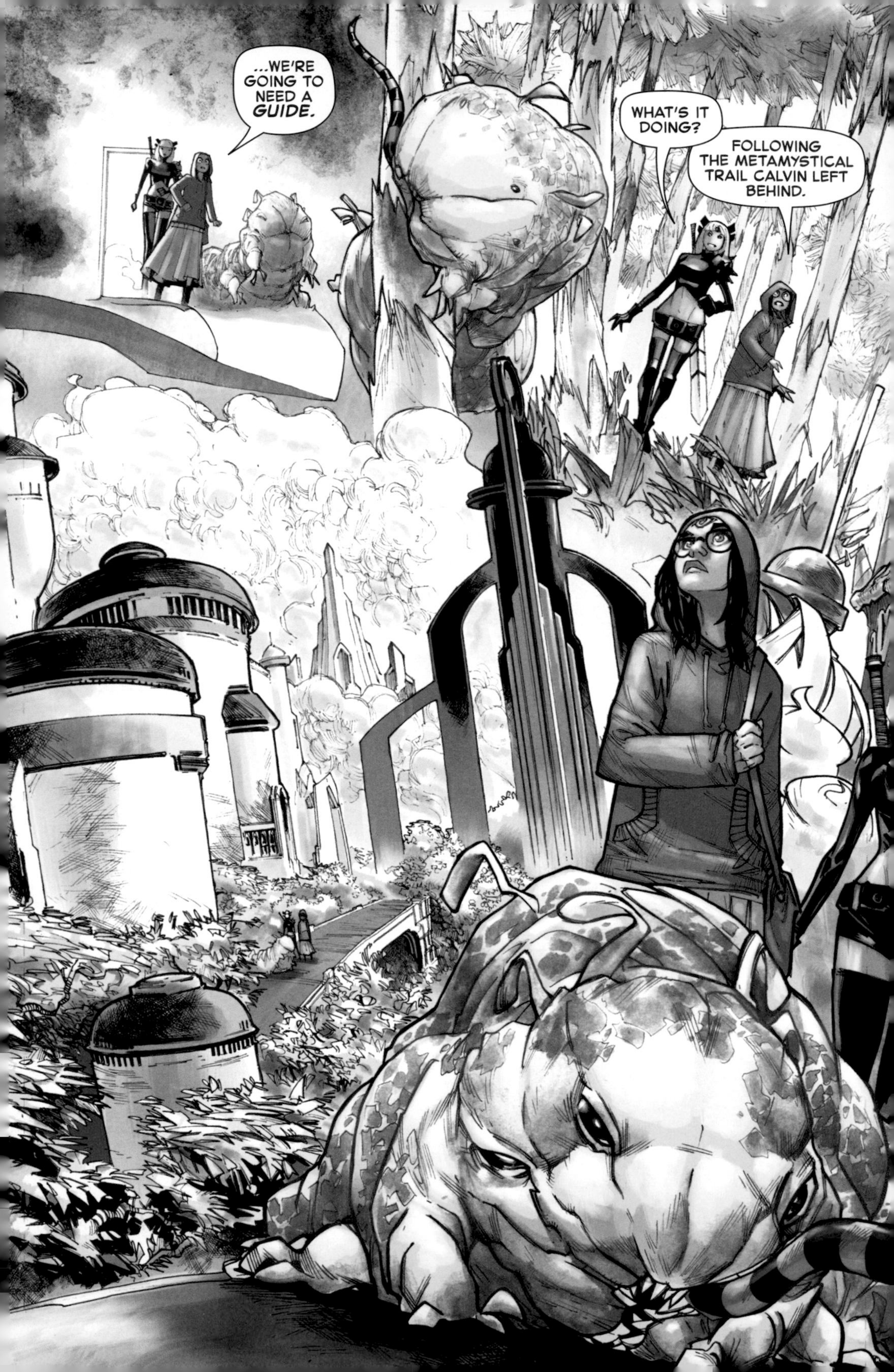
...WE'RE GOING TO NEED A GUIDE.
WHAT'S IT DOING?
FOLLOWING THE METAMYSTICAL TRAIL CALVIN LEFT BEHIND.

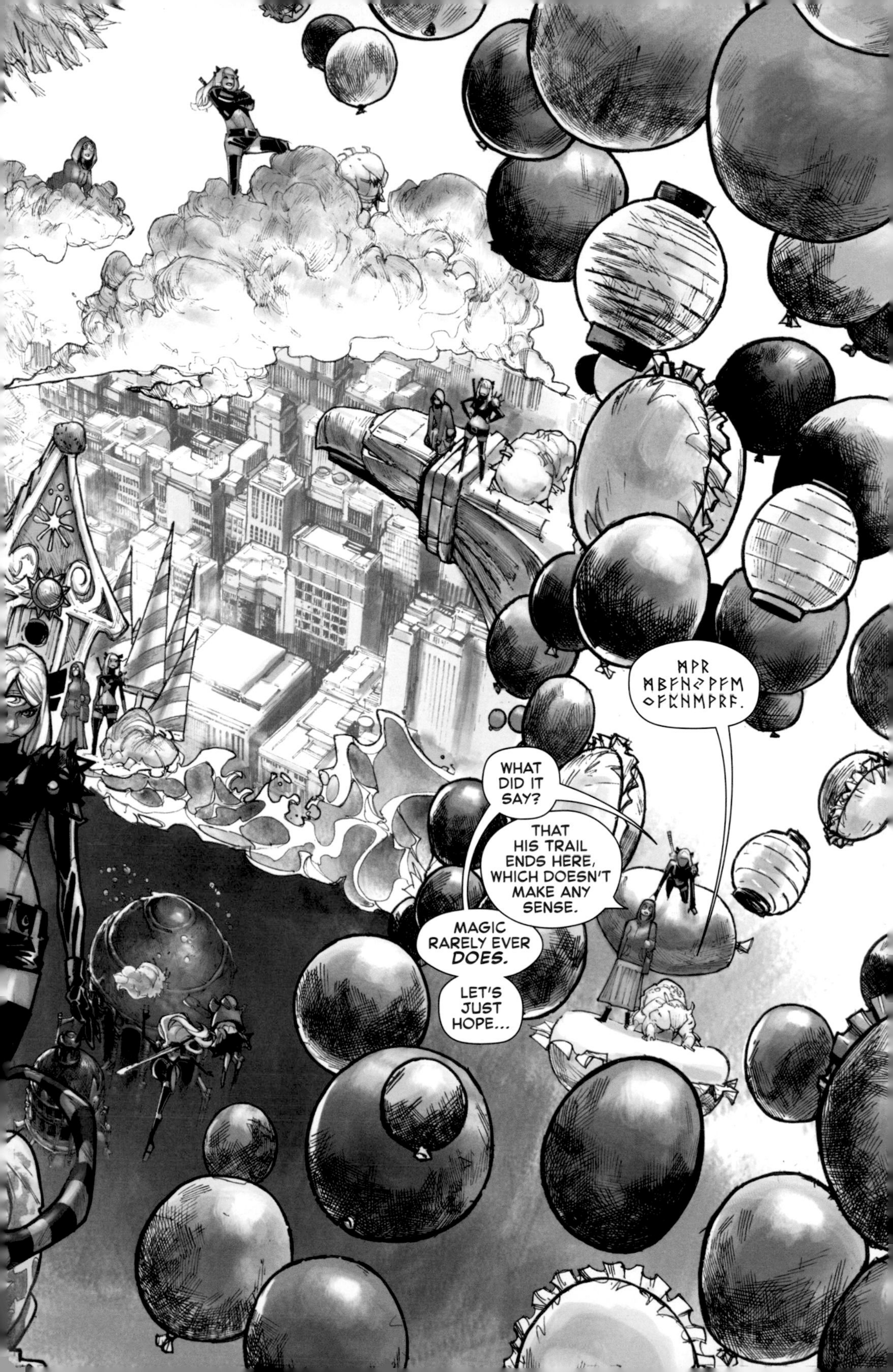
WHAT DID IT SAY?
THAT HIS TRAIL ENDS HERE, WHICH DOESN'T MAKE ANY SENSE.
MAGIC RARELY EVER *DOES.*
LET'S JUST HOPE...

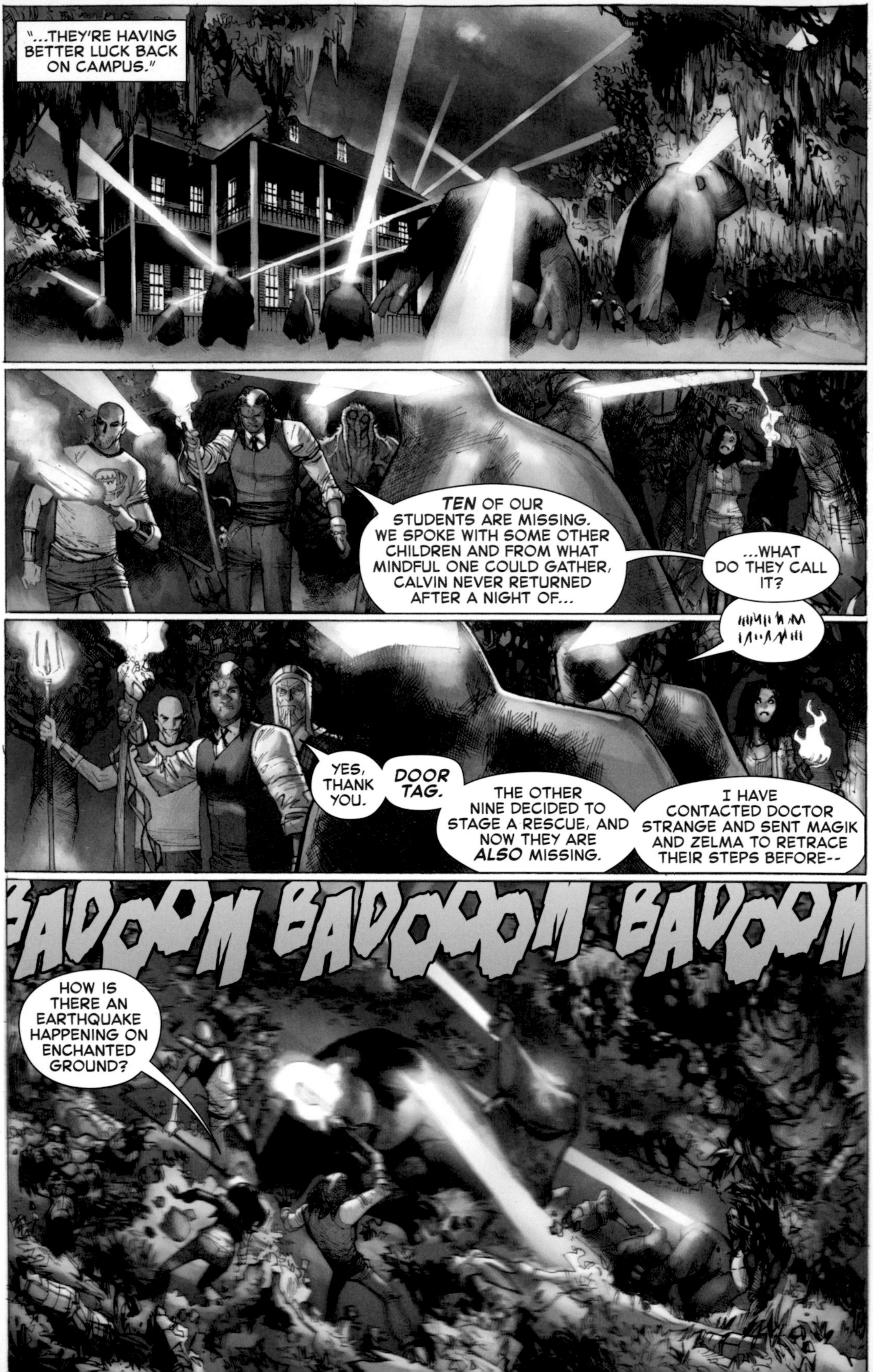
"...THEY'RE HAVING BETTER LUCK BACK ON CAMPUS."
TEN OF OUR STUDENTS ARE MISSING. WE SPOKE WITH SOME OTHER CHILDREN AND FROM WHAT MINDFUL ONE COULD GATHER, CALVIN NEVER RETURNED AFTER A NIGHT OF...
...WHAT DO THEY CALL IT?
YES, THANK YOU.
DOOR TAG.
THE OTHER NINE DECIDED TO STAGE A RESCUE, AND NOW THEY ARE ALSO MISSING.
I HAVE CONTACTED DOCTOR STRANGE AND SENT MAGIK AND ZELMA TO RETRACE THEIR STEPS BEFORE--
BADOOM BADOOOM BADOOM
HOW IS THERE AN EARTHQUAKE HAPPENING ON ENCHANTED GROUND?

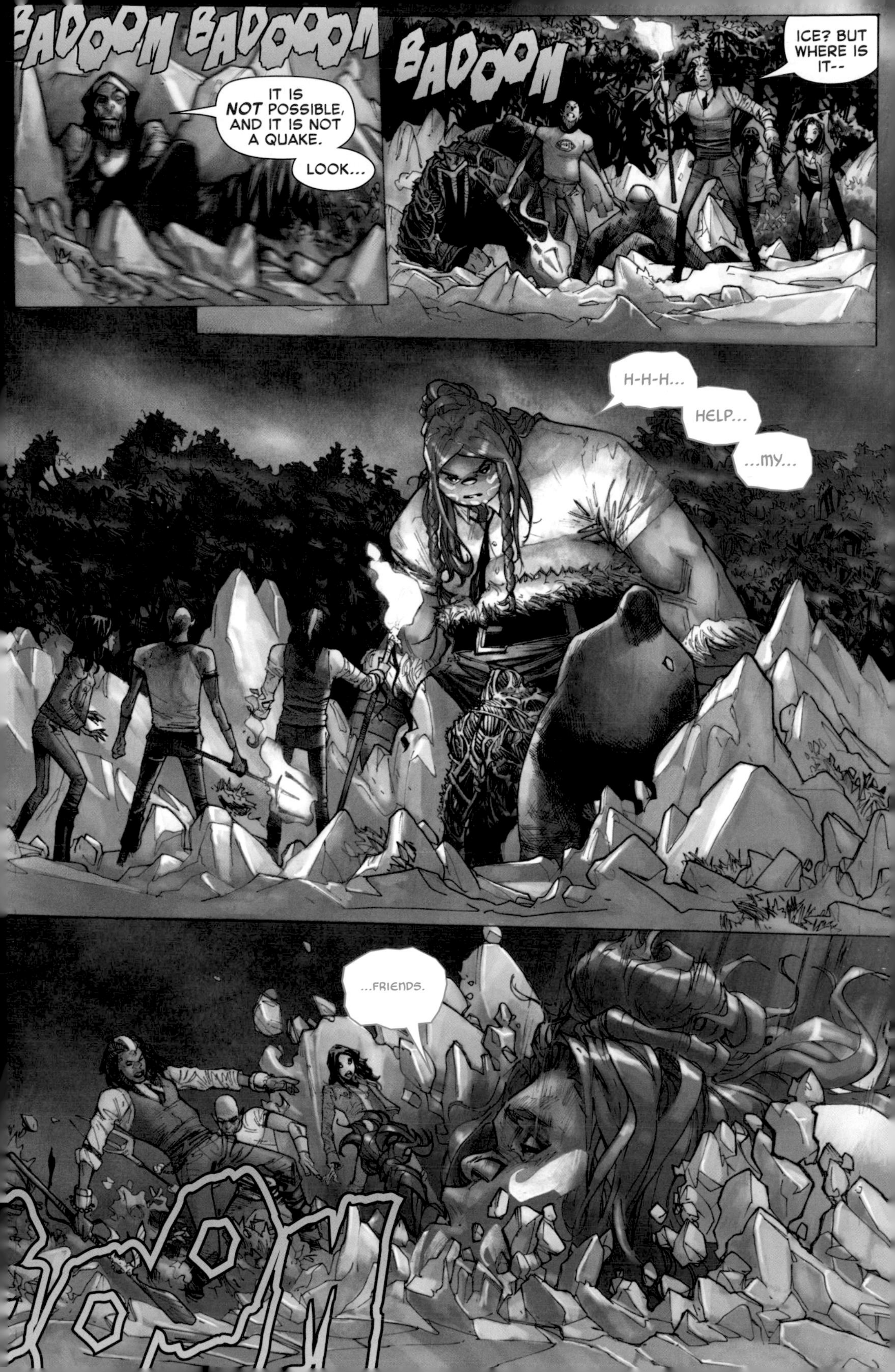
BADOOM BADOOOM
IT IS NOT POSSIBLE, AND IT IS NOT A QUAKE.
LOOK...
BADOOM
ICE? BUT WHERE IS IT--
H-H-H...
HELP...
...my...
...FRIENDS.
VOOM

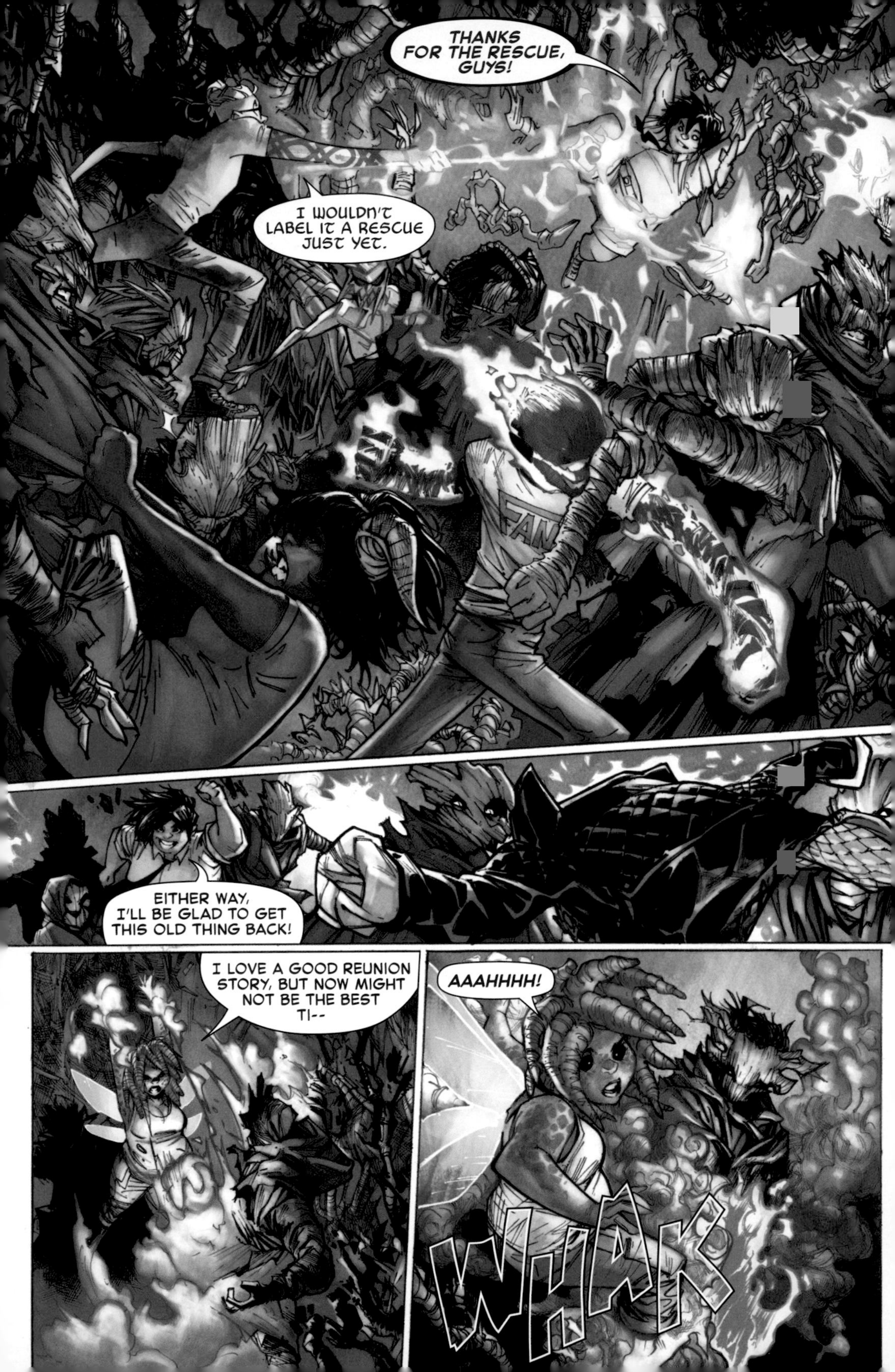
THANKS FOR THE RESCUE, GUYS!
I WOULDN'T LABEL IT A RESCUE JUST YET.
EITHER WAY, I'LL BE GLAD TO GET THIS OLD THING BACK!
I LOVE A GOOD REUNION STORY, BUT NOW MIGHT NOT BE THE BEST TI--
AAAHHHH!
WHAK

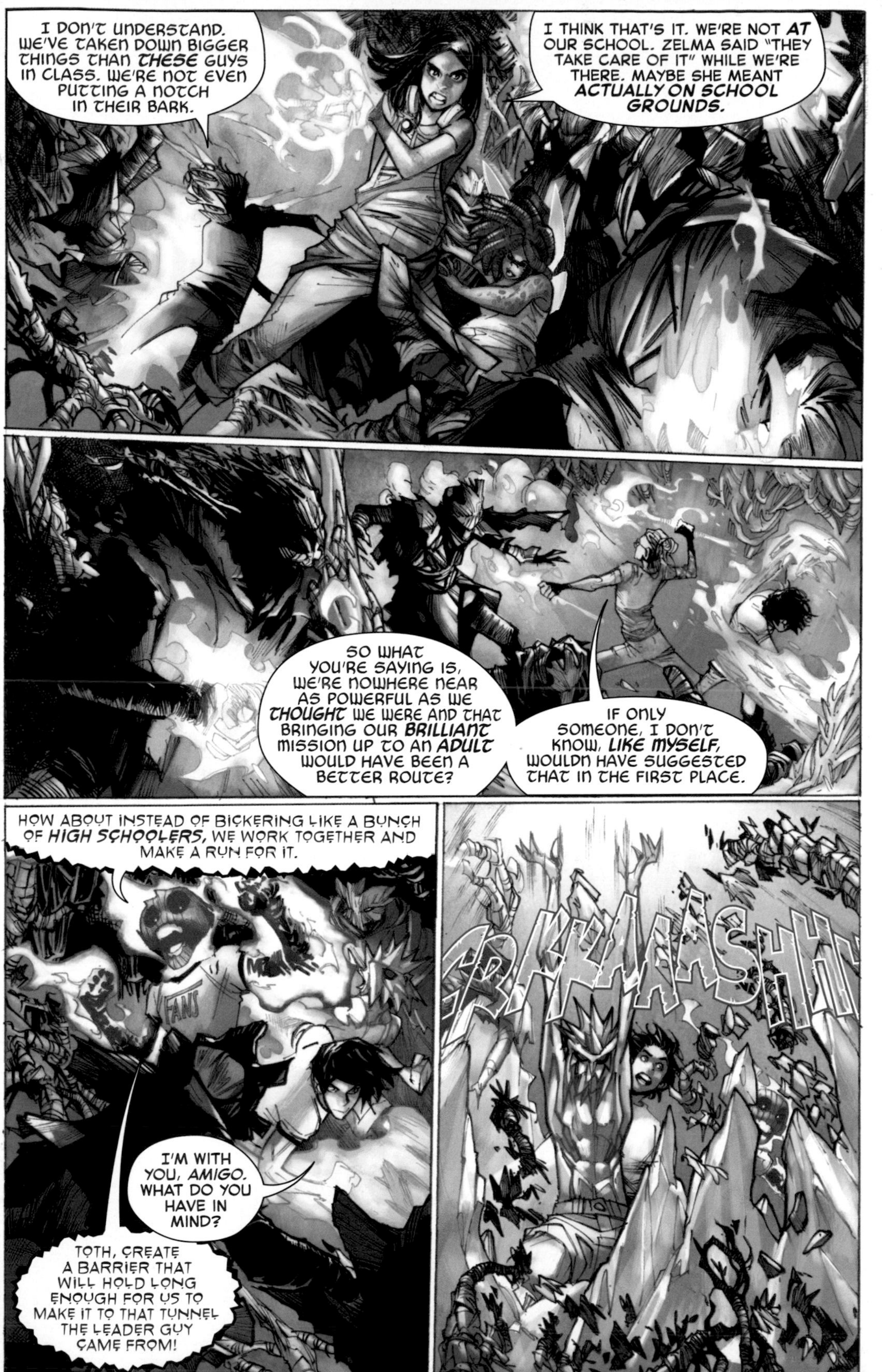
I DON'T UNDERSTAND. WE'VE TAKEN DOWN BIGGER THINGS THAN *THESE* GUYS IN CLASS. WE'RE NOT EVEN PUTTING A NOTCH IN THEIR BARK.
I THINK THAT'S IT. WE'RE NOT *AT* OUR SCHOOL. ZELMA SAID "THEY TAKE CARE OF IT" WHILE WE'RE THERE. MAYBE SHE MEANT *ACTUALLY ON SCHOOL GROUNDS.*
SO WHAT YOU'RE SAYING IS, WE'RE NOWHERE NEAR AS POWERFUL AS WE *THOUGHT* WE WERE AND THAT BRINGING OUR *BRILLIANT* MISSION UP TO AN *ADULT* WOULD HAVE BEEN A BETTER ROUTE?
IF ONLY SOMEONE, I DON'T KNOW, *LIKE MYSELF*, WOULDN HAVE SUGGESTED THAT IN THE FIRST PLACE.
HOW ABOUT INSTEAD OF BICKERING LIKE A BUNCH OF *HIGH SCHOOLERS*, WE WORK TOGETHER AND MAKE A RUN FOR IT.
FANS
I'M WITH YOU, *AMIGO*. WHAT DO YOU HAVE IN MIND?
TOTH, CREATE A BARRIER THAT WILL HOLD LONG ENOUGH FOR US TO MAKE IT TO THAT TUNNEL THE LEADER GUY CAME FROM!
CRKKAASHH

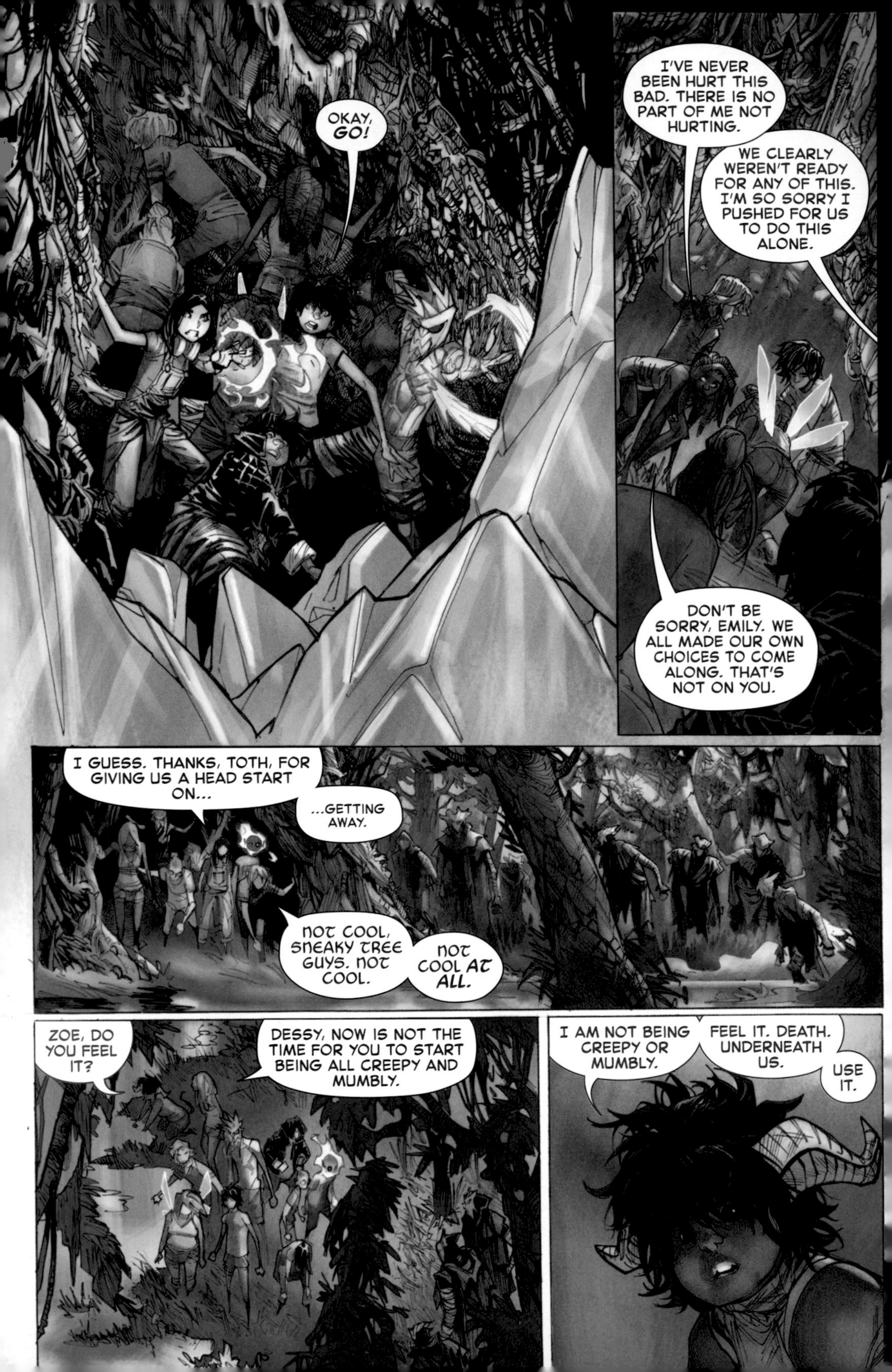
OKAY, GO!
I'VE NEVER BEEN HURT THIS BAD. THERE IS NO PART OF ME NOT HURTING.
WE CLEARLY WEREN'T READY FOR ANY OF THIS. I'M SO SORRY I PUSHED FOR US TO DO THIS ALONE.
DON'T BE SORRY, EMILY. WE ALL MADE OUR OWN CHOICES TO COME ALONG. THAT'S NOT ON YOU.
I GUESS. THANKS, TOTH, FOR GIVING US A HEAD START ON...
...GETTING AWAY.
NOT COOL, SNEAKY TREE GUYS. NOT COOL.
NOT COOL AT ALL.
ZOE, DO YOU FEEL IT?
DESSY, NOW IS NOT THE TIME FOR YOU TO START BEING ALL CREEPY AND MUMBLY.
I AM NOT BEING CREEPY OR MUMBLY.
FEEL IT. DEATH. UNDERNEATH US.
USE IT.

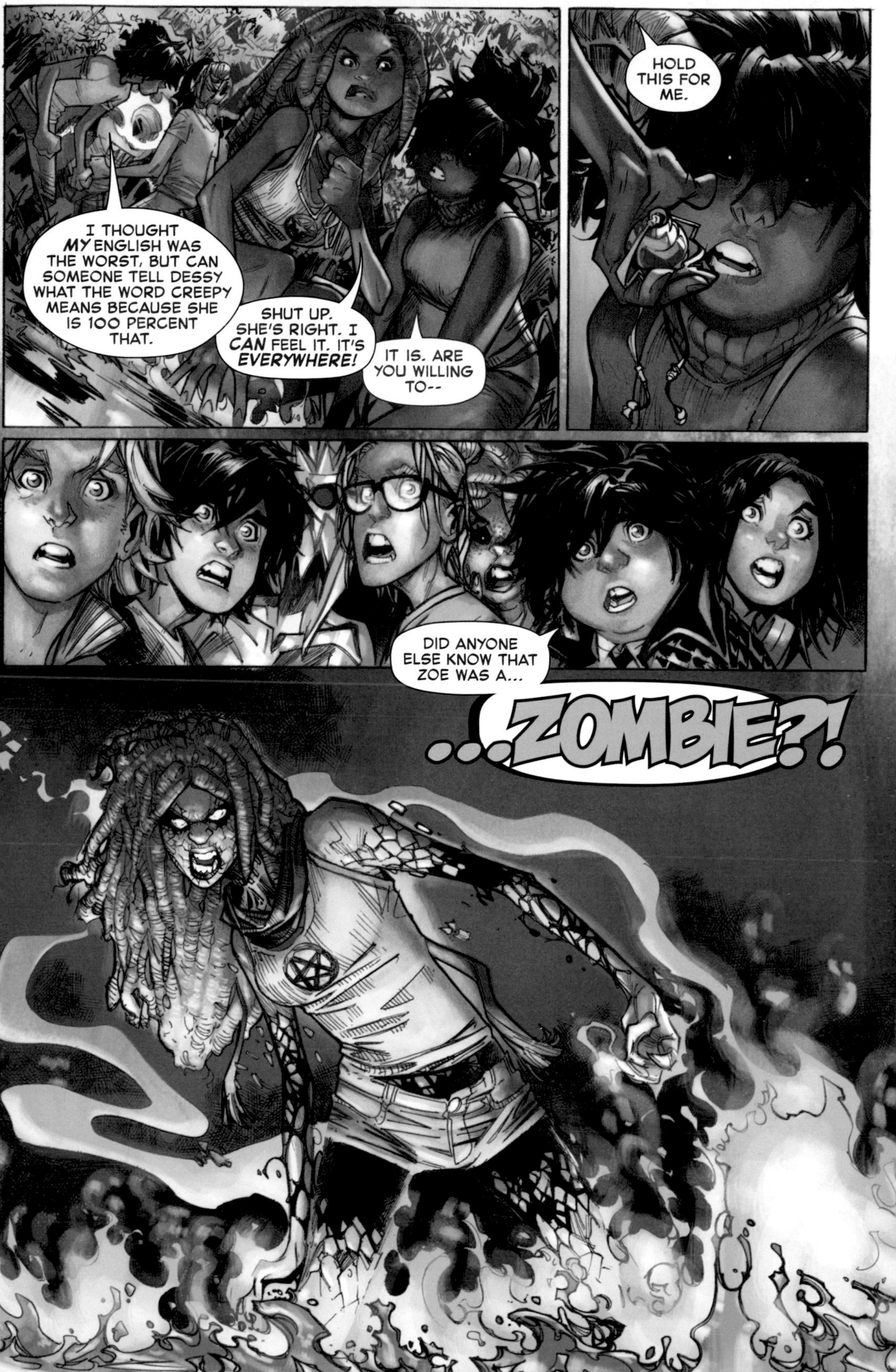
I THOUGHT MY ENGLISH WAS THE WORST, BUT CAN SOMEONE TELL DESSY WHAT THE WORD CREEPY MEANS BECAUSE SHE IS 100 PERCENT THAT.
SHUT UP. SHE'S RIGHT. I CAN FEEL IT. IT'S EVERYWHERE!
IT IS. ARE YOU WILLING TO--
HOLD THIS FOR ME.
DID ANYONE ELSE KNOW THAT ZOE WAS A...
...ZOMBIE?!

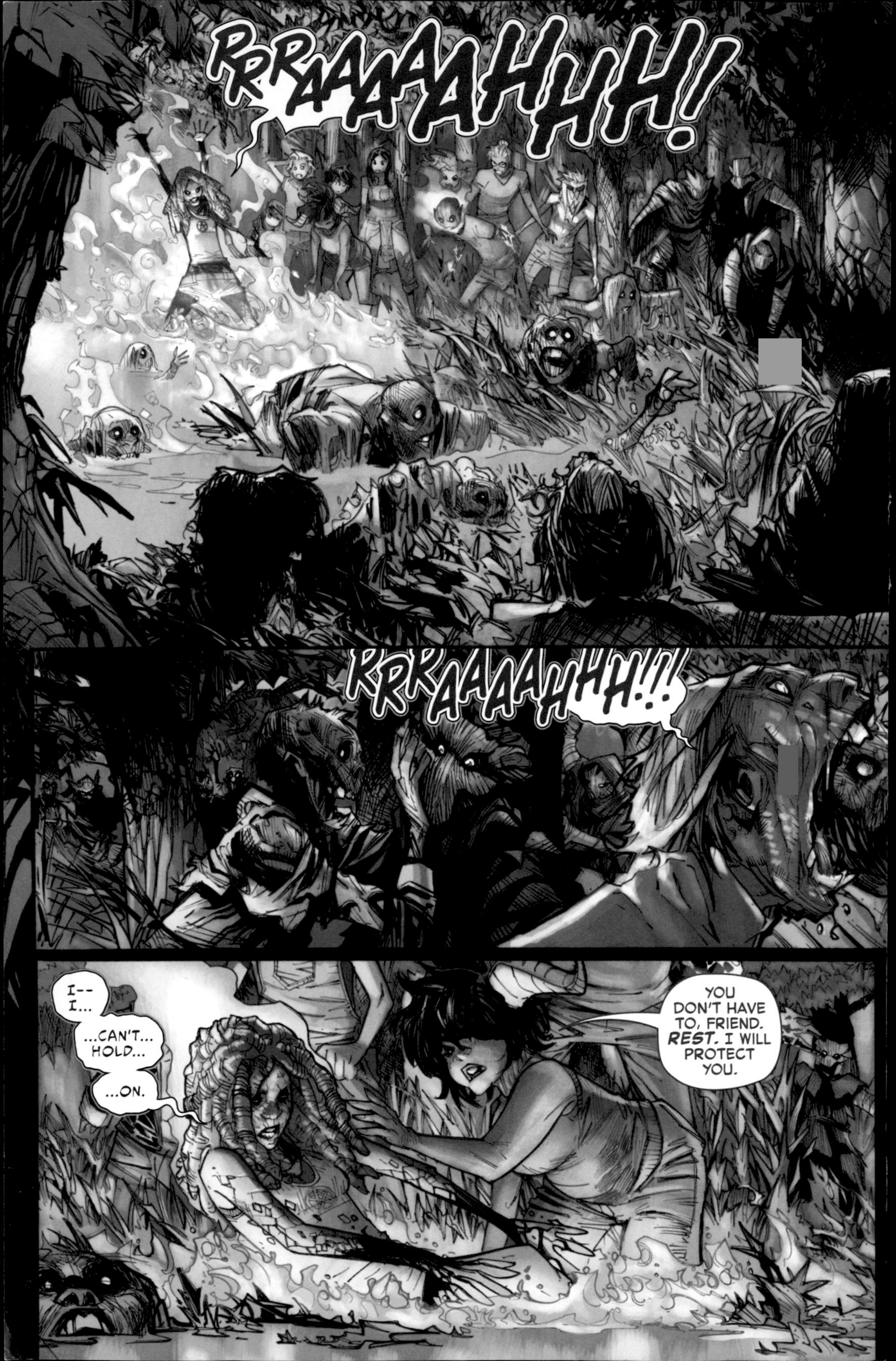
RRRAAAAAHHHH!
KRRAAAAHHH!!!
I-- I...
...CAN'T... HOLD...
...ON.
YOU DON'T HAVE TO, FRIEND. REST. I WILL PROTECT YOU.

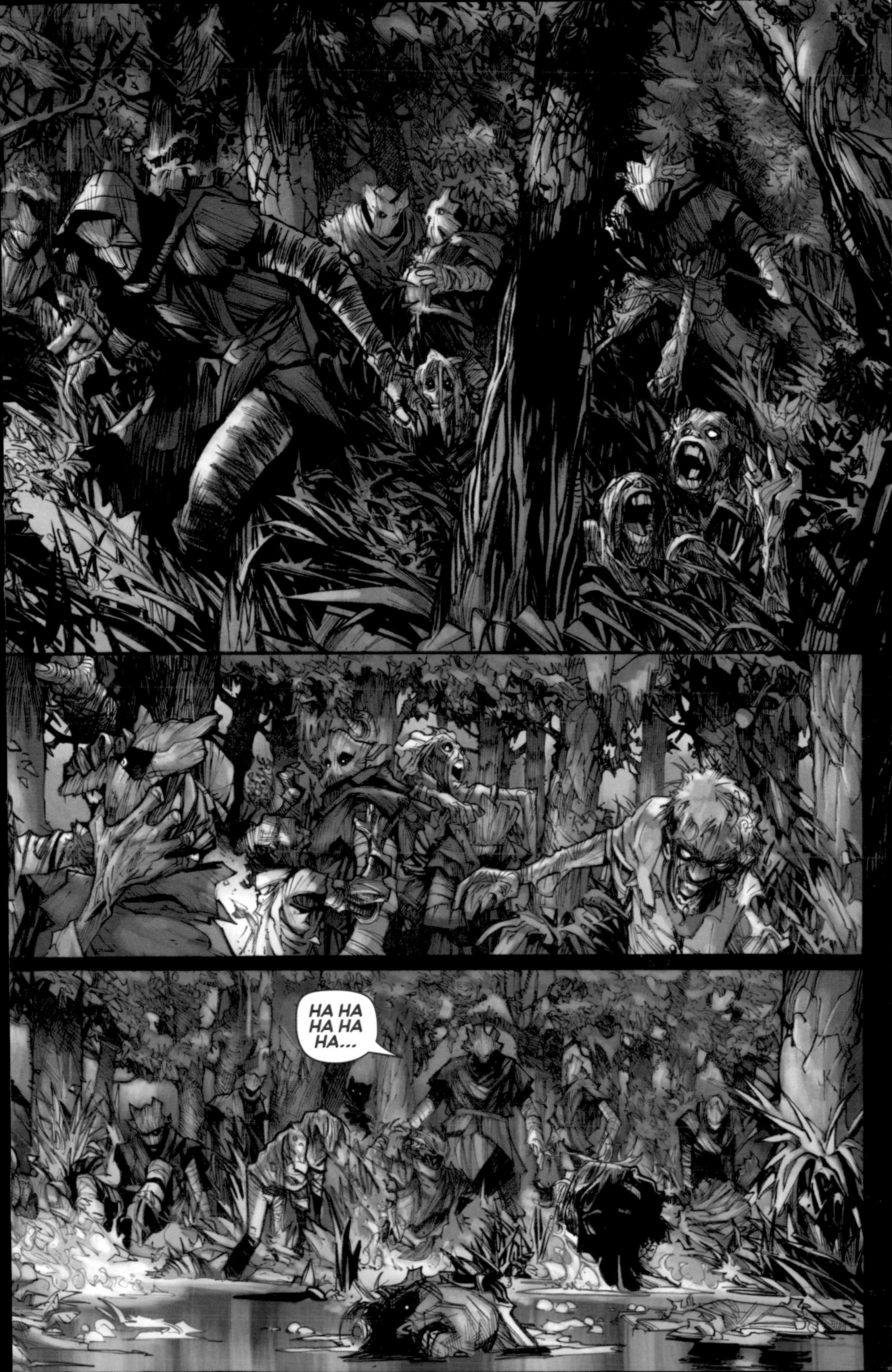
HA HA
HA HA HA
HA...

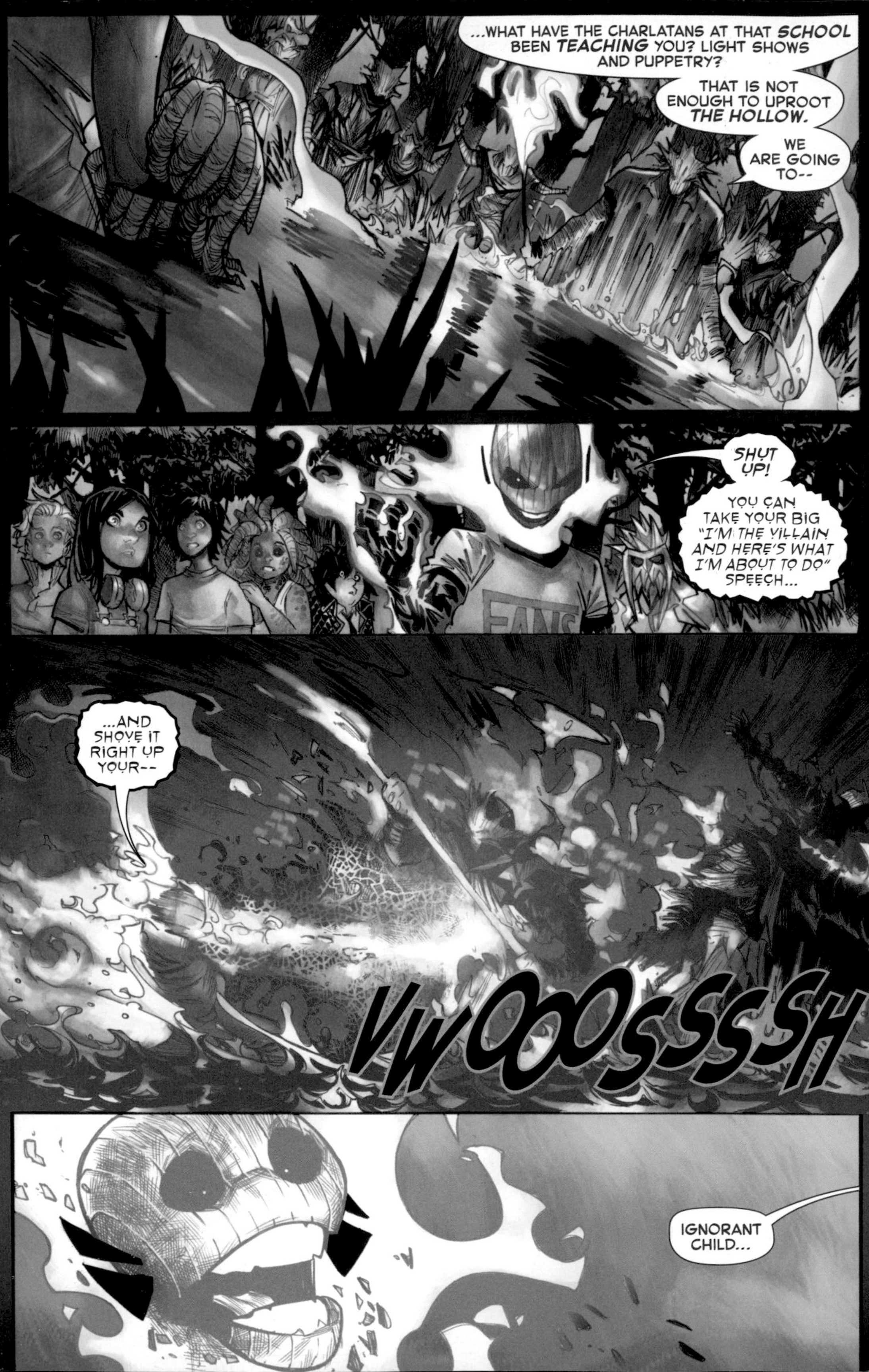
...WHAT HAVE THE CHARLATANS AT THAT SCHOOL BEEN TEACHING YOU? LIGHT SHOWS AND PUPPETRY?
THAT IS NOT ENOUGH TO UPROOT THE HOLLOW.
WE ARE GOING TO--
SHUT UP!
YOU CAN TAKE YOUR BIG "I'M THE VILLAIN AND HERE'S WHAT I'M ABOUT TO DO" SPEECH...
...AND SHOVE IT RIGHT UP YOUR--
VWOOOSSSSH
IGNORANT CHILD...

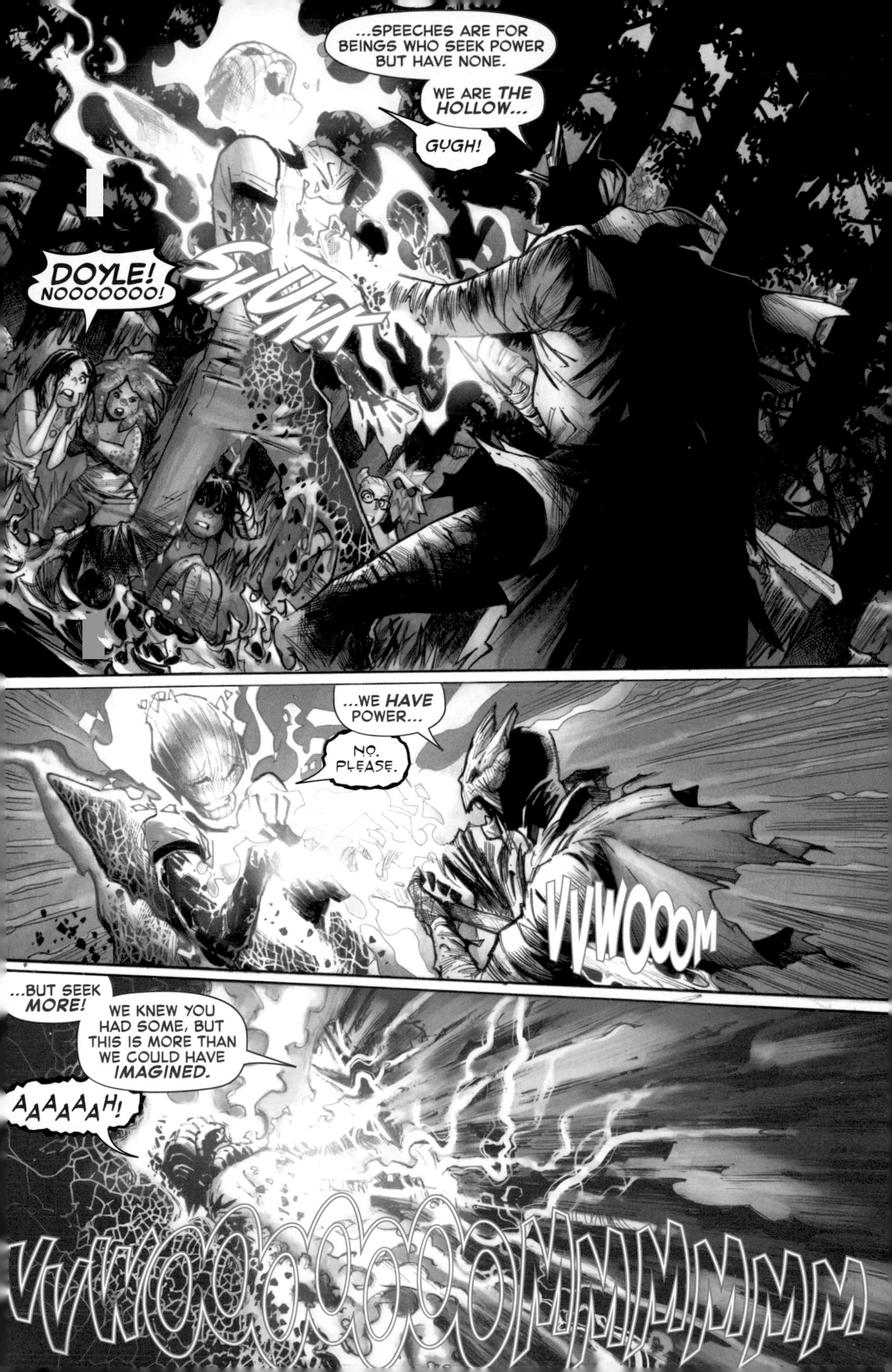
...SPEECHES ARE FOR BEINGS WHO SEEK POWER BUT HAVE NONE.
WE ARE THE HOLLOW...
GUGH!
DOYLE! NOOOOOOO!
SHUNK
...WE HAVE POWER...
NO. PLEASE.
VVWOOOM
...BUT SEEK MORE!
WE KNEW YOU HAD SOME, BUT THIS IS MORE THAN WE COULD HAVE IMAGINED.
AAAAAAH!
VVWOOOOOOOOMMMMMMMM

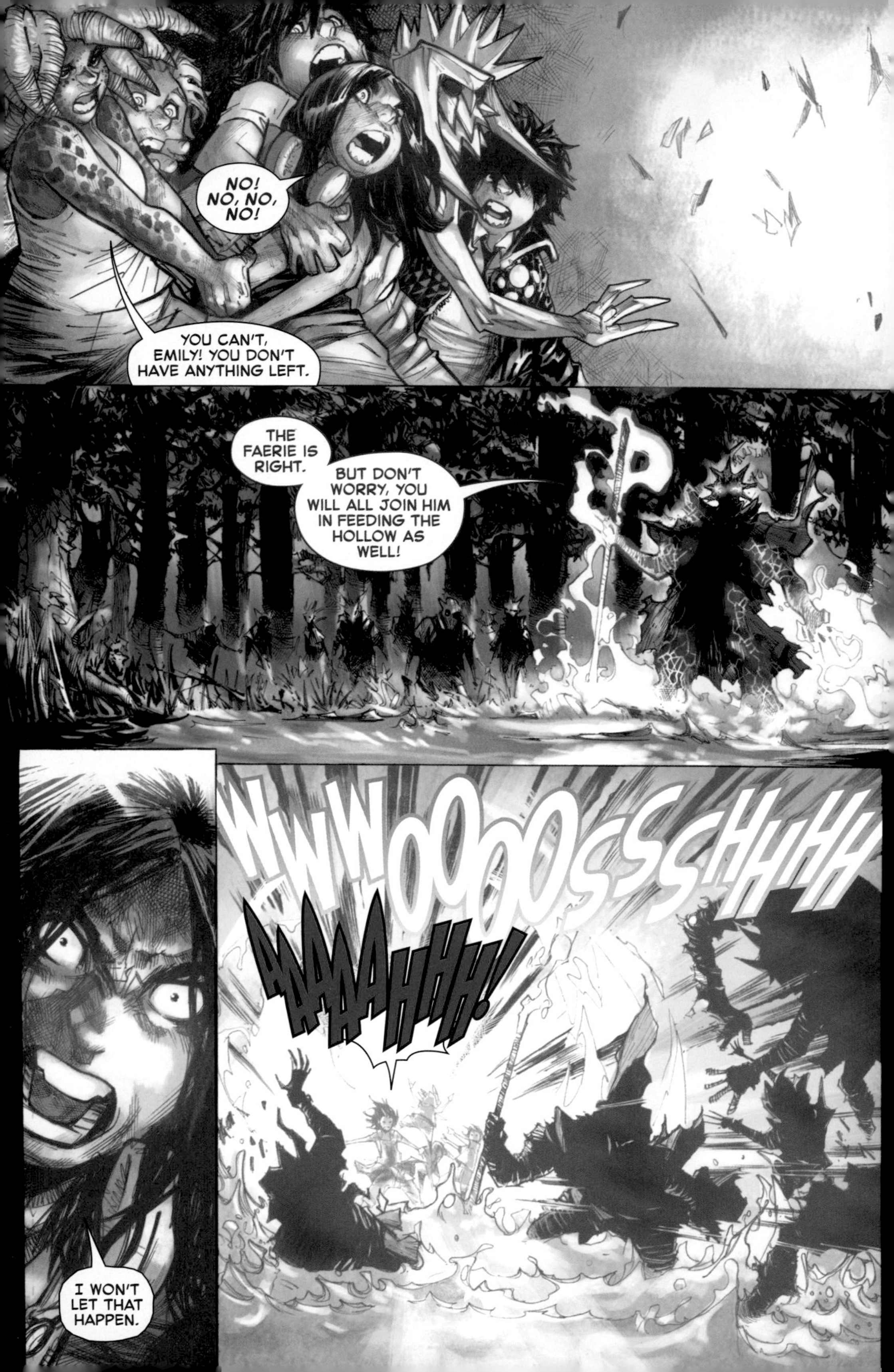
NO! NO, NO, NO!
YOU CAN'T, EMILY! YOU DON'T HAVE ANYTHING LEFT.
THE FAERIE IS RIGHT.
BUT DON'T WORRY, YOU WILL ALL JOIN HIM IN FEEDING THE HOLLOW AS WELL!
I WON'T LET THAT HAPPEN.
WWWOOOOSSSHHHH
AAAAAHHHH!

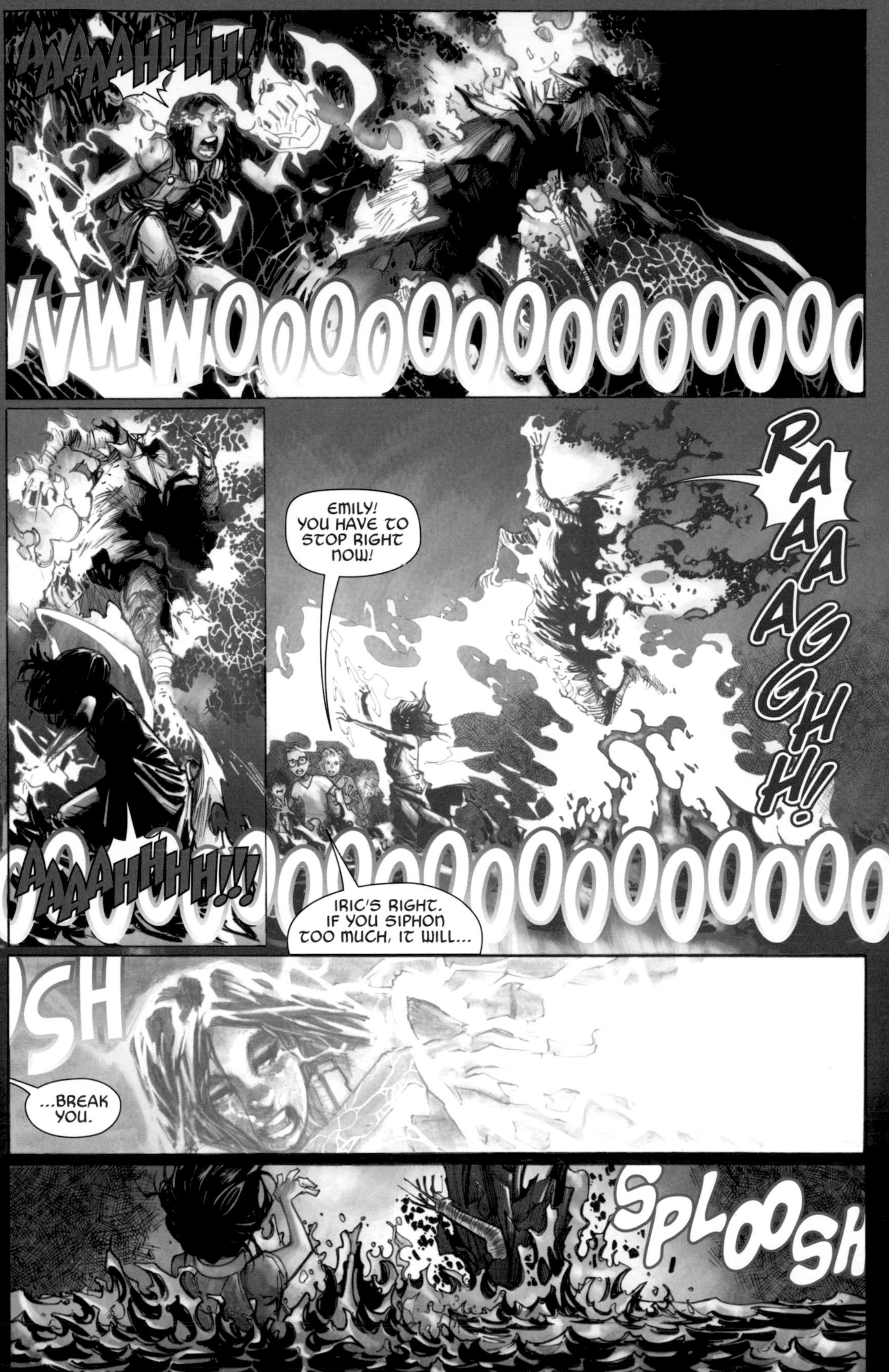
AAAAHHHH!
VWWWOOOOOOOOOOOOOOOO
RAAAAAGHHH!
EMILY! YOU HAVE TO STOP RIGHT NOW!
AAAAHHHH!!
IRIC'S RIGHT. IF YOU SIPHON TOO MUCH, IT WILL...
OSH
...BREAK YOU.
SPLOOSH

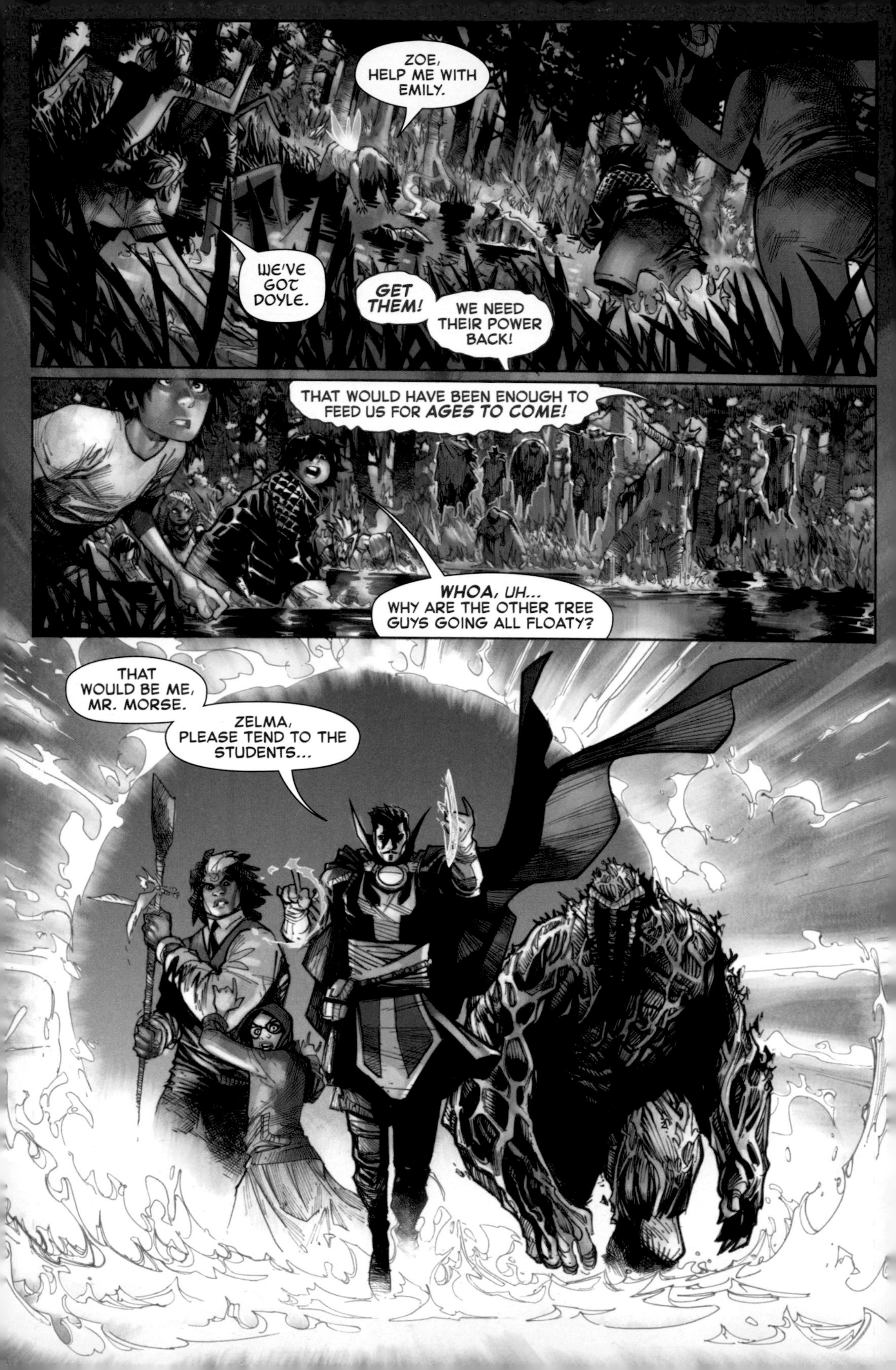
ZOE, HELP ME WITH EMILY.
WE'VE GOT DOYLE.
GET THEM!
WE NEED THEIR POWER BACK!
THAT WOULD HAVE BEEN ENOUGH TO FEED US FOR AGES TO COME!
WHOA, UH... WHY ARE THE OTHER TREE GUYS GOING ALL FLOATY?
THAT WOULD BE ME, MR. MORSE.
ZELMA, PLEASE TEND TO THE STUDENTS...

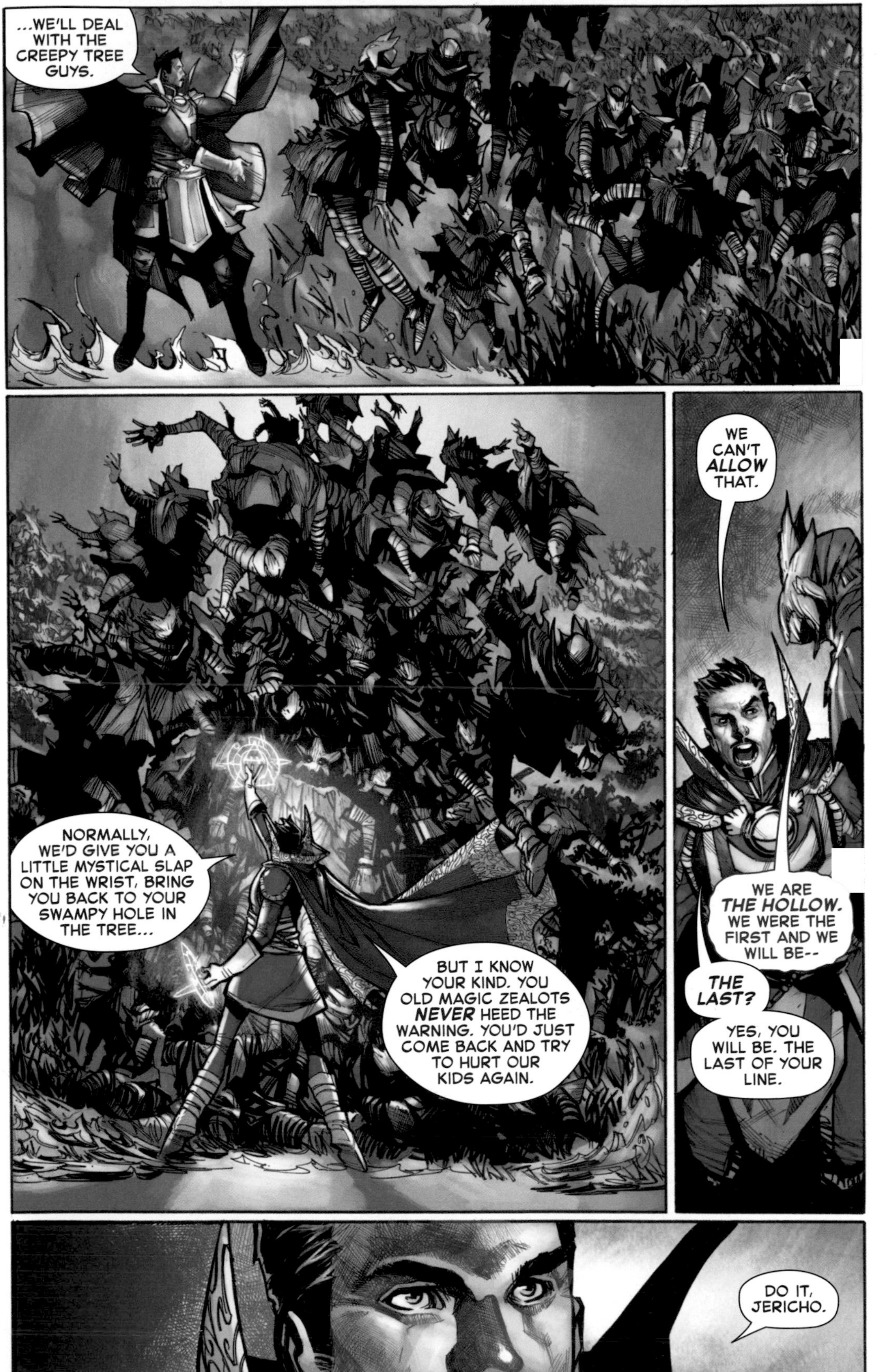
...WE'LL DEAL WITH THE CREEPY TREE GUYS.
NORMALLY, WE'D GIVE YOU A LITTLE MYSTICAL SLAP ON THE WRIST, BRING YOU BACK TO YOUR SWAMPY HOLE IN THE TREE...
BUT I KNOW YOUR KIND. YOU OLD MAGIC ZEALOTS NEVER HEED THE WARNING. YOU'D JUST COME BACK AND TRY TO HURT OUR KIDS AGAIN.
WE CAN'T ALLOW THAT.
WE ARE THE HOLLOW. WE WERE THE FIRST AND WE WILL BE--
THE LAST?
YES, YOU WILL BE. THE LAST OF YOUR LINE.
DO IT, JERICHO.

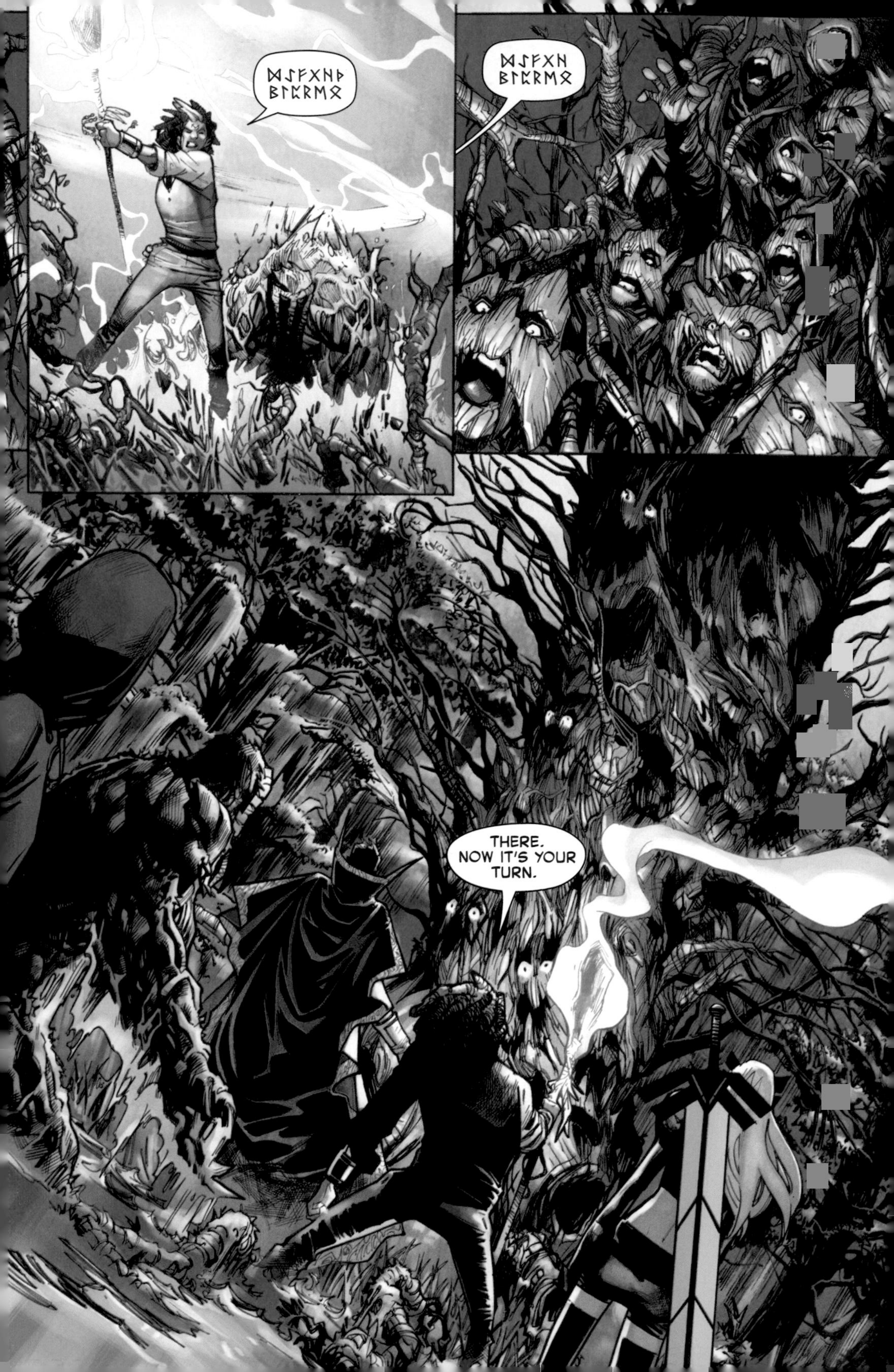
THERE. NOW IT'S YOUR TURN.

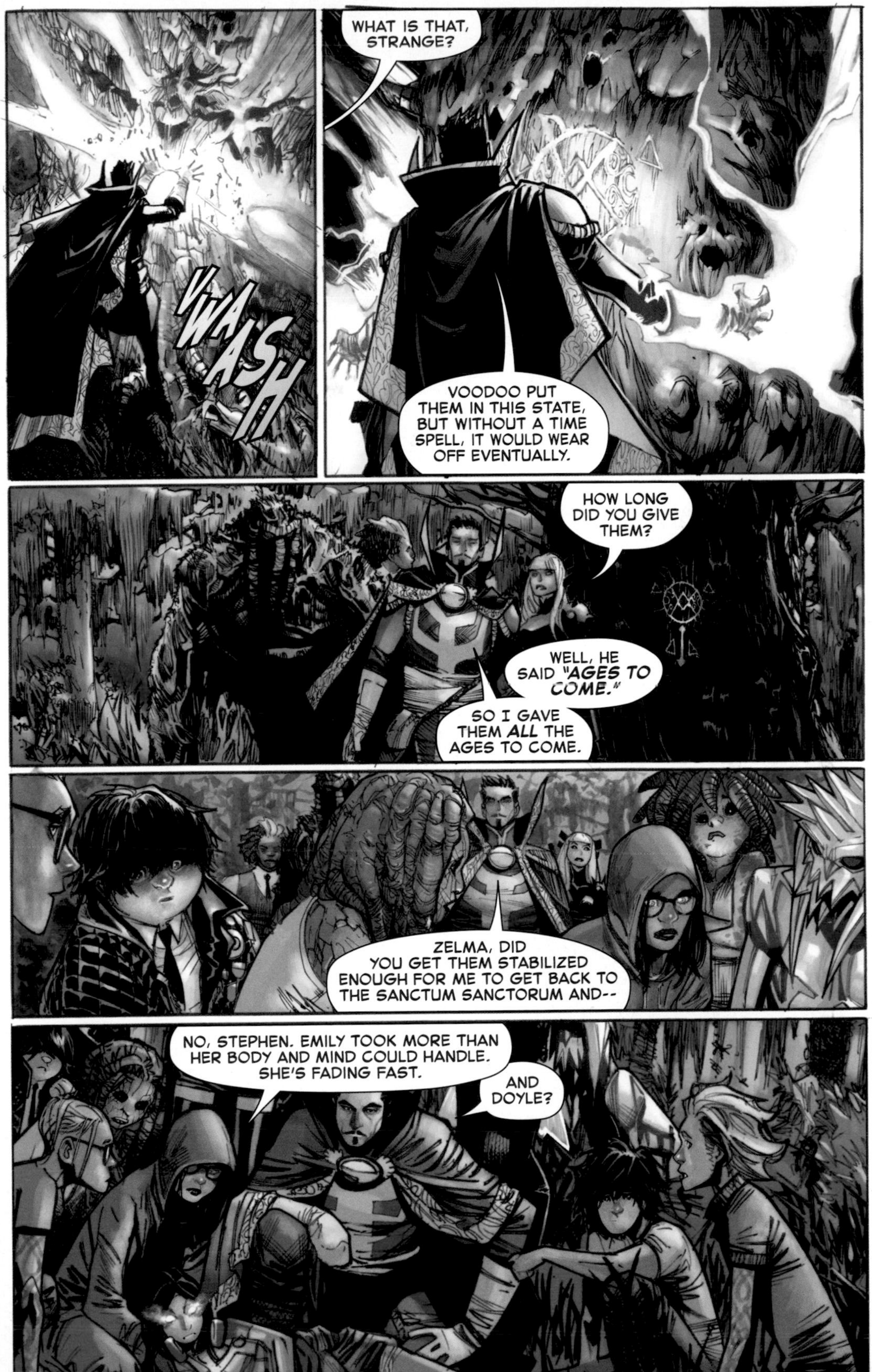
VWASH
WHAT IS THAT, STRANGE?
VOODOO PUT THEM IN THIS STATE, BUT WITHOUT A TIME SPELL, IT WOULD WEAR OFF EVENTUALLY.
HOW LONG DID YOU GIVE THEM?
WELL, HE SAID "AGES TO COME."
SO I GAVE THEM ALL THE AGES TO COME.
ZELMA, DID YOU GET THEM STABILIZED ENOUGH FOR ME TO GET BACK TO THE SANCTUM SANCTORUM AND--
NO, STEPHEN. EMILY TOOK MORE THAN HER BODY AND MIND COULD HANDLE. SHE'S FADING FAST.
AND DOYLE?

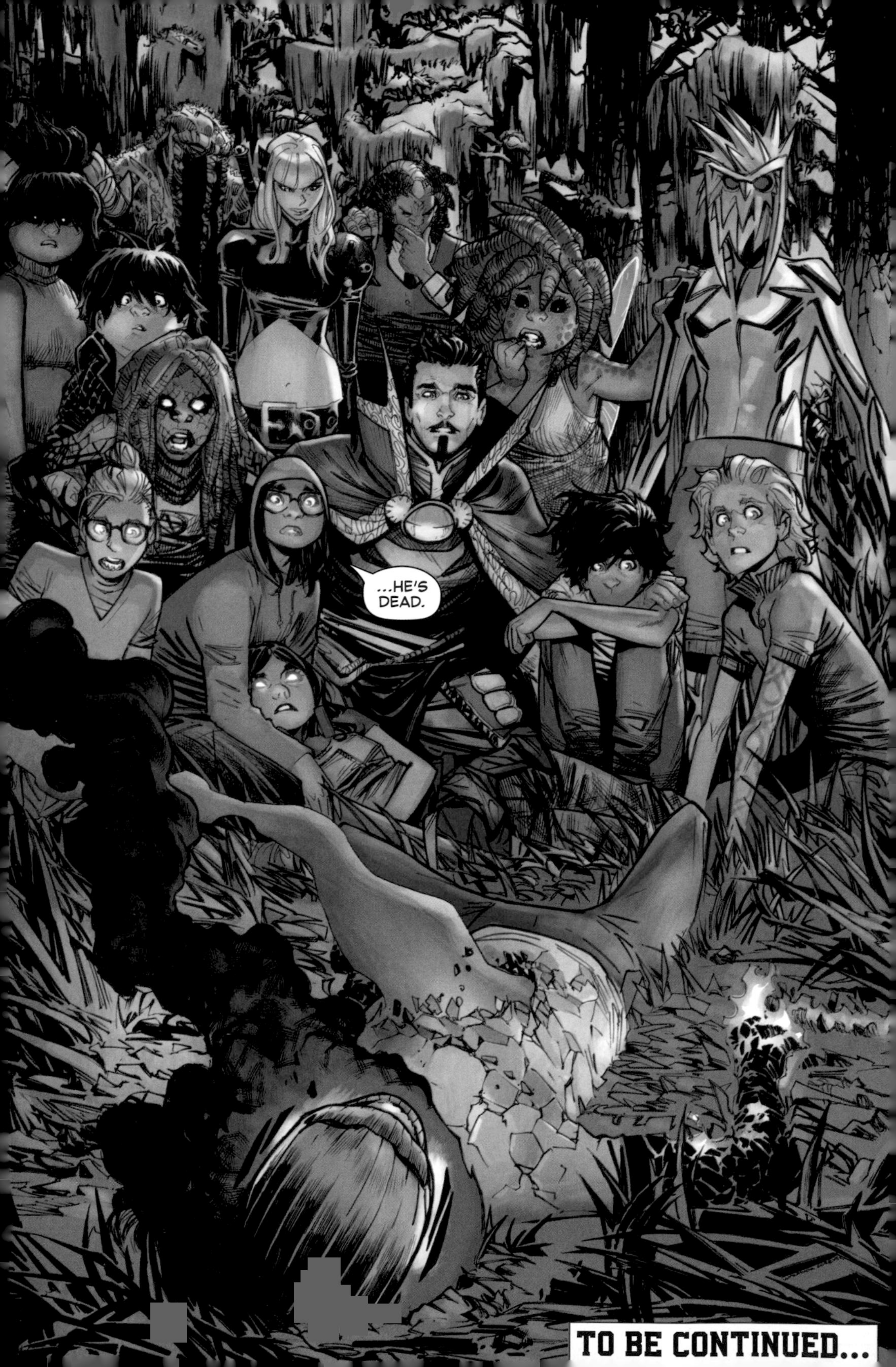
...HE'S DEAD.
TO BE CONTINUED...

The STRANGE ACADEMY

Theatre Group Presents...

THE TEMPEST

Starring

ALVI BRORSON *as* **PROSPERO**

NASIRAH NOORANI *as* **MIRANDA**

SHAYLEE MOONPEDDLE *as* **ARIEL**

GUSLAUG *as* **CALIBAN**

GERMÁN AGUILAR *as* **ANTONIO**

HOWARD SCOTT *as* **FERDINAND**

WHEN?
December 9 – December 13, 2020
8:00PM CST
(Earth/Midgard Times and Dates)

HOW MUCH? $25 USD *(Earth/Midgard Currency)*

WHERE? **THE SIMON WILLIAMS AUDITORIUM**

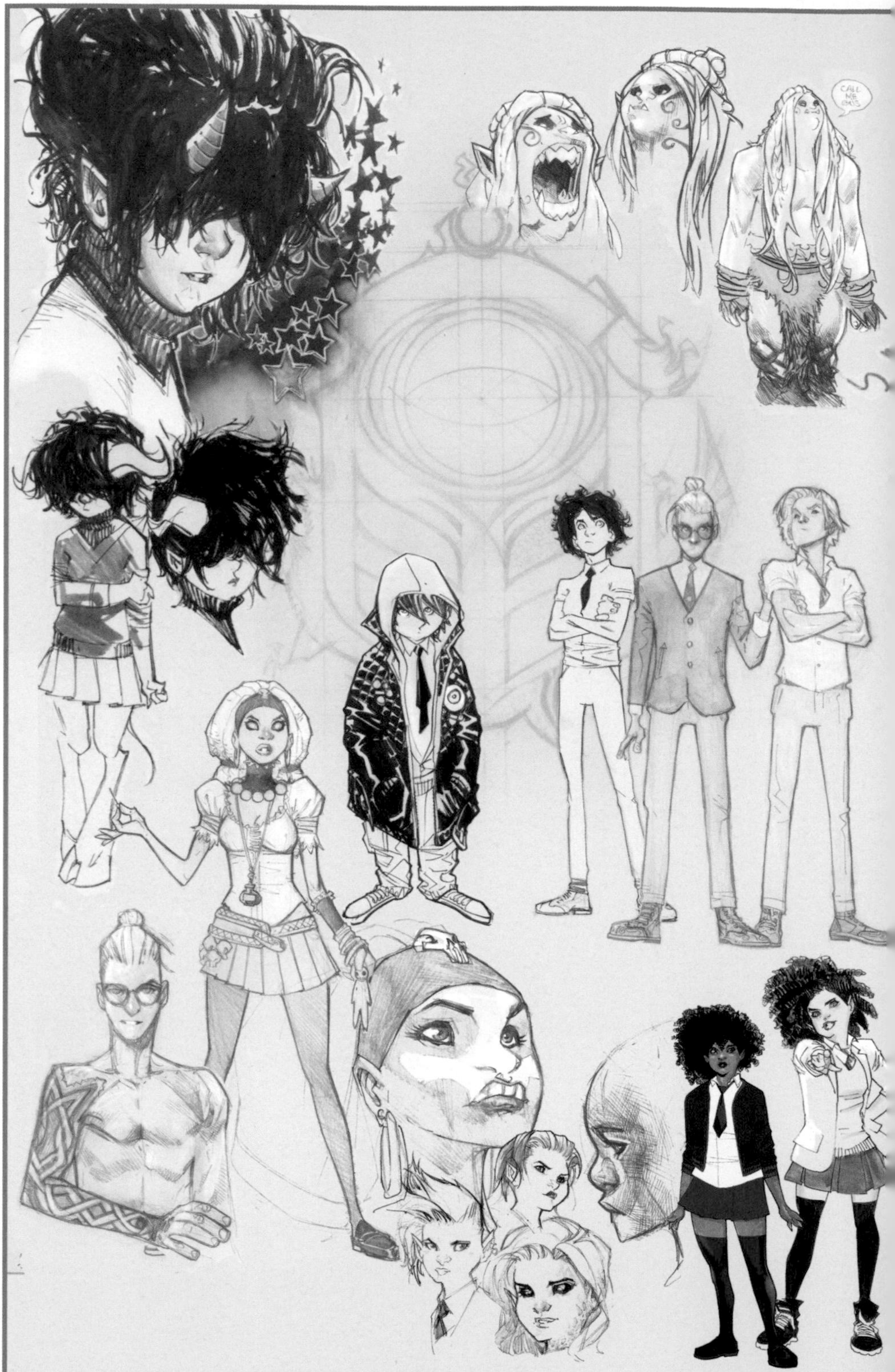
CALL ME

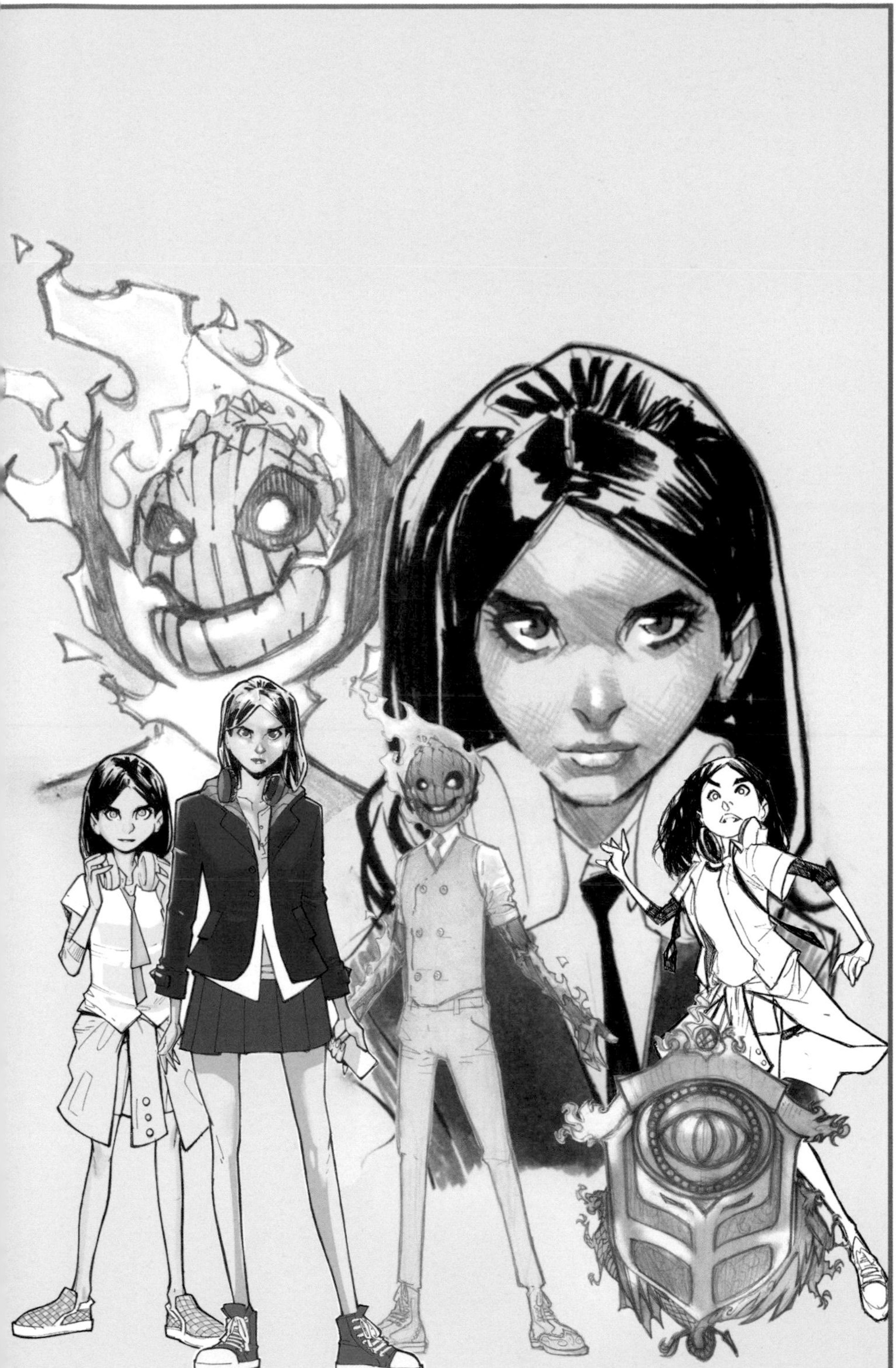

#1 DESIGN VARIANT BY **Humberto Ramos**

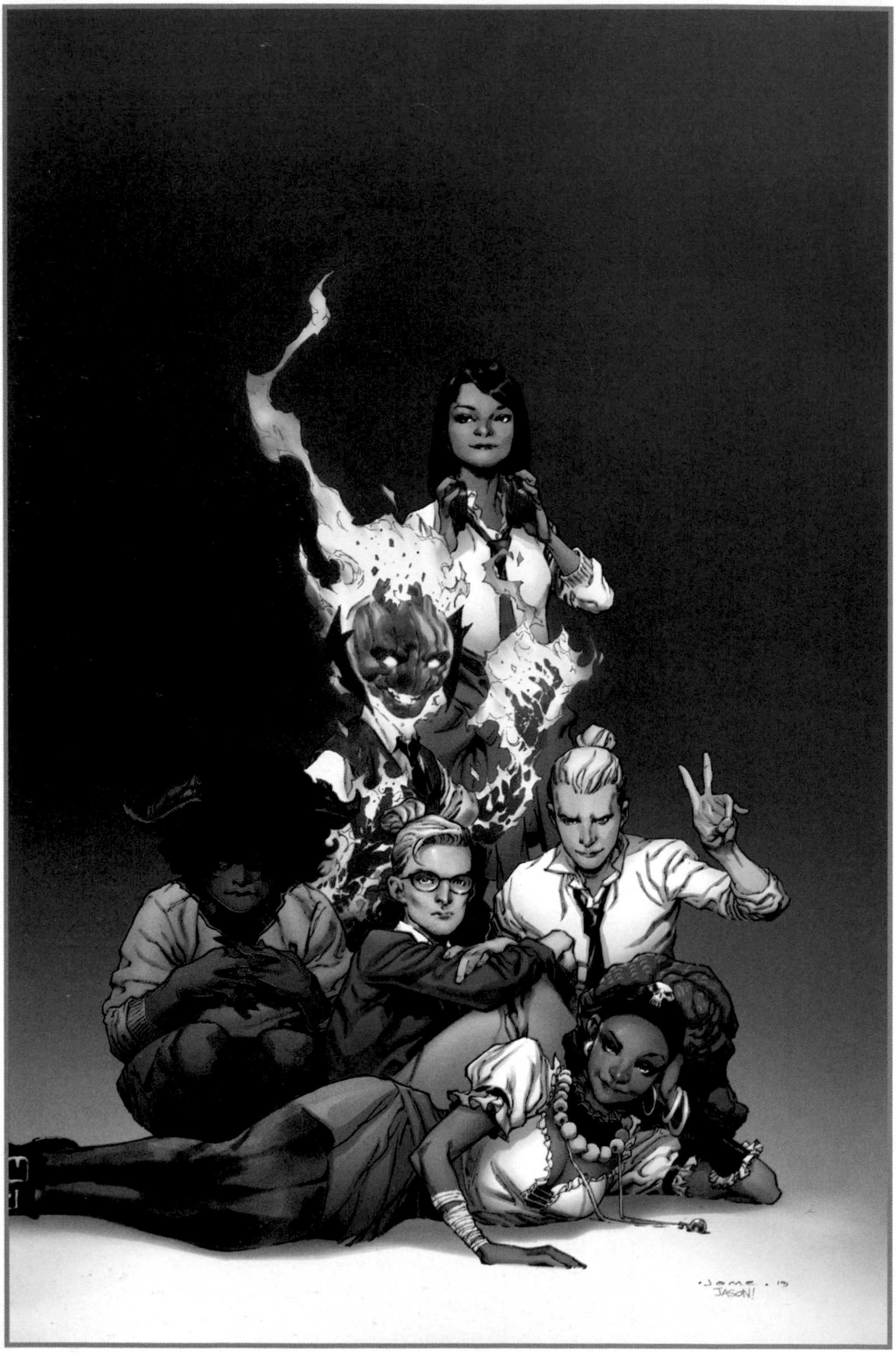

#1 VARIANT BY **Jerome Opeña** & **Jason Keith**

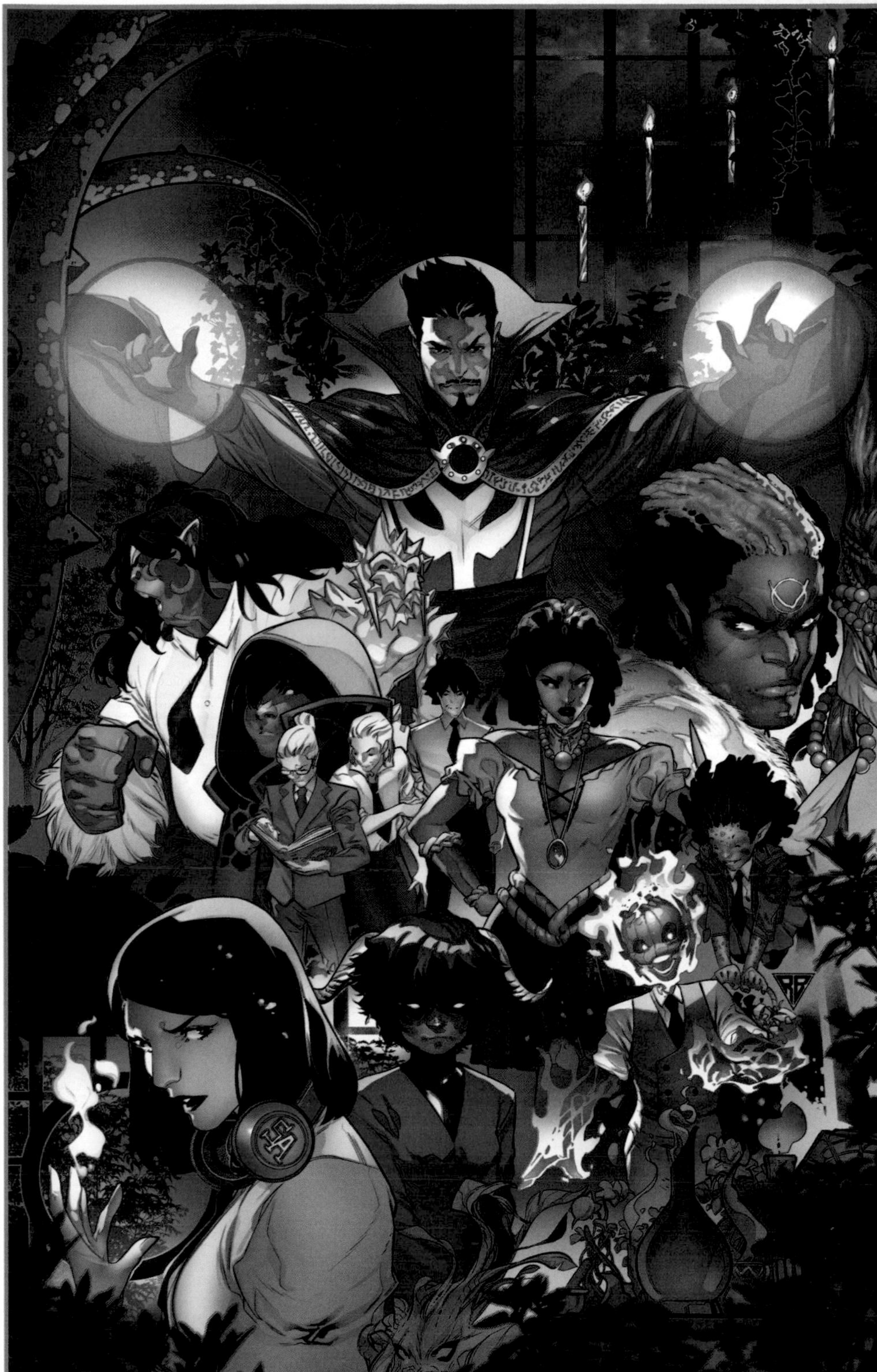

#2 VARIANT BY **R.B. Silva** & **David Curiel**

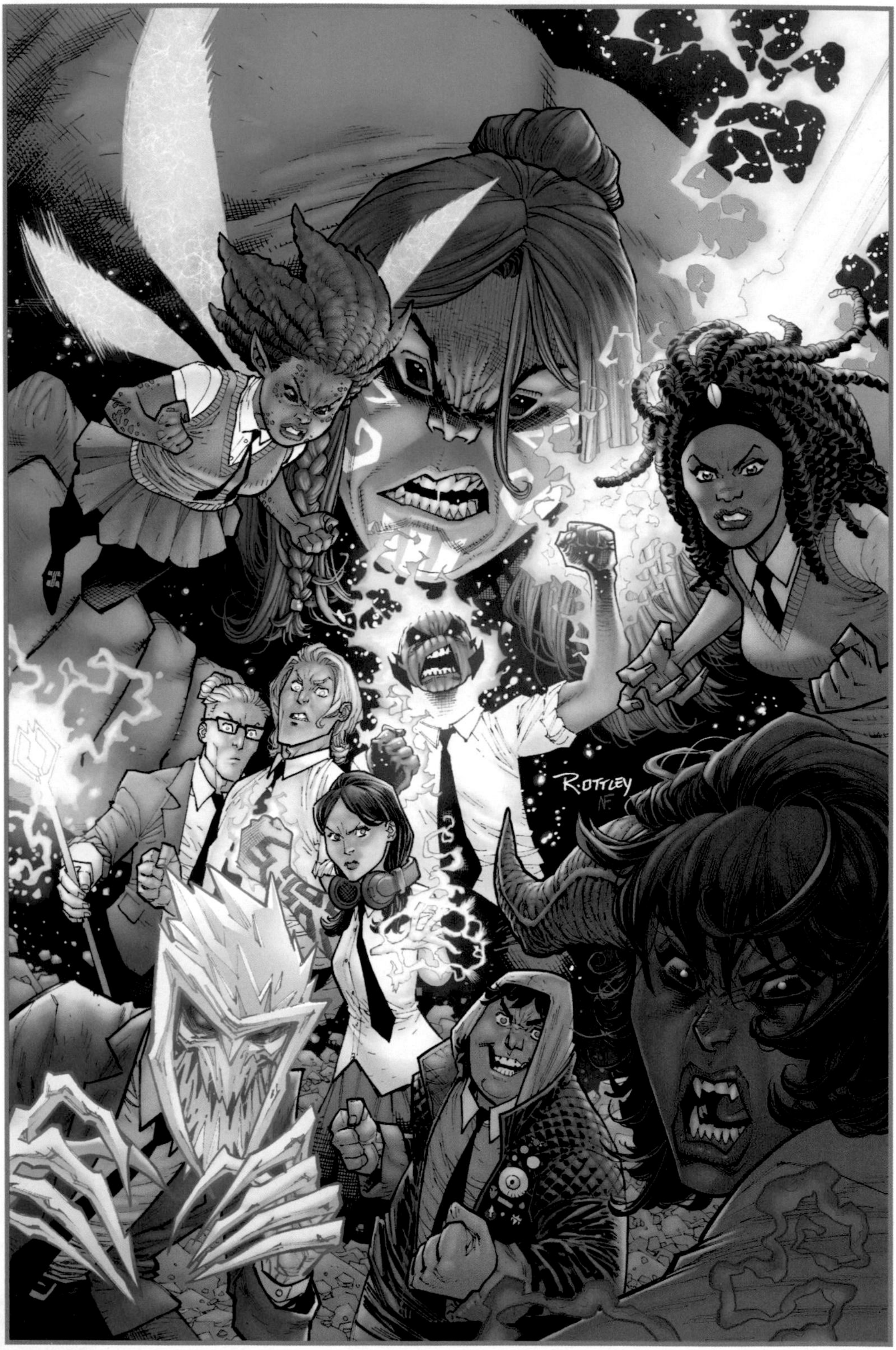
R.OTTLEY
NF

#3 VARIANT BY **Ryan Ottley** & **Nathan Fairbairn**

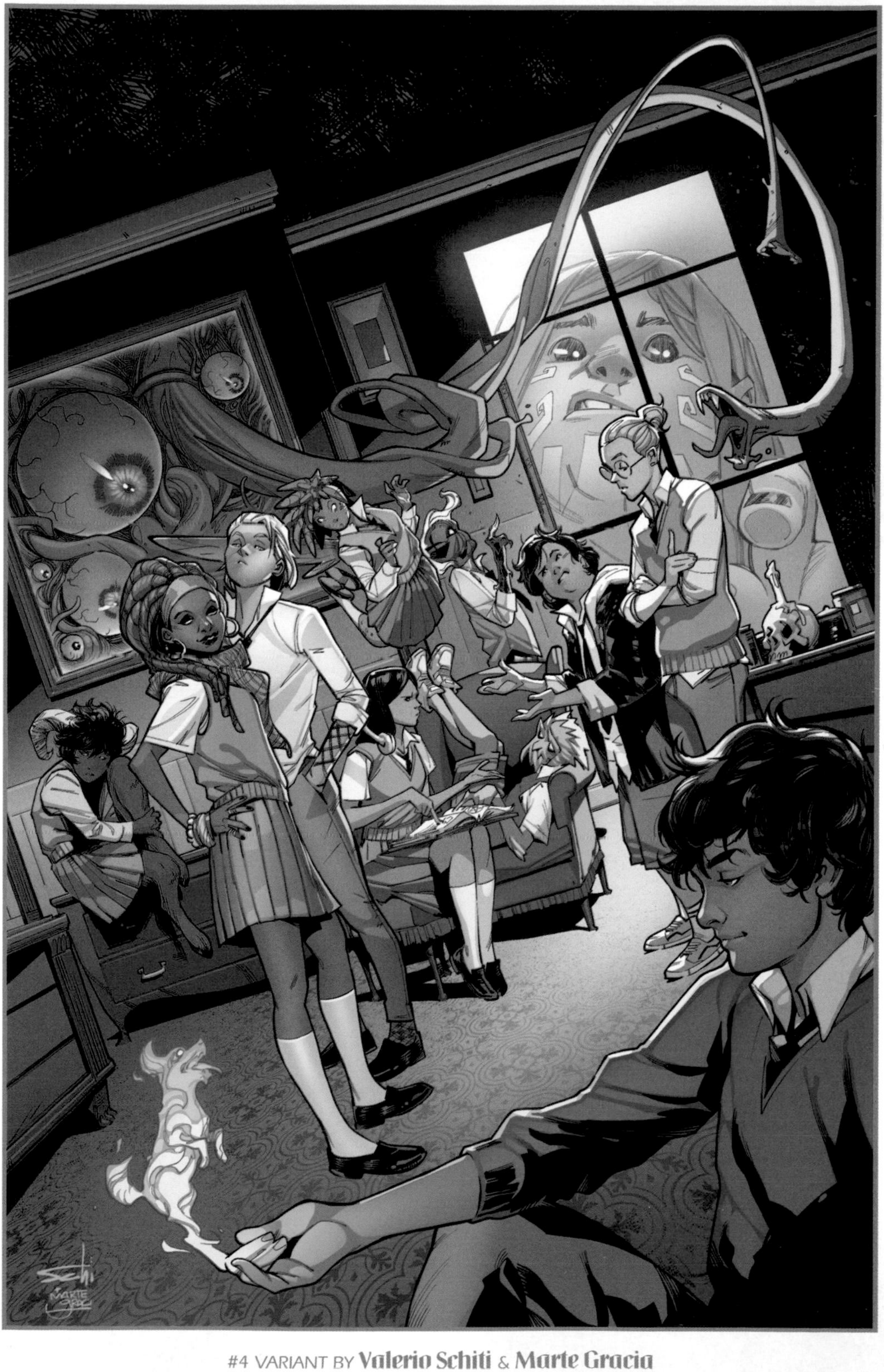

#4 VARIANT BY **Valerio Schiti** & **Marte Gracia**

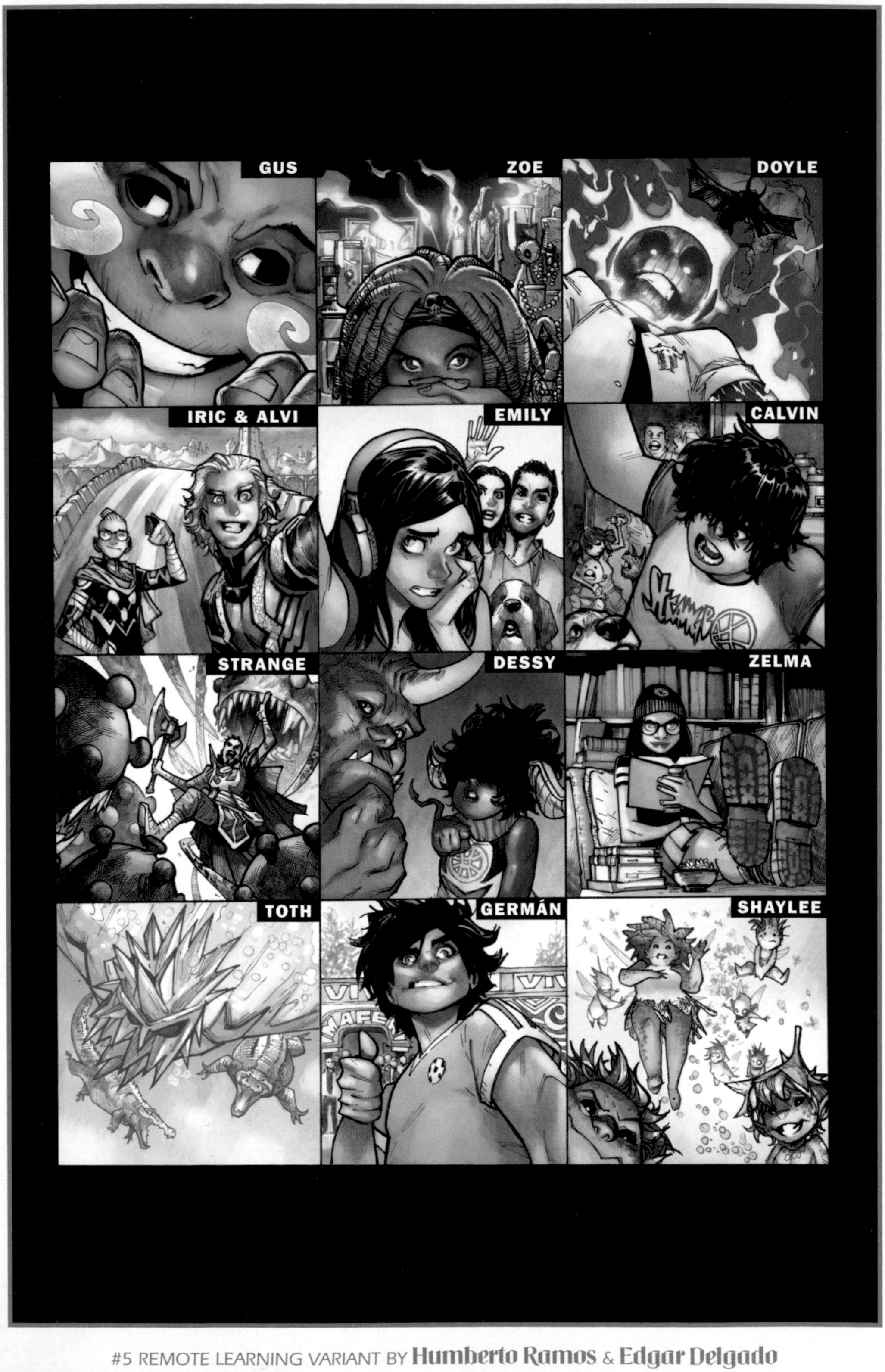
GUS
ZOE
DOYLE
IRIC & ALVI
EMILY
CALVIN
STRANGE
DESSY
ZELMA
TOTH
GERMÁN
SHAYLEE

#5 REMOTE LEARNING VARIANT BY **Humberto Ramos** & **Edgar Delgado**

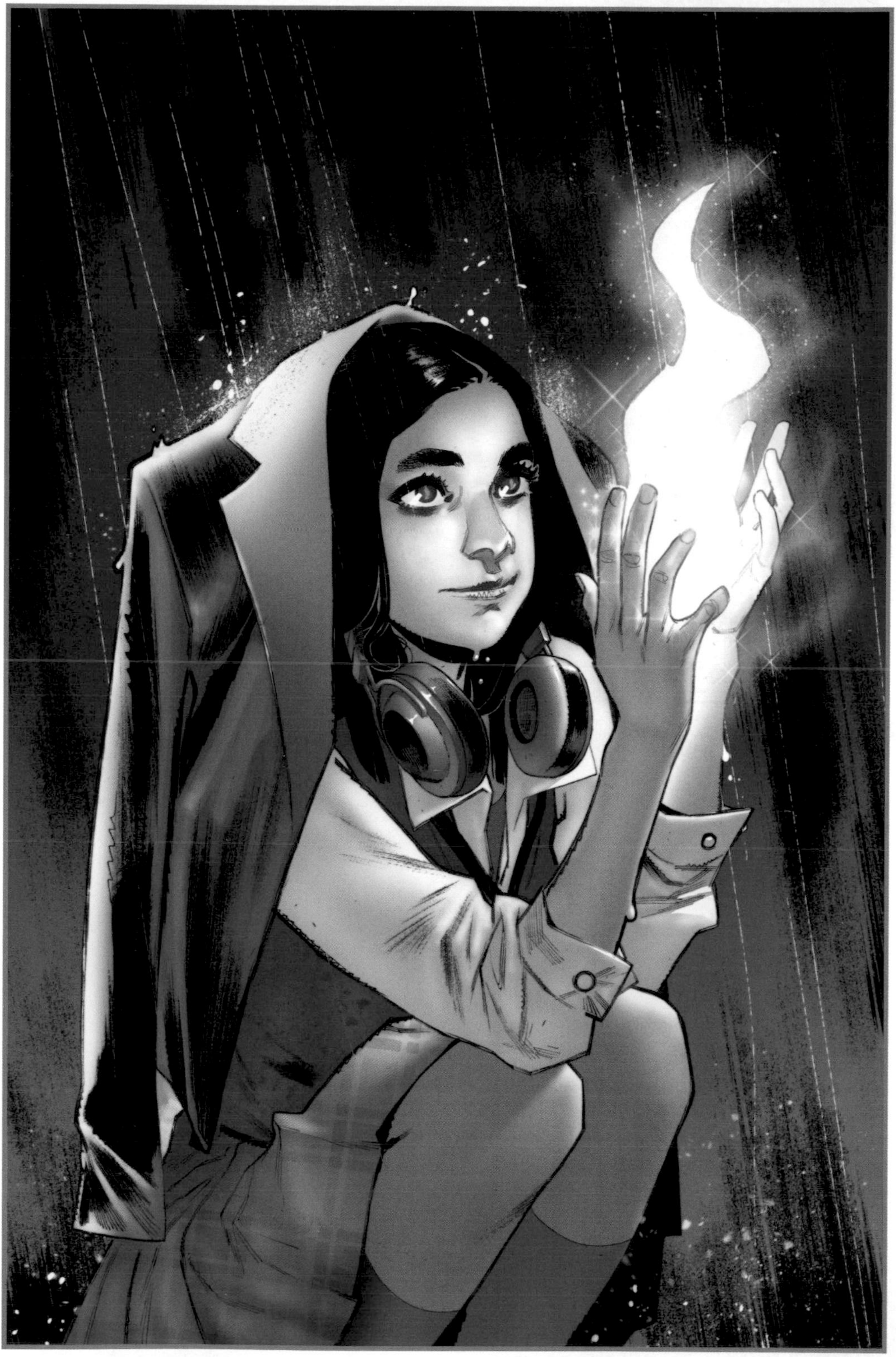

#6 VARIANT BY **Sara Pichelli** & **Edgar Delgado**

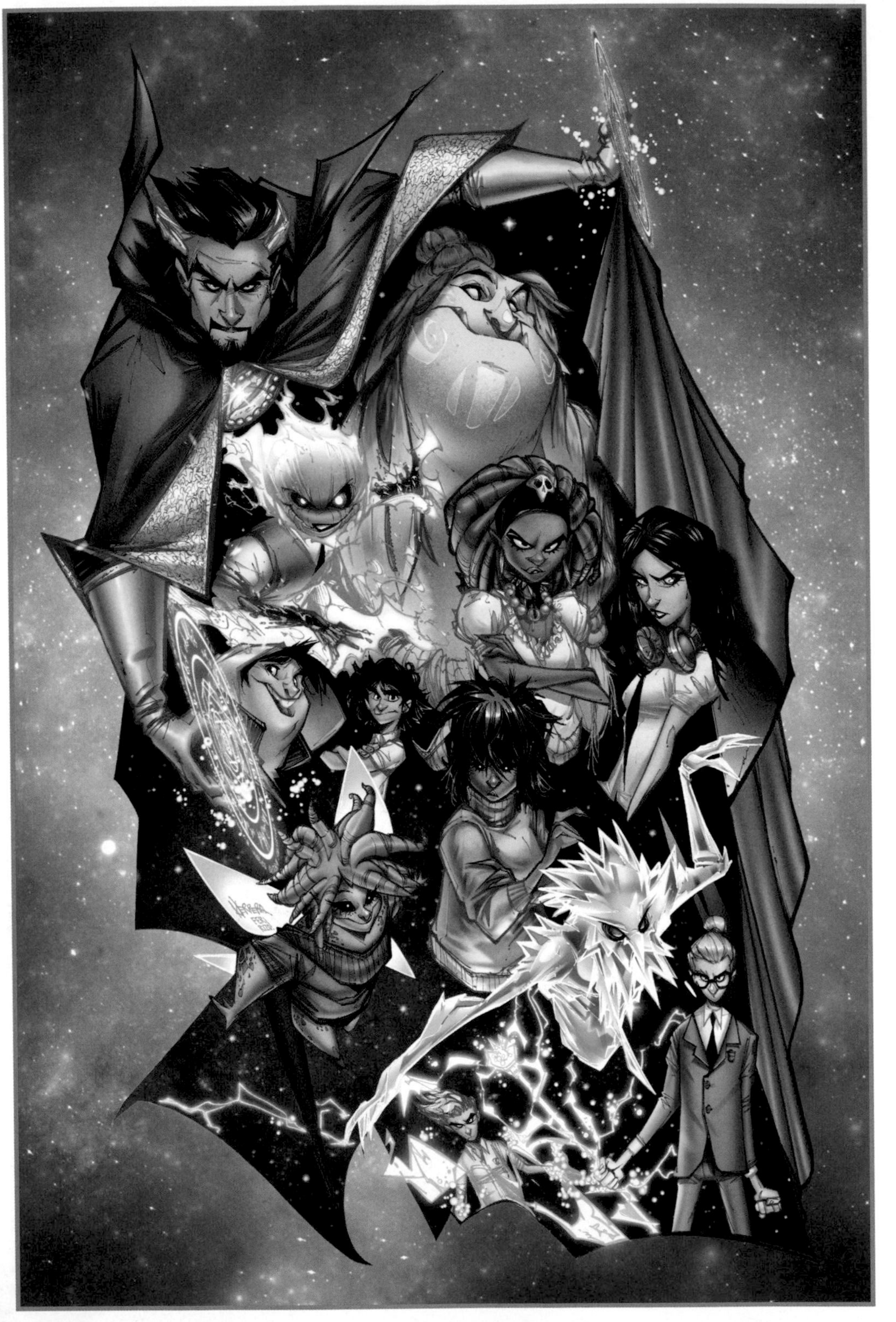

#2 SECOND-PRINTING VARIANT BY **Francisco Herrera** & **Fernanda Rizo**

#2 SECOND-PRINTING VARIANT BY
Humberto Ramos

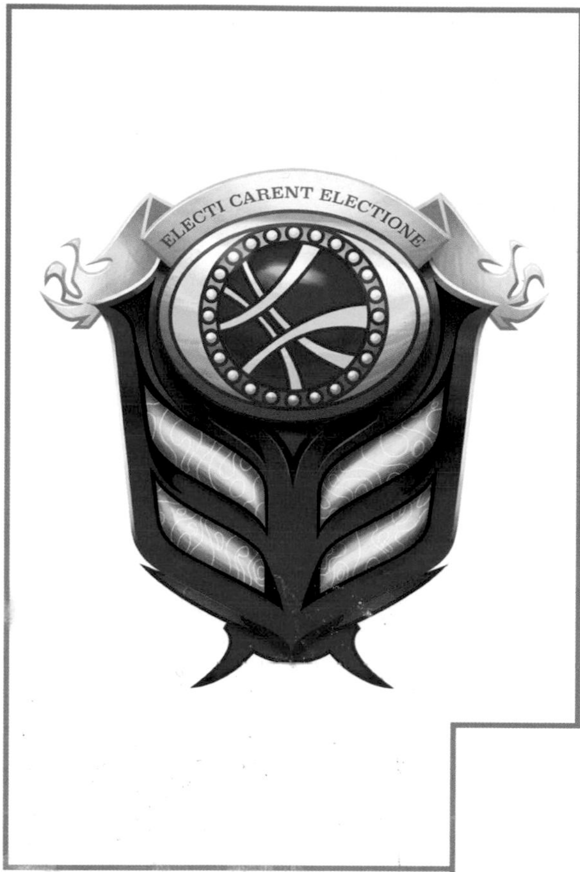
ELECTI CARENT ELECTIONE

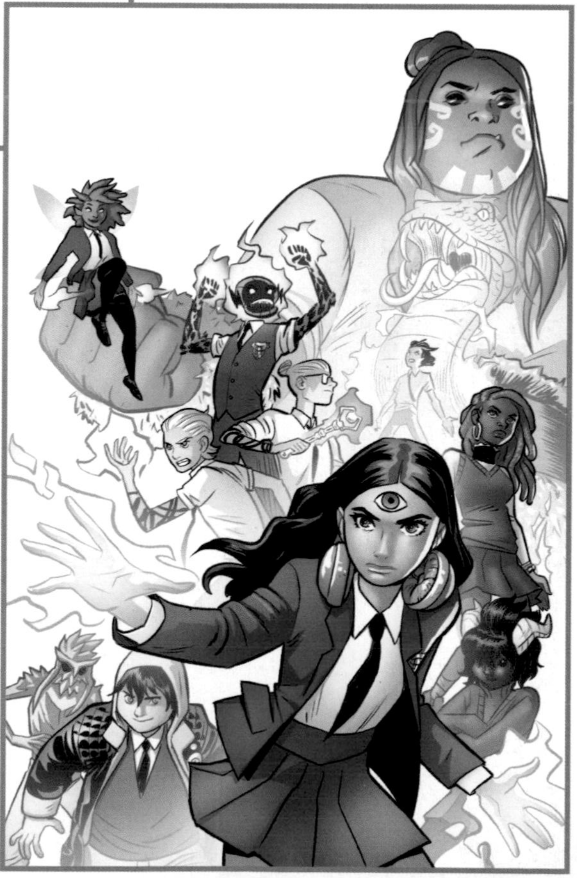

#3 SECOND-PRINTING VARIANT BY
Natacha Bustos & Edgar Delgado

Emily Bright

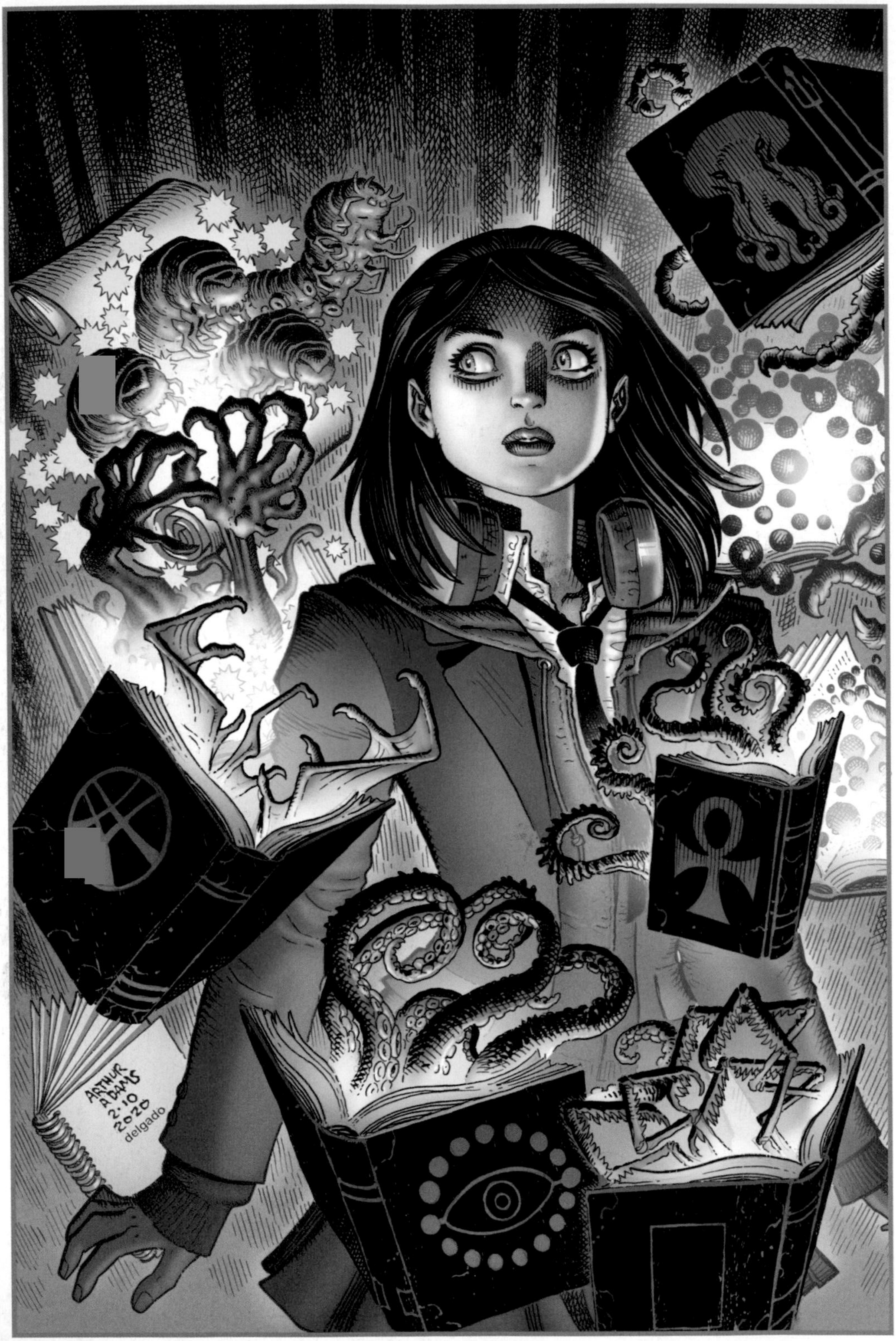
ARTHUR ADAMS 2·10 2020
delgado

#1 CHARACTER SPOTLIGHT VARIANT BY **Arthur Adams** & **Edgar Delgado**

Doyle Dormammu

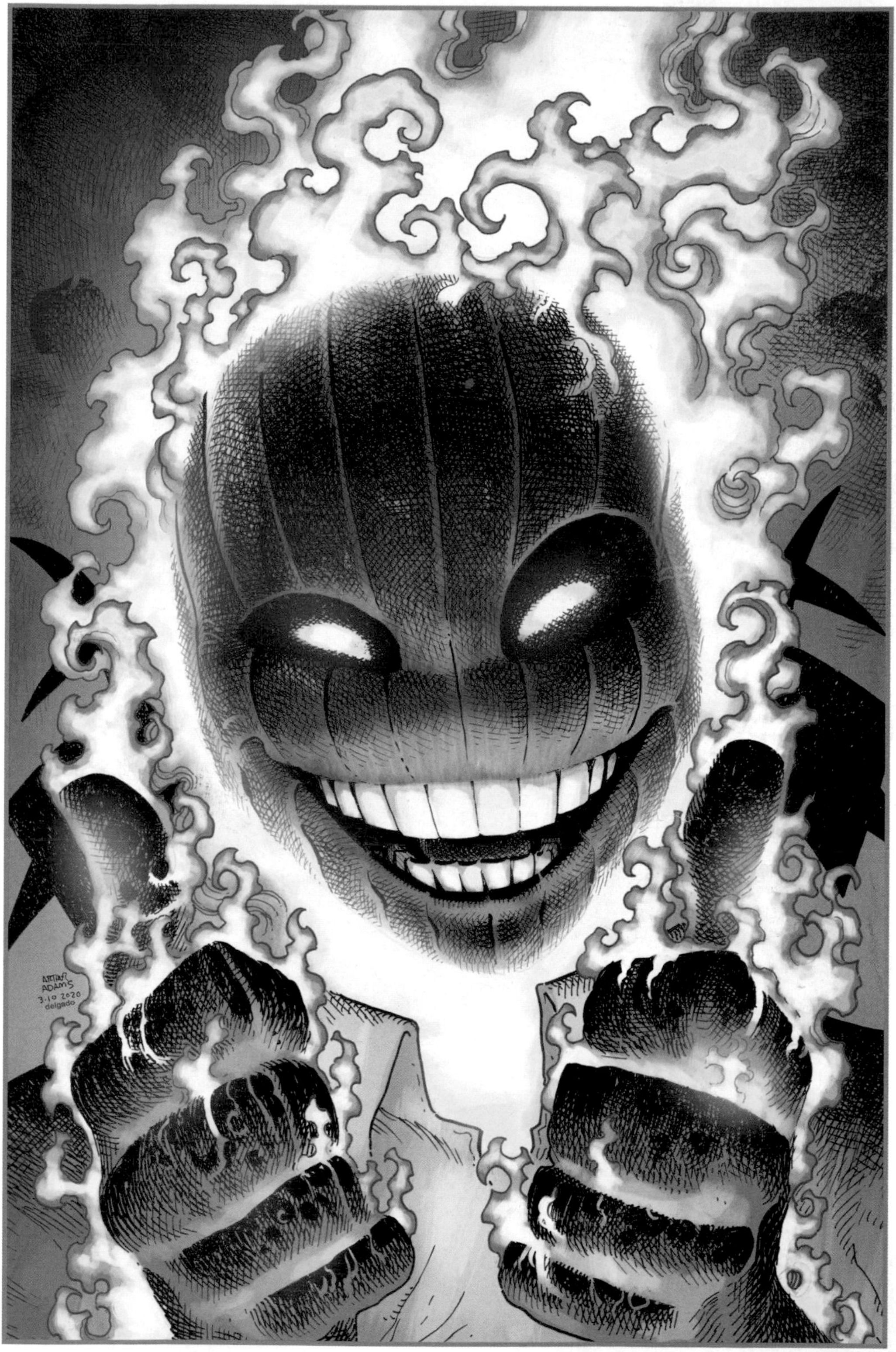
ARTHUR ADAMS 3-10 2020 delgado

#2 CHARACTER SPOTLIGHT VARIANT BY **Arthur Adams** & **Edgar Delgado**

OCT 2021

Shaylee Moonpeddle

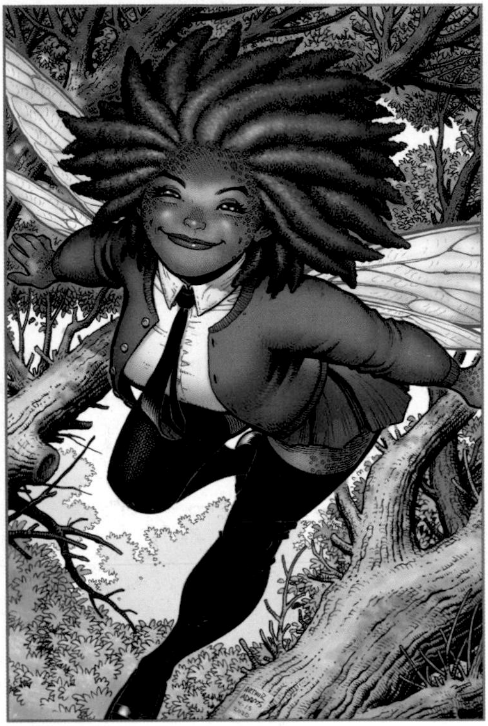

Zoe Laveau

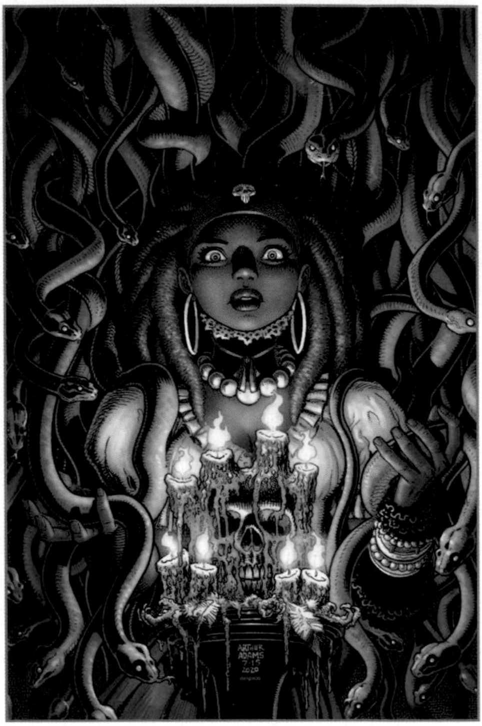

Calvin Morse

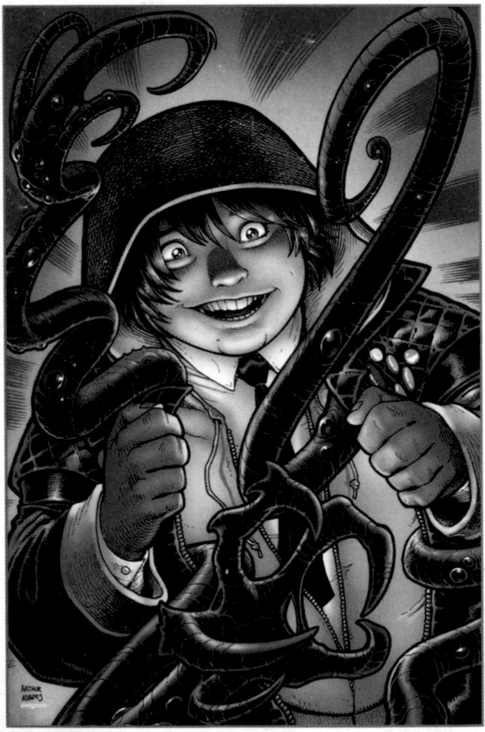

Iric & Alvi Brorson

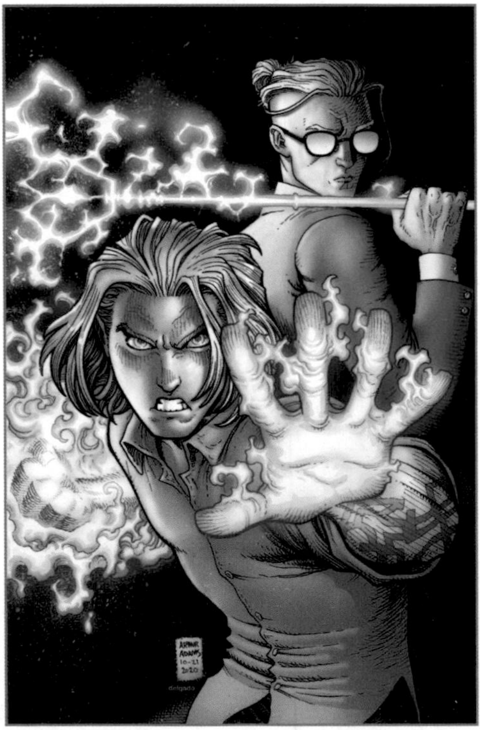

#3-6 CHARACTER SPOTLIGHT VARIANTS BY **Arthur Adams** & **Edgar Delgado**